one
hundred
percent
lunar boy

A NOVEL BY STEPHEN TUNNEY

one
hundred
percent
lunar boy

A NOVEL BY STEPHEN TUNNEY

MACADAM CAGE

MacAdam/Cage
155 Sansome Street, Suite 550
San Francisco, California 94104

www.MacAdamCage.com

Library of Congress Cataloging-in-Publication Data

Tunney, Stephen, 1959-
 One hundred percent lunar boy / by Stephen Tunney.
   p. cm.
 ISBN 978-1-59692-368-3
 1. Teenage boys—Fiction. 2. Moon—Fiction. I. Title.
 PS3570.U47O54 2010
 813'.54—dc22

                                                        2010022878

Printed in the United States of America.

10 9 8 7 6 5 4 3 2 1

Book and jacket design by Dorothy Carico Smith.

For Anne, Julien, and Sophie

The only birds that live on the Moon are hummingbirds. They are lunar white and the size of dogs and they travel across the lunar landscape in vast clouds. Their wings vibrate something inside the inner ear that makes one feel euphoric, as if they are floating. During those fleeting moments when they kissed, he wondered, *am I inside a cloud of hummingbirds?*

The fact that he kissed her had made the train ride bearable. And that was saying a lot, as the Sea of Tranquility line was easily the worst subway on the Moon, especially late at night. It must have been close to one AM when the ancient plastic and aluminum monstrosity stopped in the middle of nowhere, forcing Hieronymus to sit for hours in the hot and crowded subway car. The bright florescent lights flickered on and off. Periodic announcements from a cackling speaker explained the reasons for the delay, but no one listened as nearly every person squeezed in with him was drunk. Everyone in that loud, sweaty mob must have been returning from parties or concerts or other nocturnal events. Some were loud, some were sleeping, a couple were sick. Two or three fights broke out, and there was even singing. Still, he hardly noticed them. Earlier that evening, at an amusement park, under the luminous Earth, he kissed a girl, and this delightful memory blocked out the debauchery all around him. She was beautiful in a way he had never known before. She was a foreigner. A tourist. She was from Earth.

He arrived home at five in the morning, had a terrible shouting fight with his father, stumbled into his room, and passed out. He slept for seven hours and then woke completely disoriented.

Through his grogginess, Hieronymus tried to remember the previous night. Not that there was much difference between night and day. The sky was always the same reddish tone of the artificial atmosphere. Dusky dawn color is what the Earth-born called it. She called it that. She. And what was her name? What kind of a young man was he to kiss a girl, and the next morning struggle to remember her name? It's not like he was drunk—he wasn't. He peered out from under his covers at the clock on his messy desk. It said twelve. His forgetfulness must have been from other places than lack of sleep.

There was a strong smell of motor oil coming from somewhere. He tossed his covers aside, shocked to find himself not only still dressed, but covered in a strange industrial filth. Greenish gunk, dirt, grime. His white plastic jacket lay on the floor, stained in motor oil, with a huge rip in its side.

He had also fallen asleep with his goggles on. Usually he'd have to wear them all day long and then toss the Pixiedamned things off to the side before going to bed each night. He hated them. They were ugly and utilitarian with black rubber straps. The lenses were slightly purple. At least when he was alone in his room he could be free of them, but everywhere else, he had to wear them. It was the law.

But it was because of the goggles that he had met the Earth girl. Slowly, the memories floated in. The evening reassembled itself.

She had an Earth name. The kind of name you never heard on the Moon because it was so trendy on Earth and Lunarites were always a little behind the curve when it came to fads like that. It was a sentence for a name. When she first told him, he pretended not to let on how awkward it was, but after a few minutes with her it seemed completely normal, and now he lay there in his bed, fully clothed and furious with himself for not remembering.

He was about to take his goggles off and go back to sleep with wondrous dreams of the kiss they had shared when it suddenly came back to him. Not the girl's name, but that other, terrifying thing they did together. The illegal thing.

He covered his face with his hands.

He was only sixteen and already his life was over. Was he mad? Was he completely out of his mind? What he did with that girl was so far beyond forbidden. If the authorities found out, he would be sent to a prison on the far side of the Moon with an automatic life sentence. He would disappear. Those rotten goggles—the same goggles that attracted the Earth girl also attract the police. They set him apart. They inform all of Lunar society that he is one of *them*. A One Hundred Percent Lunar Boy.

Hieronymus took several deep breaths.

His first line of thought was that he was in trouble with his father but not with the police. Not yet. He looked at the clock again and reasoned it was over twelve hours ago that he last saw her. He dropped her off at her hotel and caught the last subway out of LEM Zone One, far away on the other side of the Sea of Tranquility. The police were extremely fast in cases like this, and he was counting on her parents believing her totally false alibi, which he found unlikely. The girl was covered in dirt. A lump of automotive grease meshed into her hair, she was completely spaced out after what they had done. What kind of parents would not call the police?

Indeed, they broke the law. Actually, he broke the law. He was responsible, not her. He didn't want to do it, but she convinced him otherwise. He tried to explain it was a crime, but she was sure they would get away with it. He told her she would get hurt, but she disagreed—she was a strong and daring young woman from Earth who could take anything the Moon tossed at her. She was wrong, not about being daring, but about everything else.

At least they kissed before they did it.

In his bed, terrified of even moving, expecting to hear police sirens from the highway outside growing in volume before twenty officers burst in through his door to drag him away, he wondered how many times a day this happened. To others just like him. Other One Hundred Percent Lunar People.

His special status was not completely rare, but unusual enough to be a curiosity, one generating stares and questions and rumors. Borderline abnormal. A shameful thing to be. There were many others just as shameful as himself—One Hundred Percent Lunar Boys, and Girls, and Men, and Women. Thousands. They all wore goggles. They *had* to wear goggles. *They were forced to wear the goggles, every last freakish one of them.* It was that, or exile to the far side of the Moon. Hieronymus cursed his life and the limitations that had always defined it.

He sat up. He lifted the goggles up off his face to rub his weary eyes. He glanced over at his window. Something happened just outside the glass. Actually, something was about to happen, and he quickly put his goggles back on. He was right. A hummingbird, this one very large, came by the window and tapped its long beak on the window pane, begging for food as these annoying creatures often did. He tossed a small pillow at it, and the bird flew away. None of this was a surprise. With his goggles off, during those few seconds, Hieronymus saw the entire thing played out in shadow-like forms before it happened. The goggles filtered out his natural visual ability to see physical actions and movement before they occurred. This was true of all One Hundred Percent Lunar People, and why the Lunar authorities created laws to keep their vision suppressed. Normalized. As if they were normal people, which they were not.

One of those laws was very clear. Never look at another human being without the goggles. That was the law he broke last night. He looked at her. And if he were to be discovered, the consequences would be severe.

The girl from Earth with the sentence for a name. He'd never met a teenager from the Motherworld before. She was vivacious and demanding and intelligent and she knew about the phenomenon. Had she been from the Moon, he would have easily brushed her off, but her accent and the way she walked and her naïve Earthling's enthusiasm captivated him. He was weak. He could not resist. She wanted him to look at her with the goggles off.

Which he did.

And as a result, he knew he would never see her again.

He broke the law. When the goggles came off, he knew exactly what was going to happen to anyone he looked at. He knew what was going to happen to her. And it made him terribly sad.

Two more hummingbirds slammed into his window. They fluttered away disoriented, and Hieronymus suddenly remembered her name. Windows Falling On Sparrows. Her name was Windows Falling On Sparrows. He whispered it to himself. The breath of her rediscovered name passed through his lips, solidifying, for a moment, the last image he had had of her: her hand on a staircase banister as she looked at him one last time before disappearing up the stairs of the filthy, badly lit hotel lobby.

Windows Falling On Sparrows.

He gazed out through the window. A horizon of neon-covered towers under a red sky. The Sea of Tranquility was full of tower blocks, and from where he was, he was part of the same massive skyline of repeating skyscraper clusters. Endless housing projects. He lived on the eighty-eighth floor of a tower just like them with his family. It was rare that his father ever yelled at him, but when he'd finally gotten home at the insane hour he did, his old man really blew his top. Ringo Rexaphin was aware that the subway often broke down, and had it not, his son would have arrived at a decent hour, but that was not exactly the point of his baritone, high-volume yelling. *Why, why, why put yourself in that position? Why subject yourself to the whims of others? That subway is over three hundred years old!* His father had lectured him through his own half-closed sleepy eyelids, furious he had to wait up all night. And he was right. The Lunar subway was notorious for its late-night breakdowns or accidents, and sometimes, and seemingly for the Hell of it, the trains would be pulled for maintenance. Randomly. *On a whim.* One that could leave anyone stranded for hours. And the crummy old subway system was not just known for its mechanical failures—it was also a place of violence. Robberies, rapes, brutal stabbings. His father was particularly on edge because just the night before, a couple from Plagston Heights had been murdered on the exact same line Hieronymus had traveled on. Their train broke down between two suburban stations in the middle of the Sea of Tranquility. Three cruel men with stockings on their faces climbed aboard and attacked the couple, who, unfortunately for them, were the only passengers in the subway car. They chopped the poor woman's head off. And the man: his eyes were gouged out. A gruesome discovery for the next morning's commuters…

Hieronymus had paid special attention to this story, and to the others like it. He was aware of the details during his grueling ride. It made him a little bit paranoid. The man with the plucked-out eyes? He was a One Hundred Percent Lunar Man. What really interested the detectives—and the press—was the fact that the man's eyes were nowhere to be found. The murderers had stolen them. They did not take any money or valuables, but they took his eyes. They even left behind the fellow's goggles.

The police knew what it was all about, and it was not too difficult to figure out. The color of those eyes were the exact same as all the eyes covered by all the goggles that all the One Hundred Percent Lunar People were forced to wear. The color was highly unusual—the only place one could find it was in those eyes. It was not just any color or any mix of colors—it was something altogether new. It was the fourth primary color. And because of the extreme and hysterical reactions exhibited by anyone who actually saw this eye color, the color itself was illegal.

Hieronymus Rexaphin's eyes needed to be covered up because they were the fourth primary color. And simply looking at the fourth primary color caused profound temporary disruptions in the cerebral cortex. And so many people wanted to experience that…

I'll pay you fifty dollars if you let me have a peek at those eyes beneath your goggles.

Go away.

Listen, Hieronymus, I won't tell anyone if you just allow your goggles to slip off. I just can't imagine what a fourth primary color looks like. You have to let me see…

No way.

I'll kick your ass, goggle-freak, if you don't let us see what's behind those goggles!

Leave me alone!

That girl from Earth had also turned out to be a bit too curious for her own good.

He lay back in his bed. Certainly, if the police had found out, they'd be here by now.

He had kissed her. *Why couldn't it have just stayed at that?* Like normal people who just kissed each other and then maybe a bit more, but certainly not something as extreme and as unlawful as what then transpired?

They kissed. It was the most wonderful thing that had ever happened to him.

And then it was ruined.

She kept insisting. She was not just beautiful, she was everything beautiful should be, and she was from another world, and she seemed to be so intellectually together, and the sound of her voice drove shooting stars through his heart, and there was a quality to her that made him think she would be strong enough to see the color of his eyes with no consequence, but he was dreadfully wrong. He wanted to be a normal young man just this once. He was not, and life had seen fit to remind him of it. He allowed her to lift his goggles off, and then it happened, and it took hours for her to return to normal. It nearly destroyed them both. He thought about that part. How she went completely insane and it was his fault. And while it was happening he felt so horribly helpless.

Windows Falling On Sparrows.

He buried his head in his hands.

What had happened to her? She was a mess. Had her parents believed her? Was he a coward not to explain to them himself? Yes. He was a coward. He'd endangered her life, he should have turned himself in to the police, but, what the Hell, he had to catch his train, so he walked her safely back to her hotel, and then ran as fast as possible to the subway station. He was a very fast runner. He was so fast that, unknown to him until yesterday, some students called him *The Phantom* because he would always sprint to his classes at a remarkable speed. And last night, he ran from her hotel as if his life depended on it. He was convinced the police knew all about the evening's illegal transgressions—and that they were hunting him. All he needed was to get to the train. As fast as he could. He did not even have the time to call his father, who would be furious by this time anyway for not knowing where the Hell Hieronymus

was. He had to get on that train! He sprinted past the drunk-filled casinos and prostitute-infested bars, past the shambled buzz houses and
junkie dens, past the decrepit remains of the first LEM to ever land on
the Moon—it was over two thousand years old—past partying crowds,
past beautiful models out on the town with rich boyfriends, limou-
sines, intersections of crowded traffic, flashing cinemas, clubs where
loud bands inside played rhythmic and insanely noisy music, he almost
stopped when he saw the taxi stand but he remembered that he had almost no money left so he had no choice, it would be the Lunar Subway
System, Sea of Tranquility Branch, the most notorious of them all, a
dreadful train his father always told him to avoid, but he had to take
it and he had to run if he was going to catch the last train back to Sun
King towers, where he lived.

He succeeded. But the ride back was a slow-moving disaster. A hot
and suffocating disgraceful wreck of worn-out plastic and cracked aluminum. He arrived home at five o'clock in the morning.

* * *

Windows Falling On Sparrows lay in the strange bed. The police had
been both rude and kind to her, especially that strange detective with
the face that looked like a plastic doll with mismatched eyes. Of course
they were rude because she did not cooperate, and the doll-policeman
knew she was lying before she had even opened her mouth. She stared
at the ceiling, unable to sleep. She would begin to doze off, then…that
color…would nudge her from the place where her dreams began, and
she would sit up in her bed breathing heavily, trying desperately to see
it again. She was in a state of both terror and bliss. Then she would
remember him and start to cry.

Her parents had been outraged when she showed up late and
looking like she'd been hit by a leaking oil truck. Her behavior was
erratic—she could not finish sentences, and she refused to answer her
parents when they asked her what in Pixie Hades had happened to her.
Her mother began to scream at her father for allowing her to wander
out by herself on this dreadful, horrible Moon. Her father called the
police because he was certain she had been attacked or some sinister

gang-types had forced her to take drugs. When the police arrived, they spotted the signs immediately—she had been exposed to the fourth primary color. She refused to admit it, and the evening for this poor family from Earth went from awful to extremely terrible as the police became vicious and highly disrespectful. They had heard there was a One Hundred Percent Lunar Boy at the amusement park with a girl who fit her description. The police always kept tabs on One Hundred Percenters—just in case something like this happened.

If I had not shown you my eyes, none of this would have happened.

I don't care.

Are you sure?

Yes. And besides, I talked you into it. It was my idea. I can't say I remember everything that happened. I can't remember your eye color. I wish I could.

It's impossible to remember. Your mind won't allow you to remember.

That's sad.

No. What is sad is that we will never see each other ever again.

I don't believe you.

That is what I saw when you took my goggles off.

Then you are wrong.

I can't be wrong, but I wish I was.

We should test this out.

What do you mean?

Let's agree to meet here, on this very spot, tomorrow night at eight o'clock.

You won't even be on the Moon by that time. You will be on a Mega Cruiser going back to Earth.

You are wrong. My parents and I are not scheduled to leave the Moon until Sunday morning. We are not going to Earth—we are traveling out toward the rings of Saturn. I will still be here tomorrow evening. Come back and meet me here.

It will never happen. Instead, there will be an event that you cannot imagine that will force you and your parents to return to Earth.

You are wrong. Your prediction of the future cannot possibly come true.

It is not a prediction. It is a fact. The color I see does not exist in linear time. What I can see is the same thing as a shadow from the future. It cannot be changed…

Agree to meet me here tomorrow night.

I cannot agree to what I know is false.

Agree anyway. Agree because we kissed.

I agree to be here tomorrow night at eight o'clock.

Sitting up in her bed, she covered her face with her hands. Nearly all of the things he'd told her had come true. Since that terrible episode between her parents and the police, everything had changed. Their vacation faded into nothing. Cancelled. Hieronymus was correct—they were going back to Earth. If only she had not insulted that detective with the sweaty plastic face, they might have let her stay with her parents. Instead, she was here—in this steel room. Machinery all around. She will never tell them his name. Never. His wonderful, unusual name. They knew she had seen the eyes of a One Hundred Percent Lunar Boy; she wore it on her face as clear as the anguish of a star-crossed lover. They knew. This was their world and they knew, but they would never get his name from her. She was a woman from the Motherworld, and the secret of his name became her all-protected child, never to be given away to these diluted people of the artificial terraformed satellite, and especially that strange, confused man with the artificial skin and the nervous eyes, of which only one was real. Back to Earth she had to go. Expelled.

She closed her eyes and tried to remember it.

The color. Equal to red. Equal to blue. Equal to yellow. But with no name.

The memory was gone.

She could not remember the color, but she remembered how they kissed. And now that was ruined, too.

Before she left for her trip to the Moon, a friend of hers sent her an article that was making the rounds in the media. It was written by a journalist who was known for his inflammatory rhetoric…

NEVER LOOK ONE OF THEM IN THE EYE
by Warren Gladpony

Your mind will short circuit. Your eyes, the rods and cones of each retina, will scramble to accept a color outside the normal spectrum of red and yellow and blue. You will experience temporary psychosis. You will hallucinate. You will be reduced to a state of extreme helplessness akin to that of a newborn child at the moment of birth. This is what will happen to anyone who attempts to view the fourth primary color. The only known examples of this color can be found in the eyes of a certain minority of lunar inhabitants commonly referred to as One Hundred Percent Lunar People. These people, if they can even be called that, have a questionable place in the human race. Not only do their eyes have this abominable color that is crippling to look at, but these agents of the devil, these demons, have the ability to see the fourth primary color all around us. The governments of both Earth and the Moon don't want you to know this. They have declared that the fourth primary color is a myth, that it does not even exist. The lunar authorities are confused in their application of this law, as they require this inhuman segment of their population to wear goggles that filter out a color that they claim does not exist. At least these goggles serve as a warning—should you be unfortunate enough to visit the Moon, you must avoid all contact with those wearing them. These people have no place mixing in with the general population. Just one quick look at the hideous color of their eyes will result in a mental and physical seizure that will shut down your brain. You will suffer temporary madness.

The viewing of this color is so traumatic that your mind will have to reboot itself and, in the process, erase and reject all memory of it to carry on with its previously normal functions.

And these devils—that is only a part of it. It has been documented, and proven, that because these dangerous creatures have the ability to see the fourth primary color, they can also see projections of future movement. This new color exists in a dimension unrestrained by time. They can see how the fourth primary color leaves trailings and shadows of all movement, backward as well as forward.

Avoid them. It is an outrage that the government does not simply round up these abominations and destroy them. They should all be destroyed—before they destroy the rest of us.

She did not finish reading it, as it was nothing more than a paranoid hateful diatribe. And if anything, it helped to fuel her curiosity on the subject. After all, there was that other rumor—the one claiming only One Hundred Percent Lunar People had the ability to pilot Mega Cruisers.

*   *   *

Hieronymus got up from his bed again. He had a terrible headache. His room was not very big—a bed, a desk, four blank walls, a window. As he turned his head to look outside at the neighboring towers, a shadow fell upon him. It was another Mega Cruiser from Earth passing above. He wondered if she was on it until he realized it was most likely heading in, looking for a place to dock. The sky behind it was red. On the Moon, the sky was always the exact same tone of red. The artificial atmosphere was only a thousand years old but somebody had mucked it up good when they terraformed the Moon back then. He knew that on Earth, it was possible to guess the time of day simply by the character of the sky—its lightness, its darkness, its in-between. But the Moon's sky was always the same—a bland netherworld red. A red sky with a landscape covered in neon lights—every building on the near side of the Moon was covered in neon tube lighting, including the tower he lived in with his family. Exactly why it was neon, he had no idea—it was an aesthetic decided upon hundreds and hundreds of years ago. Everyone forgot why that was. The reason became lost through the centuries, like so many other things.

He watched the clouds of hummingbirds in the distance. There was only one kind of bird on the Moon: hummingbirds. They thrived in the artificial environment where so many others had failed. They were huge. An adult hummingbird was as large as a dog. They traveled across the landscapes of cities and wilderness in gigantic clouds. They lived everywhere, sometimes even under the ground. They were all, without exception, bone white. Lunar white. Colorless, hovering creatures. Half bird, half dream. They were often scavangers, and their long beaks were perfectly suited to retrieving trash from garbage bins. They were known to silently enter apartments and steal the dinner right off of plates the minute you had your back turned.

From afar, a traveling cloud of hummingbirds resemble a swirling white dragon as large as any Mega Cruiser, shifting, changing shape, dispersing, then re-forming again.

They were as numerous on the far side of the Moon as they were here.

There was a prison there. On the far side of the Moon. A special, secret place just for the One Hundred Percent Lunar Boys and Girls and Men and Women who broke the law—and not just any law, but specifically the law against deliberately showing their eye color to a normal person.

Nobody liked the far side of the Moon. It was nearly deserted. There were no apartment towers there, no cities, no trains, nothing. A handful of research stations with a few scientists. A single highway called Highway Zero crossed the entire thing. Grazing fields for wild animals. Strange farms run by robots because no one could stand to live there. The Moon was a place of extremes: the side that faced Earth was overpopulated and highly urbanized and illuminated with neon, and the side facing away from Earth was bleak and dead and full of shadows and fear. And a prison.

If she had betrayed him, he would be there by now.

He decided to begin his belated day. He went about gathering the clothes he thought he should wear. What a pity his favorite white plastic jacket was destroyed. He had left it on the floor, as he did with all his things. He found a shirt—wrinkly, but not stained and not smelly. From under his bed he retrieved a pair of crumpled pants he had only worn once. It then took him twenty minutes to find a matching pair of socks.

He tiptoed into the hall, heading for the bathroom. It was going to take an extremely long shower to get all that automotive gunk off of him.

He silently passed his parents' bedroom. His father was still sleeping. His mother was awake, but still in bed, crying. He was used to that. It was all she ever did.

Her name was Barbie. She too was from Earth. Because she spent every minute of her life crying, Hieronymus had never enjoyed a single conversation with her. Whenever he tried, she looked away, her face crunched up, tears spilling from her eyes, a miserable portrait of a never-ending state of misery. For years, Hieronymus thought it was because of their life on the Moon and that dreadful law—Quarantine Directive Number Sixty-Seven, the one preventing all parents of One Hundred Percent Lunar Children under the age of eighteen from ever leaving the lunar surface—that she was a woman so filled with tears.

His fault, in other words.

Ringo never wanted Hieronymus to think that.

"There is a reason why your mother is like that, Hieronymus. It has nothing to do with you. It has nothing to do with our living on the Moon. She was like that on Earth. For a long time."

"If that were the case, Da," Hieronymus once asked his father, "don't you think that after all this time you might consider sending her to a psychiatrist? She seems pretty miserable."

Ringo shrugged his shoulders as he always did when avoiding responsibility, which was something he was pretty good at.

"No," he replied. "She's not that bad off—she's just going through a rough patch."

Hieronymus did not believe him and concluded, naturally, that this rough patch had begun the day he was born.

The doctor held him upside down.

The doctor, even before spanking the goo-covered infant on the behind, knew something was off, something was slightly unusual about this baby.

The doctor held the newborn higher and glanced directly into its newborn face, only to suddenly squint his own eyes shut and turn away with a slight dizziness—like someone fearful of heights confronted with a thousand-meter drop.

Looking away, his face collapsed in sadness. His loud, resigned sigh was enough to warn everyone in the room of the inevitable announcement.

"Madam," he said. "Your son is a One Hundred Percent Lunar Boy."

Barbie had already been crying, so there was not a noticeable change in her. But the nurse who stood just next to the doctor was overcome by her own curiosity.

"How can that be?" she exclaimed loudly as she took the upside-down Hieronymus from the doctor. "Let me see…"

It happened so quickly. Everyone reacts differently. This nurse, Oxcelendra Marlin, was completely unprepared, and the doctor blamed himself entirely for not warning and training his staff in case this should happen—in case they should happen to deliver one of *them*.

She looked into the two tiny open eyes. She saw it. The color with no name. Not a simple mix of other colors—a new one. Primary.

She went into a sudden and extreme panic, and she felt as if the inside of her chest had collapsed, as if her body cavity was no more than a bag of crumpled-up paper. Someone took the baby from her. She knelt and placed her hands on the tiled floor. She remembered a prayer from her childhood. She chanted it out loud.

Jesus and Pixie, how your hour is bright.
Oh Pixie, Fairy of the Lord, I tunnel in my tracks
through fire, and flood and smashed automobile
He sees the colors of salt and blood
through his eyes, the demon portholes
witness him and his eyes that slay the normal light….

This nurse, suddenly mad, stopped reciting her unusual prayer. She knelt straight up and held her head between her hands. She tried to control the horrific fear that brought her groveling on her knees in front of the staff she normally had complete authority over. But they had not seen those eyes. The simple placement of his two irises, their positioning so completely normal. A color at once bright and from the void. She thought to herself, *is this what it is like for a blind person, sightless from birth, to suddenly see colors for the very first time?* No. A blind person would understand. This was more like being a dog. A beast who lives in a black and white world who suddenly gets a glimpse of color—and is unable to articulate what it means. *Nothing like yellow! Nothing like blue! Nothing like red! Nothing like green or orange or purple! New! New!* Her headache became intolerable. The doctor, her colleagues, they became intolerable as well. That baby—beyond intolerable. A bearer of light, but a light from the void. All else was dimmed, the collection of horrible people around that horrible infant became shadows, and the ceiling above reminded her of a bucket of combustible fuel. As a young girl, she once had her eyelashes and eyebrows burnt off while staring into a bucket of fuel that suddenly ignited, and her face received a sunburn, and she wondered as she looked up into the ceiling, *how long will it be before the combustion happens again?* Alas, it already had, for she actually saw the color that everyone secretly spoke about, and she had no idea exactly what it meant, as no one did. No one, nobody on the Moon or the Earth, understood what this meant. All they could do was hide from it. Pretend it did not exist. Never give it a name.

She heard voices. New people had entered the chamber, and one was a tall fellow she used to know when she worked in the operating room on the fortieth floor. But in her state, she could only ascertain the familiarity of his voice, and with it a certain degree of trust she felt as his form approached her. With his shape were several others. His voice was deep. *Oxcelendra, oh Oxcelendra, keep still, breathe deep, Oxcelendra, this will pass. It happens to everyone, the first time and every time. In a few moments you will be back to your old self, just breathe deep, your mind cannot keep it. Already the color is fading—your mind cannot process a color it cannot accept, Oxcelendra. Would you like to hear a story, my dear Oxcelendra, of the first time I saw this color? There you go; lie down on the floor. I was twelve and my older sister had a cruel friend who was one of them, and as a joke he took off his goggles and forced me to look at his eyes and I saw that color and I ran and hid under a table in a public restaurant. But eventually I was okay, and I reported him to the police and the cruel friend was sent away...*

Oxcelendra Marlin lay curled into a fetal position under a nearby window. No one bothered her once she fell asleep.

The doctor was already gone. Barbie was still crying, and a nurse stroked her head, which was protected by a paper hood and completely soaked in tears. Through her moist and squinting eyes, she saw another nurse walk away with her baby, who was already fitted with an infant-sized pair of goggles.

Endless stripes of neon covered the walls of the corridor. Ringo had to stop every twenty meters or so—neon was nothing new to him, but sometimes he got a little sick of its overuse on the Moon. It occasionally made him dizzy. He was angry at himself for not being present for his son's birth. If he were present, somehow, perhaps Hieronymus would have been born with normal brown or blue eyes and there would not be the massive unknown he was now wandering into. If he had been there, this would not have happened. But instead, he was at his cursed job overseeing the hydrodynamical particle converter just at the moment the zoning sequence began to blow off a few red lights. Even if Barbie had called him (and she did not, as she long ago had stopped communicating) to let him know she had suddenly gone into labor, it would have been impossible to leave at that exact moment.

He was one of only thirty-seven Ulzatallizine Hydro physicists on the Moon who knew how to transfer particle reactions into Hydro-Extraction salvage points—were he to leave at that exact moment, just as the acceleration modules were setting off alarms, it would have meant immediate termination, and correctly so, as such a move would have proved how terribly selfish and irresponsible he truly was.

Four years prior, another fellow of the exact same position left his post during an identical crisis and the resulting catastrophe ended the lives of four hundred and fifty-eight workers, thirty engineers, two dozen administrators, and six thousand inhabitants of a housing complex located just above the Ulzatallizine Extraction and Processing pump. It was a catastrophe caused by one man's stupid and selfish negligence—he had rushed home to see a goddamned tellball game between A.C. Tycho and Fecunditatis. He lost his job—and then he killed himself. Ringo took this event to heart. But still, he could not help but feel his absence in the birthing chamber added to the factors that tipped his son into the population of lunar inhabitants who were obliged by law to wear those dreadful, unattractive goggles.

He entered her room. Like the hallway, this place too was lit with neon. Barbie lay in her bed, on her side. Weeping. Her eyes were closed. Two rivers of tears, one from each eye, soaked the pillow behind her head. The only consolation he could muster was the bland normalcy of this. Her crying. Even if Hieronymus had been completely normal, she would still be crying.

She cried every day.

She hated living on the Moon, but she had not been particularly happy on Earth, either.

Ringo looked down at her.

Earth.

Suddenly, a forbidden place.

Not that he was in much of a hurry to go back. Since he and Barbie had taken up residence on the Moon, he had only been back once—one quick visit in the three years they'd lived here.

But now.

Quarantine Directive Number Sixty-Seven.

Eighteen years. They could not leave the Moon for eighteen years. Their life on Earth, their memories, instantly became a fleeting, half-remembered dream. Suddenly that was eons ago. Strange discolored images from a world now thrust into the far-away. Students at the university. She sat a few desks away from him in one of his classes. Her hair was bright red. Her accent. She took forever to tell him where she was from. He pursued her. The first time they kissed, a tree collapsed in the wind just three meters away, and they ran back to the party they'd escaped from, convinced it was their fate to be lovers.

Barbie is such a silly name, he told her. Oh, and yours, what kind of a name is Ringo?

The stove worked on and off. They had a cat who died—he buried it in a muddy field outside the small house they lived in when he was in graduate school. She wrote a novel; it was published. She earned her degree in Chlorination Reversal and worked for a time at a geological institute where a man named Filby tried to seduce her but instead got himself beaten up by Ringo, who used to be very jealous. They all became excellent friends—Filby married Ringo's sister. Ringo had very black hair. And his eyes were copper brown. Or velvet brown, as Barbie used to say, as they reminded her of the velvet couch her grandmother slept on. He once got drunk and wrote some embarrassing poetry he destroyed before Barbie could find it. A yellow kite—the wind forced it into a nosedive. Thieves stole their bikes. They were married at a shopping mall, before and after a pair of robberies. Ringo's father died in a mudslide. How many lovers did you have before we met? Several. How many is several? Several is a number I cannot remember because these past loves just don't compare to you.

Sometimes, people called the Moon the round rock.

Eighteen years on the round rock.

And it was worse for their son.

No One Hundred Percent Lunar People were ever permitted to visit Earth. Period.

An entire life condemned to the Lunar surface. His son. In exile. Forever.

Barbie finally opened her eyes, and quickly she looked away. Out the window, the sky hung in its usual, never-ending twilight of artificial red. It never changed color, never became fully day or night. Always in-between. From here, the new parents could see all the neon-covered skyscrapers of South Aldrin City humming with a billion grains of endless human activity. A lone hummingbird hovered close to her window. She stared at it. It knocked on the glass with its beak, probably thinking she might give it food. Barbie only stared at it, and seconds later, the hummingbird flew away. One of the skyscrapers in the distance appeared to be experiencing a power outage. None of its lights were on— it just stood there, bland and blank, a dark pink slab among the gaudy urban decoration.

She turned her head slightly, just a few centimeters, to look up at the muddy brown Earth. A ball of twinkling lights and smoke and filth. An abomination. An eyesore. An example for any world never to become.

Eighteen years.

As she stared up at the diseased object, in her ears, she understood someone had entered. She had no interest whatsoever in whom that person could be. She did not even know if it was a man or a woman, and she didn't give a damn. She continued to stare out the window. And whenever any cloudy snippet of conversation made its way into her ears, she tuned it out.

"Yes," said Ringo. "Our son's name is Hieronymus."

"A very nice name," said the social worker, smiling. "Did you or your wife choose that name?"

Ringo's voice was resigned and unfocused. And he hesitated, as if he were hiding something, something he wanted to speak about but simply couldn't.

"I chose it on my own. My wife has not been herself lately—she waved me away when I asked her what we should name our baby. She refused to be a part of the decision."

He looked up and noticed the social worker was sitting next to him. Her name was Joyellenbacx and she was wearing a suit made of aluminum paper, and her shoes were very chic—bright red with drawings of grizzly bears etched into the shiny plastic. She wore a women's tie that had a matching grizzly bear printed on it. She had large black eyes. Her hair was black. She smiled, and Ringo managed only a half-smile. And that was because he found her to be attractive—if she was only neutral in his eyes, he would have given her a neutral glance. With no smile at all.

"Why did you name him Hieronymus?" she asked, her smile unwavering, yet sincere.

"Oh. Well, you see…I was thinking that…you know, she might…" His eyes glazed over with suppressed tears. "That name, that name, is… well, I wasn't thinking very clearly when I filled in the birth registration."

"And is your wife okay with your choice of name?"

"I think so. I told her yesterday. I can't always tell if she is paying attention. I'll ask her. Barbie? Barbie, do you like the name I picked for our son? Hieronymus—remember? Our son's name is Hieronymus."

Barbie sobbed louder for a few seconds, then with her limp, barely living, horribly pale hand, she waved him away and continued weeping, her face deep in the moist pillow, no longer interested in the window and the landscape and the tower with the power outage in the distance.

"It's fine with her," Ringo said, as if his wife had somehow communicated something other than *go away*. "She likes the name."

Joyellenbacx continued to smile, but not as sincerely as before. After a moment's awkward pause, she began to speak in a hushed voice.

"Your son," she continued, "suffers from lunarcroptic ocular symbolanosis, also known simply as LOS."

"Yes," replied Ringo, his voice barely audible. "I know."

The social worker was about to start in with the usual—that the misinformation surrounding those with LOS was completely untrue, that their son would indeed have a completely normal life. One Hundred Percent Lunar children always grew up to be completely normal One Hundred Percent Lunar adults. They got educated side by side with other kids. They got jobs and they got married. They had children like everyone else. They were citizens, and on the Moon their rights were equal to all other citizens. On the Moon, that is.

But she saw he was a very well-informed man. He was less interested in the statistics and clearly worried about his son's health.

"Is LOS a disease?"

"No. Not at all. Your son is extremely healthy."

"So there is nothing wrong with him."

"Correct."

"Well, if LOS is not a disease, what is it?"

"We don't know. Lunarcroptic ocular symbolanosis began to show up about two hundred years ago. There are theories as to why some are born with it, but nothing has been proven. It is simply the ability to see a fourth primary color."

Ringo already knew. But the idea was too abstract for him to grasp its social and even political implications.

"I don't understand what the big damn deal is. So what? My son can see a few colors that the rest us can't. If that means he's just a little less colorblind than most of humanity, well, so be it—I can't imagine why he is forced by the law to wear those ugly goggles, and I especially don't appreciate or understand why he is condemned to live his whole life on the Moon! You yourself said that he is healthy—that this is not a disease!"

Joyellenbacx waited for Ringo to collect his thoughts, and to calm down a little. Actually, he and his wife were taking this news fairly well compared to others. Two weeks ago, a man and a woman in Brothersoftang attacked her while having an identical conversation to this one. They could not accept their daughter's eye color. They were now in jail, their daughter in an orphanage. He used to be the manager of a bank in William's Hamlet. She was the Lunar liaison for the C.R.Z. Corporation. They had both been born on the Moon and reacted as horribly as any uninformed Earthling.

Ringo noticed the woman sitting next to him was holding an umbrella. He had not seen one in three years.

"What are you doing with an umbrella? It *never* rains on the Moon."

"I know." She smiled. "My husband brought this back for me. Water fell from the sky. He used this to protect himself."

"Believe me, it's not a big deal—it's actually a pain in the ass if you get stuck in it."

"Rain. A world where water falls from the sky. It's hard for me to imagine that."

"So you've never been to Earth?"

"I was born there, but we moved to the Moon when I was only a few weeks old."

"Well, you're not missing much. And rain is highly overrated. It's only good for the farmers—and even they think it smells bad."

"Which is why it is so important to carry an umbrella."

"You won't need it here on the round rock."

QUARANTINE DIRECTIVE NUMBER SIXTY-SEVEN

It is hereby stated that all Lunar Citizens shall comply with the regulations listed below in accordance with Lunar Law. Failure to comply shall be punishable within strict interpretation of Lunar Criminal code 489B.

All Lunar citizens legally identified as bearers of Lunarcroptic Ocular Symbolanosis (hereafter referred to as LOS) shall be permanently restricted to the surface of the Moon. Any attempt to visit Earth or the terraformed colonies on Mars, Venus, the Thirty-Seven Asteroid Confederation, the League of Jupiter Moons, the Cooperative of Saturn's Moons Assembly, or any inhabitable or uninhabitable colonial entity within the legal frontiers of the Solar System shall be punishable by no less than twenty-five years imprisonment.

Any Lunar Citizen bearing LOS who attempts to breach the national planetary border of the Moon shall be subjected to criminal penalties.

All Lunar Citizens bearing LOS must strictly adhere to the following social regulations while residing on the lunar surface among the local population.

Schmilliazano lenses MUST be worn at all times. A list of acceptable goggle manufacturers can be found at any hospital, school, or mayor's office. Failure to wear Schmilliazano lenses is considered a criminal act.

IT IS ILLEGAL to show one's uncovered eyes to any Lunar or foreign citizen. Failure to comply will carry with it SEVERE criminal penalties. No exceptions are permitted, including family members and close friends and spouses.

The purposeful showing of one's eyes will be considered the equivalent of assault in the context of the law.

It is illegal to attempt any visual reproduction of the so-called fourth primary color.

It is illegal to attempt to name or classify the so-called fourth primary color.

It is illegal to speak of the existence of the so-called fourth primary color.

The so-called fourth primary color does not exist.

Ringo stopped reading the dreadful document that she had politely handed to him. He ran his fingers through his thick black hair.

"Why does this even exist? Why aren't people outraged by this? *Why?*"

Joyellenbacx shrugged her shoulders, somewhere between compassion and resignation. And a hidden measure of contempt. *No one cares why until it happens directly to them,* she thought. *Including yourself, Mr. Rexaphin. Did you really give a damn about this until you yourself got sucked into it? Of course not. Were you ever outraged when it applied to others? I doubt it. But now that it has happened to you...*

One of the broken neon stripes on the wall behind her sizzled and blinked on and off. She started to speak. She had said this all before and knew it all by heart. It was technical. She hated herself as she recited it.

"The first recorded case of lunarcroptic ocular symbolanosis occurred two hundred and seventeen years ago. It fell upon a girl—her name was Eleanor Biie. She only lived to be about nine before the people in her town killed her. Her mother had already committed suicide and her father was reduced to a mumbling idiot. No one had any proper explanation, and it is public record how the shock of the girl's eye color created the most inexplicable mayhem wherever she was, starting with her own home. You are aware, I suppose, of what happened at your son's birth. A nurse stared directly into your son's eyes. She experienced a short circuit at the most profound neuro-perceptive level. Your son has an eye color that cannot possibly exist. The human body and mind can only reject it if one sees it. It is an intrusion of the cognitive assembly of human perception. And her reaction was indeed normal. The mind uses its eyes as its first communicative portal of sensation with the outside world. But eyes are only organs—flesh, made of normal body tissue. For millions of years, humanity and, most likely, its animal predecessors relied on a sensory schemata dependent upon only three colors: yellow and red and blue. A fourth primary color disrupts the basic three-color tripod of our visual relation with the world. We cannot comprehend the fourth primary color, especially when it is shown to us. And because people cannot comprehend it, they invent their own surprisingly crude reasons for its existence. Totally logical people accept farfetched mythological and religious explanations. And historically, this has gone in both directions. Some of the early One Hundred Percent Lunar People were thought of as gods or demigods. Others were condemned as being agents of the devil or something like the devil."

But Ringo could not bear to hear any of this. The more she spoke, the more technical and awful and pseudo-scientific and fanatically religious the whole thing began to sound. She lost him. He stopped listening. In the middle of her last sentence, he got up and walked out.

She ran to the door and caught sight of his back as he walked away down the long neon-lit corridor. She ran to catch up with him.

"Mr. Rexaphin! Wait!"

He turned around, his body stiff as if he were a wooden board revolving. Two wet lines ran down his face from the tears he had successfully kept locked up until his back was turned.

"Mr. Rexaphin, there is something else. Something you have to know. Something you must tell your son once he is old enough to understand."

His dark brown eyes stared into hers, resigned, defeated.

"Sir, this is painful information I am about to give you. But it is true. And your son must be aware of this. It is very important. Your son must never become friends with any other child or person with LOS. Never. All LOS citizens, for their own good, must avoid one another."

"Why," he began, his voice barely a whisper, "why might that be?"

"If two people with lunarcroptic ocular symbolanosis look at each other without their goggles on, they…"

"They fall in love like normal people?" he asked bitterly.

"No. They die."

Lunarcroptic ocular symbolanosis was rare—but not quite rare enough. It lay somewhere on the horizon, an ancient phantom from the dark, barely inhabited far side of the Moon. It would sweep in through the open window. It would leave a ball and chain on whomever it chose. It chose Hieronymus Rexaphin. Stay. Stay here. Its breath was older than the craters that had long since been filled with the water of melted comets.

chapter two

She was an excellent friend of his.

Her goggles were not as ugly or utilitarian as most—*her* frames were translucent and stylish.

She also dyed her hair blue—as long as Hieronymus had known her, and that was since the third grade, she was the little girl with the electric blue hair.

And through all the school years that followed, her hair never changed. It was always blue. And it rhymed with her name, which was Slue. Sometimes people called her Slue-Blue. A nickname.

She was the girl with the blue hair.

And it was secretly and deeply important to her that people noticed the electric blue hair first.

It was the essential part of her fashion scheme to distract from the initial impression she was a One Hundred Percent Lunar Girl.

Slue Memling was the same age as Hieronymus. They were both sixteen. There were only five kids in their entire school of two thousand students who were classified as bearing lunarcroptic ocular symbolanosis, but none of them ever spoke to each other. By habit, or by force of nature, or by two hundred years of social engineering, the ones with the goggles habitually distrusted and avoided their own kind. And of course it was always in the back of their minds. The unspoken spectre. To look at each other without the goggles. Death in the neighborhood, in the area, whenever a pair of goggles pointed in the same direction. Final punishment for daring to imagine.

They were all so ashamed of themselves. The inexplicable eye color hidden behind their goggles made them all desperately wary of who they really were.

Slue was the exception. She succeeded, by way of her hair color, her fancy (imported from Earth, made in Italy) goggles, and her sheer enthusiastic force of personality, in putting her One Hundred Percent Lunar stigma several notches below the cosmetic attributes she invented. And it worked extremely well—the first thing everyone noticed was her blue hair. And her eyewear was too chic to be classified as anything but high fashion. Lunarcroptic ocular symbolanosis was not the first thing people thought when encountering Slue.

You're kidding! Slue-Blue's a One Hundred Percent Lunar Girl? How about that! I had no idea!

She was tall. She was very striking. She was very funny. An excellent student.

All the boys were in love with her.

Hieronymus had forgotten, but Ringo remembered the time his son came home from school back in the third grade.

Da, there is this really beautiful girl in my class! She has blue hair, and she is just like me. She wears goggles too…

Hieronymus himself was not immune to her undeniable charms, but he kept it tucked away and hidden, annoyed with himself that he had let their friendship slide into this confidential yet platonic, brother-sister-like point of no return. He secretly, ever-so-slightly fancied her—but it was too late. The definitions were made: she was his excellent friend, and just a friend, and in that static zone it stayed. And probably for the better.

Still, there were always those repressed thoughts whenever two One Hundred Percenters just happened to pass each other on the street or in a corridor or got stuck face to face on a crowded subway car. It entered his mind, phantom-like, every time he saw her.

Of course it's not true! We won't die! We can look at each other! We can!

And what would we see, if we did look at each other without the goggles?

They may have both thought that, but the question never came up between Hieronymus and Slue. Whenever they were together in class or in the cafeteria or the library, the other students stared, but only for a few seconds. *How unusual—two goggle-freaks actually talking to each other.*

And except for the goggles—and what they meant—Hieronymus was almost a normal student. Almost a typical high school student. In a typical public high school. On a typical part of the Moon. Almost.

But.

He led a double life of the most bizarre proportions.

Extreme Academic Schizophrenia was how his guidance counselor once described it to his father during a parental meeting. "Your son excels in some classes. In literature, for example. Ancient literature. He is beyond the other students. In fact, I would recommend that he begin university coursework just so he won't get bored. The same is true for his standing in history class. In philosophy, well, he might as well teach the class himself. He is astonishing. Your son has the makings of an excellent researcher in the humanities, should he someday decide to go into those fields."

Ringo was ready to pop open a champagne bottle and do headstands.

"But that's wonderful!" He laughed.

"That part *is* wonderful, yes, indeed it is, Mr. Rexaphin."

"Gagarin University, here we come!" Ringo thrust his fist into the air, and the guidance counselor went red with embarrassment.

"Well, not so fast, sir…"

The meeting went downhill from there. And, of course, Ringo blamed himself. He was essentially a mathematician and a scientist. He had failed miserably to transmit any of this inherent knowledge to his poor, suffering son.

"By law, as a public school funded by the taxpayers of the Sea of Tranquility, we are obliged to place Hieronymus into the remedial math class and the remedial science class and at least one remedial industries class. Your son may be at the top of his class in the humanities, but in science and math, he is at the very, very bottom."

"Very bottom?"

"Lower than the scum at the bottom of the math ladder."

"That's terrible."

"He will never graduate if he continues on his current course—he won't even be allowed into the next grade, he'll be held back. But if we move him to the remedial section, he will at least pass those classes. His average will improve."

"This is horrible. My son…in remedial…"

"He will have a schedule unlike any other here at Lunar Public 777. Half his day will be spent with the smartest, brightest, most intellectually curious in the entire school—the Advanced Honors class. The other half of his day will be spent with…"

That evening, Ringo tried to find a private school for Hieronymus. He knew someone who knew someone who knew someone who knew the admissions officer at Armstrongington Academy. He swallowed his pride without a thought, and after twisting a thousand conversations twenty-six-seven ways, he secured a quick last-minute interview.

I'm sorry, sir.

He failed for two reasons. He couldn't afford it. And even if he could, they still wouldn't let his son attend their fine institution. The reasons?

I'm sorry, sir. These are the worst math and science grades ever submitted by any applicant to Armstrongington Academy I have ever seen in all my years as an admissions officer.

Hieronymus attracted the worst kind of attention within seconds of walking through the broken-hinged door. Mess. Overturned tables. An odor he'd never smelled before. Not a teacher in sight. Chaos and noise and sudden stares flooded in his direction, because he was new and be-cause of the goggles. Sucked into a strange mini-world of anarchy and gaudy clothes and bizarre idiomatic expressions he could not under-stand. He was immediately surrounded, and three of them swarmed on him. His first day in the remedial section was quick and violent.

Is it true that you can see the future of anyone you look at without your goggles?

Let go of my arm!

Is it true, goggle-freak?

No. It's nothing like that!

I heard that when you take your goggles off, you can see colors that no one else can see. And that some of those colors show where people went and where people will go. Is that true, goggle-freak?

Stop calling me that, you filthy Loopie.

What, goggle-freak?

Let go of my arm before I really kick the skuk out of you.

You're going to kick the skuk out of me? I'm two years older than you, goggle-freak. I'll wipe the wall with your ugly face.

Leave me alone.

Leave you alone? Not till you show us your goddamned eye color, and then you tell me who is going to win tomorrow between Gratons and Wool so I can get my bets right.

It doesn't work like that, you fool!

Oh, no? Show us, then!

It was never even a scandal because it was so well covered up. No one cared about Lester—not even his own parents, who never bothered to go to the morgue to identify his body. And the other thugs who helped Lester pull the goggles off were too terrified to speak of it, of that color and what it did to them. No charges were pressed against Hieronymus—after all, they had attacked him, and on his first day in remedial math. The teacher was fired because the teacher was respon-sible, and the teacher had already been driven out of the classroom by the students. Hieronymus was fourteen at the time—he did not know these kids. They were completely out of control; they had already been through a succession of teachers who could not handle them. They, the boys and girls of remedial math, were not really a class of teenage children. They existed as a collective amorphous soup of instability. They were but a constant barrage of physical and verbal tornadoes. They struck without warning, out of boredom, out of malice, out of love. One side of the brain could not talk to the other side. There was only shouting and shouting and shouting. They were full of mockery, and they had lives at home so miserable they loved being in school even more than they hated it. They beat each other up, they beat up kids from other classes, they robbed people, they drank alcohol, they took drugs, they went to jail, they destroyed property, they wrote graffiti, they lied about everything to everyone, they threatened teachers, they were sent to psychiatric hospitals, they became prostitutes, they became pimps, they became gangsters, they became pregnant, they dreamed of expensive consumer items, and they blew whatever money they came by on clothes and shoes and hats and jewelry. They lived deeply, *but only* in the brief moment that existed during the time it existed. No peripheral vision, no yesterday, and no tomorrow. No attention span. No short-term memory. They discarded everything except whatever was self-destructive; they swam in currents so illogical not a single moment of reason could last before drowning in a violent whirlpool of chaos. Hieronymus was alone in a class full of these kids. They swarmed upon him. They grabbed him, they threatened him, they pulled off his goggles.

You can't look at the Devil in the eye. And that boy is a demon who carries the Devil in his eye. All of those Hundred Percent kids are demons. They don't know it, but they are demons.

That's not true. You know, and I know, that Lester was high on Buzz. Him and those other two losers were smoking Buzz in the utility closet and they overdosed and Lester died.

That's what the police say, but that's not what I heard.

What did *you* hear?

That that boy—the one with the goggles—already killed a few kids, and that they put him here with us as punishment.

I don't believe that. He probably got sent here because his grades in math really suck. Which is why you and I are here. Because we suck in math.

I'll bet he doesn't suck in math. And what does it matter—those guys with the goggles can kill anyone at will and the police will do nothing about it because the Devil is involved, and the Devil has a way of making things look perfectly fine. And they kill people that no one likes. Skukheads like Lester. Do you think anyone misses that scumbag? I hated him. I'm glad he's dead, but I stay away from that boy with the goggles anyway because he can kill you and me with just one look from those eyes with the Devil's color in them.

Man, you are really flying sideways.

I may be flying sideways, but I know a demon when I see one and that boy is one of them. He was sent here like bait, like the cheese in a mousetrap. He was sent here to clean out the nest, to kill off guys like Lester, and he can get away with it because the Devil protects him, and the Devil is in league with the goddamn innacawsing principal.

He quickly placed the goggles back on his face, and then he looked, knowing full well what had happened.

Lester, the boy who had demanded he take the goggles off, was on the floor, dead, his eyes wide open, an expression of pure terror chiseled into his face. The two other boys directly involved in the assault were down on all fours, slowly crawling away, one of them crying and mumbling incoherently, the other one praying just as incoherently. The floor itself was a filthy checkerboard linoleum tile. Several chairs lay on their sides. One of the boys stopped crawling, turned around, and sat, his face so turned inside-out with the harshest dead-fish-in-the-butcher-shop look of extreme physical disconnection, and he simply bellowed out loud with a despairing sound Hieronymus never thought possible from any human being. The other students piled themselves against the wall, terrified beyond belief—and, for the first time, silent.

He looked down at the dead kid. This kind of thing had happened before—getting picked on by bullies, getting the goggles torn off, and the result was always similar to this. Except no one had ever died before.

The principal, two policemen, a detective, and a forensics expert arrived at the scene. Shortly afterward, they were joined by another figure—a completely silver mechanical man. A rescue robot. He moved into the classroom as gracefully as a ballet dancer. He pointed his featureless face at the huddled students and a humming sound vibrated upward and out of him as he quickly scanned the assembled group, measuring their heart rates and nervous systems, making sure none of the human beings were experiencing trauma or shock from witnessing the untimely death of a classmate. He was so shiny that all the students saw their own reflections in his body and in his blank visage. The forensic expert took blood samples from Hieronymus, the dead boy, and the other two, one of whom had discovered a corner in the shabby room. The blood samples were placed into a small handheld machine for immediate analysis. The detective stared at Hieronymus, then turned to the principal.

"You let creatures like this take classes with regular students?"

"It's the law. We have to integrate them into the student body."

"This is the first time anyone's ever died from this."

"Died from what?"

"You know what I'm talking about."

"Oh, the color that doesn't exist."

The detective glared again over at Hieronymus. Hieronymus glared back. This was a very strange-looking man. His face appeared to be made from sweat-dripping plastic, as if it were a mask molded to look as real as possible, but failing because it was so hot and uncomfortable. The result was a sad fakeness, a department store mannequin's face with a moving mouth and a sad, angry eye behind the covering. An odor of lanolin hung in the air. A portrait of unpleasantness. Nobody liked this man. The other cops couldn't stand him. But he was an expert in these cases, and Lieutenant Dogumanhed Schmet was perturbed that this dangerous, inhuman creature with those eyes was not in handcuffs. One of the police officers had already recorded Hieronymus' statement. The other students were interviewed, but they, being who they were, gave twenty-five drastically different versions of what had happened.

No one cared what those psychopaths thought anyway. The whole scene had been captured by the classroom surveillance system, and it was clear Hieronymus had been hassled, then assaulted. The dead boy, Lester, had grabbed the Schmilliazano lenses while the other two held the One Hundred Percent Lunar Boy.

The forensics expert spoke to the detective after his analysis machine beeped with its result shown on its tiny, old-fashioned screen. "Okay, so the dead boy has a load of Buzz in his blood, along with traces of E-94—he was raring to go. His levels indicate overdose. Those other two? They're going to the hospital right now, and Goggles over there," he pointed to Hieronymus, "is clean."

"Do you think that boy's overdose could have been triggered by something?" the detective asked.

"Sure. It was triggered by him taking too much Buzz and mixing it with E-94, which is probably the most jackass thing one could possibly do."

The detective pointed to Hieronymus.

"You see what we have over here."

The forensics expert, a balding man who combed his black hair over his shiny wet skull in the exact same way men have been doing for centuries and centuries, was extremely careful with his words.

"I see a boy, probably about fourteen years of age."

"You know what happened. I want you to include in your report that even though his goggles were torn from his face involuntarily, the fourth primary color in his eyes triggered the overdose in the Buzz-head who's about to go to the morgue."

"Officially, the fourth primary color does not exist."

"I don't care if you think it exists or not—I want you to make the connection that that boy's overdose was caused by the fourth primary color."

"His overdose was caused by the ingesting and inhaling of too many illegal drugs. There is nothing in his blood sample that remotely suggests influence by any visual stimuli. I am not going to include details in my report that are not scientific and true, that cannot be presented as evidence. And in the eyes of the law, this so-called fourth primary color does not exist."

Annoyed and unsatisfied, Lieutenant Schmet then turned to the rescue robot.

"Belwin!" he shouted over at the machine. "Come here!"

Belwin, his silver form a marvel of anatomical engineering and chrome-plated minimalist style, moved eloquently toward Lieutenant Schmet.

"Yes, Lieutenant Schmet."

"Belwin, please scan the dead boy, and scan the creature over there with the goggles."

"Technically, Lieutenant, the expression 'creature' is not legally accurate when addressing the student with the Schmilliazano goggles."

"Whatever. Scan them both and tell me the extent to which the dead boy's death can be blamed on his exposure to the fourth primary color."

"Excuse me, Lieutenant, but there are only three primary colors: yellow, red, and blue."

"Belwin, are you familiar with lunarcroptic ocular symbolanosis?"

"Only insofar as whenever I perform feats of rescue, should I come across accident or fire victims who are wearing Schmilliazano goggles, I am obliged to make sure the goggles remain upon their faces. It is a safety consideration that I do not understand, yet am programmed to follow most stridently."

"Enough with the fireman shoptalk, Belwin. Kindly scan the cerebral cortex and optic nerve connections of the dead boy. Is there a rupture among the perceptionary axis that can be used as evidence pertaining to trauma from exposure to the fourth primary color?"

"Lieutenant Schmet, I am happy to assist you in all rescue operations. However, I am afraid that I will be of little use as an evidence gatherer. My scanning results only concur with my human colleague from the forensics department, which is that the overwhelming presence of the aforementioned illegal chemicals caused the death of this poor student. At this point, it is purely hypothetical for you to suggest that an unimaginable color could have thrown this deceased young man into a state of deadly trauma. And legally, there is no backing for it, as according to my legal statutes that guide my interaction with the human population, no fourth primary color exists and, therefore, it is outside my own understanding, as well as the understanding of the law and how it is applied to incidences of any criminal investigation. I say this not only as a machine, but as a machine who sympathizes with your curiosity of the perceptive conundrum. I do not see colors at all, as I am not a living entity, but I can imagine that were I a living being, I for one would be shocked to see any color at all, as I do not know what colors are, except as hypotheticals on the spectrum analysis data

I am fed, which, by the way, only informs me of three primary colors. And three is the legal limit. You yourself are outside the law to suggest otherwise, and you may have to put yourself under arrest if you persist in confronting the civilian population about colors that, indeed, do not exist within the laws that govern our legal responsibilities when interacting with the population of our society."

Schmet stared at the robot and saw his own unpleasant reflection in the slab of shiny metal where a face could have been constructed. He had one brown eye and one blue eye. They moved in unison, but not quite, as one was real and one was false. His real eye shifted to the boy with the goggles, and he made an intensive mental note to remember this one, this fish that got away.

That afternoon, Hieronymus was sent to his next class: ancient literature. He sat with his fellow students and entered into a class discussion on *White Jacket* by Melville and how it compared with Credolpher's *Rhythm of the Scron*. The teacher was immensely pleased with Hieronymus. And the other students, so adult-like, so respectful, were astonished by his on-the-spot analysis of these old classic works as well. Slue was there—she was in all the Advanced Honors classes. She always felt a strange, suppressed pride in her fellow One Hundred Percenter whenever he started speaking of these dead authors and the relevance of their ancient words and how they tied in with one another and how they tied in with the current social and political and cultural spectrum of their own lives, today, on the Moon. Hieronymus even quoted, verbatim, lines from *White Jacket* in its original language, free of translation, and when he finished it, he explained what it meant, and some students were so moved they went through great lengths to hide the moisture in their eyes.

No one thought of the dead boy on the other end of the school who was at that moment getting transferred to the Sea of Tranquility central morgue. No one ever found out about it. It was a non-event, just like the non-color.

The next day, when Hieronymus returned to remedial math, the incident was completely forgotten. But the other students, despite their ever-rambunctious behavior and destructiveness toward everything, avoided him. They feared him. He was a demon, or some kind of ghoul who could kill with a glance.

Hieronymus didn't even have to touch them if he wanted to kick their ass—he did it by just looking at them.

Two years went by. In all that time, nobody knew of his double life. Of his *extreme academic schizophrenia.* He dreaded someone would find out. Especially Slue. He was a master at avoiding the subject of *wait, what math class are you in?* Or *wait, where do you go for half the day?* Or the trickiest question of all, *wait, what were you doing on the second floor hanging out with those Loopies?*

Loopies.

Everything in the teenage world has a derogatory name. Always a put down. People categorized, given a label that, no matter what, stays and stays and stays.

Was that you I saw walking down the corridor with those Loopies?

Is it true that you have a twin brother who's a Loopie?

I passed by the Loopie class and I couldn't believe it—I thought I saw you in there with them.

The Loopies were what everyone else called them. If you were in *that* class, you were a Loopie. Even the teachers used the expression. While visiting the main office, Hieronymus once heard a substitute teacher being told that *sorry, today you get the Loopies,* and the sub just sighed and cursed and complained that *it is going to be a long day today, I can't believe that I'm stuck with the Loopies again, those kids are really horrible, oh innacaws it, on second thought I'm not doing this, no way* and the sub stormed out and the payroll secretary had to make a few more phone calls to find another substitute teacher. *Hello, this is Lunar Public 777, we have a call for a last-minute substitution, are you available. Yes? Good. Well actually, you will be subbing for section 241…yes, uh, that is correct, that is the Loopie section, but—wait, you just told me that you were available…*

Nobody wanted to teach the Loopies. Some teachers did not even last a day. Substitutes never wanted to come back. That troubled class full of troubled kids went through at least fifteen teachers a year. Not counting the endless times substitutes had to be called in because teachers simply walked out.

—

Luckily, most of the students at Lunar Public 777 were not of the Loopie persuasion. Hieronymus was aware of this fact, but for half of every school day it seemed to him he was living in a world of Loopies. Their highly vocal concerns and reactive behavior over every tiny detail in front of them, their need to shout constantly about inane things that would never matter in a middle-class setting, their extreme physicality, their inability to stay seated for more than thirty seconds, their abusive name calling, all of it, the rudeness and the anarchy and the idiomatic expressions he failed to understand, the whole Loopie experience began to take a strange place in his heart. He was quietly becoming a part of their existence. Sitting in that crowded class placed him in a very privileged spot: he could observe, only because they left him alone—and they left him alone because he was a killer and a demon.

He took advantage of the easy work and he was the only one in class who bothered to do any assignments. He scored very well on the remedial exams and quizzes. With time, the students gradually stopped ignoring him, and through the ear-aching chaos, he found out he had some friends. Many of them had qualities he found lacking in some of the kids from the Advanced Honors class. None of the Loopies were pretentious, for example. They were all brutally, horribly honest. They never pretended to like you. Beneath the shifting waves of illogic and anarchy and cruelty and sentimentality was a code—the Loopie Code—and after his first few months among them, he began to understand the basics of it and how to communicate with them. It was fun. He became "the smart one" in class, and slowly, ever so slowly, some of the Loopies actually put the occasional schoolwork question to him. Once that started to happen, he almost became a type of liaison between the students and whoever the teacher happened to be at the time. He became one of them. He even had a Loopie name. The Loopies, in line with Loopie reasoning, simply dropped the first three syllables from Hieronymus. He simply became Mus. He was the Loopie who proved the schoolwork in remedial math and remedial science was not the problem, the problem was with the *goddamned way the innacawsing wrackball teacher was looking at my EEE shoes, what, does he think he can find foot houses that can crimp his pan-handle like that?*

As his social status in the Loopie world rose to new heights, he was a little worried his cover might be blown—that he was not fully a member, that he was only there for half the day. They had no idea he was in the Advanced Honors class. Would his carefully cultivated status, his rise from victim to demon to semi-tutor, be compromised were they to discover his secret?

The concept of *extreme academic schizophrenia* was outside the understanding of the Loopies. But indeed, what would they do if they found out? Nothing, of course, because they had a million other concerns, like avoiding their abusive stepfather or getting the same pair of massively wicked Chromo-cufflinks that Blonzo Clangfor of Alphatown United wore. But that was not the question. *Would the Loopies stop trusting me if they knew...that I was also...a Topper?*

A Topper. Among other Toppers.

A dreaded, hated group. Total snobs. Brainy. The polar opposite to the Loopies. Perfect students, extremely adult-like in every way, logical, and not ashamed to quote poetry at the snap of a teacher's finger. Obedient, but ready to challenge a teacher if the teacher said something stupid. They were loved by the faculty, and the substitutes fought over the rare assignment to teach a Topper class—and indeed, that was a rare thing, because the teachers of Toppers never called in sick.

They were the Advanced Honors class. Hieronymus was a star among them.

Mus! Was that you I saw in the auditorium yesterday with all those Toppers?

I heard that Mus has a twin brother—in the Toppers class! Can you believe that?

The expression Toppers was not their own invention any more than the moniker Loopies originated from the Loopies. These labels were the work of all those students in the middle, the overwhelming bloc of boys and girls who were neither Toppers nor Loopies. Hieronymus never got to know any of these—he only befriended those on the fringe.

The kids in the middle, the big fat majority of average Joes and Josephines, had equal contempt for the Toppers and the Loopies. They felt physically threatened by the Loopies and intellectually threatened by the Toppers. To them, Hieronymus Rexaphin was an inexplicable phenomenon—they were not sure if he was even a student. Because of the scheduling of his classes, he often had to run through the crowded halls of Lunar Public 777, his goggles fixed to his face, sprinting from one academic end to the other, from Toppers to Loopies or Loopies to Toppers, dodging all the average kids, the non-crazies, the non-geniuses, the non-criminals, the non-prodigies. They called him names sometimes. They knew all about his extreme schedule simply by watching where he ran to and ran from and he didn't care if they knew, they all lived in the purgatory of teenage existence. He ran through them every day, several times a day, and they insulted him, *hey goggle-freak are you a Loopie or are you a Topper,* but he smiled and he wore their insults as a badge of honor because he knew their animosities were based on a peculiar kind of jealousy: There was no nickname for those in the forgotten, mediocre middle.

By the time he was sixteen, after two years of living the *extreme academic schizophrenic* dream, he had accumulated quite a number of friends from both worlds, and among them, he had two absolutely excellent friends. Slue, of course, was his excellent friend from the Toppers, who, like himself, also just happened to bear lunarcroptic ocular symbolanosis. On the other end of the spectrum, there was Bruegel, his excellent friend from the Loopies. Bruegel had no idea what lunarcroptic ocular symbolanosis was. In fact, it did not even occur to him that Hieronymus wore those goggles for any reason at all except that they looked cool.

Bruegel was a type of prince among the Loopies. He had as many social problems and family miseries as any of the others in that den of frazzled youth, but, unlike most, he never chose violence as his first or second option to solve anything. Which is not to say he was never kicked in the face after breaking a classmate's nose with his hammer-like fists—Bruegel never followed violence, but violence had a way of following Bruegel. He was big and burly and with his unkept mop of dirty blond hair, maintained a peculiar joviality among the swirling chaos around him. His expression was always perplexed, amused, and, most of all, innocent. He was dirty, but never in a repulsive way—indeed, his dishevelment was more like that of a knight who fell off his horse and landed in a pool of mud—and if an aristocratic Loopie could even be imagined, complete with an aristocratic sense of naïve ragtag splendidness, it was Bruegel.

He failed every subject, every year.

He was very, very easily distracted.

He often exploded into remarkable bouts of enthusiasm for things or ideas in direct contradiction to the teacher's plans.

Some teachers thought he was a lousy student but a brilliant and likable fellow nevertheless—other teachers thought he was just the worst thing to ever walk into their classrooms. The girls could never decide if he was handsome or horrible.

Hieronymus liked him immediately.

Every time Bruegel walked into a classroom, the room became smaller, and his voice, naturally several decibels above the din, dominated all sound. He was constantly being told to *shut up!* or to *lower the volume of your noisy trap!* but it failed to register. In the world of the Loopies, Bruegel and his way of speaking transformed whatever classroom he entered into a tempest of cacophony—with himself at the center.

"Hieronymus!" he shouted across the crowded room. Bruegel was the lone member of the Loopies who never called the One Hundred Percent Lunar Boy "Mus." He found shortened names to be somewhat beneath him. "Hieronymus, you would not believe what happened to me today on my way to this den of un-learning…"

"Bruegel!" shouted the exasperated teacher, already overwhelmed by the waves of noisy disrespect.

Non-plussed, Bruegel continued.

"A woman came up to me on the subway—I think she was from some kind of religious organization. She rang a bell and she wore this really bizarre hat and she wanted me to give her money. She waved a book at me."

"Bruegel!" the teacher shouted.

"She was good looking, but too old for me—and she was really weird. She was talking about Jesus and Pixie."

The teacher, whose name was Mr. Flustegelin, who had only been with the class for two weeks, and who was already completely burnt out and close to quitting, shouted at Bruegel again.

"Bruegel, you are late and you are disrupting this class!"

This was both true and untrue. Bruegel was indeed incredibly loud. And if the teacher had been successful in controlling the class, the accusation that Bruegel was disrupting the class would have certainly been a legitimate complaint. However, as the noise level had already crossed the acceptable limit before Bruegel's arrival, it appeared the teacher was picking on him unfairly. And most likely because Bruegel never attacked teachers—he was a safe reprimand.

"My dear sir!" Bruegel shouted. He never bothered to learn any of the names of the teachers—he only addressed them as *my dear sir* or *my dear madam,* and because he was aware of his own limitations in vocabulary, he often made up words to make himself sound smarter than he thought he was. "Your quadrangulations on the vobis articulations exiting from my oral sector are most excrustinghating! I am not the solitary sens-being-boy in this room who is a torrent-builder of volume! I suggest you punish my classmates first before you rally your aquizations and stolligahazen against me!"

The class roared. Some students felt the teacher unfairly did not notice their own uncontrolled contributions to the general din of noise. Bruegel's pseudo talk only acted as a type of volume switch for everybody, suddenly shifting the cacophony into an upward direction.

"Bruegel, you are the loudest in this room!"

Bruegel ignored the teacher, and before he could continue shouting across the room to Hieronymus about his inane encounter that morning on the subway, he turned to a girl named Clellen, who sat a couple of meters away from him. His voice was just as loud as it had been when speaking to Hieronymus.

"Clellen, did you watch *Sweaty Servants* last night? I thought the girl who played Roxanne looked just like you."

"Shut up, Bruegel!" Clellen shouted, obviously insulted. "I look nothing like that sling-shot! You got your typhoon sucking backward again, penguin buster!"

"I meant it as a compliment," Bruegel yelled back, laughing with both mockery and affection. By the time he finished his sentence, there was an altercation on the opposite side of the room, with one Loopie already smashing another in the face with a huge metal belt buckle he was using like a pair of brass knuckles. Mr. Flustegelin ran over to the fight in an attempt to break it up, but instead tripped over a student's foot. The student, despite having his whole leg jutting out, sitting in the most improper fashion, actually did not intend to cause Mr. Flustegelin to fall, but was still, nevertheless, outraged the teacher did not see his leg. The minuscule bit of pain that momentarily flashed through his toe caused this student to roar and scream the worst accusations at the poor embattled teacher who lay on the floor, his own skull throbbing from slamming onto the hard surface. The crying student, seizing a moment of self-righteous outrage, hopped over to the teacher's table, picked up the tablet screen that the wounded adult had been using for his lesson plan, and smacked the stunned Mr. Flustegelin directly in the face just as the man was getting up.

"You abusive, student-hitting monster!" he shouted. "You broke my toe! You broke my toe!"

With every shout of the word *toe*, he smashed the tablet down on the man, who lay in a fetal position, covering his head with his arms to shield himself from further blows. Within seconds, other students joined in on the assault, surrounding their teacher, whom they hardly knew because he was new and could never control their class even for a second, and kicked him as if he were a bag of diseased rats.

Bruegel took no part in this attack, but instead smashed open the lock on an old closet with a hammer he had smuggled into the school, and within moments was tossing all kinds of small plastic tools and data cards and student tablets all over the room, singing a popular song. *Someday it will rain on the Moon and when it does, I'll reign on you.*

Hieronymus hid under his desk. Soon the security guards would arrive as they always did, nearly every hour, it seemed, as scenes like this were common in the Loopie class. He quietly took out his own secret mini-tablet, where he was preparing an exposé on *The Confessions* by Jean-Jacques Rousseau for his philosophy class. He had just finished reading it, and in its original language no less. He wanted to sprint out just as the guards showed up with their batons and nets and stun-gas.

He hated to be late to class because of this kind of thing.

Moments later, like a sailor arriving in a calm port after a swirling tempest at sea, he would arrive in philosophy. Or history. Or literature. No one in those classes had any idea of his other life among the mad. And the mad had no idea of his other life among the intellectuals. He stepped in and out of both worlds seamlessly. He belonged in both, and his eyes bore the color that belonged nowhere.

chapter three

Hieronymus and Slue had entered the media-viewing rotunda to gather some research materials for an exposé they were collaborating on— the project was to be an examination of *The Random Treewolf* by Naac Koonx. Hieronymus had already collected a myriad of critical opinions and notes on this well-known classic, and his own analysis on it was already beyond all reproach—however, thanks to his father's brother, Uncle Reno, he had discovered something about *The Random Treewolf* of which he was certain not even his professor was aware. He couldn't wait to see the look on Slue's face once he showed her.

It would blow her One Hundred Percent Lunar mind.

He and Slue sat down together at a table in the center of the huge room and plugged into a data terminal. They took out their tablets and launched their stylo-points.

"Well…" he began as about twenty noisy students from an art group walked past them heading for the pigment distribution terminals.

"Well, what?" she answered.

"Well, I think we got stuck with a very boring assignment," Hieronymus lied as he played with his stylo-point, drawing a small translucent box in the air, then drawing a cloud shape inside that, then clicking on the cloud where it animated itself with a tiny cartoonish lightning bolt, lines suggesting rain falling beneath it.

Slue looked at it for a second, then waved across it with her own stylo-point, erasing it.

"Get serious, Hieronymus."

"Why did you erase my rain cloud drawing?" he asked with obviously fake indignation.

Slue was about to lecture him on the obvious—that as One Hundred Percenters, they had never seen rain, nor would they ever experience the sensation of rain for it never had and never would rain on the Moon. She was about to get all serious on him, have a stern goggle to goggle chat on their plight in life, until she realized he was already open to page 42 of *The Random Treewolf,* his stylo-point busy underlining whole sentences in the translucent floating graphic in front of him.

From her tablet, she activated and pulled up her own copy of the same novel. She stared into the translucent image of the page before her—with a wave of her hand and the correct amount of clicks from the stylo-point in her fingers, she adjusted the opacity of the image in front of her. She began to read, starting also at page 42—until she realized *her* page 42 was extremely different from the page 42 Hieronymus was reading and making notes on.

"Hey, we're supposed to be working on the same book."

"We are," he answered, his focus never leaving the page image in front of him.

"No, we're not," she insisted. "Look at your page 42. Now look at mine. They are extremely different."

He never took his eyes off the work in front of him, nor did he give Slue the satisfaction of looking in her direction as he spoke. He knew she would sooner or later come to this realization. In fact, her reaction was all going exactly to his plan.

"We are both reading *The Random Treewolf* by Naac Koonx," he blandly reported.

"No, *I* am reading *The Random Treewolf* by Naac Koonx. You are reading something entirely different!" Her voice had begun to increase in volume, and he smiled. Some students at another table turned to stare at her.

"Shhhh…" he whispered at Slue.

Another crowd passed through the rotunda. "Hi, Slue!" A boy walking among them called to her. His voice echoed above the mashed sounds of a hundred conversations and she glanced at him for a quick second. Bob. Big. Athletic. Not a Topper. Okay student, but completely bland and nondescript. He "liked" her and she truly wished he didn't. He emerged from the shadows with fifty other faces, smiling, staring at Slue as if she were pleased to see him. But she was indifferent, and the smile she tossed back at him lasted as long as her glance. Bob's class transversed the rotunda, briefly illuminated by the room's circular dark yellow globe light above, then their walking forms disappeared into the shadows at the opposite end. She'd say hello to him later. After this crisis over the book was resolved.

She whispered, but even her whispering was heard a few tables away.

"You are not reading the same book as I am. Our pages are remarkably different!"

"Same book, Slue."

She dragged her chair closer to Hieronymus and the floating image of the page in front of him, then nearly thrust her face into the letters as she pointed out the obvious discrepancies to his amusement.

"Look at what you are reading!" she said, circling some text in the middle of the page with her stylo-point. "Who is this character Neef? And what is this business about the donuts in the back seat of the pelican push cart? And look! Look at that line, that sentence! *The candy-fine ran-ran bungled over her top nose as she told Paul how much the clouds at dawn resembled the veins in his hard-boiled, hungover dirty filthy bloodshot eyes, oh nuclear explosion, oh nuclear explosion, oh nuclear explosion, oh, spinning top, rop and mop!* How can you sit there and tell me that that is the same novel?"

She barely had a moment to let that last sentence leave her open mouth, her teeth slightly horselike at that moment, the blue strands of hair waving on either side of her lips as she made her determined point, when there was another greeting from another male admirer.

"Slue-Blue! Slue-Blue!"

Both Slue and Hieronymus looked away from their work as another large class of students passed into the media-viewing rotunda. Again, there was a fellow, tall and athletic looking, who smiled in Slue's direction as he walked with his classmates through the rotunda. Jim. A star second backer on the Lunar Public 777 tellball team, he thought every girl in the Sea of Tranquility found him irresistible. Indeed some did, but Slue was not among them. And yet, there he was, just like Bob, convinced she was somehow interested in him. She gave Jim the exact same fake smile she had given Bob, then turned back to the contested book.

"As I was saying, Hieronymus, you are not studying the assigned text. Which, frankly, is your own problem. But being that we are working in groups and you and I are supposed to collaborate on this project, I guess you must think it's very funny to pretend to be reading the same book as I just to get me upset."

What didn't help matters much was the fact that Hieronymus had a big smile on his face. He was about to explain the game to her at last when, for a third time, a voice called out her name.

"Slue! Slue! Slue!"

Once more, a large group of students entered into the rotunda and, as usual, there was an athletic guy whose head jutted up slightly from the bustling crowd of teenagers. This young man had an ear-to-ear grin on his face—an expression seemingly cut from an identical mold as the other two. This was Pete. Pete was also on the tellball team. And not only was Pete on the tellball team, he was also the team's captain. He was also on the track team. He was a young man who liked teams a lot. Everyone in school liked Pete, but at this moment, Slue did not even bother to smile at him—she just turned herself back to the text, utterly and totally and completely embarrassed.

"Slue, why do those guys think you like them?"

"Shut up, Hieronymus."

"No, seriously. It's like you have a fan club here that only accepts barrelhead athletes."

"I don't know why they think I like them."

"Well, you must have *something* to do with it."

"Those boys are just dumb. I don't know why they look at me like that. I don't even flirt with them or anything."

"Maybe you flirt with them by accident."

"Don't be stupid."

"Maybe Bob or Jim or whoever dropped something like, I don't know, a coin or a rubber band or something, and you just said something completely bland and neutral like, 'Excuse me, you dropped your rubber band,' and to them, that was some kind of sexy flirtatious signal." When Slue glanced sideways at Hieronymus, she saw by the curvature of his mouth, the tilt of his neck, and the tone of his voice that he was being as sarcastic as a bloody Pixie in Hades.

"Your head," she stated, articulating very slowly, "is somewhere… on the…far side…of the round…rock…stupid…"

Hieronymus turned around to see Pete still trying to get Slue's attention as the large group he was stuck with continued to shuffle through the media-viewing rotunda.

"Slue! Hey, Slue!"

Slue pretended to be deaf, but Hieronymus stared back at Pete. Then it occurred to him. This was the third huge group of students to pass through this normally quiet zone of research and study. Some kind of event must have been going on in the school, and they had no idea what.

"Hey, you! Guy with goggles!"

"Are you talking to me?" Hieronymus called back, almost shouting.

"Yeah. Tell your sister to look over here!"

"She's not my sister."

"Whatever. Can you tap her on the shoulder?"

"Tap her on the shoulder? What's that supposed to mean?"

"Just do it."

"What, tap her on the shoulder?"

"Yeah."

"I don't know, that's sort of a tall order. I know for a fact that she doesn't like to be tapped by anyone, especially me."

"Don't be a rectumexit. Just do it."

"I'll do it for five thousand dollars. I was originally going to charge you three thousand, but then you suggested that I'm being a rectumexit, so the price went up."

"Don't make me go over there, phallic-brain."

"Actually, I'm trying to make you come over here so you can tap her on the shoulder yourself."

"I can't go over there. No one's allowed to leave the line. Which means your nose stays on your face for a little while longer."

Hieronymus paused for a second. Those threats meant nothing to him—and Pete must have thought Slue was wearing headphones to block all the noise out, for during their shouting-across-the-room conversation, two more classes came into the rotunda and the normally quiet library-like space was suddenly as noisy and chaotic as the cafeteria. Hieronymus stole a quick sideways glance at Slue—actually, she was working extremely hard to pretend she did not hear the exchange over *shoulder tapping*, pointing her face away from Pete, straining not to laugh.

More class-sized groups of students entered.

"Hey, shoulder-tapping guy! What the Pixie is going on?" Hieronymus sincerely asked his new nemesis. "Why are all these classes passing through the rotunda? Where are you all going?"

Pete only gave him a disgusted smirk.

"Go innacaws yourself, goggle boy."

"I'll make you a deal," Hieronymus said, not impressed by the big guy's insult. "How about if you tell me what's going on, and then I'll tap your girlfriend here on the shoulder—I'll even knock her headphones off so you can just speak to her directly. I'm sure she would love to hear the eloquent way you go around asking people to tap each other on the shoulder."

As expected, Pete had not the slightest notion Hieronymus was being sarcastic. He only followed through as if this was a serious, actual proposal.

"It's a school assembly. Something to do with dental hygiene. Everyone is supposed to go with their classes. Why aren't you and Slue with your homerooms? Everyone is supposed to go. There. I told you. Now tap Slue. We're about to leave. Tap her on the shoulder, and do it quick."

Hieronymus didn't give this a moment's thought. He turned slightly, tapped Slue on the shoulder with an exaggerated, mocking gesture that completely flew over Pete's head, and she pretended to be surprised, pretended to take tiny objects out of her ears, pretended not to know what to expect as she swiveled herself around, pretended to be surprised, pretended to be pleased to see the larger form of Pete standing with his class, then pretended to smile in his direction as she waved. Pete waved back. Hieronymus also waved at Pete, and Pete waved at Hieronymus, and all bad feelings were instantly erased. As if they were all friends.

"So what's *his* name," Hieronymus asked with slightly cruel grin.

"That. Is. Pete."

"Pete? That big guy who threatened my nose is named Pete?"

"He didn't threaten your nose."

"He did."

"He did not. He only says things like that. He's really very sweet…" That last word rolled off her tongue with a certain tone of regret.

"So you *know* him!" Hieronymus teased.

"No, I don't know him."

"But you just said that he was very sweet! How would you know that he was sweet or not if you didn't know him?"

"I just know him a little bit."

"A little bit. Did you ever kiss him?"

"Are we going to work on this project together or not?"

"I think you kissed him."

"I never kissed him and I don't think it's any of your business"

"I think you know indeed that it is my business—and you know why."

"You are such an idiot."

"All of us One Hundred Percent Lunar kids have to stick togeth—"

"I knew you were going to bring that up!" At this point, the noise level of the rotunda had decreased significantly as the last groups of students shuffled themselves out, and the discussion between Slue and Hieronymus once more became a public spectacle.

"We are NOT friends because we are both members of the LOS community! That has *nothing* to do with *anything*!"

There was an astonishing silence after that last syllable. A small group of students at the next table glared at them.

"*LOS community?*" Hieronymus gasped, his expression incredulous, embarrassed, amazed, and disgusted all at the same time. "Where does *that* come from?"

"LOS. Lunarcroptic ocular symbolanosis! What are you, utterly and completely *ignorant* about *everything* in your own life!"

"No, it's the *community* part that bugs me."

"There is no name for us as a group! Have you ever wondered about that?"

"What are you talking about? Everyone calls us One Hundred Percent Lunar…"

"Exactly! Have you ever wondered about that stupid expression?"

"No, but come on, LOS community sounds like a place where frail elderly people go to stay away from…"

"One Hundred Percent Lunar Boy, Girl, Person, whatever is a derogatory expression that others invented for us. Do you know where it comes from?"

"Slue, I don't know, and I don't want to know," he lied.

"Ninety-four years ago there were camps on the far side of the Moon. It was where they stuck all of us. It was during a time known as the Regime of Blindness. It's not spoken about in schools. It is denied, and the deniers have been in power for generations…"

"I told you, I don't want to know this!"

"Of course you don't. It's been erased from the history books."

"Then how do you know? Who told you?"

Slue stared at him, unable to speak, the answer unable to launch itself from her gut.

A cruel laugh came up from Hieronymus—it sounded cruel, but actually, it was sad and, at its center, just plain jealous.

"Did one of your boyfriends tell you that?"

Hieronymus realized things with Slue were suddenly falling out of hand—and he was squarely to blame. He always liked to tease her. Two minutes earlier she was trying so hard not to laugh when he was mocking Pete. How quickly it had shifted into this. She was standing—her hands were clenched into fists. Her blue hair matched the short jacket she wore over a black t-shirt. Black and blue. In ancient times, blue was a sad color. It was associated with melancholy. Slue-Blue. Slue-Blue. For the first time, he quietly damned everything in his life for the simple fact he could not see her eyes. As they really were—without the purple lenses. He could see the shapes of her eyelids and he saw her eyelashes, the dark dots of her pupils and the whites of her eyes—but without the color of the iris, her eyes were denied. As were his own.

They stood frozen. They were about to talk about it, she wanted to, she wanted to tell him *we will not die if we look at each other with our eyes uncovered* but he stopped her—how long could humanity live on the Moon and remain human? There was no percentage below One Hundred. Either you were human or you were something else entirely. The Moon was a stone in space. The air they breathed was artificial. The water they drank came from melted comets. She dyed her hair blue. They were working on a project together. She stood. They were always told never to look at each other, never to speak to one another, but that was a lie from somewhere and Slue knew things he did not know and he was afraid to find out. It was obvious by the silence they fell into. The other students were staring at them. Her hands were still in fists. The lenses over their eyes prevented the subject from progressing. He savored this sight of her…

He was about to confess that everything in his life revolved around her, and *Ha, I'll bet you didn't know that, Slue—I myself could not grasp it, not till now, the moment you stood, your fists clenched, the slow reactive movement of your hair, you spun, I revolved with you, I had no idea that I was your satellite, but I am, there is no gravity in my life without you...*

Hieronymus spoke in a voice she could hardly hear. He looked at the place where her shoes met the floor.

"My mother stays in bed all day. And all she does there is cry."

Slue's fists relaxed.

"She's done that for sixteen years. I've never had a conversation with her."

Her fingers extended and pointed to the floor.

"She wears a raincoat to bed. A plastic raincoat."

Slue sat down.

She looked straight ahead. He was all wound up. All his own details he kept to himself. She knew nothing about his mother—she had assumed his mother was gone. Dead, or far away on Earth; she never saw her, and she never asked because Hieronymus always behaved as if it was only himself and his father.

The Regime of Blindness. She will tell him. He knows it's true.

Slue sat there for a long time looking at him. Through his goggles, she saw him blink both his eyes. She knew he was not looking at anything, and she waited for him to speak again, and his lips did move, but nothing came out. He reached up and brushed something imaginary from his hair. He was about to apologize, but he couldn't. *I'm sorry, I'm just jealous, those boys don't have goggles covering their eyes...*

Dear Hieronymus, I did not know this about your mother. It was your secret. I have a secret, too. But I can't tell you. Not yet. It's about my older brother, Raskar. You remember him? He lives in the District of Copernicus. He's an attorney, and he works in the Lunar Federal Court, and he has accidently discovered some things that are unimaginable. Things that have direct consequences for you and I. What the government and its corporate partners are doing. My parents are terrified that he is going to get arrested, but they are even more terrified of what may happen to me if his ear and eye on the truth are disrupted. He has joined an underground society, secretly gathering evidence that all is not right here on the Moon. All is not right, but one thing is for certain: The lies began when they told us all we can never look at each other. That's what they fear the most. You and I, and others like us, looking at each other.

Eventually, she asked him a question. It had to do with their project.

"You really aren't reading *The Random Treewolf*, are you?"

Hieronymus shook himself out of his wandering mind. Of course. Their school project. His page was still illuminated and hanging in midair only inches away, next to her page. The texts were entirely different.

"It was a surprise I wanted to show you. We really are reading the same book by the same author, but…" He paused. "My copy is a direct translation of the original edition. What we have in the library here in school is the standard version that students have been studying for at least one hundred and thirty years. I found out that this book has been 'updated' three hundred and forty-eight times in the past nine hundred years."

Slue was astonished, and she reacted in her usual manner whenever she was astonished at anything—she shrugged her shoulders with a noncommittal "So?"

"It is a completely different book," he replied. "It is evidence of the crime of 'updating'."

"The crime of 'updating'?" she whispered. With her stylo-point, she flipped the book imagery back to the title page. It read: *The Random Treewolf* by Naac Koonx (Natalie Koolmahn) Translated from the Ancient American English by Reno Rexaphin.

"Reno *Rexaphin?* Any relation?"

"My uncle. He's a Professor of Ancient Literature at Quadroff-Maxant University on Earth. But he comes to the Moon quite often for research. He's here now, as a matter of fact. I saw him two days ago."

"He comes to the Moon—to research ancient literature?"

"Of course. The Moon has the largest paper book library in human history."

"Paper books? Here on the Moon?"

"Yes. You didn't know that?"

"I never imagined such a thing."

"It's not exactly a secret, but it's not open to the general public either. Only researchers like my Uncle Reno have access."

"Where is this library?"

"On the far side. Inside of a mountain. It's more like a vault, from what I hear. But it was the only way to save all of these ancient books from being lost forever."

"They sent them here to the Moon?"

Hieronymus recalled the long conversation he had had with his Uncle Reno. Reno Rexaphin had made a name for himself in the tiny world of academics by discovering most of the current editions of classic literature made available to the public today bore almost no resemblance to their original editions that had one time existed on paper in their original languages.

Reno concluded that gradual laziness, anti-intellectualism, and fuel consumption were to blame for what he considered to be this colossal human tragedy.

"Hundreds of years ago, the Earth ran out of fuel," he'd explained to Hieronymus during his last visit. "Then some idiot discovered that old paper books, with their highly combustible paper sheets, made a fine substitute. No one cared that this meant destroying millions of copies of novels—because nobody read them anymore. Literature itself had been transferred to a digital format, but it was done badly and carelessly and the experience of picking up a book and flipping through the pages was lost. Books were considered these archaic things, taking up space, no longer readable because the general vocabulary of humanity had diminished to such a pathetic level that nobody understood them anyway. Great works of literature were lumped together with common magazines and newspapers. Burned as fuel. And nobody, absolutely nobody, cared. Books became akin to the organic matter of dinosaurs and prehistoric forests that eventually became oil. Those who protested this were openly mocked."

Slue looked at Hieronymus as he explained what his uncle had told him—how, at last, a movement was begun to bring the last copies of books to the far side of the Moon, how the hidden library was constructed, how through the centuries that followed, it grew into the largest vault of human endeavor and archiving in history. They kept millions—maybe even billions—of paper books there. Many of them written in languages that didn't even exist anymore.

"Do you think your uncle would let us come and see this place?" she asked.

"As long as he's there, I don't think there would be any problem at all."

"I have never seen a real paper book in my life," she half-whispered.

"Nor I," replied Hieronymus.

They looked at the image of the title page again.

"When did your uncle translate this one?" Slue asked.

Hieronymus smiled. "My uncle did this while he was in graduate school, twenty-something years ago. It was one of his first. He was surprised when I told him you and I were assigned to make an exposé on *The Random Treewolf*. It is a book he knows backward and forward— and then he suggested, because he was able to get me this copy right here, that if we really wanted to have fun and get an outstanding grade, we should use the original-original-original version that he translated himself from the first twelve-hundred-year-old paper edition."

"Paper edition?" Slue sighed almost dreamily. "Extraordinary. He knows what it's like to read a book where the words are printed on paper pages…"

"I guess it must be a little like having rain on the Moon," added Hieronymus.

They looked at the two sets of text in front of them. Slue's copy suddenly appeared to be very plain, short, and uninteresting when compared to the image floating in front of Hieronymus, where the sentences described things they did not fully understand, and passages appeared to be written for the beauty of themselves, and the images they provoked, and the sounds they made as the words were echoed in the reader's mind.

The version translated by his uncle had three times the number of pages. There were entire chapters and numerous characters nowhere to be found in the modern version. The more they directly compared the two, the blander and more superficial the standard version became. Slue pointed out an idiomatic expression she knew for a fact was invented only a century earlier. As they directly compared the two texts, their task, which started out as a type of detective game, soon evolved into a tragic comprehension of cultural and intellectual loss.

"According to my uncle, the real interesting part is not so much the physical condition of the paper books, but the gradual deterioration of their meaning through the centuries. Meaning, that as languages changed, ever so slightly, literature itself became less understandable— as vocabularies shrunk, and as generations passed, entire novels became incomprehensible.

"There was a hemorrhaging of words and meaning, and instead of publishers protecting their original works, they began to slightly 'update' novels for younger generations. Entire books were shrunk to accommodate the dumbed-down, shrinking vocabularies of the population. And once they started chopping words, they started chopping paragraphs. Then they started chopping pages. Novels by this time were no longer produced on paper, so it was easier to cut them in half without having anyone notice. And nobody cared anyway.

"Nobody cares now. You and I care because we're in the smart kid section—but all those students who passed through here on their way to the auditorium? Would they be the least bit curious to know that the original version of *The Random Treewolf* is three hundred and forty-nine pages and the copy we all read in school is just under a hundred?"

Before Slue had a moment to contemplate this amazing discovery, there was a rude interruption. The disturbing ruckus of a desk falling over.

The Loopies entered the rotunda. About fifteen of them. All of them loud, shouting, laughing, and fighting.

Hieronymus froze.

His two worlds collided with a cacophony of smashing glass and crashing furniture. He had never been cornered in one room with both Toppers and Loopies at the same time. They didn't mix.

"Look!" one of them shouted—this was a shaggy little guy named Plennim. "Look who's here! It's Mus!" Plennim had a scratchy voice, and his eyes were bloodshot. He wore a white shirt with a sizeable oil stain on its front.

"Mus! Muuuuuss!" bellowed a fellow whose long beard reached the middle of his chest. Jessker—one of the worst. He had a tattoo of a third eye on his forehead and he carried around his neck a small silver box on a chain. He had the annoying habit of going up to people and opening the top of the box just under their noses, insisting that they "Smell! Smell!" and the odor that wafted up out from the inside of this cube was, without fail, always horrendous.

Within seconds, two Loopies started wrestling, and another table was smashed when one boy jumped up on it for no apparent reason other than to check and see how the traction under his shoes would grip.

In front of Slue's disbelieving eyes, Hieronymus, with a wave of his stylo-point, quickly shut down the floating image of the book project he had been eagerly discussing with her just seconds before and stood up. Two very attractive girls walked over to him. One was dressed in a flannel pajama, and she wore rollers in her hair. Her large eyes had the most unusual allure to them, unfortunately spoiled by the bruise on her face. This was Clellen. The young lady just next to her was shorter and her name was Tseehop. Tseehop had long black hair to her knees. She wore white jeans with red polka dots. On her black t-shirt was a drawing of a man on a horse holding a submachine gun. The man's eyes were plucked out. So were the horse's.

"Mus!" Clellen cooed, batting her eyelids as soon as she came face to face with Hieronymus. "Mus, we missed you in math today."

"Yeah, Mus, where were you?" added Tseehop. "Debbie and Johndon were thrown out of class for making out—"

"They were doing a lot more than making out, Tseehop," Clellen said, her eyebrow raised. "He had her shirt up over her neck and she had her hand in his—"

But Tseehop didn't let Clellen finish her sentence.

"Did you cut class?" she abruptly asked Hieronymus, fake-inquisitor style.

Hieronymus' grin widened. He then said with an enthusiasm Slue had never heard before, "Yes! I always cut math on Tuesday. You know that!"

Slue froze as she sat looking up at this unfolding spectacle. Hieronymus knew these Loopies. He *knew* them! They knew *him!* They had an affectionate nickname for him! Mus! They called him Mus! He had a Loopie nickname! An ugly-sounding Loopie nickname! Mus! So vulgar, like they couldn't even bother to attempt to pronounce his whole name.

And what was all this business about cutting class? Hieronymus is *not* in any *Loopie* classes! That would be impossible. He's a Topper.

Slue shook her head. It was like she was in a horrific dream all of a sudden.

When she looked up, the noisy spectacle had only gotten worse.

Clellen put her arm around Hieronymus and touched the end of his nose with her pointer finger.

"So," she continued in her coquettish voice. "When am I going to get to see what you look like without those goggles—I heard you have the most gorgeous eyes…"

Hieronymus touched the end of her nose. Slue was amazed at how *familiar* he was toward this girl.

"Now who told you that, Clellenie-clel…"

"Oh, word gets out. Some girls…have seen…your…eyes…"

Was this really Hieronymus? Slue wondered. *Talking and flirting with…Loopies?*

She quietly and quickly put away her research. She felt numb. Three of her classmates from another table several meters away, stared wide-eyed at her, terrified. They were also Toppers, and they were be-having as if they were about to get pummeled by these criminal types who hadn't even noticed them yet.

One scared Topper boy, Poole, silently mouthed, *Let's go!* repeat-edly. But she was frozen.

The counter where the librarian normally sat attracted the atten-tion of three Loopies, who quickly took out screwdrivers and magic markers. With a loud blunt cackle of laughs and obscenities, they pro-ceeded to carve and mark up and vandalize the main desk with a de-structive abandon Slue never thought possible.

One boy punched another directly in the mouth.

A tall boy in a trenchcoat went up to Tseehop and they started kissing, first standing, then passionately crashing upon a table where another group of terrified students got up and fled.

Slue looked back at Hieronymus.

"Clellen, my naughty she-cat," he said to the strange girl in the rollers. "You know that if these goggles ever come off for any girl, it would be you…"

"Mus," she laughed, "You are suuuuuuch a liar…"

Clellen began to stroke his face with wide, affectionate sweeps of her hand, which had the number "10" tattooed on it in dark green ink. She was obviously trying to kiss him, and Hieronymus glanced at Slue as he made a slight effort to resist.

Another table crashed. The boy with the traction shoes jumped off his second wreck.

The two wrestling kids shifted gears and hurled the crudest and most vicious insults at one another, making Slue wince. And then, out of the blue, from another corner, two extremely tall Loopie girls in rag-gedy velvet tuxedos began punching the Hell out of each other, and within seconds there was blood flowing from one of the girl's noses. Nobody cared, including Hieronymus.

"Show me!" Clellen laughed.

"No!" He laughed back.

"Show me!"

He covered his eyes with both palms, and Clellen wrapped herself around him tighter, as if she were an octopus trying to open a cartoon treasure chest. They immediately fell to the floor, and Hieronymus' attempts to get her off him were clearly lackadaisical. He seemed to love this little game she was playing with him, and they rolled around as if they were lovers on a haystack, Clellen laughing and Hieronymus mildly protesting between giggles.

Slue got up from her seat and walked toward the Toppers who were slowly walking backward out of the room, taking long silent steps to avoid getting the attention of these hoodlums. She joined them, and as they all left, Slue was suddenly overwhelmed by an emotion she could not fully comprehend. She stopped. She walked back into the rotunda by herself and went up to the rolling forms Hieronymus and Clellen on the floor.

"Hieronymus," she called out to her changeling friend. "Hieronymus, I'm going."

She immediately regretted bringing attention to herself. Silence swept through the room as every Loopie stopped their destructive, noisy behavior and looked at Slue.

Only teachers called him Hieronymus. And Bruegel, but he was not there.

Then Clellen and Tseehop exploded in excitement.

"Ohmygod! Ohmygod! This is SSSSOOOOOO CUTE!"

Clellen jumped up from the floor and in two seconds was uncomfortably close to Slue's face. "You are so cute!" she exclaimed, as if she were a little girl in a toy shop picking up a stuffed doll she wanted. "A One Hundred Percent Lunar GIRRRRRL! And you know Mus! You even call him Here-on-uh-mus!"

The boy in the trenchcoat sat on the desk just next to where Slue stood. He reached up and poked her elbow.

"I didn't know Mus had a sister. Are you his sister?"

Tseehop was more direct.

"Hey, you must be Mus' girlfriend! I'll bet you both take your goggles off when you're sliding in each other's sweat!"

Slue froze. She was surrounded by these criminals. *Why do they even allow people like this in school?* She glanced at the students destroying the counter. A loud crash thundered out from the lounging area as more furniture was destroyed. *Where are the teachers?* she wondered.

Hieronymus slowly got up and sauntered over to the gathering around Slue. Even the way he walked was drastically different when he was among this riffraff.

The trenchoat boy shouted unnecessarily loudly over to Hieronymus.

"Mus! How can this girl be your hop-on if she's also a goggle-freak like you? I thought all you goggle-freaks hated each other."

Hieronymus pushed himself through the crowd and placed himself between Slue and Clellen.

"Everyone," he announced to the Loopies. "This is Slue."

"Slue!" Clellen exclaimed. "That's a sexy name. I love your hair!"

Slue nodded. The big bruise under Clellen's face was extremely difficult to look at.

"How do you know Mus?" a boy in the back shouted.

"Uhhh," began Slue, obviously scared. "I've known Hieronymus since the third grade."

"How come you're not in our class?" demanded another.

Slue had no answer for that, so she just looked away.

Two or three other Loopies came over. One of them, Jessker, clutched the silver box around his neck. As soon as he saw Slue, he did what he always did when he met someone for the first time. He opened up the lid of the tiny box and held it up to Slue's face.

"Smell!" he demanded in a sharp, nasal voice. "Smell! Smell!"

"What?" Slue gasped, terrified.

"Smell!"

"What am I supposed to smell?"

"Oh, go ahead!" Tseehop interjected. "Jessker here wants to be a perfume maker when he grows up. He's always trying out his new creations on everyone."

Slue was about to take a sniff, then stopped herself.

"Wait. This isn't some kind of 'drug thing,' is it?"

Within the eruption of laughter that followed, she heard several voices assuring her *no, no, this is not a drug thing, no, no, don't worry...*

She looked over at Hieronymus. He had a broad smile on his face.

"It's totally safe, Slue. Jessker is a true artist of odor."

She leaned forward. The small silver box was very pretty, but Jessker's fingernails upon it were horribly dirty, with purple gunk under each finger nail. She parked her nose over the open top.

She sniffed.

And then she nearly vomited. It was an odor of rot she never even knew existed—of soiled fermentation, musky, dead, and sour and intense. It was by far, for that quick half second, the worst moment in her entire life. Whatever that odor was, it made her see death and the rotten oblivion it left in its wake.

"Ugh!" she cried out loud, humiliated. "Ugh! Ugh!"

The Loopie crowd burst into hysterical laughter once more. All of them, laughing at her, including Hieronymus, who had his arms around Clellen, both of them balancing each other to keep from toppling over.

The offending Loopie with the beard, Jessker, had already disappeared.

Slue's eyes were all watery behind her goggles. "You are sick!" she screamed at them all. "Sick! Sick in the head!"

"Let's see your eyes!" someone in the crowd yelled out.

"Yeah," another Loopie added. "Mus won't show us his eyes, you show us yours!"

This only inspired a counter reaction from some other Loopies.

"No! Don't tell her to do that!"

"Let's see them!"

"Don't! She takes those goggles off, we're all dead!"

"That's not true, you know. I heard that the eye color makes you high."

"It makes you dead. That's what it makes you!"

"Remember what happened to Lester two years ago!"

"Lester died of an overdose of Buzz!"

"He died of exposure to the devil color!"

Four of them began swinging at each other with fists.

Tseehop shook her head back and forth, staring up at Slue.

"You, fungelina, are in a lot of trouble. You call us sick. Then you get four of us to fight over you. You really must be some kind of demon."

Slue was petrified. Hieronymus stopped laughing and started to walk forward, slightly worried.

"I think she's a demon, too," an extra-loud voice from the destroyed counter announced. "Just like Mus. He's a demon. A demon from the far side of the Moon."

"Wait, you're a Topper," Plennim piped up with his scratchy voice.

"And how do you know that Slue is a Topper?" Clellen interrupted, fists on her hips, turning to face the scratchy-voiced boy with the oil stain on his shirt. "Mus would never be friends with any snobs like that!"

"Maybe, maybe not," Plennim said. "All I heard was that there was this hot-looking One Hundred Percent Lunar Girl who had blue hair who was in the Topper classes."

Clellen shook her head. "You're on Buzz, that's what's up your face, scratchy."

Plennim was quick with a retort.

"I'm not on Buzz, you kazzer-bat!"

"Who are you calling a kazzer-bat, you little lice baiter!"

"You, ping-slud, go wrap yourself in a big fat kank!"

The ensuing fight between Plennim and Clellen diffused the uncomfortable attention Slue was getting from the assembled Loopies. She was amazed at the chaotic way they all communicated with one another. One sentence, followed by a retort, followed by overwhelming physical action in the form of violence or wrestling. Everything was extreme. Strange insults she had never heard before. She had no idea what they were talking about. She watched the fight between the boy and the girl—it was horrendous, loud and brutal, and the other students barely paid attention to it after the first twenty seconds. Hieronymus finally went up to her, a slightly embarrassed look on his face.

"I'll bet, I'm sure, this is probably a little strange…"

"Loopies?"

"I…you see, I am really bad in math. And science."

"Loopies."

"They're not really that bad."

Slue looked beyond his shoulder and watched Clellen poke Plennim in the face with the end of a chair leg.

"I am obliged by the school to take remedial math and remedial science. And remedial shop, and home preparation. I spend half my day in the Loopie section."

Slue stared at him, and her breathing quickened. She quickly turned her back on him and left, at first walking, then running.

—

The next day, Slue spoke to the teacher, requesting that she be assigned another partner to work with on a completely different book. The teacher paired her up with the boy named Poole, who was absolutely pleased to collaborate with the beautiful blue-haired girl.

She refused to even look at Hieronymus, never mind speak to him. She was determined to never speak to him again.

Two weeks later she sat in the back of the classroom and watched as Hieronymus gave his dissertation on the two versions of *The Random Treewolf* all by himself. Her throat felt heavy with a slight choking sensation. She disliked him now. She even wondered if she hated him. He spoke to the class with such a marvelous exactitude. It was both wonderful and brilliant, and for the first time in her life she was glad to have those goggles covering her eyes, preventing the others from seeing how incredibly moved she was.

chapter four

Windows Falling On Sparrows could not wait to get away from her suffocating mother and her doltish, dimwitted father. Managing to last the entire fourteen-hour journey from the Earth to the Moon, confined to a small family cabin, stuck with them, was a genuine miracle.

True, what a fantastic thrill to ascend into the sky like that. To keep going and to look out the window and watch her city shrink into a glimmering puddle of lights till it just meshed with all the other puddles of lights on the surface of the worn-out continent she came from. It was a profound experience, entirely ruined by her mother asking dumb, nosy questions about school exams, homework, and that boy in her class named Cornelius. *He's a really nice boy, you should go out with him instead of some of the riffraff you seem to be interested in.* Endless questions that were so utterly boring. *If you haven't noticed, Mom, we are in space, for the first time in our lives, can we please NOT talk about my school or who you think I should date?* It was a tall order. Her mother, Exonarella, had such ambitions for her youngest daughter that she often slipped into the very tiresome mode of living vicariously through her sixteen-year-old. She was a nervous woman. She wanted her daughter to be successful and independent, and, as a result, just like Windows

Falling On Sparrows' two older siblings, all she managed to do was to drive her away with her constant micromanaging of every detail of the poor girl's life.

The family cabin vibrated. After two thousand years of space travel, leaving the Earth's atmosphere was still leaving the Earth's atmosphere. Sedenker, Exonarella's husband and the father of the suddenly annoyed I-hate-everything teenager, was vastly relieved that he had taken an extra strong dose of E-94, a prescribed drug for space travel. It was excellent for those with motion sickness who might normally vomit during their first space flight. It blocked out all anxiety. It also blocked out his nagging wife, who immediately turned to him after finishing her argument with Windows Falling On Sparrows.

"When are you going to get a job?" she demanded.

They felt the vast ship turn and thrust as the view of stars in a hazy purple field replaced the filthy clouds they rode up through.

"You're asking me about that now?"

"I don't know how we are going to survive next month," she declared with a sudden urgency.

"That's why I think," her husband said under his breath, "this whole vacation to Saturn is one of the dumbest things…"

Predictably, that remark made her angry.

"No. I'm sorry! We are not getting into that again. My brother got us these tickets for free. We should be grateful to him. How often in life do we get a chance to do something as wonderful as this?"

Sedenker passively sat back, which was something he was very good at. *Thank God,* he thought to himself as his wife launched into one of her non-stop lectures on his many shortcomings. *Thank God I have motion sickness so I can get that dose of E-94 and I don't have to listen to her for a change.* He looked in her direction. Her mouth moved with furious intention. When he couldn't hear anything, she was the most beautiful woman in the world.

The family was indeed on their way toward the rings of Saturn, to a resort on Titan called Chez Cracken San. They were riding in the *Ragmagothic Chrysanthemum*, a vast Mega Cruiser. Several thousand passengers were on board. The three of them had a small family cabin all to themselves, which was fine for the quick journey to the Moon, but Windows Falling On Sparrows was already dreading the three-day trip to Saturn, where they would be cramped in there together, her mother in her face, inquiring about this, lecturing about that, dreaming out loud about everything else. And her father—the complete opposite. So stuck inside his interior depressive neurosis, they could go ice skating on the rings of Saturn and he wouldn't even notice. He'd been without a job for three years. When she forced herself, she had vague memories of a happy and contented man she used to call Daddy. But this guy, all he did was look for jobs and get nothing. Loser. Hard to believe it was the same man.

"Did you take E-94, Daddy?"

"Yes I did, Windows Falling On Sparrows."

"So you took drugs."

"In my case, it's not drugs. It prevents me from getting sick when going up into space."

"But you've never been in space before, so how would you know?"

"I get sick when I ride the bus. I think that's a pretty good indicator."

"Your eyes are all red."

"I guess they are."

"If you take E-94, then you smoke Buzz, you can die from an overdose."

"Is that so? Well, no need to worry about me, then. Its not like I'm going to go around smoking Buzz anyway."

The magnificent curvature of the Earth suddenly appeared as they broke through the highest clouds, leaving the atmosphere. It was an overwhelming sight for the family. Their first time in space. They all grew quiet. Strange muffled sounds were heard within the body of the Mega Cruiser. The window afforded a view that all the media imagery in history could never truly capture. There they were, finally, off world. The initial feeling was always the same. Wonderment. Followed by a dreadful realization of extreme and total self-insignificance. Followed by a profound sense of accomplishment. Followed quickly by a return to whatever Earthbound petty worries and personal bickerings and mediocre obsessions occupied the individual before this enormous leap past the stratosphere and into the heavenly forever, filled with billions more stars than the vague few one can see from the muddy, soot-choked planet.

Sedenker took Exonarella's hand in his own and he inhaled a deep breath through his nose.

"This ship smells wonderful, doesn't it?"

She glared at him for two contemptible seconds, then focused on her daughter.

"Is Cornelius your boyfriend? Yes or no."

Because the family had these free tickets, they were subjected to certain inconveniences that usually came along with anything that might be as cheap as an all-expenses-paid trip to Saturn's rings. They were allowed almost no luggage. There was a set time period and a set schedule of flights that could not be changed. There were only three tickets available, so the couple's older two children, their son, Squirrels Running On Highways, and their other daughter, Dolphins Tangled In Nets, were told to stay at home, which they agreed to with a surprising enthusiasm. In fact, when her parents told Windows Falling On Sparrows she would be the one taking this long voyage with them, she slammed her bedroom door and screamed how it *wasn't fair!* and sulked for days. Sedenker and Exonarella thought she was simply being a drama queen over nothing, but in fact, she was annoyed at missing, again, all the secret wild parties her two older siblings were going to organize the moment their parents left the apartment.

Her dismay was short-lived, disappearing as soon as she understood the itinerary, which her mother almost canceled the trip over.

"We have to stay on the Moon for two days!" Exonarella complained. "In a hotel in LEM Zone One! That horrible, sleazy place! What was my brother thinking! How can he give us tickets like this! I want us to go directly out to Saturn! Not spend a moment in that hellhole!"

"These are free tickets," Sedenker commented. "I don't think we should complain."

"It's a horrible place," his wife shot back. "A wicked den of thieves and prostitutes and sick people. I'm canceling. I'm calling my brother, and we are not going."

"Okay," was her husband's reply, as he honestly did not care.

—

Exonarella was a woman of many prejudices, and Windows Falling On Sparrows could never understand where she got them from. Her mother was never clear as to exactly why she had such a negative opinion of the Moon, especially since she had never been there herself. Windows Falling On Sparrows, on the other hand, was thrilled by the prospect.

The Moon. A bad place.

On the other hand, Chez Cracken San, a resort over by the Rings of Saturn, was guaranteed to be a touristic, shopping-mall experience of living death. Exactly the kind of place her mother would love. A plastic, prefabricated, and controlled environment with piped-in music, about as exciting as an elevator. No wonder her uncle gave those tickets to them—only losers went to places like that. Only adults, especially older ones, went on these voyages. She would be the only teenager, surrounded by lecherous middle-aged men in toupées who wouldn't stop staring at her while their brain-dead wives all chatted with each other about their sons and daughters and which ones went to medical school and which one was a lawyer. She was going to suffocate to dear death, especially knowing her older brother and sister would have moved all the furniture out of the living room and turned their flat into a non-stop rave festival by then. *Everyone* was going to be there, except her—*she* would be stuck between Mom and Dad and their dumb petty arguments over nothing. Confined to close quarters with her overbearing mother and passive-aggressive father…

Rings of Saturn? So what? SO WHAT!? I'll go there when I'm old!
Touristic. Waste of time.

But the Moon. Especially if they were really supposed to stay in a hotel in the infamously sleazy LEM Zone One! It would be easy—she would escape from her parents and wander around LEM Zone One just like the girl in that film *Blood Crater*, the one starring Janet Xan, who infiltrates a Sea of Tranquility mob family and ends up killing three hundred gangsters in a casino lobby. Or like the woman in *Cheap Cheat Chuck-Off*, who starts off as a prostitute who gets stabbed by her pimp, only she comes back later and cuts his head off then kills all of his henchmen with a machine gun, also in a casino. Windows Falling On Sparrows was a big fan of violent Lunaxploitation films, so the chance to see this infamous part of the Moon was very compelling. All her friends would be so jealous.

And there was also another reason.

She had a deep fascination with One Hundred Percent Lunar people. What she had heard about them was both remarkable and strange. At school, for years, there were endless rumors about these bizarre people who lived on the Moon, that they had to wear goggles because there was a color in their eyes no one was allowed to see. That they saw invisible colors enabling them to look into the future.

And, the most fascinating rumor of all: One Hundred Percent Lunar People, with their ability to see all of that, were the only ones who were able to pilot all the fast stellar ships, including the Mega Cruisers. Only their eyes could transform the bending of unseen light across outer space into safe passageways through the solar system. Only they could see the pathways of the planets over the incredible distances.

All of this was just rumor. But she did have a friend of hers named Slaquenn who, as it turns out, had a cousin who was a One Hundred Percent Lunar Boy. And something terrible indeed happened to that boy to support the rumors.

Her friend nervously explained it one day. She was a classmate. It happened during a field trip their school took into the countryside to explore the overgrown ruins of a city that had been destroyed several centuries earlier. The two of them wandered off from the rest of the class. The air smelled of the usual mix between burnt plastic and sour foliage. Slaquenn insisted Windows Falling On Sparrows follow her to an isolated area because she had something really important to tell her. Windows Falling On Sparrows assumed it would be nothing more than her latest secret crush on some unobtainable boy. She followed Slaquenn to a spot beneath an ancient elevated highway, its concrete and steel structure now just a collection of cracks and rust. Sufficiently isolated, Slaquenn told Windows Falling On Sparrows the incredible story of her cousin.

Don't tell anyone what I am about to tell you, Windows Falling On Sparrows. I have to be quick, and I have to tell you before I change my mind. I have a cousin. His name is Bik. He is ten years older than we are. I never really knew him, but I did visit him once, a long time ago on the Moon. The Moon, by the way, is a very weird place. Never go there. Anyway, Bik is my father's nephew—the son of his brother. Don't tell anyone this, but Bik is what they call a One Hundred Percent Lunar Boy. I never completely understood what that really meant, but these are people who are born on the Moon and can somehow, and no one knows why, see colors that normal people cannot. They also have to keep their eyes covered because if you look at them in the eyes, you can get brain damage or you can become crazy. This is all a big secret. These people, like my own cousin, are not allowed to leave the Moon. The last time I saw him was nine years ago. I was seven. He was seventeen. I traveled to the Moon with my parents to visit our relatives there. It was a very nice visit, but it was strange to meet my cousin, Bik, who always wore these strange goggles. I was very young, and I just thought he was about to go swimming. Right after we left, Bik got himself into a load of trouble. He was arrested for purposely showing his eyes to someone. He was sent to a prison on the far side of the Moon. No one was allowed to have any contact with him. Not even his family. His parents tried to visit him, but they were threatened with arrest if they continued to try. Then, the government insisted that Bik had never existed in the first place. All records of him, his school records, his hospital records, everything vanished. His mother was committed to a psychiatric hospital for imagining that she had a son. His father, my uncle, was sent to prison for subversion. He's been there ever since. Meanwhile, Bik has been officially erased. The lunar government is very stubborn, and eventually, after years of trying to find out what happened, my father gave up. Then, just as we were ready to accept the harsh reality of Bik's disappearance and the imprisonment of his parents, something else came up to throw us all into excessive turmoil. Six months ago, my aunt, this is my father's sister, who is also Bik's aunt, had to fly to Mars for some kind of business meeting. She was on a Mega Cruiser. Halfway out there, the ship collided with a comet, and an S.O.S. was sent out. A rescue ship was called. Luckily, the damage was not too severe, but the passengers were all herded into lifeboats anyway just in case things got worse. Now, usually during a voyage on a Mega Cruiser, passengers are never, ever allowed to come into any kind of contact with the actual pilots—you know, the people behind the steering wheels who directly drive those things. No one knows *why. Some kind of law. However, during an emergency, all that protocol breaks down, and my aunt found herself squeezed in with the captain and fifty others inside one of the ship's front corridors. Everyone was in a panic because of the comet—my aunt said that everyone was convinced that that Mega Cruiser was about to fall apart. So thought the captain, who was highly agitated. He was yelling and barking orders at the entire panicking crew. Then he demanded to see the pilots. He shouted out loud, "Bring me those Pixiedamned goggle-eyed One Hundred Percent Lunar idiots who have ruined my ship!" and then she couldn't believe it, from a hatchway, her nephew, my cousin Bik, shows up with another One Hundred Percent Lunar Man. The captain threatened to toss them back to the prison on the far side of the Moon. "What good is your wacko vision if you can't even see a comet—that's why we have you creatures driving our ships! To avoid this!" My aunt tried to get my cousin's attention, but he was dragged away, and the captain realized that he had spoken too much in front of too many passengers. Later, after the emergency was neutralized and the passengers were transferred to another ship, my aunt made thousands of inquiries and she came up with the same brick wall each time—that her nephew never existed, and no, the pilots are not One Hundred Percent Lunar People.*

But you see, that is another lie. My cousin is an indentured servant. That's what happens to One Hundred Percent Lunar People. The corporate government sets up the law so that sooner or later, they trap and arrest as many of them as they need. Then they are sent to a secret prison on the far side of the Moon. They train them to be pilots, and force them to fly those giant ships, because no one else can. They force them to do it—my parents and my aunt believe that the government and their corporate partners are afraid of the One Hundred Percenters becoming a united political force, so they keep them subjugated like that—using their talents to pilot their ships because once it is clear how powerful they really are, all travel inside the solar system will change. That's why there are all of those strange stories about them being demons and crazy. The "powers that be" want everyone to be afraid of them and for the One Hundred Percenters to be afraid of each other...

Windows Falling On Sparrows was flabbergasted by Slaquenn's incredible story and at first only pretended out of politeness to believe her.

She thought the idea was beyond silly, but she also found herself thinking about it more and more as the school year progressed. She did her own research. The only official information she could find was that indeed, some people on the Moon suffered from a mysterious condition called lunarcroptic ocular symbolanosis. But that was it. No additional information could be found for anyone on Earth. A few weeks later, she asked Slaquenn what that meant, but at that point Slaquenn refused to speak about it. Then, when Slaquenn and her family disappeared out of the blue, Windows Falling On Sparrows reached the only viable conclusion—that everything her friend had told her about her cousin, the One Hundred Percent Lunar Boy, was ultimately, one hundred percent true.

Unexpectedly, during her own voyage to the Moon, she came face to face with a chance to test this theory. It got her into a bit of trouble, but it helped confirm her suspicions.

Everything became quiet. The Earth loomed through the window, but smaller as they flew away at an incomprehensible speed. Her father, despite her mother's non-stop berating and criticizing, fell asleep. Most likely, he took another pill of E-94. Once he was out, Exonarella followed suit, suddenly falling asleep just next to her husband as if physically connected to him, as if whatever medicine he had taken somehow entered her bloodstream as quickly as his. She rested her head on his shoulder, eyes closed, childlike.

Windows Falling On Sparrows sneaked away, anxious to explore this wonderful ship, and determined to find a few answers to this nagging question…

She wandered through the long, crowded corridor. All the tourists were up and about. This particular Mega Cruiser was supposed to have an extraordinary observation deck, but none of the wandering crowds knew where to find it. A group of boys who were obviously in a party mood said some flattering things to her as she passed, but she only smiled at them and continued. She was, at this moment, not particularly interested in boys or observation decks. She had her own agenda—finding out what the pilot looked like. Finding out if the pilot was a…

She passed and dodged around the annoying gawking crowds. She believed she was heading in the direction of the bridge. That's where they would be. The drivers, the pilots, the captain. All she wanted was to take a quick peek—see if anyone sitting behind a steering wheel or a joystick or whatever they used in massive space vehicles like this actually used, just happened to be wearing the telltale goggles. She was not sure what she would do with this information. But it was her latest obsession. And her obsessions had to lead her somewhere.

She left the crowds behind her. This ship was truly gigantic and the corridor she was in, known among the passengers as *The Spine*, as it ran the vessel's entire length, was extraordinarily long. Along with the occasional crowds of gathering tourists, small electric cars appeared and disappeared from the myriad of port holes and sub corridors.

Then, from nowhere, a large human figure clothed in a one-piece jumpsuit made of wrinkled paper and hundreds of miniature metal antenna stepped out directly in front of her. A security guard. He asked her where she was going.

"I want to meet the captain," she demanded.

The guard, who wore a white plastic shield over his mouth that had three small blinking red lights, studied the bold teenage girl.

"Sorry, miss, but nobody sees the captain unless it is an absolute emergency." His voice was bored, and she thought he appeared to be staring at something on her forehead instead of looking at her in the eyes.

"Can I meet one of the pilots?"

"Absolutely not. No one is allowed to meet any of the pilots under any circumstances."

"Why is that?" she asked, sensing a validity in her suspicions.

"Mega Cruiser pilots are extremely busy and they have to be free to work outside the concerns and questions of teenage passengers."

"Really?" she remarked. "Are you sure it has nothing to do with the fact that the only ones who can pilot Mega Cruisers are One Hundred Percent Lunar People?"

"What?" The security guard was genuinely perplexed by this.

"It's true, isn't it, that all pilots of Mega Cruisers are One Hundred Percent Lunar Men or Women?"

"No. That is an extremely silly idea."

"You know that it is not at all a silly idea. You know that it is fact. Please answer. In order to successfully pilot ships through the solar system, you must be a bearer of lunarcroptic ocular symbolanosis—true or false?"

"You are arriving at an outlandish conclusion, miss."

"Do they wear their goggles when they pilot ships like this? Or, do they take their goggles off just before starting, peering off into the void, able to see the past and the future all at once, able to visually navigate the vast reaches—"

At that moment, an oval door slid open across the passage and three figures stepped into the brightly lit corridor. All three wore the distinctive black shiny rubber suits known to be worn by the cockpit crews of extremely fast spacecraft. One was a man, the other was a woman. The third, walking between them, had so many hoses protruding from nearly every part of the body it was hard to tell at first that this too was a male. But the most interesting thing was the helmet this man wore—like a shiny black egg, covering his entire head. The other two wore no such head gear, and they appeared to be guiding him, as if he could not see…

"I tell you, Reginald," began the woman to the man beside her. "You are not missing a thing down there. Earth is a burn-out. It smells like rotten eggs and burnt plastic…"

"I'll bet it beats the far side of the Moon, Peggy," replied a voice from behind the faceless helmet.

"Well, you'll never find out, Reggie," added the man on the other side of the masked one who, like the woman, was helping him walk forward. "You'll never be allowed down there, so don't bother worrying about it."

The girl froze. They must have entered the ship right after takeoff, probably at the orbital refueling station about two hours earlier.

She shot past the security guard and ran directly up to the middle figure.

"Excuse me," she said to him in an excited, breathless manner. She could see her own reflection in the man's shiny helmet, her own black hair falling over her dark eyes. "Are you a One Hundred Percent Lunar Man?" she asked.

There was no answer. All three of the rubber-clad crewmembers greeted her inquiry with desolate silence.

"You are all dressed as cockpit crew, but you," she directed her

voice to the fellow in the middle with the hidden face, "you're the actual pilot—you are a One Hundred Percent Lunar Man, are you not?
I just overheard what you three just said. You were just talking about
not being allowed to go to Earth. And yet here you are, wearing a Mega
Cruiser pilot suit. Is it true, the rumor going around, that only One
Hundred Percent Lunar People can drive the big, super-fast ships across
the solar system?"

The woman gave a worried glance over at the egg-shaped helmet as
the bold girl from Earth continued.

"Are you wearing Schmilliazano goggles under that mask?"

The security guard finally intervened and uttered something
about spoiled teenagers as he grabbed her wrist, scanned the ticket-
bracelet she wore there, then escorted her the entire thirty-five-minute
walk back to her cabin, woke up her parents, and informed them their
daughter was lost and disturbing the crew of the Mega Cruiser. They,
as expected, were terribly annoyed at having been roused out of their
slumber, and as a result, forbid their daughter to leave the cabin until
they approached the Moon, which was, at that point, only about eight
hours away. This reprimand had but a null effect and she only smiled as
she sat down into her deeply cushioned travel sofa. The Earth appeared
smaller and smaller through the window. The actions of the security
guard and the reaction of the crew, for her, validated the rumors and
everything Slaquenn had said—that the pilots of this Mega Cruiser, and
thus all Mega Cruisers, were off limits, and for only one reason. They
were beholders of lunarcroptic ocular symbolanosis. They were able to
see things normal people could not imagine.

Her mother was thoroughly disgusted by the crappy little hotel where
they were scheduled to stay for two days.

It was called the Hotel Venice.

It was cramped. The walls were paper thin. All the carpets were
damp, and the entire building, situated in the exact center of the red-
light district of LEM Zone One, smelled of mold. The room itself was
tiny. There was a double bed and a cot with a very thin mattress next to
a cracked window. Exonarella complained she must have been having
an allergic reaction to something because her throat felt very scratchy.

Outside, the blinking neon sign illuminated a street below where about every third person was a prostitute. She screamed in shock when she discovered a huge hummingbird hovering just outside the window, tapping on the glass, hoping to get a treat. She pleaded with her daughter to shoo the wild beast away, but Windows Falling On Sparrows opened the window and gave it a cookie she'd brought along from the Mega Cruiser before waving it away. Meanwhile, Sedenker made himself comfortable on the bed and smiled at his distraught wife, as he often did whenever her face exhibited profound repulsion.

"Not bad!" he declared. "Totally free!"

"And if you had a job, we'd be able to walk away from this hellhole and find ourselves a decent hotel!"

Her husband continued to smile as he shrugged his shoulders. This made Exonarella even more angry.

"Go ahead and smirk, you self-satisfied, overweight oaf! Is this your idea of a nice hotel? A place to bring your youngest daughter? Did you see all of those prostitutes outside and in the lobby? And what was that disgusting creature outside, tapping on our window? I swear, if I don't die of an allergic reaction to whatever this moldy odor is, I will die of a heart attack from the shock over what a terrible husband and father you are! How can you sit there and do nothing while your daughter is exposed to prostitutes!"

"Mom," Windows Falling On Sparrows interjected, "I think I can handle the sight of a few hookers."

"I am handling the sight of those hookers very well myself, if I may say so," added Sedenker, his smile growing even wider.

That remark only brought upon Exonarella's wrath in full seismic spectacle.

"You weak, weak, worthless man!" she shouted as she grabbed one of their small bags of luggage and threw it at him. "When I am dead tonight from allergies, heart failure, and the inevitable knife wound that I am sure I will get from the gang of thugs or pimps who are planning to break in here tonight and rob us, you will know that it is your fault, you complete mediocrity, you poor excuse for a man, you lazy, doltish, passive life-waster! My mother was right about you, I can't believe I am married to such a loser! An unemployed charlatan! May you rot in the gutter! You have ruined my life! Look at me now! You have ruined—"

Windows Falling On Sparrows made a quick announcement that shut her mother up quickly.

"I'm going out," she said very matter-of-factly, as if they were back home on Earth.

"What?" screamed her mother. "You're going out? Where are you going? This is a HORRIBLE neighborhood!"

"I want to go see the LEM. You know, the original. The LEM."

"LEM? LEM what? I have NO idea what the Jesus Pixie you're talking about!"

"They call this area LEM Zone One because right around here is where the first people from Earth landed two thousand years ago. The ship was called the LEM. There are still parts of it left. I want to go and see it."

"Have you any idea how dangerous this area is?" Exonarella shouted.

"Oh, let her go," Sedenker said. "You're driving her nuts. You're shouting like a madwoman. Those are mostly tourists out there." Then he turned to his daughter. "Don't be gone too long. Remember where the hotel is. And whatever this LEM thing is, if they have any media images for sale, bring one back."

She felt very much the Earthling as she walked through the filthy, neon-lit streets. Her mother may have been right. There were riffraff in every direction, sinister-looking prostitutes and strange-looking men with harsh expressions staring at her as she walked past. Voices asked questions she could not answer because their accents were too thick and too full of idiomatic expressions that made no sense to her.

"Hey, Lilac, you want to take a jumble in the crankinfranker?"

"Hey, Earthvox! Sweet collider, come over here and let your Yo-Yo fall in my fingers of love…"

She definitely stood out. Earthlings always traveled in groups, and here she was, alone. Her steps gave her away. They were extra bouncy, as the gravity here was noticeably lighter than at home, and everyone she passed walked more naturally than her—they were completely used to it. In fact, she was not really interested in the LEM at all. That was just an excuse to get the Hell out of that cramped hotel room—she herself barely knew what the LEM was and, truthfully, she didn't care. She wanted to find it because then she could get a bearing on where her hotel was, and then stay out just long enough until her parents got to bed, then sneak in after they'd fallen asleep. She couldn't stand their fighting. That was pretty much the only reason she was out in the streets of this notoriously dangerous part of the Moon pretending to search for the remains of a history long ago forgotten.

She walked between two men dressed in odd white suits covering their bodies and faces. They were passing out tiny electric cards with information on them. The electric cards were just translucent sheets of information you held in your hand, and they always dissipated after a few minutes. It had something to do with the LEM—and those white outfits were just costumes of the early space suits the explorers had to wear way back in ancient history before the Moon was terraformed. They were standing among the crowds, advertising a museum—a LEM museum. Not too many were interested.

The monstrously tall casinos towered above her in the red sky, almost every inch of them covered in glowing neon. This was a quality of the Moon she appreciated—the presence of neon on just about every manmade structure. She was enthralled with the thousands of hummingbirds swarming high above in their shape-shifting masses. The sky was bathed in a perpetual glow of twilight, with odd wisps of green cloud-like forms drifting high above. It reminded her of festive summer evenings.

She walked on. To her left was a woman in a green-sequined dress, marching along with a pet gorilla on a leash. The gorilla had white fur, and it was tall and slim and walked very upright, like a man. She had heard there was a sizeable population of white-haired gorillas living on the Moon, but she had no idea there were some who were kept as pets— she had heard they lived in the mountains and in caves and on the far side of the Moon. She thought of her friend's cousin Bik. When he was sent to prison on the far side of the Moon, did he ever see Lunar gorillas like this one?

She kept her eyes open. Where were they? Where were the One Hundred Percent Lunar People?

She was looking.

—

She walked past a neon-covered vehicle consisting of a single giant wheel with a sphere within its circumference—the wheel had a colossal knobby tire on it, and the sphere was where the driver and the passengers sat—like a miniature planet Saturn on its side. This was typical of all cars on the Moon. She had seen thousands of them on the elevated highway earlier, just after landing. She was worried and repulsed by the tremendous number of drunk people among the crowds, and was alarmed to see how many of them climbed into those big Saturn-shaped cars. The police, all of them wearing their distinctive stovetop hats and capes, appeared not to give a hoot about the drunken drivers, or anything else for that matter. They didn't even intervene when one man very casually smashed a half-empty bottle of beer in another man's face. An arm's length away from this scene, a woman pushed her young child in a stroller as a gigantic stray moose, incredibly tall and as white as the gorilla that had just passed, lifted his leg and urinated like a dog on the edge of a banister over the concrete steps leading into one of the casinos.

Suddenly, the girl from Earth felt slightly frightened. She heard her mother's shrill voice in her memory's ear, and wondered if her annoying parent was right about the Moon.

There was a loud disturbance at an outdoor café just meters away from her. A waiter served a sitting couple their dinner. As soon as the waiter left, and as soon as one of the customers turned to open her bag, three gigantic, dog-sized hummingbirds swooped down out of nowhere and grabbed the food right off their plates and took off. The following commotion was very loud, as everyone present exclaimed and yelled over who was responsible, the shocked patrons accused the management of allowing wild animals to steal their dinners, the managers shouted and insulted the waiters for being careless, the waiters fought back and demanded apologies because it was management's fault, others customers at the next table demanded that they all keep it down, the police were called, glasses fell over and accusations flew in every direction as the atmosphere at the outdoor restaurant suddenly became heated and unpleasant.

As she squeezed herself away through the crowd, she thought about her mother. Safe and sequestered in the hotel room. She wouldn't budge from there until they were ready to leave for the Chez Cracken San. Her father might venture out once or twice. But they would both remain fearful, and Windows Falling On Sparrows began to understand why.

She wondered if she was the only Earthling in the area, but that didn't seem possible. Almost all the Mega Cruisers stopped on the Moon before heading out. And LEM Zone One was a truly historical spot, despite the mess and the confused human debauchery growing all around her the farther she wandered from her hotel. Certainly, there must have been tourists here—or did nobody give a damn anymore? She remembered only a third of her classmates in school even knew what the significance of LEM Zone One was. Most thought it was just a place on the Moon where a lot of casinos were all lumped together—which, indeed, it was.

In the distance, beyond the neon-covered casinos and hotels arching up into the red sky, was a long horizontal object, at least a kilometer in length, resting atop a skyscraper-sized tower of concrete and steel tubes all festooned with blinking red lights. Her Mega Cruiser. *The Ragmagothic Chrysanthemum.* Shaped like a colossal, god-sized sturgeon, it sat, filling its tanks with Ulzatallizine pumped up from the Moon's interior. Only lunar Ulzatallizine could propel ships like the Mega Cruisers out to Pluto and back. Ulzatallizine was the only reason humanity emigrated to the Moon in the first place. The entire economy of the Moon revolved around it. No one really knew exactly what it was, but it was powerful. It created millions of jobs. It opened up the solar system. It was nectar. It was holy water. It was the wind in the sails of ten thousand ships all shaped like sturgeons, all moving forward at wondrous speeds never before imagined, humanity leaving behind the cradle it ruined with filth and detritus and waste and selfish stupidity.

There were endless arrays of flexible tubing and hoses running up from the concrete tower and into the belly of the *Ragmagothic Chrysanthemum.* Umbilical cords, feeding. Clouds of hummingbirds traveled through all these appendages, undeterred by such complicated arrangements in the sky. She wondered how much Ulzatallizine was pumped up into that monstrous vessel. All ships heading out to the far points had to do this. It was unavoidable. They were all obliged to stop on the

Moon. The final gas station. Here was where they picked up their petrol.

And most likely where they also picked up their mysterious pilots. The One Hundred Percent Lunar kind.

She passed a man who had just fallen on his back. His eyes were blood-shot and his nose was bloody. The door of a noisy rundown bar was just swinging shut, where inside, she heard the sound of men laughing. Not far from this inebriated fellow was a middle-aged woman sitting on the edge of the road under the red light of the sky, crying so hard all the mascara from her eyes formed two long black rivers down her gray, wrinkled cheeks. A younger man sat next to her, dressed as a woman, with a blond wig and a mini skirt. He appeared to be trying to comfort her as she sobbed, mumbling incoherently about losing everything—*EVERYTHING*—at blackjack.

A woman—obviously a prostitute by her clothes, not to mention the official badge she had pinned above her breast indicating she was safe and legal as all Pixie Hades and state certified to be disease-free—ran up to the Earth girl.

"Honey, my watch broke—do you know what time it is?"

Windows Falling On Sparrows nervously glanced at her watch, but realized she was still on Earth-time.

"I, uh, it's…my watch is…"

She was surprised at how frightened she was. After a moment, the prostitute grew impatient and asked someone else, a tall man in a tattered tuxedo, with his watch on the proper time.

The Earth girl's head was buzzing. There were adults all around. Smelly, sleazy, drunken, bored, desperate adults. She hated it—she hated them. And suddenly, she lost interest in seeing the very first space-ship from Earth, the LEM or whatever the hell it was called. She simply wanted to go back to the safe hotel where her parents were waiting for her, and then go to sleep before continuing on her pointless vacation to Chez Cracken San, annoyed she was missing the excellent party her older brother and sister were no doubt currently having, a hundred friends crammed into their apartment. *I hate my life,* she seethed. *I hate my parents and I hate the Moon and I hate this stupid vacation…*

She walked another five meters and everything changed. She had come upon a clearing—a large city square at the feet of the skyscraping casinos. And there it was—like a beaten-up spider with three legs instead of eight, a dilapidated hexagonical structure. The first LEM, or at least the remains of it.

It sat tilted in the dirt.

It was over two thousand years old and the crowds of people shuffling past hardly noticed it. The poorly maintained pile of metal parts sat dwarfed amongst the metropolis of blinking neon all around it. Hummingbirds picked at some of the garbage that was discarded under it and around it. It was obvious to Windows Falling On Sparrows that half the people who swarmed around it had no idea what it was.

As she approached the thing, she realized some people were climbing on it. They were all teenagers, about the same age as herself. They were not on holiday as she was.

She approached them.

That is when she came upon him. She couldn't believe he was interacting with all the other kids as if there were nothing different about him, as if he were normal. But there he was—a little taller than most of the other kids, thin, almost wiry, wearing the white plastic jacket that was considered so cool and fashionable for teenagers on both the Earth and the Moon. He was without a doubt, to her eyes, handsome, with high cheekbones, a strong jaw and aquiline nose, and the disheveled thick hair on his head not in any way long enough to hide the purple lenses of the Schmilliazano goggles that hid his eyes. He was climbing up onto the ancient space vehicle and jumping off just like all the other kids, and she moved toward him as if he were a magnet and she a floating girl of iron.

Forget the ridiculous pilot with his hidden face, this was a real live One Hundred Percent Lunar Boy, and she was determined to meet him.

chapter five

Hieronymus was surrounded by kids he did not know. He knew their faces, but nothing more. Some of them stared at him.

They were on their way to LEM Zone One—a school field trip. He was crammed into a highway transport vehicle with about a hundred other students from Lunar Public 777. With only a couple of exceptions, they were all kids from the middle sections. The Loopie section, his science and math group, were supposed to go, but the substitute teacher assigned to that nightmare of a class could not prevent the vast majority of them from cutting as they all headed out to the transport vehicle. Only two other Loopies besides himself, Clellen and Bruegel, bothered to make the trip. They sat in the back of the transport. It was rare for Bruegel to be seen mixed in with "normal" students, and Hieronymus noticed outside his element, he was strangely quiet. Clellen was far more sociable—her hair was no longer in curlers, but on this day was all gelled up into a bizarre configuration of wet-looking circles—and she either went up to groups of kids sitting together on the transport and tried to join in on their conversations, or she sat next to Hieronymus and Bruegel, sulking and blurting out, "Hey! What are you looking at?" whenever someone's glance would happen to pass in her general direction. Everyone steered clear of these three, and over the din of chatting, Hieronymus heard the occasional *Loopies! I can't believe they stuck those Loopies in here with us!*

The journey from Lunar Public 777 to LEM Zone One normally took about an hour and a half on the national highway. The traffic was moderate, however, and at one point they did experience a serious back-up and were stuck for twenty minutes—further up, there had been an accident. The highway patrol and several ambulances showed up, and by the time the student transport vehicle passed the scene of the tragedy, the students were treated to a terrible sight. Three vehicles lay twisted beyond all recognition. Broken glass scattered all over the concrete. Huge burning puddles of spilled fuel tossed pillars of black smoke into the air. Five sinister mounds of blood-stained white sheets were lined up side by side next to the smashed cars. It was obvious what was under the sheets—they were not large enough to cover the feet of the victims they intended to hide.

One hummingbird hovered close to the transport window as they slowly passed. Bright white. Almost mechanical. The size of a dog. The medics at the accident scene were busy shooing the pestering creatures away from the awful scene.

The transport continued on its way once the traffic had cleared. For its passengers, it was a fairly tight fit, as most of the seats had been constructed close together. There was an aisle the students sat on either side of, and the windows provided excellent views of the outside world.

Hieronymus turned to Bruegel.

"*You're* quiet today," he said.

Bruegel grinned defensively as his eyes scanned the passing countryside.

"I'm quiet on the outside today, Hieronymus, just quiet on the outside. But here," he knocked his knuckle against his shaggy-haired skull, "there is a storm brewing…right here…"

"I see." Hieronymus laughed. "So your mouth and your brain decided to trade places?"

"His mouth and his brain," added Clellen, "are two sides of the same hollow blow-horn we have to keep listening to over and over no matter which one he crates on the plumb side…"

"Clellen, if I wanted to hear your opinion I would not have flushed the toilet this morning."

Hieronymus could see these two were about to start spinning at each other with the usual avalanche of infantile jokes turning into insults turning into violence when, suddenly, an outsider intruded on their little bubble of Loopie-World.

"Hey!" someone shouted in their direction. "Hey! Goggle-guy!"

Hieronymus looked up into the mass of students sitting in their transport seats, only to see a moderately familiar face poke itself up—a large fellow, athletic, bigger than the rest of those around him. He stood up and, with an ear-to-ear smile on his face, began to walk toward the back where Hieronymus and his two comrades were sitting.

"Hey! My man! Goggle-guy! Remember me?"

At first Hieronymus drew a complete blank—and then it returned. Of course. Pete. A barrelhead. One of Slue's friends, whom he met in the media-viewing rotunda just three weeks earlier. The one who wanted him to tap Slue on the shoulder. The one who had threatened to take his nose off. Hieronymus waved.

"Hi," he said with zero enthusiasm.

As Pete got closer, Bruegel shrank a little, and Clellen instantly took an interest in the newcomer, instinctively adjusting her gel-clogged hair.

"Hey!" Pete smiled widely as he reached the rear of the transport where the three were sitting. "Mind if I sit with you guys?"

"Sure," Hieronymus mumbled, moving over slightly so as to make more room for Pete, who was wearing a tellball jersey with the words Sputnik Spiders emblazoned across the top, a tarantula-like creature with bloody fangs printed in fiery colors just under it.

"I like your shirt!" Clellen said with extraordinary over-enthusiasm.

"Thanks!" Pete took his place next to Hieronymus. "I think the Spiders are going to really clamp down on the Jackson Craters next week. Don't you think so?"

Hieronymus and Bruegel each gave an affirmative shrug, not knowing what Pete was talking about. Clellen commented with a gigantic and vivacious "OHHH YESSSSS!" while waving both her arms in a strange show of celebration. Clellen knew less about the tellball tournaments than anyone there, but she didn't want Pete to know that. The newcomer smiled quite genuinely at her, and then he introduced himself, his eyes mostly on the bubbly Clellen, who was relieved the big bruise on her face had faded a long time ago.

"I'm Pete, by the way."

"Very pleased to meet you, Pete." Clellen giggled as she shook his hand. "I'm Clellen."

"Clellen is a lovely name," he replied.

"And this is Bruegel, and that guy over there with the goggles is Mus."

"Mus?" Pete looked perplexed for a second. "I thought your name was Hiker-a-mous, or something like that. Slue always mentions your name, but I can never get it right…"

A burning, sad thought entered Hieronymus' mind. *Slue always mentions*…said with such matter-of-fact familiarity. Slue wouldn't speak to him now. And with that one single casual sentence, Hieronymus understood indeed, she was now spending time with this fellow right next to him.

"Hieronymus is actually how it's pronounced."

"Oh, I'm sorry, man. I'm not really good with names that have more than one syllable."

"Don't worry about it—it's not exactly common, so a lot of people mispronounce it."

"That's why we call him Mus," Clellen added.

"Yes," Hieronymus grinned a half smile. "A lot of people call me Mus. You can call me Mus if you'd like."

"I don't know." Pete laughed in a friendly way. "I think I need the challenge—everyone I know has names like mine—Pete or Bud or Ken or even Slue, you know Slue, with only one syllable. You have a really cool name. I should just make the effort to remember it."

Hieronymus was struck by how sincerely friendly this Pete was toward him—and toward the other two as well. They had only met once before, and the encounter had been less than sociable.

"Anyway," Pete continued, looking down at his triple-sized V-RR100 shoes. "I Just wanted to come by and tell you I'm sorry I was such a rectumexit a few weeks back at the rotunda."

This was out of the blue. It completely shocked Hieronymus.

"What are you talking about?" he replied. "You weren't being a rectumexit at all," he lied.

"Well, I was pretty rude to you, ordering you around like that to tap Slue on the shoulder. I didn't even say please, and then I even suggested I was going to break your nose, or something like that."

Hieronymus couldn't remember the last time he had ever felt so embarrassed—and at the same time, redeemed—considering the minuscule amount of time he had even spent thinking of this guy since the last time they met. And in fact, the more he looked at him, the more he could not help but sort of like him. After all, if Slue hung out with this Pete fellow, he couldn't have been all that bad. Modesty suggested he be gracious toward the apologizing oaf.

"Look, I was the one being a wise guy—I could have just as easily tapped her on the shoulder when you first asked me, but I was being a schluck. And you were in a hurry."

"Yeah, but in retrospect, I forgot that Slue is a really serious student, and she doesn't like to be interrupted when she's deep into her intellectual stuff. I was intruding."

"No you weren't," insisted Hieronymus, who found it strange that he was engaged in a bizarre apology contest with Pete. "What kind of an intellectual is one who can't be tapped on her shoulder, Pete?"

Pete had no answer for that, but he looked off into the passing countryside with an expression of contemplation.

"Well, anyway, Slue explained the whole thing to me, and I realized that I was not very nice to you—or her— that day."

"Don't worry about it, Pete."

"You're a really good friend of Slue's, aren't you?"

Hieronymus shrugged his shoulders. "I've known her since the third grade."

"She talks about you a lot."

"Have you seen much of her lately?" Hieronymus asked, slightly nervously.

"Yeah, a bunch. I took her to the tellball previews between Lovettown and Gagarin last Saturday. She loved it."

"Really? I had no idea that Slue was even interested in tellball—or any sport."

"Oh, she gets into it if the game is good. We have a deal going—she comes with me to see games and sports and stuff like that, and I go with her to museums and films and poetry readings. I've opened up her world to athletics, and she's opened up my world to…you know, old films, novels, even paintings, and all this music I never heard of before. And you know what we totally agree on? My car. I have a three-year-old Prokong-90. It's in great condition! Slue loves my car, and I think our favorite thing to do together is go for long drives under the Earthlight during the wee hours when the highways are empty."

Hieronymus forced himself to smile and paused before he spoke.

"That's great, Pete."

"I even read that book you just did the presentation on in your class last week. Slue made a copy of the one your uncle translated—it was really great. Very bizarre, but great."

"I'm very pleased to hear that, Pete. You know, Slue was supposed to work with me on that one but she just quit, out of the blue, and worked on another book with another student instead."

"Yeah, she told me that."

"She just stopped speaking to me."

"Really?"

"Yeah. In fact, it started right after we saw you at the rotunda. How long ago was that—three weeks, right? She's ignored me since. Until two seconds ago when you told me that she made a copy of *The Random Treewolf* for you, I had no idea she even listened to my dissertation on it."

Pete shook his head, laughing.

"Man, she wouldn't shut up about it. She thought it was the most brilliant thing she had ever heard."

Hieronymus said nothing. He only stared ahead, then out through the window at the passing neon-covered apartment complexes in the distance.

Pete leaned in a little closer.

"Look, man, I really have to ask you something."

"Sure, Pete. Anything."

"I know that Slue is in the Topper classes. I know that you have to be really, really smart to get into those classes. Usually, it seems that if someone is in one Topper class, they tend to be in *all* of them. Like Slue. Now the other day, she told me something totally unbelievable about *you*." Pete lowered his voice to a whisper so that neither Bruegel nor Clellen could hear him. "Slue said that you are only in three Topper classes, and that the other half of your subjects you take with the... Loopies?"

Hieronymus smiled, then raised his eyebrows in such a way that jiggled the goggles on his face. He was expecting a weird question on lunarcroptic ocular symbolanosis, or on the fourth primary color, or on the goggles, but of course, it was the old Toppers and Loopies thing once again.

"This is true. I am a Topper, and I am a Loopie."

Pete was impressed and astonished.

"I've seen you running through the hallways, sprinting through the crowds of kids just walking to their classes. Everyone talks about the goggle-guy—sorry, I mean One Hundred Percent Lunar Boy who's in both the best and the worst classes and who has to run the entire length of the school just to get to his classes on time. It's you, isn't it?"

"Yes, Pete, that's me."

"You know, you're incredibly fast. That's why you are both a mystery and a legend among the bulk of the students. We just see you zip right past. I'll be walking to class with five or six others, the hallway will be really crowded, we'll be talking about normal stuff, like last night's game or something, and then all of a sudden, *whoosh!* This *phantom* darts right past us, a tablet and a stylo-point in his hand, and in the blink of an eye, he's gone. It happens every day. Nobody knows who you are because you are in no one's class and you don't seem to associate with anyone who is not a Topper or a Loopie. When I met you three weeks ago in the rotunda, I had no idea that you were *The Phantom*. You're that fast."

Hieronymus was not sure where Pete was going with this story— but the big fellow appeared to be genuinely impressed with his running abilities, which, till this moment, he'd never considered in any kind of way.

"Listen," Pete continued. "Tryouts for the track team start in three weeks."

"Oh…" Hieronymus suddenly understood what this was about.

"Me and some of the other guys, after making fun of *The Phantom*— that is, making fun of you—realized that you were a lot faster than any of us. You would be such an excellent sprinter for our team."

"I thought you were already on the tellball team?" Hieronymus asked, surprised and flattered by this unforeseen appreciation for a talent he did not even know he had had.

"I am. But the season is almost over. And we were knocked out of the semifinals by Lunar Public 64, so we're not even playing anymore. However…" He paused. "With *The Phantom* on our track team, I think we can have an unbelievable next season."

"*The Phantom…*" Hieronymus considered it. "I like that. And it sure beats goggle-guy."

Pete laughed, gently slapping himself on the forehead.

"Sorry about that."

For the rest of the transport ride to LEM Zone One, Pete stayed with the three representatives of the Loopie world, talking to Hieronymus and especially Clellen. Bruegel was uncharacteristically shy. Clellen had her flirt siren on, blazing and blaring, and Pete was happy to accommodate her.

"Do you like being on the tellball team?" she asked.

"Sure," he answered. "Do you like being on the Beautiful Girl Team?"

Clellen laughed and slapped him on one of his biceps.

"Stop it! There is no Beautiful Girl Team!"

"Really? You should start one. You'd be captain…"

"You!" She laughed as she slapped him again, this time on the shoulder, before changing the subject only slightly.

"Do you think I'd make a good cheerleader?"

"Cheerleader?" Pete asked.

"Yeah, you know, all those ring-top girls really getting their frazzles on, doing shake-shake on the ring-side while the boys just get the inna-caws-drive going on the other teams' ace ball!"

"What?" Pete asked, his middle-class brain unable to comprehend Clellen's last sentence.

"You know, buck." She laughed, standing up in the aisle and throwing her arms in the air. "Cheerleaders!" She shouted as she started to do this incredible dance while singing a song, her body gestures and leg-kicking both violent and sexual and clumsy and utterly copied from ancient films when cheerleaders actually existed on Earth, their image exploited and exaggerated for reasons long ago forgotten…

Superman, superflux
I'm a sloppy, out of luck
meet me in a pick-up truck
go-packa-macka-facka
Ring-arounda-rollie-pollie
roll-me-with-your-holy-rollie
I'm a sloppy silly slut
go pack me in the gut

Hieronymus and Bruegel hardly paid any attention to her. Clellen performed this and a thousand other identical routines about five times a day in their classroom. Pete, on the other hand, had never seen anything remotely like this in his entire life.

"Wow!" He cheered, applauding with his big hands. "I like your song!"

She jumped up in the air and landed on his lap, where she immediately placed her open mouth on his, giving him an unbelievably long, wet, tongue-thrusting kiss.

"My gosh!" Pete exclaimed, his face flush with excitement. "I am *so* joining the Loopie class!" he yelled so loud half the entire transport could hear.

Moments later, the transport arrived at LEM Zone One. Hieronymus noted to himself that he alone among the four knew what the LEM actually was—the others simply didn't care. Pete stayed with the Loopies, chiefly because Clellen kissed him a few more times, and as they walked to the site of the ancient broken spaceship, he went out of his way to introduce Hieronymus to some of the other kids, saying things like, *this is Hieronymus The Phantom. I got him to join the track team!*

A hundred students arrived at once. They disobeyed all the rules regarding the old metal ruin from Earth. They climbed on it, they jumped off, they wrestled, and they all threw things at each other. The teachers yelled and when the kids got themselves in order, the teachers explained what had happened on this very spot two thousand years earlier. The students quickly got bored and some of them began to goof around again—this was a story they had all heard hundreds of times before, and they were more attracted to the glittering casino lights in every direction and all the strange adults crowded around than a pile of broken-down metal vaguely resembling a giant spider sculpture. One boy found a rusted can of beer that had been tossed under the LEM and shouted out loud, *hey, do you think they left this here too?* and everyone laughed. Hieronymus climbed up and jumped off the contraption a few more times, running around with Bruegel and Clellen and Pete.

He was standing on top of the thing when he saw her. She was looking directly at him, walking in his direction.

The girl from Earth.

He froze. The way she walked. Her face. He had never seen anything like her.

chapter six

It is not a disease. It is inexplicable.

There is nothing wrong with me. They gave it a name that sounds like a disease, but it is nothing of the sort. I don't know what it is. But I am certain that there is nothing wrong with me.

What do you see when you take your goggles off?

I'm not allowed to talk about it.

But you do take your goggles off.

Sometimes. At night when I sleep. When I wash my face.

So you sometimes can go to the window, like in the middle of the night maybe, and look out.

Yes.

What do you see?

I see everything that normal people can see. And then some.

And then some. What does that mean?

I am not allowed to talk about it. If I am caught, I will be sent away.

I've come all the way from Earth.

Then you will go back to your normal life on Earth and forget you ever had this conversation with me. You will forget you ever met me.

Do you know that only One Hundred Percent Lunar People can

pilot Mega Cruisers?

What are you talking about?

It's true. If you want to pilot a Mega Cruiser, you have to be able to see whatever it is that you see. I heard they pilot all the ships in the entire solar system and they don't wear goggles when they do it.

I don't believe it.

It's just a rumor. But I think you would know right away if this idea makes any sense. Certainly, at some time in your life, you have looked up into the sky, into the forever that is the same outer space that we see on Earth. You just told me that you sometimes looked out your window at night. How could you not have looked into the sky? What do you see?

What do you see?

Here she was. Beautiful was too cheap a word. She was an image. A revelation. Fragile. Invincible. An orchid. A silver antenna. She was electricity. She was a fairy. She was a firefly, a silkworm, an imp, a demon, a goddess. A black-eyed, black-haired girl from another planet, from the sphere just above their heads. He felt himself unable to breathe as soon as he came upon her approaching form. He was standing on the lopsided contraption of junk that had at one time carried the first human beings to the Moon. There was a crowd of people, students and tourists, and from them, she emerged, an apparition, her eyes already on his, making him feel childish, her other-worldliness inherent in her awkward walk, her gaze belonging only to him.

She climbed up the ladder the ancients had once climbed down. She did it with the ease of someone from a world where the gravity is harsh, and thus, here on the Moon, can practically float.

He could not move. He was paralyzed with such pleasure as she approached him. Surrounded by the buzzing neon lights of the casinos, standing on a junk pile, an archaeological contraption, broken, *so hard to believe that humanity had once tossed this thing here—a symbol, an endeavor of such high expectations,* it rests crumbled and surrounded by tourists, half of whom do not even know what it is, she walks upon it as if it is her altar, constructed eons ago to mark her arrival on this spot, at this particular time.

She walked right up to him and his world slowed to a halt. Silence enveloped the atmosphere. Huge hummingbirds hovered in the air as she approached.

Humanity took a breathless pause.

Her lips moved.

"Hello. I'm from Earth. I saw you from over there. Are you a One Hundred Percent Lunar Boy?"

"Yes, I am."

Her smile widened. A volcano split the Moon in two, but all he saw were her wonderful black eyes. Her accent when she spoke…

"I would love to speak to you. Do you have some time?"

"Yes. Yes I do."

His comrades from school quickly became insignificant. They were transformed into shadows, gray and brown and fading into the neon lit cityscape. There was only her. She was from Earth, the forbidden place. She was the most astonishing thing he had ever seen and she came from the tumultuous world of his ancestors.

"What would you like to talk about?"

You can not comprehend what it is that I can see. It can not be explained in words.

Everything can be explained in words.

Not this.

As they walked away from the ruin of the LEM, only Bruegel and Clellen and Pete noticed. Pete, being the by-the-book kind of guy he was, immediately expressed concern that his new friend Hieronymus could get into trouble by cutting. Bruegel, who by now had warmed up to the tellball player, explained that in this case, leaving was not really cutting, but it was more or less deciding independently when to pursue academic pursuits, or, in Bruegel's pseudo way of making up words to sound more educated, it was a fluxitation of the romular behavioral mode ingrained in the Lunar constitutional triad that allowed for immersions and slegisonic sidemorgraphic thinking in a carpikular sense. Pete thought this explanation sounded logical, especially when Clellen interrupted again and gave him yet one more extraordinary, spine-tingling, outrageous kiss on his open mouth with her wondrous yet bad, very bad and beautiful lips. Pete felt his heart palpitate. *Where did you learn to kiss like that?!* he exclaimed between breaths. As the rest of the class made their way to a nearby museum, Bruegel and Pete and Clellen snuck away to a bar—Bruegel had a fake ID and Pete had a few extra dollars and so they ordered several rounds of beers and the three of them got quite drunk before making their way back to the transport three hours later for the ride home. Hieronymus was nowhere to be found. None of the teacher chaperones made any effort to locate him because he was, in that circumstance, just one of the Loopies, and who really gave a damn about those criminals, that's all they do is cut class anyway. The bus ride home was uneventful except that Pete and Clellen got a little out of control in their making out. Bruegel fell asleep, and luckily for him, when he finally got back to the apartment he shared with his mother, she did not notice the smell of alcohol on his breath because she herself was pretty smashed as it was, passed out on the living room floor. Clellen was dreading what her father might think if he caught her again with the stink of beer on her lipstick-smeared mouth, so she bought a pack of mints and ate them all—luckily, at the moment she arrived in her own flat, her father was busy in his bedroom with one of his girlfriends, so Clellen did not have to test her mint-flavored scheme of covering drunkenness. She sneaked into her room and locked the door by shoving a chair under the doorknob. Pete had never been drunk before in his entire life and he was physically unprepared for his body's own adverse rejection of it—not to mention his parents' horrified reaction to the spectacle of their son puking up the unmistakable bile of stinking excess in the living room.

That night, Ringo Rexaphin was beside himself with worry when his son never came home. He called the school, but no one even knew Hieronymus was missing. He dreaded the idea of calling the police. He did not trust them, and they were notorious for singling out One Hundred Percent Lunar People and charging them with the crime of Ocular Assault when, in fact, nothing of the sort happened. Still there was this terrible thing that had happened on the subway just the night before, and he was worried beyond all reason. He spent the night pacing the apartment. Several times he got so worried he almost hyperventilated.

He had never known such anxiety. He drank three glasses of whiskey. It changed nothing, and he didn't even feel it.

Finally, at five in the morning, Hieronymus walked in. His father yelled a lot and almost smacked the sixteen-year-old in the face—but his relief that his son was finally safe at home quickly pushed the possibility of this far away. It was Saturday morning. Hieronymus slept until noon.

Have you ever imagined what a fourth primary color might look like?

I have tried to imagine, but I can't.

There are three primary colors. Red, yellow, and blue.

I know.

Try to imagine what a fourth one might be like.

Green comes to mind.

Green is just a mix between yellow and blue. Try again.

Purple? Is purple the fourth primary color?

Wrong again.

Is it a brownish mix?

It is not a mix at all. You don't mix any colors to get it. It's primary.

What you are saying is impossible. Logically, there is no fourth primary color.

There is a fourth primary color. I know. I see it. There is probably a fifth and sixth one too. There may be an infinite number of primary colors. We don't see them. You only see three. I can only see four.

Does it hurt to see this color? Does it give you a headache?

These goggles give me a headache.

Why must you wear them? It seems to me to be a very excessive measure.

I am required by law to wear them.

That seems like a very unfair law. What would happen if you all decided to refuse?

There would be a mass hysteria like you wouldn't believe.

Why would anyone get hysterical over people taking their goggles off?

You would get hysterical if I took my goggles off.

How could you say that? You don't even know me.

It doesn't matter. You will become totally hysterical if I take my goggles off.

Prove it. Take your goggles off.

No. I will go to jail if I do that.

None of what you say makes any sense.

But it does. My eyes are the color of the fourth primary color. Your brain will short-circuit if you even look at it.

Show me.

I can't. I have already broken the law by talking about it.

Show me your eyes.

The last person who looked at my eyes died.

I won't die.

No, but you won't be the same ever again.

Good.

They had to keep walking in order to maintain this conversation. He had known many people from Earth before, but they were all adults. She was a teenager. Someone his own age. He was amazed at the graceful way she walked beside him—as if she were a dancer, almost floating, the peculiar way her arms swayed at her side. He was enthralled with her delightful accent. She told him exactly where on Earth she came from, but he had never heard of it, and it hardly mattered to him because the experience of listening to her speak was in itself a musical treat.

They passed a gigantic casino experiencing a catastrophic emergency—hordes of gamblers were leaving in large groups and a fire truck swerved almost onto the sidewalk, the firefighters rushing out and charging into the casino lobby. As they passed, deep inside, way beyond the lobby, orange tongues of fire sizzled out of control. From inside this cauldron, excited, panicked voices could be heard, and as they tried to pass, a crowd gathered.

The spectators prevented some of the firemen from getting their equipment from out of the fire truck, and three men who appeared to be together got into an argument with the fire chief—they were offended he had dragged a huge filthy coil of hoses from the truck and deposited it just in front of them. As they argued, there was an explosion from inside the casino, and the flames suddenly grew with a bright intensity.

One of the three men, dressed in a flashy bright blue blazer and a hat of brushed aluminum, flustered with indignation at the sloppiness of the firefighter.

"You have a tremendous amount of nerve!" he complained. "Those hoses are filthy! You almost got them on our shoes!"

The fire chief shouted orders into a tiny, old-fashioned wrist-mounted radio and ignored them. He was joined by another fireman as they grabbed more bulky pieces of equipment and dumped them just next to the hoses. This caused another self-righteous outburst from the same spectator.

"Excuse me!" the fellow with the aluminum hat shouted. "Our shoes were almost stained by your carelessness!"

The chief had no time for this. There was another explosion, and the other fireman addressed the concerns of the spectator.

"Sir, kindly move away. You are preventing us from dealing with this emergency."

"No. You move away. You move these hoses out of the way. I am not walking into that filthy street with these new shoes, which your careless fire chief almost stained with those disgusting hoses."

As he said that last sentence, three new firefighters rushed past him from another truck that had just careened onto the scene. In doing so, they brushed against one of the other three complaining men—this being a fellow who wore a wonderfully exquisite wrinkled paper suit of bright white. The three of them moaned at the large black greasy soot mark this left behind across the gentleman's shoulder.

"Look at that! Look at that!" shouted the man in the aluminum hat. "What are you going to do about the stain on my friend's suit?"

The firemen were too occupied with their immediate worries of preventing the entire casino from going up in flames to pay any attention to this rude dandy. Three or four silver figures showed up—rescue robots—mannequin-like, faceless machines designed to walk through fire and locate trapped people. They reported to the chief, who told them to run up to the tenth floor, the fourteenth floor, and the twenty-ninth floor. As he said that, there was a shattering of glass, and looking up, three hysterical faces began shouting and screaming from the twentieth floor. "Track those voices!" the chief yelled to the last robot who ran into the spreading flames, "I think they might be on twenty…"

The fire was spreading fast, and the chief grumbled to another fire-fighter about the cheap and hazardous materials used in constructing these skyscrapers. An orange ball of light exploded on the sixth floor, and a fire marshal said to the chief, *what the hell were they keeping up there?* And the chief said, *this looks a little like arson, don't you think so?* Three firemen were carried out, suffering from smoke inhalation—a collapsing beam had fallen on them, ripped away their breathing equipment, and forced them to inhale the insanely hot, soot-filled air. As they were transported on their emergency gurneys, the back of one fireman's coat brushed against the checkerboard trousers of the complaining fellow with the aluminum hat who had refused to budge from his spot. He looked down and saw the soot stain across his pant leg and fell into a screaming fit about his pants and his shoes that were almost marked and his friend's paper suit, which was ruined. The firefighters ignored him as more human screams filled the air. That only encouraged the man, who persisted, despite the mortal danger in every direction, to create an enormous distraction with his ridiculous ranting. Finally, the fire marshal told him, *you know, you are really in our way. I am sorry that your clothes got stained, but I think you should have known better as you are standing right in the middle of a fire zone and you are just preventing us from carrying out our responsibilities, so won't you please move over there across the street? I am warning you, not only will you get arrested as soon as the police arrive, but you will only get more soot marks on your clothes if you don't leave.* This was a fruitless plea. The three furious men stood in their spot without moving and declared they would stay glued to the sidewalk until someone from the Sea of Tranquility Fire Department wrote them a check to cover the cost of dry cleaning their unfairly soiled clothes, and just as the gentleman in the aluminum hat made this loud and vocal demand, his face round and red with the most extreme anger, his moment of standing his ground proved to be a fatal one for him and his friends. Thirty floors above their heads, there was another loud crash followed by a massive object falling, falling and screaming—it was a man, a four-hundred-pound man, who had leapt from his apartment to escape the flames. He landed directly upon the three complainers and crushed them all on impact, in particular their vertebrae columns and their skulls. The crunching sound was louder than the fire-alarm-and-screaming cacophony, and despite the instant deaths of the three stubborn gentlemen, the four-hundred-pound window leaper emerged from this freakish accident completely intact. He had no problem whatsoever with the fire marshal's request to stand across the street.

The girl from Earth began to cry, and Hieronymus put his arm around her, a genuine protective gesture—he was taller than her, and he had already seen death happen right before his own unshielded eyes. This horror scene had reminded him of the way he killed Lester two years earlier. He felt the girl trembling, and he wished they had not wandered down this particular street. The day was ruined. Her shoulders were shaking, and her eyes were full of tears.

"I'm so sorry," he said.

"Those poor men, those poor men. I've never seen dead people before. I can't believe what happened. One second they were alive, then one second later, they were crushed under that falling man! If only they had listened to the fire marshal, they would still be alive!"

"Yes, but then that big fellow who had fallen upon them would be dead. They gave their lives to him."

"Horrible," she cried. "Death is horrible!" Then she held him tight as they walked through the crowd, fighting it like fish swimming upstream, through all the currents of the gawking population heading toward the spectacle of the fire, which was getting out of control under the red sky. More fire trucks came roaring up the avenue, passing them and then heading toward the unfortunate, burning catastrophe.

She was truly scared. He was also scared, but for different reasons.

"I watched those men crumble," she moaned. "Three men, crushed like insects—I can't believe how their backbones snapped like that, their skulls…"

Tears streamed down her face. Sirens wailed. A man walked past wearing a black derby. He turned to smile at her, but she nearly fainted as he had only one eye—the other was just a long-ago healed eye socket with bland skin coating its cavern interior. The fellow had a handlebar mustache. When he opened his mouth, a miniature baby hummingbird on a leash of dental floss flew out and hovered next to his ear, never able to fly away as the other end of its line was tied to the man's front tooth.

She covered her face with her hands. "This place is awful," she moaned.

"What hotel are you and your parents staying in?" Hieronymus asked.

"It's called the Hotel Venice. It's on Ratugenbar Avenue."

"I'll take you there."

A vehicle with three drunken tourists veered off the street and smacked into an iron footbridge. The three human beings inside were not wearing seat belts, and at the moment of impact, they flew forward like three ragdolls and smacked themselves upon the interior windshield, bloodying their faces with broken jaws and cracking the glass. Hieronymus was about to run over and help, but the Earth girl grabbed his arm and said, "Enough. I have seen too many terrible things for one night." And so he walked away with her.

The girl from Earth was so upset by all these random accidents. She felt as if the Moon had toppled off its orbit and was causing all of these terrible coincidences to occur just to chase her away.

Your eyes are the color of the fourth primary color?

Yes.

Is that why you keep them covered?

I don't keep them covered. The law keeps them covered.

If this law did not exist, would you still keep them covered?

I don't know.

I would like to see this color. Won't you show me?

I can't. It will make you completely hysterical.

After everything that's happened tonight, I'm already hysterical.

It's against the law. And there are police everywhere. I'm always hassled by the police because I'm a One Hundred Percent Lunar Boy. If I look at you with my goggles off, I will be charged with assault.

I want to see this color.

Find someone else.

No, I want to see your eyes specifically.

It's not going to happen.

Don't you want to see what I look like with the fourth primary color?

They got lost. Hieronymus was not completely certain where her hotel was. It was somewhere in their vicinity, among the hundreds of hotels they kept passing. It was easy to take a wrong turn and simply end up wandering in circles. Tourists blocked their every step, and these were not just visitors from Earth, but tourists from all over the Moon, clogging the streets looking for casinos and bars and night-clubs and restaurants and prostitutes and drugs. LEM Zone One was only a name. No one knew nor cared what its historical significance may have been—it existed at this point in time as a quasi-lawless free-for-all, a gambling hole, an adult playpen, a place where losers went to fulfill loser dreams.

They walked through an alleyway leading to an illuminated area. The Earth girl looked through an open door that led into a dark hallway. A man with a rubber snake in his teeth was on all fours, chasing a small white mouse with a hammer. He caught her from the corner of his eye. "What's wrong, you never saw a chaincarresser before?" he said.

She nervously walked away and with Hieronymus, exited the alleyway into a sea of bright blue lights. An amusement park...a Ferris wheel...twirling rides...a roller coaster...a lake with small boats shaped like mechanical dogs.

What is your name?

You won't believe what my name is.

That's not true. I am ready to believe whatever you tell me.

My name is Window Falling On Sparrows.

Excuse me? Did you just tell me that your name was...an incredibly silly sentence?

Yes. Windows Falling On Sparrows.

Is that just your first name? Or is it your entire name?

It is only my first name. And you? I have just spent hours walking around with you, asking all sorts of personal questions, and I don't even know your name.

Hieronymus.

That name is also unusual. I have never heard it before.

My father named me that. He never told me where he got the name from.

And your mother?

I have no idea what her opinion of my name is.

—

Determined to rid themselves of the evening's horrible surprises, the two teenagers entered the amusement park—a festival of light bulbs and giant moving insects. The first thing they saw was a crude rink surrounded by a fence. The rink was only fifty meters in diameter, and inside, two large moon moose were viciously fighting. Moon moose were very similar to their relatives on Earth, except their fur was a highly unnatural, bluish white. They were also much bigger than their Earthling counterparts and far more aggressive. Their ancestors were brought to the Moon almost a thousand years ago, and they thrived mostly in vast herds on the far side. Another factor that differentiated them from their cousins on Earth was that they were omnivorous—and sometimes cannibalistic when the food supply ran out. Windows Falling On Sparrows ran to the barrier and stood among the jeering crowds, some with dollars in their hands. Big, crude men and women, all with fleshy faces, excitedly watching these two massive beasts ram each other with their magnificent antlers. The animals themselves were frightening, almost prehistoric creatures. Never in her life had she ever witnessed such a display of illiterate vulgarity. They yelled bizarre idiomatic expressions. Every face, either stupid looking or ugly. That crowd, even worse than all the cretins she met by the casinos. She stayed close to Hieronymus. The two moose rammed each other, circled each other, charged, and then rammed each other again. Deafening cheers and boos. The man next to her waved his fist full of paper Lunar dollars. He smelled awful. He was filthy and his clothes were of the worst sort—shiny blue running pants, flannel shirt. Drunk, he gave her a threatening look with his wet, bloodshot eyes. Just behind him, a skinny woman with translucent gray hair and a face full of lines took a sip from a flask-shaped bottle, threw it into the rink, then inexplicably, with her tongue, licked the rust covered fence post.

Hieronymus saw the look of disgust and fear on the face of poor Windows Falling On Sparrows. He thought this was a pretty awful place, too, but he was used to this—standing at the fence, watching the two moon moose fight it out was not a hell of a lot different from a typical day in remedial math class.

—

If you took off your goggles, what things would be colored by the fourth primary color? For example, to you, would green become something different? Does white become your new color? Does black become something new?

It is nothing like that. This color exists as a translucent. It is a fading trail that is left behind by movement. All movement leaves it behind. This color also appears before the movement occurs. It fades into existence, the object moves through it, it fades away.

That is senseless. That is mad, and you are either insane or you are lying.

To look at the world without these lenses, when there are people all around and there is movement in every direction, can be jarring and confusing.

What you are describing is incomprehensible.

I agree. You cannot comprehend it.

If you looked at me, you would see a trail of this color? You would know where I walked in from?

That is true. And depending on the light in the air, if your trail does not fade too quickly, I could retrace your steps for a long distance. The problem is that everyone else's trail would collide with yours. And the movement of everything else, too—cars, animals, falling objects.

And you also see a trail of where I am going?

This is true.

If I were to walk away, you would know the direction I was going to take.

Yes.

So you could see into the future.

Sort of. I know what direction you are going to take. I could see exactly where you will go before you have even decided to go. I could see the direction that everything will take in my field of vision.

It sounds like a lie. It sounds like a phony lie that psychics claim to be true.

I am not a psychic. I cannot read your mind. But without these goggles, I can tell where you will go. It is scientific. It is proven, and for me, it is as clear as day, because this color exists as powerfully as yellow and red and blue.

But how can you possibly see movement before it happens?

I can see it because I can see the fourth primary color and the fourth primary color does not exist in the same time schedule as the other three primary colors.

Time schedule?

We can only perceive of time as moving in a linear direction. We are human beings. Our bodies age progressively, in one direction. And, for us, color is only a part of the linear world. Colors all fade with time unless they are replenished with fresh ones. Our eyes perceive the colors and the types of light that help us to navigate properly through our own existence. But we are also as perceptive as worms are to us when we are forced to consider the limitations of our own mechanisms of contact with the world outside ourselves. We are arrogant enough to imagine that our own perception of reality is the final one. We are arrogant enough to assume that there are only three primary colors because that is all we can see, and therefore, no other colors can possibly exist. We are arrogant enough to imagine that time travels only in a set and measured direction because we age and break down and eventually stop working. We are arrogant, but we are no more arrogant than the parasite worm who lives in the intestines of a moose— for, to that parasite, there is no more reality than its dark existence among others like it, never knowing more than what its perceptions indicate to it, never knowing that, in fact, its whole world rests deep inside a strange beast that fights with another beast while drunks and other assorted riff- raff bet over which moose will win the stupid fight.

My ability to see the fourth primary color is only a peek into the general reality that is denied us by our own crude organs. If I can see this color, then I can see what will happen before it happens because the color exists in the genuine reality of time itself. I am no more than a viewer, but I see this color and its place in the actually existing world in much the same way that anyone who looks up into the night sky will see the lights of stars that no longer exist. This color cannot be seen by you or most people because it has no place in the normal experience of human rapport with reality. But it is real. It is as real as we are. As those animals fighting over there. As real as the planet up there where you come from. It is real. The fourth primary color has no name because it is not allowed to by the people who cannot see it. But it exists. The fourth primary color exists. And contrary to their stupid law, it is lunarcroptic ocular symbolanosis that does not exist. I have no condition, nor do I have a disease. I am not a mutation. I can only see what most others can't.

This was the first time in his life he had ever explained any of this forbidden subject to anyone. As he spoke, he knew that at any moment, he could be arrested. However, the amusement park was noisy and, from what he could gather, completely lawless.

They went to an aluminum pizza stand and ordered slices. They stood at the counter, the bright white light bulbs strung in a line above their heads. He watched her eat, the way she folded the slice in half, the way she blew on it, her black eyes glistening. They shared a secret. He committed crimes against the state by even talking about himself. But she had an extraordinary aura of trust about her. He did not believe she would get him in any kind of trouble. She told him that the pizza on Earth was a completely different thing than what they ate.

If you show me the color of your eyes, no one will ever find out.
  Everyone will find out. Starting with the police.
  Do you see any police here?
  I refuse to show you my eyes.
  I think you want to. I can tell. You want to show me your eyes.
  Why would I want to show you my eyes?
  Because you like me. You fancy me.
  This...is...true.
  Then why don't you show me your eyes.
  Because it might hurt you, and I will be sent to prison.
  I won't get hurt. I am very strong. I am from the Earth. The gravity there would be too much for everyone you know. I can take it. Have you ever met an Earth girl before?
  No.
  Have you ever kissed an Earth girl before?

Hieronymus bought a booklet of tickets and they went on some of the rides. The first one was a twirling contraption called the tarantula, and it actually did resemble a giant spider, except it had about twenty legs instead of only eight. Along with every other ride, it was covered in light bulbs. Hieronymus had never seen so many light bulbs in his life—they were considered archaic, outdated, and even dangerous. They walked around and entered into a house of mirrors and soon left, laughing at each other's distorted images. After that, the two of them went onto the roller coaster. They sat in the front. During the long steep climb to the top, he looked around. Colossal white hummingbirds hovered in the air and traveled upward with them. The world of neon stretched off into forever, through the Sea of Tranquility. The glittering casinos. The flowing rivers of endless, illuminated traffic working its way across webs of elevated highways—thousands of Saturn-on-side cars jammed together and following each other like industrious ants pretending to be fireflies. More hummingbirds, farther away, journeyed in fast-moving clouds through the distance. Millions of them, everywhere. They saw the glowing silhouettes of cities and towns in the distance, apartment complexes, craters filled with water, concrete and steel Ulzatallizine pumping stations, refineries, and tall docking stations for the many Mega Cruisers that floated in the distance, massive sturgeon-shaped vessels, either ascending into the red sky or slowly searching for places to land after their impossibly long voyages from everywhere far away. Windows Falling On Sparrows pointed to one of them with her long finger. "Look," she said, with a very slight tinge of sadness. "That's my ship—that's the *Ragmagothic Chrysanthemum.*"

The roller coaster began its sudden jolt downward, and they held onto each other.

You want to show me your eyes.
> *Yes. I want to. But it is forbidden.*
And that is all the more reason why.
> *I have never purposefully shown my eyes to anyone.*
So I will be the first. Intentionally.
> *Yes. But you may never forgive me.*
I will never forgive you if you don't show me your eyes.
> *I will be the first.*
And I will be the first that you have ever intentionally shown them to.
> *I hope we won't regret this.*

If we do, it doesn't matter. I'll go back to Earth. You will continue your life here. We'll forget about each other if it turns into something we regret.

My heart is racing. I can't wait to see you, to look at you without these goggles on.

I can't wait to see your eyes and their color. Feel my heart. It's racing just like yours.

The boy from the Moon and the girl from Earth discovered a small alleyway between two old abandoned brick buildings. Holding hands, they ran into it. It led to a very secluded yard, completely dark except for the reflected light from the Earth directly above them. They were alone, surrounded by walls and three or four hummingbirds, one of which started to circle around them. Outside, the twirling lights of the nearby rides revolved, churned with the music of a thousand bells.

They faced each other, holding each other by the arms. First they kissed for a delightfully long time. Her mouth, from so far away. Both were fairly new at this and the slight awkwardness was wonderful in and of itself. Their noses touched. He felt her breath air as it mixed with his own.

They could not stop. His spine was on fire. He felt her fingers on his arms.

Never in his life had he ever felt so completely alive.

They continued to kiss.

Then their faces parted. The Earth hung directly above. It cast a blue light on her as she looked at him.

She reached forward and with her fingers, she lifted his goggles up and off his face.

chapter seven

It was a disaster. She was completely unprepared for what she saw, and he was beyond irresponsible for allowing it to go this far. But he couldn't help it—he really liked her. She liked him also. But as soon as he saw her face crumple up into a pit of inhuman confusion just a second after seeing the fourth primary color, he knew he had done a very bad thing.

She saw the color. Both disks. Black pupil in the middle of each iris. Each iris a circle filled in with—that color. Yes, it was a primary color. As individual and as different as red and yellow and blue. How could she look at it? There was no reference. It was profoundly alien and profoundly normal, as it was a color and no more, but it was also an outsider color. After a couple of seconds, her eyes began to hurt, and she felt as if she had looked directly into the sun. There was a clicking sensation in her head. Those two circles of color. Was it a color or was it a disruption? This boy, this strange boy just in front of her, he brought this color to her. How could she ever forgive him? He stood, a god, a creature. He was not a human being. He was a stone. He came from the center of the Moon. With his eyes, he did not have to touch her to crack her head open with this intrusion, she felt so utterly displaced from herself, inside-out, her peripheral vision closed, only a pinpoint of the world visible in front of her, to focus on that dreadful intrusion, that color, that horrible porthole into both Hell and Heaven, all movement disjointed. She swore she could feel chemicals shifting and mixing. She thought of those men who were crushed just a few hours ago, the way their spines collapsed as if they were a stack of wooden coins covered in red strawberry syrup. Her own spine felt the same way, wobbly, unable to maintain itself, and her mouth was dry, and her teeth were just crystal objects about to break. Her physical self, her lungs barely functioned, her heart worked in overdrive, and her brain did not work at all. She was a blank vessel. Her tender tears flowed out from her eyes and into a world where water does not fall from the sky. What was she doing on the Moon for God's sake? What was she doing in this unnatural, manmade place? It was a false world, and that boy was false. He was a false human with his false eye color, and he tricked her with his good looks and his exotic goggles. He must be a demon or he must be some kind of strange god from the far side of the Moon. She never believed in God or any type of god, but what else but a god could he be? A god of the underworld. That color, both wondrous and nauseating and crippling, that was him. He and that color were one and she wanted to kill him and she wanted to worship him because she hated him and she loved him and now she was forever attached to him. She'd seen his eyes, and she cursed herself for being so stupid. He warned her but she was so goddamned cocky and sure of herself and this was what happened and forever after she will know that she is half-blind as she now fully understands that the world contains a fourth primary color. She has seen it, but only for a second. It is real, but she would never see it ever again and the existence of this color confirmed that human beings are so pitifully limited in their communication with the world, and she resented the boy in front of her for spelling this out with just a blink of an eye.

She felt herself collapse.

Her own eyes rolled so far back into her skull that her optic nerves vibrated with painful strain.

She bit her tongue. She tried to scream but could only mumble. She wrestled with herself. She could not remember her own name; she could not remember where she was. She only knew that she was in a small yard with brick walls on all sides and the muddy brown Earth directly above and, off to the side, the glowing edge of a nearby Ferris wheel twirling, the light bulbs blurry. She could not focus as her eyes were uncontrollable. She shouted words she did not understand. She tried to pull her own hair out, her fingers went into her ears to get at that insane ringing. The brass bell inside her skull. The silhouette of the boy-god circled her as she writhed on the filthy ground. He did not know what to do. She screamed at him. She tried to close her eyes, but that mad fourth color stayed imprinted, and she could not get rid of it. She crawled over to one of the brick walls and as she tried to smash her head against it, she was taken into the god's arms.

He struggled with her on the ground, but when he spoke to her, she could not understand because she could no longer place words with meaning and she could no longer place sounds with words. He held on to her mad thrashing form and he became all covered in dirt as well. They were both filthy and clouds of dirt rose in the air as they tussled against each other as she desperately wanted to smash her head against the brick wall, and he desperately wanted her to be completely still and stay alive and wait. And she suddenly understood what he was saying. He was asking her to wait. *The color will fade, your mind will reject it completely, wait, you will go back to normal, you will be exactly who you were, but you must ride it out, you must wait, you must wait…*

Two hours later, she sat next to him on a boat in the middle of a crater lake. They were covered in dirt, her hair matted with an industrial grease that she had rolled into. The abandoned yard they had chosen for their tryst had been filled with broken car parts and puddles of black oil. Hieronymus' white plastic jacked was covered with black spots and had a large rip in it from a sharp slab of broken windshield glass propped among the rusting junk he fell into. One of his fingers was in terrible pain—she had bitten it. The whole experience was far worse than either had imagined. He wanted to take her to the hospital and then turn himself in to the police, but she wouldn't allow it. Instead, as soon as she felt fully recovered, they left the small yard and wandered aimlessly through the amusement park. When they found the dock where small boats shaped like floating dogs were rented out, they decided to row out as far as possible into the middle of the circular lake. They wanted to be away from everyone.

The water was completely still, and under the dark red sky, appeared almost black.

Both of her knees had been badly scratched. She leaned forward and looked at the water, the glowing amusement park on the distant shore. She did not face him as they sat side by side, the oars making a small splashing sound as he drew them into the boat. He looked up at a distant floating Mega Cruiser. They were alone on the lake. From far away, the muffled sound of music. The occasional cackle and roar of the roller coaster. She could not look in his direction. He looked at her sad lump of matted hair.

"I love you," she said to him.

Hieronymus never told Windows Falling On Sparrows how happy he was to look at her and at the world without those damn goggles. The fourth primary color made him feel good—made him feel normal and complete. It was a sigh of relief to see things as they really were without those goggles filtering everything. Sadly, it was a moment of pleasure that lasted only a couple of seconds. Her reaction to his eye color had been thoroughly awful and he himself was surprised at how badly she handled it. And he knew that this type of thing was going to happen just before it did—when his goggles were off his eyes, he saw everything laid out in front of him, almost like a road map. He knew she was going to have a bad reaction, but it was too late because she had already seen his eyes. He saw the path she would take—the color trail bouncing itself off the walls, through the junk piles, intersecting with his own future trail of color where he would tackle her down, trying to prevent her from hurting herself. He was relieved to see ahead of time that her episode of confusion would be limited to the yard, as he could see her color trail as it left, but side by side with his—a calm, less confused marking of the same color. And then he had seen something profoundly sad. He didn't know how this was possible, but he recognized her trail of color from far away—it was a distinct and powerful one. He saw it rise up into the sky from somewhere off on the horizon and head directly toward Earth. This line of ascension he knew would happen soon. He was able to read these trails of colors with a natural exactitude simply by their intensity, by the steadiness of their form. The longer he looked up into the sky, the more he saw countless other trails of movement emerge. The trails of Mega Cruisers, the trails of thousands of other smaller vehicles, and indeed, the largest trail of them all—the one before and after Earth itself, soon filled the cosmos. But he was not concerned by them. The unwritten, unspoken language of pure color already conveyed to him the inevitable—that she was leaving the Moon extremely soon, and she was not going to Chez Cracken San with her family—she was going to go back to Earth, and she would be leaving very soon.

The water was black, and he looked at her lump of knotted, filthy hair. The rowboat hardly moved. There were no waves nor current. All was still. It was completely artificial.

"You don't have to answer me," she continued. "I know you love me, too."

He said nothing. She was right. He hardly knew her. But he loved her so tremendously, even though the words could not form themselves.

"Don't you want to know what I saw?" he asked her.

"It is irrelevant to me what you saw. What is more important is what we did."

He reached forward and caressed the back of her head. His fingers were already covered in grime and blood, so it was pointless to wonder if he was making her hair any worse than it already was.

"You look like a complete wreck. What are we going to tell your parents?"

"*We* are not going to tell them anything. You are going to bring me back to my hotel. I am going to tell them that a gang of thugs chased me and that you rescued me. And we had to hide in that yard."

It did not occur to Hieronymus until that moment that he himself was very far from home. Certainly, his school transport had already left. He was on his own, and he had almost no money. "Do you live around here?" she asked him.

"No. I live on the other side of the Sea of Tranquility."

"How will you get home?"

"There's a subway."

"Will you be in trouble if you get home too late and looking like that?"

"Yeah. My father will have a fit. He always waits up for me. I just wish he would just go to bed and let me stay out as long as I like, but that's what he does. He's a pain in the ass."

"Well, he can't be as bad as my mother…" Windows Falling On Sparrows was about to recite a list of complaints against her overbearing mother, and had they been on Earth, that's what she would have done. But instead, she looked at the black water in front of her. It sat still. No waves, no ripples. Just the division of element between gas and liquid. Then she remembered something from her science class: On the Moon, water and air had a strange relationship to each other. Because the atmosphere was artificial. And it was put in place by artificial means. And it was maintained artificially.

"You speak a lot about your father," the Earth girl said. "What about your mother? Do you have a mother?"

Hieronymus looked that the back of her head. At the incredible mess it had become.

"I…I don't really know. My mother. I don't really know my mother. I have lived in the same apartment with her all my life, but she has *never* spoken to me. She's actually mad. She stays in bed all day. All she does is cry. She wears a plastic raincoat in bed. She's…well, she is…it is impossible to communicate with her…"

Windows Falling On Sparrows listened to him describe his mother.

He knew a little about some of the things she had done in her life before she turned into what she was now. She once worked in a geological institute on Earth. She was born and grew up in so-and so, before this or that disastrous event led her to leave her country. Then she met Ringo. She was very secretive about her past. There were some major things, one in particular, that she could not bear to tell Ringo about. But it haunted her, and eventually Ringo found out, and he did his best to make her happy and to put it behind her. She tried to rebuild her life, and so they got married. For a short period of time, she attempted to become a writer, and she even succeeded in getting a novel published, but it failed to go anywhere and so she quit that. It went out of print and all traces of it were lost. Then, one day, she and Ringo were offered positions on the Moon at an Ulzatallizine refinery station. It paid well, and they figured that they would spend five years on the Moon, then return to Earth. But into their third year Lunar-side, she began to slip. She was already pregnant and so naturally Ringo just thought it was related to that, but by the time Hieronymus was born, she was pretty far gone. She lost her position at the refinery station, and because her son was registered as a bearer of lunarcroptic ocular symbolanosis, she was condemned to spending the next eighteen years on the Moon.

"That is a very sad story," said Windows Falling On Sparrows, still unable to look away from the black water in the crater lake.

They walked to the foot of the Ferris wheel. There was a line of tourists waiting their turn, and the Ferris wheel itself looked extremely unstable. It was covered in light bulbs. It had been painted several times over, as there were peeled-off sections where a layer of maroon could be seen under the layer of turquoise it was currently covered in. They had no intention of going on, but they wanted to mark this spot. This was where they would meet the following evening. At the foot of the Ferris wheel, at eight o'clock. He told her that it would never happen. He knew that she would be gone, very soon, placed on a Mega Cruiser and sent back to Earth. She didn't believe him. He promised her anyway that he would be there.

"Wouldn't it be wonderful if you were proven wrong," she said, the revolving light bulbs of the moving wheel reflected in her black eyes.

"This would be a great thing," he sincerely agreed.

They eventually found the Hotel Venice. She still wouldn't allow him to walk her up the stairs and explain to her parents why she was in the worst shape possible. Even the hotel clerk and the hookers who were hanging around could not believe how horrible the teenagers looked. *Would you like me to call you an ambulance?* the clerk asked, a little wary as he realized Hieronymus was a One Hundred Percent Lunar Boy. One of the prostitutes shot an angry look at him. *Did you do this to her? You looked at her with your goggles off, didn't you, creep?* He ignored her and walked Windows Falling On Sparrows to the stairway.

She turned, one of her hands on the banister. She looked at him, but neither spoke a word. He wondered what she was going to look like some day, and he had no doubt that she would still be as beautiful in fifty years as she was at that very moment, looking at him so questioningly.

He had the urge to beg her not to leave, but then where would they go? What would they do? A hummingbird hovering close to the chandelier cast a strange, flickering shadow on her.

She blinked both of her eyes very slowly, then she turned and walked up the steps.

He knew he would never see her again. He cursed his own certitude. To be wrong. *Oh, to be wrong!*

Were all One Hundred Percent Lunar People as paranoid as he was? As he ran out the hotel lobby, the clerk strained his neck to watch him. He probably contacted the police. Hieronymous was a guilty bastard for not taking her to the hospital right away. But then, if he did that, it would mean having to admit that he had purposely done it.

He ran. He looked like a strange homeless man running in ripped rags, speeding away from one dirt pit and into another. Considering the dregs who surrounded him, all the prostitutes and junkies and addicted gambling losers, this was an extraordinary accomplishment. He sprinted directly into traffic, challenging the drunken drivers to apply their brakes for the speeding phantom in goggles. He ran through the flashing neon streets of LEM Zone One, past the tourists in their sheeplike formations, their tasteless attire, their bland way of staring at things as low and pre-fabricated as casinos with an expression of wonderment. *Where do these people come from?* Hieronymus wondered. *And why would they come here of all places?* Of course, he got his answer as he sprinted past the LEM itself, the thing from Earth. It used to be the main tourist attraction, but now it was only a pile of junk that nobody cared about, and soon it would probably be replaced with a chain drugstore. He swerved to avoid running into it, and he also dodged any kind of visual contact with the police, because this time, he could not lie his way out of trouble, because he did it, he did it, he really did it—what a stupid jackass thing to do, *jackass!* He had endangered that girl's life, and he risked getting thrown into prison, never to be seen again.

Beyond two neon flashing skyscrapers, the underside of a Mega Cruiser passed slowly, a behemoth floating directly above, and he was reminded of what she told him, and what might indeed be happening to all of those One Hundred Percent Lunar Boys and Girls who disappear into the criminal justice system. Was it true? He imagined how the ability to see the fourth primary color would be applicable in the cosmos. He was so used to repressing it that he felt guilty just contemplating this idea. The world of neon passed him by. The annoying hummingbirds hovered out of his way the faster he traveled. He sprinted on sidewalks, and he sprinted through gardens and dilapidated storefronts. He turned a corner onto a residential street, and within seconds, he found himself running through an incredibly chic part of town. Expensive cars, expensive apartments. Expensive jewelry on the middle-aged women who were out walking their dogs. Some regarded him with extreme fear—he must have looked like such a freakish criminal in his goggles and torn white plastic jacket that was completely destroyed by oil and filth. Again, as he passed onto a busy avenue known for its chic nightclubs and fashion models and movie stars, he figured that, once again, a call was made to the police that *one of them* was running amok in *our* neighborhood. He realized how absurd it was that he should be hunted down like this, that they needed his type to drive the Mega Cruisers. Of course, maybe that was why they hunted him down—so they could lock him up and then force him to use his eyes for them like a high-tech indentured servant, a slave. That's what they wanted, to make him a slave who had to keep his mouth shut. To use him like captured men and women were used for centuries in the pre-ancient times, his talents exploited, his vision exploited. They needed his vision, as his vision was the vision of outer space. He had been born in the cosmos. The Moon was not a real place, but he was a real human being. And so what do human beings do but grow thumbs? His eyes, his vision, had a pair of thumbs that no one else but the explorers of the heavens could contemplate. It was not a question of looking at objects and people and predicting which direction they would walk in, and it was not a question of how freaked out people got when they saw your eyes—the real question was none of that, as he had the vision of a true stargazer and his eyes were for looking across the vast reaches where the curving of time and space made sense to those who could see it in front of their faces—he was one of them, and all else was unfocused.

He ran down the concrete steps of the Lunar subway. He paid with cash, which was highly frustrating because he only had a couple of crumpled-up dollars, and the machine kept on rejecting them while other rushing late-night commuters and tourists passed with such ease through the fingerprint machines. He heard the train arrive in the station. The clumsy toll machine finally accepted his last dollar. He charged down the steel steps, and he almost slipped. He made it to the train just as the rickety doors were closing. The crappy slug made of ancient plastic lurched forward in its claustrophobic tunnel. He was a long way from home, but if the train maintained its schedule, he'd be home in an hour and a half, and thus, only a little past his curfew hour. He sat. He looked around. Nearly everyone was sleeping. They were all drunk, or they were junkies who were nodding, face forward, eyes half closed. The train smelled. The lights blinked. The walls were festooned with advertisements that changed every ten seconds on worn-out screens. The screen directly opposite him, hanging over the half-sleeping form of a drunken college student, had a huge gash across its middle, and a sticky material ebbed out in gelatinous bulbs.

When she entered the tiny hotel room, her parents were aghast at her condition. Their daughter looked as though she had been through a mudslide and ended up trapped under a truck. Her mother became hysterical. Windows Falling On Sparrows had planned a long monologue about having been chased by a group of thugs, but in the bright lights of the hotel room, which her parents had kept on, staying up, worried about where their daughter was, she became confused. She wandered over to the bed and lay down. She was about to speak when a flashback of the color, one that lasted only a millionth of a second, sailed quietly through her mind, and she widened her eyes. Her lungs raced with air. *No!* she thought. She was suddenly afraid the color would return and stay in her field of vision, and that would be the end of herself as a sane person. She vaguely heard her mother's hysterical screaming and her father's calm yet determined voice, at that moment unusually precise, asking her, "What happened? Did somebody do something to you?

What happened? What happened?"

Her black eyes strayed from light to light. She could not look at them. She found their faces to be alien and frightening. Her mother rushed to her side with a damp cloth and wiped the side of her face with it, the cloth instantly filthy. Her father kept repeating himself, and when her mother bellowed with another nervous exclamation, it was as if she were speaking a completely foreign language. Windows Falling On Sparrows attempted to speak, but only a few words came out. Her mouth was dry. All she could think about was that spot in front of the Ferris wheel. She was going to meet him there again, tomorrow night at eight o'clock.

Her father was convinced she had been assaulted. Her knees and the palms of her hands were badly scratched. Who could have done this to her? What was that stuff in her hair? What kind of horrible ordeal did they put her through! *I am going to kill them with my bare hands! I am going to kill them!*

She squinted and heard the loud cannon-like sound of her mother's voice berating her father. She could not decide if she wanted to see or hide from any more flashbacks of that color that nearly drove her completely mad.

Her parents quickly understood that they had made a terrible mistake by calling the police. Two of them arrived wearing their characteristic stovetop hats and unfashionable capes. One of them had long hair and extremely large, feminine eyes. The other officer was a short burly man who needed a shave. Exonarella noticed his extremely tiny hands. The burly one spoke in a very rude and direct manner.

"We received a report that your daughter has been assaulted. Where is she?" Before Sedenker could even answer, the officers brushed past him and stopped in their tracks. They saw Window Falling On Sparrows sitting up on the edge of her bed, blinking into the overhead light, completely unaware the police had arrived.

The officers knew immediately. One of them activated a small device on his wrist and spoke into it.

"Lieutenant Schmet, this is Officer Krone. I'm upstairs at the Venice. I think we found our Juliet, but there is no sign of Romeo. I repeat,

Romeo is not anywhere in sight. You want to come up here and ask her a few questions?"

Exonarella's blood pressure charged through her body, her infuriated brain about to explode like a hand grenade at this presumptuous officer.

"How dare you call my daughter Juliet! That is not her name!"

"I understand that, Madam, but that is only police lingo between ourselves. Not to be taken personally. Lieutenant Schmet is on his way—he's a police specialist in these matters, and he will have some questions for your daughter."

"What do you mean, 'these matters'?"

The two officers looked at each other, and then the effeminate one with the big eyes spoke up.

"We are not certain, but we believe your daughter my have been the victim of a very particular type of assault that is specific to the Moon."

"What?!" Exonarella screeched. She turned around and smacked Sedenker in the face. "You let her go! I wanted her to stay here, and you let her go and see that damn LEM thing!"

"Don't you ever hit me again, you insane shrew!"

"I hold you responsible! You! You allowed our daughter out into that den of prostitutes and gangsters and all sorts of heathen scum! And now here she is, out of her mind because she has been attacked! Attacked, and it's your fault!"

Sedenker walked over to Windows Falling On Sparrows.

"Who did this to you? WHO DID THIS TO YOU?" he shouted.

She looked up and began a sentence, but forgot the first few words of it before she reached the middle. She turned away, not because she intended to be rude to her father, but because for a split second, she thought she saw the fourth primary color. This time, she wanted her mind to accept it, to become one with it, to see him again.

Detective Dogumanhed Schmet was indeed a type of expert in this. More than an expert, actually. He had a keen personal enthusiasm for the law enforcement side of lunarcroptic ocular symbolanosis. He didn't care about its scientific or its social issues. His own mission was extremely clear—if one of *them* is caught showing their abnormal and dangerous eyes to any normal person, they will be arrested. That's that. He was delighted to spend endless hours on and off duty guided by his obsession with the LOS population. What happened to them after he took them off the streets was of no concern to him—he just knew that his life's mission was that of a sentinel, a lonely floating angel who had set out to protect the Moon from these abominations, even if it meant legally catching them one by one. And he had a very good record in this respect. Fifty-eight confirmed arrests of various sorts, all of them within the same parameter—a citizen with lunarcroptic ocular symbolanosis showing his or her eyes, on purpose, to a citizen without lunarcroptic ocular symbolanosis. That was their weakness. They had to show their eyes—they could not resist. And he was always there to reel them in.

His enthusiasm was legendary in the world of Lunar Law Enforcement. That is not to say he was liked. Most policemen he came into contact with secretly detested him. They did not like his strange, manipulative manners toward his fellow officers and toward members of the public. They also did not like the way he smelled, which was inexplicable, but probably related to his unusual, fake-looking skin. And his eyes. One was false, one was real, and they were different colors. It was terribly disconcerting. But still, he was a legend.

He let himself into the hotel room without knocking. He did not say hello to the hysterical mother nor the flustered and shouting father. He simply nodded to the other two police officers before walking to the girl. He paused for a second as soon as he saw her. There was something so familiar about her. Impossible. She was a teenager from Earth. He had never been there.

"Hello. My name is Detective Schmet of the Sea of Tranquility Police Department. Your parents called because they believe you have been roughed up by some thugs or a gang, but officers Rondo and Krone over there suspect something else entirely, a different kind of assault, one that can only happen on the Moon. Just by looking at you, I am inclined to believe them. So tell me, where is he? Do you know his name?"

"Who?" she asked, looking up at the newcomer.

"Come on. The boy with the goggles who showed you his eyes."

"I don't know any boy like that."

Detective Schmet sighed. The girl was truly intimidated. His pasty white skin was moist and wrinkled as an olive upon his artificial-looking face. She thought he was made of warm rubbery wax. The heavy odor of lanolin lingered around him. His hair was bright yellow, and there was that one blue eye and one brown eye. He wore a suit of plush turquoise velvet. On one of his hands, there was a tattoo of a cat's face, screeching, a mouse's tail protruding from its fangs.

"Maybe you do not know any boys like that. How could you know any boys at all on the Moon? You just arrived here a few hours ago, and according to your passport information, which I took the liberty of checking just after the officers here alerted me to your presence, and indeed they alerted me and me specifically because I keep close tabs on a certain phenomenon that exists here on the Moon...What was I saying— oh, yes—according to your passport information, you have never been to the Moon before. Of course. So it is indeed an accurate answer if you do say that you *don't know any boys like that,* because you don't. But that brings me to my next question. A general question. Answer truthfully. Do you know what a One Hundred Percent Lunar Boy is?"

She hesitated.

He moved forward. He could smell guilt. Withholding information was a noisy endeavor, and he could see it in her shaking left index finger, in her eyelashes, and in the edge of her earlobe that twitched, her earring shifting.

"As in One Hundred Percent Lunar Person?"

"Yes."

"Those are the people on the Moon who wear those goggles with the purple lenses in them."

"Right. Congratulations. You know something that most kids on Earth don't. Now, answer this next question. Why do they wear those goggles? The purple-lensed goggles. Why?"

"Because their eyes are very sensitive?" she answered, knowing full well that he saw through her lame, unimaginative answer.

He smiled.

"You are a very smart and intelligent young woman. I knew before I entered this room that I was going to meet a very special, inquisitive teenager. Now, how did I know that? Because there was something that was flagged on your passport information. The type of thing that gets sent right away to my office. Just in case. What I saw on your passport information was a report by a security guard on the Mega Cruiser you and your family flew in on. The *Ragmagothic Chrysanthemum*. Beautiful name for a ship, by the way. According to the security guard, you, Windows Falling On Sparrows, demanded to know if the pilots of Mega Cruisers were One Hundred Percent Lunar People. You appeared convinced of the outlandish notion that only One Hundred Percent People could pilot Mega Cruisers, and then you went on to declare some purely phantasmal concepts over why. You used the expression lunarcroptic ocular symbolanosis, which proves that you indeed have a very keen interest, and knowledge, in this subject. Best of all, you took it upon yourself to confront a pilot crew who just happened to be passing in a corridor—I believe they were on their dinner break. You asked one of the pilots if he was a One Hundred Percent Lunar Man. You even asked him if he was wearing Schmilliazano goggles under his helmet. Now, there is nothing wrong with being interested in any particular subject, and you are certainly allowed to maintain your spectacular views, however, this short, documented history of your confrontation with the crew only reveals to me, an officer of the law, that you are also withholding information regarding a dangerous criminal who has assaulted you and will most likely assault others before we finally catch him. So please, when I ask you a question, don't play dumb. I know that you know that I know that you know that you have a keen interest in the subject of One Hundred Percent Lunar People. Well, I have a keen interest in that very subject as well, and I understand how it makes complete sense, that once here on the Moon, you may indeed sneak away from you sweet parents here, your calm and reassuring family unit that makes you feel like a wonderfully secure human being, and wander the streets of LEM Zone One, where if you happened to meet one of those One Hundred Percent Lunar People, you might get some answers to the questions you were denied on the Mega Cruiser. Yes? Is that not right?"

"The report in my passport is in error," she lied.

"News travels very fast on the Moon. You met a One Hundred Percent Lunar Boy. We know that there was one in the immediate area tonight. You became friendly. You already, as evidenced by your actions on the Mega Cruiser, had a deep interest in the mythology of their eyes—you know, the so-called 'fourth primary color,' and you wanted to see for yourself. He showed you."

"I don't know what you're talking about, Officer."

"Everyone wants to see the fourth primary color. Admit it. He took his goggles off…"

She could not believe how ugly this man was. But he was very perceptive, and she had to concentrate not to give herself or her lunar boy away. He spoke more, and as a defense, she silently indulged the vacant feeling that had overcome her.

"You know that his eye color is the fourth primary color. You wanted him to show you. You wanted him to take his goggles off…"

"What are you going on about?" Exonarella shouted at the detective, unable to control herself any longer. "What is all this about goggles and eye color?"

He turned his strange, artificial-looking face in her direction. Beads of sweat rolled down his cheeks as he cast a menacing glare at the nervous woman.

"You are very good-looking, but you must really be a pain in the ass to live with," he growled.

This stirred up the embattled Sedenker, who, despite the abuse he took from his wife, absolutely refused to accept any insults to her from strangers.

"Hey! Who do you think you are, talking to my wife like that? Apologize to her right now!"

The waxy-looking detective shifted one of his eyes to the shouting man from Earth. When he spoke, it was as if the words came from only one side of his mouth. Like half his lips were glued together.

"As I walked to this hotel, I heard your wife shouting from up the block. As I entered the lobby, because of your wife, I thought I was entering a lunatic asylum. As I climbed the stairs to this very room, I was getting an earache just listening to her. She is already, to my mind, a public nuisance. I am a lieutenant in the Sea of Tranquility Police Department. Normally, we arrest public spectacles of high human volume like this."

"Oh!" screamed Exonarella. "But what about all the thugs and scum and hookers and pimps and scumbags and gangsters just outside this fleabag hotel?"

"Either you let me question your daughter in front of you, or I take her down to the station and question her myself. For your information, she has been exposed to a deadly phenomenon that only happens on the Moon. Earlier this evening, I received a report that there was a boy with lunarcroptic ocular symbolanosis wandering around the amusement park with a girl who appeared to be from Earth. We immediately tried to locate them, but it was too crowded, and because of the massive casino fire earlier this evening, we were very short handed. We were hoping to intervene, to prevent this from happening. If we caught the boy actually doing it, he'd be on his way to the far side of the Moon right now. However, if your daughter is willing to cooperate, we can still locate him, and if we locate him, then we can lock him up."

Windows Falling On Sparrows suddenly spoke and all heads turned in her direction.

"You are confusing me with someone else. I never met any boy. I was by myself the whole time. I was feeling a little lightheaded because of the lightness of the gravity here. I wandered into an alleyway, and I fell down into a pile of greasy car parts. I woke up, I got lost, and then I made it back here. If I appear strange to you, it's because I am trying to adjust to the gravity. I have never been off the Earth before. The lack of proper gravity here on the Moon is making me feel very ill."

"I have a statement from the hotel clerk in the lobby. He said that a boy with Schmilliazano-lensed goggles walked with you into the lobby. He was just as filthy looking as you. Others saw the both of you together."

"Those people are all mistaken. The boy they are thinking of was actually a middle-aged man with glasses. He was a creepy stranger who followed me home. He did not wear goggles. Why are you bothering me about this when you have all those horrific adults just outside on the street? That man was probably one of them. Maybe he was a client of the many prostitutes who appear to frequent this hotel and the clerk was just thinking up an alibi."

Detective Schmet realized his fruitless inquisition was going nowhere. But the evidence, in his own mind, was doubtless. He knew. *He knew* when someone had seen that eye color. The effect did not go away easily. She so clearly had the look, but she was not cooperating.

He turned to her parents.

"I believe your daughter is holding back information. Sometimes they do this, people who have been disoriented by fourth primary color exposure. I would wager that she had a lover's tryst of some sort with this boy and now she is protecting him. It's a very romantic idea, but she is a fool to think that he is anything but a complete scoundrel. These Lunar boys are like that, you know. They take advantage of girls from Earth. She mistakenly thinks she's the first girl he ever showed his eyes to, but…" the detective turned and looked at her with the next part of the sentence, "that's probably what he tells all the Earth girls."

She stared Lieutenant Schmet directly into his eyes. She kept her face completely still, resolved to ignore whatever stupid little games he played.

Exonarella was petrified into total silence.

"So, Juliet," smiled Schmet. "Where oh where art thou, Romeo? What is his name? Where does he live? Meet me halfway. Let's make it into a game. How about a clue. I'll make you a bet. One clue from you, and I'll have him in twenty-four hours. That's how good I am."

She smiled. Her eyes brightened. Her bottom eyelids came up to meet her top eyelids for a second as she squinted at him.

"You look like a doll, Mister. I'll bet you are a doll. If you were to slice your head in half, I am sure it would be the same plasticky material through and through."

Minutes later, Officers Krone and Rondo accompanied the handcuffed Windows Falling On Sparrows down the stairway of the Hotel Venice, through the lobby, and past the clerk and seedy hookers who were gathered. The screams and shouts of Exonarella bellowed out through the entire building and spilled onto the street. The assembled regulars in the lobby heard the violent thumps of furniture crashing and mirrors shattering in her room, followed by a muffled and agonized moaning that obviously belonged to Sedenker. Moments later, Detective Schmet came strutting down the same stairs, a small hand towel covering his fist, a few drops of blood staining the terrycloth fabric. He immediately walked up to the clerk, who was highly distraught to hear the echoing screams of the woman upstairs.

"You," said Schmet with little fanfare. "Call an ambulance, one with an emergency dentist for the man upstairs married to that unbearable woman. I didn't hurt him that much, but he will need treatment. The both of them are to remain here in your lovely hotel. I am sending for an officer who will guard their door. They are under house arrest indefinitely."

"No way!" shouted the clerk, exasperated. "I want that lady out of here! I can't bear to listen to her Pixiedamned ranting anymore! I'm throwing them out now!"

"You do that and I will have the vice squad here in under four minutes, and you will be held responsible for every prostitute on this street without a health badge, of which I see there are plenty just standing around your family-friendly lobby."

Moments later, three unusual figures entered the hotel—faceless manikins of shiny metallic silver who walked with an extraordinary grace. Rescue robots. Despite their identical appearance, Lieutenant Schmet recognized one of them.

"Belwin! I am so happy to see you!"

"Lieutenant Schmet," replied the robot. "It is a pleasure as always to run into you. In fact, I was expecting to see you, as I received a fire rescue request from your own Omni-Tracker signal, but now that we are here, I am a little perplexed, as it is obvious that there is no fire."

"Indeed, Belwin, you are right that there is no fire. I must have accidently pressed the wrong button when I summoned you away from your local fire unit. I am so foolish sometimes. Oh, silly me."

"Do not apologize, Lieutenant, these things do happen."

"Yes, they do, Belwin. But I think you and your two colleagues have not wasted your time. We have another emergency here that is not fire related, but will require the astute talents of rescue robots."

"We are at your service, Lieutenant."

"Wonderful. Now, upstairs, there is a couple from Earth. A wounded man with a bloody mouth and a hysterical woman…"

"We heard her from up the street," Belwin said.

"Indeed. She is having a temper tantrum and her poor husband fell over some furniture. They are under house arrest. They are not to leave that room. I would like your two fellow robots here to attend to them, to administer first aid to the man, and to apply a sedative to the shrew he refers to as his wife. An ambulance will be here soon to treat the husband—he really injured himself, poor clumsy one. Under no circumstances are the medics authorized to transport these people anywhere. They are to remain here under house arrest as necessary witnesses for the Ocular Investigative Division until I order otherwise. Your robot colleagues are instructed to remain here and guard them."

"Understood, Lieutenant, but you do understand that this is outside our jurisdiction of duty."

"Belwin, you can check with Captain McChang over at Lunar Fire Command. He owes me some favors. He won't mind."

"Then we are at your service."

"Thank you. Now, Belwin, I have a question for you—just you."

"Certainly."

"How skilled are you as a pilot?"

Windows Falling On Sparrows could not imagine what the ugly detective was up to. She watched him exit the hotel with that incredibly beautiful robot who had no face and walked like a dancer. They were taking her somewhere. Could this be the beginning of what Hieronymus had told her? Was it happening now? The event she could not imagine?

She rode in a separate police cruiser from Lieutenant Schmet and his amazing robot. She sat alone in the back while Rondo and Krone sat up front. They both refused to answer her questions as they followed Schmet's cruiser. Both vehicles had their blue police lights flashing. Their sirens were quiet, save for the occasional *whup whup whup* as they navigated through the heavy traffic around LEM Zone One.

Within minutes, the pair of police vehicles entered a small paved field which was obviously a police facility. In the middle of the field was a ship, a sturgeon-shaped craft which, in appearance, was not unlike a Mega Cruiser, except that it was infinitely smaller. A spaceship. Large enough to hold about ten passengers.

Rondo and Krone ordered her out of the car, removed her handcuffs, and accompanied her to the waiting ship, a small Flyaround 790. Then, out of nowhere, Lieutenant Schmet appeared, walking side-by-side right next to her.

"Hello, girl," he said, not even glancing in her direction but focusing on the spaceship in front of them. He shouted out loud enough for the officers to hear.

"Thank you, Krone, Rondo. Belwin and I will take over from here."

Windows Falling On Sparrows could see the silvery form of Belwin taking his place behind the cockpit windows.

"Lovely ship, isn't she?" Schmet said with a smile.

"Where are you taking me?" demanded Windows Falling On Sparrows.

"Where do you think?"

She drifted for a moment as Hieronymus' words came back.

You won't even be on the Moon by that time. You will be on a Mega Cruiser going back to Earth.

"You're taking me to Earth, aren't you…"

"What makes you say that, Earth girl?"

"I just know it."

"You mean someone told you. Someone who could have seen your forward projection. Going up up up into the sky…"

She did not reply.

"Fret not, my little flower. He's been captured. He's already confessed to one of my colleagues."

Again, she said nothing. But her sudden glance up, the miniscule collision of several of her eyelashes on her lower lid, combined with the upper muscle over her top lip that so sadly moved in such remorse, coupled with her silence, was more than enough to convince Schmet that his little ploy, based on his extremely forward-thinking hunch, was leading him in the right direction.

They boarded. Just the two of them in the cabin. Belwin in the cockpit sat behind a separate door. They were alone, and she had difficulty looking at him. He could not stop looking at her. He was not staring at her in a lecherous way, but he had to admit to himself that there was something so oddly familiar about her, something that tickled the long-extinguished fires of his long frozen heart. He felt oddly at ease with her, as if he had known her before. Same face. A long-ago shadow. Who? Who was it? It was distracting as all bloody Hades. She buckled her seatbelt.

Schmet sat about four seats away from her. He kept his distance.

The engine started, and the spacecraft rumbled and shook just slightly as they left the surface. He had to act soon. She was on the border of trusting him. In ten minutes, she would understand that this was all a setup.

"Do you see our pilot?"

"Yes."

"He's a robot."

"I know that."

"So you see, then, that it is not true, that silly rumor that only One Hundred Percent Lunar People can fly ships into the depths of space. A robot can do it."

"So we are flying to Earth?"

"Yes, we are."

"In this ship?"

"Yes."

She turned to look out the window and it was amazingly clear. The neon-covered world of LEM Zone One was shifting away beneath a miniaturized collection of crowded avenues and city blocks and casinos and, of course, the thing that caught her eye, the Ferris wheel. Here she was, in a spaceship, not too far from where she had seen his eyes and he had seen her projected future line, and alas, it was coming true. She was fulfilling that incorruptible line he saw only hours ago, the one indicating she was going back to Earth, much sooner than she had intended.

"My parents?"

"They will be following shortly."

"Why are you coming?"

"I need to personally hand you over to my counterpart on Earth. Once there, you will spend a week in a special hospital for observation because your exposure to the color was a very severe one."

"What will happen to him? Will he disappear?"

Finally, she acknowledged it. "We will send him to a special school where people with LOS learn to safeguard themselves and the ones around them more carefully."

"I am very frightened." She looked at him. He was taken aback. She looked at him directly in his real eye. "That color…"

"I know. But it's over."

"I'm sorry I insulted you."

"Oh. It's nothing. You…you were upset…"

Of course, he had been completely unprepared for that. As soon as she apologized, and apologized sincerely, for she really believed that her Lunar Boy had been captured and that they were going to Earth, he was frozen. He was unable to continue with the clever line of questioning he had planned, hoping to extract the name of the Pixiedamned young man. It was only a hunch, and it had worked. Sometimes, the forward trail of the fourth primary color could predict a direction that lasted for hours if the person looked at was especially beloved in the eyes of the beholder. He noticed in her face, as he questioned her earlier, an unmistakable resignation, of fate, of severe melancholy. He understood very well that in order to catch someone who can see shadows of future movement, you had to somehow create the very shadows yourself, then jump in, like a cat, and catch them. This is what he did. Of course the boy knew she was leaving the Moon, because that is where her forward projection went. He must have told her this; she carried it on her face as soon as he came upon her in the hotel room. Strangely enough, none of this gave him the usual sense of satisfaction. All he had to do now was get the criminal's name, but Dogumanhed Schmet himself was unable to speak. The ship itself only took seconds to get into orbit, and he watched the girl cry and cry. He did not know what to do, and he was utterly shocked at the state he found himself in. If Belwin were not piloting the ship, he could instruct him to sit next to the girl and say reassuring things to her, but that was not the case. It was up to him. He stood up and moved closer to her so only one seat separated them from each other.

And then he slipped. So moved was he, and so uncharacteristically saddened was he, that at that tiny moment, he forgot everything and he forgot himself.

"I'm sorry, Selene…" he said.

She looked at the strange plastic man leaning toward her. His real eye must have been the sad and distracted one.

"My name is not Selene."

"Yes. I'm sorry. I'm sorry, Windows Falling On Sparrows. You just remind me so much of someone, that's all. You look exactly like her, your mannerisms are so similar to hers."

"Oh?"

"Yes. She was my older sister. You know, I used to have seven older sisters a long time ago. Imagine being a boy with seven older sisters! They spoiled me so much! I was like a prince, a child prince if you can believe that. Selene was my favorite. You remind me so much of her."

"Wasn't Selene an ancient Greek goddess of the Moon?"

"Yes. Selene was a goddess. She was."

Belwin piloted the sturgeon-shaped vessel exactly as he was programmed. Which meant there were only moments left before Windows Falling On Sparrows understood that they were returning to the Moon, and Schmet was locking her up in jail. Schmet gave up on spoiling this moment, trying to extract the name of the boy. Soon, he was going to return to his old miserable cruel and manipulative self. He would later get embarrassed and angry that, for a few minutes, he'd slipped into such sentimentality, but that was bound to happen to a man who had no sentimental life at all. She would be furious. She would feel betrayed. Rightfully so.

And so he sat next to her, this girl from Earth who jarred loose a few memories of his sister whom he missed so much, and decided to enjoy these minutes of not being himself. They looked out the window together as the neon-illuminated Moon-world passed beneath them. It glowed, and they wondered, as everyone did, why the Moon is so full of neon. An aesthetic decision made so long ago that its own forgotten reasons had fossilized. The small ship lurched itself farther, and the Moon's curvature was revealed. Only half a sphere illuminated—the other side a colossal, somber shadow. A pure, lonely darkness. Windows Falling On Sparrows tried to reconstruct the fourth primary color in her mind, but it would not return.

She placed her hand on the glass. It left an imprint, then faded.

chapter eight

Hieronymus covered his face with his hands. He felt like a criminal. He kept recalling the events of the previous evening, looking for a loophole where the police might be able to put two and three together to make five. Big question: Did anyone call the police? Would the clerk in that hotel have called the police? No, that guy was in too deep with the hooker business. What did that girl's parents do when they saw her? How could they *not* call the police? She looked positively horrible. Was she still even on the Moon? No, it was impossible. And yet he promised—eight o'clock in front of the Ferris wheel. He wanted to be wrong about what he thought he saw. Oh, how he wanted to be wrong.

Like the goddamned criminal he was, he had to quickly think of an alibi in case there was a knock on his door. But why would they knock on his door? There were thousands of others, other One Hundred Percent Lunar Boys who could easily have been there from any of the surrounding suburbs. But all she would have to do is tell the police his name was Hieronymus, and it would all be over. LEM Zone One was crowded, but he was certain that he was the only bearer of lunarcroptic ocular symbolanosis with that first name.

Would the police figure out that there was a class trip? Would they call the school if they knew that a class from Lunar Public 777 had been in the area? Even if they did call the school, he knew his name might not even come up—after all, the Loopie class was supposed to go, but except for himself and Bruegel and Clellen, they had all cut.

He had to find out. This type of thinking was beginning to drive him completely nuts. He called Bruegel on the bubblephone in his room after he took a shower. As he waited for the connection, he glanced down at the pile of clothes on the floor. He was immensely sad that his white plastic jacket had been torn and ruined by oil. He looked at it sitting there on top of everything else. It was the price paid for being so goddamned stupid…

Bruegel's fuzzy image appeared on the screen. He grinned when he saw Hieronymus.

"Hey," he said, a little bleary-eyed. "What happened to you? You disappeared with that girl yesterday. You missed all the action."

"What kind of action did I miss?"

"Well, Clellen and myself and that friend of yours, Pete, the sports enthusiast you had a long conversation with, we decided to take an alternative study lesson at some bar in the area. We got kind of drunk. Pete and Clellen were really misbehaving. I think Pete really likes Clellen a lot."

"How did you get home last night?"

"We got back on the transport along with everyone else. What about you?"

"I need to speak to you about that, as soon as possible. I think I'm in a skukload of trouble, and I have to straighten out a few things, and I need to talk to you."

"Where do you want you meet?"

"Let's meet in front of O'Looney's in twenty minutes."

"I'm kind of hung over."

"Good. I'll buy you a zag-zag. I'll even buy you a sugar wafflestomp. Just get out of that hovel you call an apartment and meet me. It's really important."

From far away, Sun King Towers looked like a gaudy red candelabra. A housing project built several centuries earlier, it was a mishmash of poorly arranged residential concrete monstrosities all clustered togeth-er and festooned with sizzling neon. Hieronymus lived in a tower in the center of the colossal housing project—Tower Ayler. The Rexaphin family's apartment was on the eighty-eighth floor.

There was a subway stop at the foot of the towers. Every morning and every evening, a congested mass of humanity squeezed itself through the single concrete stairway that led down and up from the depths. Whenever it was empty, the huge white hummingbirds ven-tured down there, flying in and out, scavenging for whatever edibles could be found on the tracks and on the platforms and often in the trains themselves. Hieronymus took the subway every morning to Lunar Public 777, although it was not really necessary. The school was only a kilometer from Sun King Towers. However, it was a bland walk through a no-man's land of concrete avenues and graffiti-covered walls just in front of the huge antenna stations that separated the housing project from the school.

Hieronymus was fond of O'Looney's—not so much because it was a wonderful place, which it wasn't, but because it was incredibly easy to get to and marvelously low tech. It was physically connected to the bot-tom of Tower Ayler. To get there, he took the elevator all the way down to the ground floor, walked through the abandoned and cavernous lobby, and as soon as he left the building, made a sharp left and walked about thirty meters and there was O'Looney's.

O'Looney's itself was a run-down grocery store and café, and for most residents it was an unavoidable eyesore on the way to the subway station. It tended to attract homeless people as it sold cheap bags of in-stant food and snacks, along with reasonably priced forty-ounce bottles of generic beer. For years, several neighborhood associations and de-velopers had been trying to get rid of it. It was a simple aluminum and washed-out Plexiglas storefront, and was the last remaining business from a bygone era, when the foot of each tower had its own economy of shops and cinemas and restaurants and cafés and bars. All that remained were boarded up ex-establishments and squats. O'Looney's stood alone.

There was always a crowd of regulars. Most of these were home-less. O'Looney's was known for attracting elderly eccentrics. No one knew why, but on any given afternoon, it was difficult to find anyone milling about or sitting in some of the vinyl booths who was under the age of seventy-eight or seventy-nine. Hieronymus figured that a lot of the people who hung out there were leftovers of the old society that existed there long ago—when the plazas and gardens and restaurants at the foot of Sun King Towers were open and enjoyable public spaces, as opposed to the bleak and paranoid vacant lots they had become. O'Looney's itself looked out onto a concrete plaza of benches and small circular platforms that were designed to hold trees, but now sat cracked and filled with dirt as the attempt to fill the area with greenery had failed long ago. The boarded-up walls of the tower's base was a spectacle in and of itself—the plastic board was extremely old, as was the graffiti upon it, painted over and over, in some areas, for many decades…

Bruegel resided in the next building, an even taller monstrosity known as Tower Zhoug. Slue was also a neighborhood resident—her apartment was situated near the top of Tower Pelikanhopper. Many of the students at Lunar Public 777 came from Sun King Towers. Others came from another complex further down the subway line—Telstar Towers, which was well known for its squalor and higher crime statistics. Clellen lived there. So did Tseehop. In fact, a large part of the Loopie class was disproportionately represented in the run-down housing complex at Telstar.

Then there were students like Pete. Pete did not live in a tower or even an apartment building of any kind. His home was but a modest single-family dwelling with a yard in the Marigold Estates section. That was on the other side of Lunar Public 777. A lot of Toppers also lived in Marigold Estates—it was considered a step up from the mundane tower existence so many lunar residents found themselves in. Needless to say, there were not many Loopies there—one or two, as of course Marigold Estates was far from upper class. Verdesker Vank Gardens was the local posh area, and none of the children from there went to Lunar Public 777—they all attended Armstrongington Academy.

For the first time, it occurred to Hieronymus how Pete must have met Slue. Many of Slue's friends lived in Marigold Estates. Pete lived there. They must have met on the subway, or at a party, or some place where mutual acquaintances could have introduced them. Something like that. But after what happened the night before with that Earth girl, his whole complicated paradox with Slue seemed so far away. As if her presence in his life had suddenly faded a notch. And the unspoken pain she caused him by refusing to work with him once she discovered his secret—that he took classes in the Loopie section seemed, in comparison to last night, practically null.

As he got closer to O'Looney's, he discovered that Bruegel was already there, waiting outside, grinning at Hieronymus as he approached.

"Looks like you had a rough night!" His friend laughed. As usual, he had that same disheveled look of a stunned knight just knocked off his horse. "But not as rough as Pete, from what I heard."

"Yeah, well…" Hieronymus was about to make comment on what else can one expect from the volatile mix of Clellen and a barrelhead like Pete but stopped himself. He walked through the usual gatherings of lost drink-ravaged men and women who always spent their entire days outside O'Looney's. One guy, his face as red as the sky, his eyes gray blue, his nose full of little purple gin blossoms, greeted the two teenagers.

"The rickety horse has a breath like black roses!" he said very matter-of-factly.

"Yes," Bruegel answered with a grin.

A woman who smelled like fermented old wine held the aluminum door open for them as they entered. Hieronymus gave her a coin.

"They call me Mad Meg! Mad Meg! Can you say it?" she cried at the both of them as they entered.

"Mad Meg!" said Bruegel cheerfully as he also gave her some money. "I can say it better than you can! Mad Meg! Mad Meg!"

O'Looney's itself lacked the usual presence of neon lights. Instead, light bulbs cast their bland gray light here, as they always had. Hieronymus thought of the strange amusement park at LEM Zone One. It too, like O'Looney's, was a land of light bulbs. Here, several hung by their wires from the ceiling, a system of illumination considered quaint and very old fashioned.

When the boys entered the café section of the shop, they noticed no one was sitting at the counter, where Chahz O'Looney, the proprietor, stood sorting through some utensils. He looked up and acknowledged the arrival of his two young customers and immediately began preparing their usual—a mug of fledderkoppen for Hieronymus, and a bottle of zag-zag for Bruegel. The boys paid, then went over to the section just in front of the grocery aisles where some ancient vinyl booths were set up. They had to be careful where they sat, because often a drunken customer could be found sleeping in one. The last time they visited O'Looney's, Bruegel almost sat in a puddle of vomit that had been left behind by an anonymous, inebriated patron. Chahz O'Looney shrugged his shoulders when Bruegel told him, in his pseudo linguistic way, *Excuse me, Mr. O'Looney, but one of your perpendiculatrix consumertedders has decided to blofigate upon your trixelliphon!* The proprietor was used to Bruegel's pretentious way of talking, and when he peered over at the mess, only said something to the effect of *best to let it dry— I'll brush off the flakes later.*

The walls were painted a muddy yellow, and whenever one glanced at the groceries, only alcoholic beverages and junk food could be seen on the shelves. Hieronymus never told his father he frequented this place—O'Looney's was a thoroughly depressing experience on so many different levels that he knew his father would be worried as to why his sixteen-year-old son chose a place where old alcoholic men and woman loitered with change in their hands, trying to decide if they had enough pennies for the vilest pint of factory vodmoonka...

A hummingbird, trapped inside, circled one of the hanging lighbulbs.

"Listen," Hieronymous began as Bruegel sat in front of him. "I might be in a lot of trouble."

Bruegel's grin got wider.

"With that girl?"

"Yes, well, sort of."

"Hieronymus, I would be very disappointed in you if you were not worried about being in trouble after walking away with that incredibly hot-looking young *foxentrotter...*"

Hieronymus looked around for a couple of seconds. What was good about O'Looney's was the simple fact it was discreet. "I let that girl take my goggles off. She saw my eye color."

Bruegel drew a complete blank. As if he was waiting to hear something interesting.

"And?" he finally asked.

"And? Is that all you can say?"

Bruegel was already distracted by other things in the shop. Like the fact that O'Looney's had a special sale on completely generic brands of beer.

"Look at that!" he exclaimed. "Generic beer! Isn't that funny? Plain cans with just the word BEER on their white labels! My mother would love that! She always told me about generic beer brands like that when she lived in Collinsberg. It's so funny! I don't know why it's funny, but it just is! Hey look, Hieronymus! Just next to the beer—they have cans of dog food! Same cans! Totally same labels! Except one says BEER and the other says DOG FOOD! Isn't that hilarious! What, is there some kind of factory where they get the same cans for everything and some guy just shovels dog food into one can and pours beer into the other? Hey, O'Looney! Mr. O'Looney! Where does this BEER and this DOG FOOD come from! THEY ARE BOTH THE SAME CANS? ARE THEY FROM THE SAME FACTORY?"

Hieronymous sighed.

"You want to quiet down?" shouted Chahz O'Looney. "I'll toss you out of here!"

Bruegel rushed over and picked up one can of beer with one hand, and a can of dog food with the other.

"LOOK! Same can! What kind of factory do these come from? Is it just a big white building with the word FACTORY written on the side?"

O'Looney usually tolerated Bruegel because the boy never stole and he always purchased a lot of beer for himself and his mother, but sometimes, whenever he got excessively loud and excited over the most mundane things, even he had to get tossed out—which is exactly what Chahz O'Looney was about to do.

There was another rude interruption.

An old man stumbled into O'Looney's. He was from the group outside. He shuffled past Hieronymus and then nearly bumped into Bruegel, who was still holding the identical cans. The newcomer walked three more steps into the beer aisle and picked up a forty-ounce bottle of yellow ale. He walked in an almost lopsided way to the counter.

"Chop-chop on the blundering pig-pie flock!" he sang out loud.

"And I see a pig-pie sucking on a tarstick!" remarked Bruegel just as loud.

Two elderly men standing by the counter got excited when they saw the fellow with the forty-ounce bottle approach, and at once, began to call him names and shout at him. Apparently, there was some unfinished business among these old hobos as several filthy red hands grabbed the beer bottle. Insults and curses were violently expressed, and all three started fighting as the bottle fell to the hard linoleum floor, shattering and splashing the malty-smelling fermentation in every direction. The fight grew. Hieronymus had never seen old men go at it like this before. Chahz O'Looney himself was a little surprised at the conflagration before him, and it wasn't until the third forty-ounce bottle was smashed over one of the gentlemen's heads that he began the tiresome effort to throw them out. O'Looney's dog, a large creature with matted dirty gray hair and bad breath, was already barking at the noisy customers.

"Get out of here before I call the police!" O'Looney wrestled with one of the boozers, who was himself caught in a biting death grip with one of the others. "Out! Out, you old bastards, and never come back!" Expelling the violent, geriatric hoodlums was proving a difficult and excruciating task.

Staring at this circus of clashing fists and mumbled screams and shattered bottles, Bruegel, who had stood in the exact same spot holding the two cans, calmly put down his generic products, casually walked over to the three fighting men, and in one seamless gesture, disengaged them from one another and tossed them out the front door as if they were three old piles of soggy newspapers. He hardly noticed that all three men landed hard on their faces, injuring themselves. He then walked back and sat down opposite Hieronymus, picking up where their conversation had broken off, behaving as if he had never interrupted himself in the first place.

"So, what were you telling me again? That girl took your goggles off, or something like that?"

Hieronymus realized what a complete waste of time it was to explain any of these details to Bruegel. Anytime he tried to explain what lunarcroptic ocular symbolanosis was, or why he had to wear the goggles, or why he was restricted to a lifetime on the Moon, all of these things were met with a friendly, blank indifference. Bruegel could not follow the complicated explanation, and even if he could, something would enter his field of vision and completely distract him. As far as he was concerned, there was no reason at all why Hieronymus wore goggles. And that was that.

But Hieronymus was not there to discuss LOS with his friend from the Loopie class. He needed a distinct favor.

"Listen. You have your driver's license, don't you?"

"Indeed I do."

"How about borrowing your mother's car and driving me out to LEM Zone One tonight."

"LEM Zone One? What are you talking about? You were just there last night."

"That is true. And I need to go back."

"I'm assuming this has to do with the girl we all saw you walking off with. What, she comes from around there? Is she a LEM Zonian foxentrotter?"

"She's from Earth."

Bruegel's eyebrows flexed upward so high on his forehead that, for a brief moment, Hieronymus thought that his large friend's skull had imploded.

"Earth?"

"That's what I said."

"An Earth girl, same age as us, was just wandering around LEM Zone One?"

"Hard to believe, isn't it."

"Well, what happened? Did you and her do any kind of pleasure particulars of the rumdangle oxmolitrex?"

"Stop throwing your fake words at me. I don't fall for that."

"Did you touch her with your lips?"

Hieronymus sighed.

"If you mean did we kiss, yes."

"Did you make out with her? Tongues?"

"Bruegel, you know I hate questions like that."

"Sorry. I forgot how uptight you are."

"I'm not uptight. What are you talking about?"

"Clellen told everybody that you were uptight."

"Clellen? What does Clellen have to do with any of this?"

"Clellen told everyone in class that you were the most uptight guy she ever made out with."

"She's a liar. I never made out with her."

"That's not what she says. She said that you were a good kisser but a lousy maker-outer."

"I think Clellen is a little confused—about a lot of things."

"So you never kissed her?"

"I kissed her, but I never made out with her."

"Well, what's the difference?"

"Big difference, you stupid idiot. *Just kissing* is when you do *just* that. Kissing. And just a few times. Under ten minutes. Making out is rolling around in addition to kissing. It's pretty straight forward."

"Clellen said you made out with her for hours at Maggie-Mag's party last month, and I know others who saw the both of you going at it and…"

"Oh, so what, Breugel, who cares! Everyone was drunk on Zhengo at that party…"

"Clellen's pretty hot."

"She is, but I think she's totally insane."

"Well, she might be insane, but I would sniff Jessker's silver box for a month just to get my tongue between her teeth! I've tried a hundred times to make out with her, but she always pushes me away as if I'm some kind of a Racker-Stang! But you've *had* her, man! You made out with her and everybody knows it!"

"Look, I don't want to talk about her. Are you going to drive me out to LEM Zone One tonight?"

"Who am I, your chauffeur? Your foot valet? Your Crinx-Balfour? You are assuming my mother is not driving her car tonight…"

"Your mother never uses that car. You told me that."

"Sometimes she does."

"Well, let's buy her a case of beer and she'll have no reason to go anywhere tonight, and you just take the keys and off we go."

"You know, I should dislocate your jaw from your face for just saying such a thing."

"Stop it. Just agree. We are going out to LEM Zone One."

Bruegel stared straight ahead.

"This girl from Earth. What is her name?"

"Windows Falling On Sparrows."

"How does that work? Is 'Windows' her first name, 'Falling On' her middle name, and 'Sparrows' her last name?"

"No. The whole sentence is her first name. I have no idea what her last name is."

"When a woman looks like that, I guess it doesn't matter what the Crack her name is. Does she have a friend or a sister? I'm not into this if there's no foxentrotter action for me. You can just zag out on the train all by yourself if you think I'm going to be the towel-holding man while you get your tongue all knotted up in that Earthling whirlpool juice."

Jesus and Pixie! fumed Hieronymus. *He is such a damned stupid crater-head!*

"Something tells me," continued Bruegel after taking a long and noisy gulp of zag-zag, "that you have no way of getting in touch with this young toaster from the Motherworld, yes?"

"All I have with her is a rendezvous point. At the Ferris wheel. In the amusement park. Eight o'clock. But something happened last night that I might be in a lot of trouble for, so I can't call her hotel."

"Well, have a good time. I'm not driving you. I hate LEM Zone One. And I am not going if there is not an additional set of ovaries for me to match up with my set of…"

"Okay! Stop! Listen. How's this? Let's give Clellen a call. You said that you like Clellen, right? Let's invite her along. We get to LEM Zone One, I'll meet the girl from Earth, and then we just pair off, and you see if you can get something happening with Clellen, okay?

Bruegel listened to this proposal, which Hieronymus thought was pretty damn clever, and after a quick contemplative moment, burst out laughing.

"Clellen! Oh, once again we return to Clellen! Hieronymus, I appreciate your offer to set me up with the Queen of Gel-Fantastique, but I have it on very good authority—actually, from Clellen herself—that she will be unavailable tonight!"

"Wait. What do you mean?"

"Clellen. She is a very bad girl. She has a hot date with Pete."

"Pete?"

"Is your brain caked with moose curd? Pete, the fellow we met on the transport yesterday who started trading tongues with dear old Clellen! Your acquaintance—the athlete boy who plays those inane games with the other barrelheads like him. It is pointless to ask her to accompany us on this misunderadventure because she is taking Pete to a motel over by Telstar Towers tonight! A motel! How sleazy and cheesy is that?"

Hieronymus looked down into his mug of hot fledderkoppen. The purple swirls on its surface dissolved into cruel fuzzy rings. The stuff was awful. Why did he drink it? Why did he come to places like this? Why was he friends with *people like this?*

O'Looney's horrible dog started barking at the homeless old men banging on the Plexiglas storefront, trying to get back in.

Then Bruegel came up with a suggestion that truly disgusted Hieronymus. And as soon as he mentioned it, the One Hundred Percent Lunar Boy knew it was going to be the program of the evening, the awful trade-off he had to make if he wanted to see that damn Ferris wheel again…

"So Clellen is out. But, Hieronymus, there is someone else I am dying to meet, and I know that you are friends with her because I have seen you with her on numerous occasions. That girl with the goggles and the blue hair…"

* * *

He hated to mix his two worlds. He hated to socially mix anything up. And now this. Not so much because he was afraid something would happen between Slue and Bruegel—he knew beyond all certainties that that was the mother of all dead ends. Slue would hate Bruegel. Period. But it was the mix between Slue and Windows Falling On Sparrows that made him curl his toes and grit his teeth. Both girls, thrown together like that in front of him. The idea bounced between the hemispheres of his brain and it went nowhere comfortable.

As he pondered that inevitable awkwardness, he barely heard Bruegel going on about how hot he thought Slue was. *That damn fool!*

Look at him, talking about Slue as if she was his girlfriend already. What an arrogant, pathetic spectacle that big oaf is making out of himself as he sits there running his mouth off, that presumptuous, pompous Loopie, talking about Slue like that, how dare he! On the other hand, it certainly would be comical to set this up. Slue, after all, has been snubbing him, so the idea that she would go somewhere with he and Bruegel was beyond all remote possibilities. She was pissed off at him. She refused to even say hello. Then he found out she'd been socializing with Pete. Of all people! Despite that misunderstanding in the rotunda, Pete was a nice guy, but also a complete barrelhead! Why, he could not fathom. Pete? He did have a nice car—a Prokong-90. But Slue didn't give a Pixie about things like that. Or did she? If he were to call her, she would just be dismissive and inform him she had a date with Pete. On the other hand, thanks to Clellen and that motel in Telstar, Pete might be…busy…

"Are you even listening to me?" demanded Bruegel, who noticed that Hieronymus was drifting off into his own daydream.

"No, not really, big guy. What were you talking about?"

"I was talking about tonight. We are going to go see the Ginger Kang Kangs."

"The Ginger Kang Kangs? What are you talking about? I told you that we're going to the amusement park at LEM Zone One."

"Only losers go there. Losers and children. No. We are adults now, adults with a vehicle, and adults with vehicles do not go to amusement parks. You will call Slue and you ask her if she'd like to come on an exciting road trip tonight with you and your pal Bruegel, who is an all-around T-Bird guy, extremely good looking and, unlike you, can actually drive a car—tell her that I have four tickets to see the Ginger Kang Kangs, who are playing tonight at the Dog Shelter, which is right next to LEM Zone One. Tell her that we will go to the amusement park to pick up your date…"

"Bruegel, hold on—the Ginger Kang Kangs?"

"They're a local band. They're really excellent. They come from Sputnik Heights and everyone says they are really happening. Clellen, for example, loves them and Clellen does have good taste in music, if nothing else. Also, the Dog Shelter is the grooviest club—very underground, so it might even be illegal. It was a dog shelter in former times.

They still have old dilapidated kennels in a separate room. It's like the make-out room. People make out in the dog kennels while the band plays in the main hall. It's really wild."

"That sounds completely sick. I'm not taking the Earth girl there. And I'm not inviting Slue to a place where people make out in cages meant for dogs."

"I see. I guess Clellen was right about you."

"Right about what?"

"You being uptight and all."

chapter nine

The public bubblephone at O'Looney's was all the way in the back and mounted to a yellow painted cinderblock wall. It had a small screen. Neither Hieronymus nor Bruegel was in the habit of carrying around portable phones or screen devices of any sort. It was a distaste for instant communication they had in common. Hieronymus hated the idea of always being cornered by a call of some sort. The obligation of answering the phone. It was a form of tyranny.

Bruegel decided to follow Hieronymus to the back and listen in on the conversation the One Hundred Percent Lunar Boy was about to have with the One Hundred Percent Lunar Girl. Hieronymus punched in the numbers. It had been three weeks since he last spoke to Slue. His heart was racing.

She answered, turning away slightly as if someone had distracted her just the second before she answered her bubblephone. He took in the image of her. Her three-quarter angle, the slope of her nose. Her cheekbones. Her jawline, her lips, and her eyebrows. Her blue hair appeared bluer that ever in the extreme palate of the small screen.

She looked into the field of the screen and recognized it was Hieronymus. She was slightly speechless.

"Oh. Hi."

"Hey, Slue. How are you?"

"I'm fine, Hieronymus. How is everything going with you?"

"It's good."

Awkward silence followed. She looked away, then back. He was not sure if she was looking at him, or looking at the edge of her screen. The electric field was blurry, and the colors were saturated, and the contrast was high. The bubblephone at O'Looney's was several decades old and in need of repair. Her face was vague, and he wondered if he looked as distorted to her as she to him. Then he thought that this was probably a good thing—they could hide behind the imperfect images they saw of each other. She fluttered on and off, and in that millisecond when she disappeared, his heart sank, and when she came back on, he realized how much he really missed her. She spoke, her voice crackling through the broken speaker.

"I…I never told you this, but I really loved your presentation on *The Random Treewolf*. It was so wonderful. I think you worked much better on it alone than if I was there. I would have just made it weaker."

"Don't say that, Slue. That's not true. I think the opposite. I think my presentation would have been a lot better if it was *our* presentation. I think there's a lot of things I missed that you would have picked up and made into something wonderful."

"Did you like the presentation I made with Poole on *Sanctified Island*?"

"Yes," Hieronymus lied. "It was very powerful."

But nothing like what you came up with, she thought.

"So. Hieronymus. Why are you calling me?"

"Well, I was wondering if you'd like to check out this band tonight. The Ginger Kang Kangs? Have you ever heard of them?"

"They sound familiar. Where are they playing?"

"The Dog Shelter."

"The Dog Shelter? Isn't that over by LEM Zone One?"

"Yea. But my friend Bruegel is willing to drive. He has a driver's license."

"Bruegel. Isn't he one of the Loopies? Oh. I forgot. You're a Loopie, or at least half a Loopie. And you hang out with Loopies."

Hieronymus cringed and looked to the side. Luckily, Bruegel had stepped away as soon as the conversation turned to their ancient literature presentations. He was already at the far end of the aisle, reading the ingredients on a box of children's cookies. He appeared to be deeply interested in the list of chemicals.

"You know, that's a really mean thing to say."

"You saw what they did to the rotunda. I want nothing to do with any of those criminals."

"Bruegel wasn't there that day."

"Are you sure? I'd hate to imagine that I'll be stuck in a car with some guy who tricks me into smelling something abominably horrible from a small silver box around his neck."

"Come on. You have to admit that that was funny."

"It was one of the worst moments of my life."

"What, smelling Jessker's horrible odor mixture?"

"No. Watching you. Realizing that you have a completely split personality. That you live in two irreconcilable worlds at the same time. Hiding it from me."

Hieronymus stared into her face on the small screen. Two people with goggles. Having a bitter discussion that only people who were meant to but never became lovers could have.

"What you are saying is true, Slue. I have tried to separate my two existences at school. I knew that nobody would understand. I knew you wouldn't. But those are the cards I've been dealt. At least the kids in the remedial section don't judge me. If they had the chance, they might rob me and beat me up—but they wouldn't judge me if they knew I took classes with the honors section."

"I'm not judging you, Hieronymus. I'm hurt that you've kept this from me."

"Look. I'm sorry. I know you're mad. That's understandable. But something came up that I really have to talk to you about."

"What? You found another book that has been drastically changed and reedited through the centuries?"

"No. Listen. How secure is your phone line?"

There was a pause in their inane conversation that was drastically deeper than everything that had transpired, and in that long, silent gap,

Slue understood immediately what must have happened.

"I...don't know...how secure my...phone line is..."

"Listen. Last night. Something happened that I should not have let happen."

"Go on."

"There was this girl."

Slue's face became utterly grim. Her head tilted down. She breathed through her nose. She looked so sad and at the same time so much like an animal who was caught with no chance of rescue, a mouse in a glue trap, a starving dog in a cage.

"I met this girl last night. She was very curious about the thing you and I have in common, but we never talk about. She...did not have a good reaction when we crossed a certain line."

Slue could not believe what she was hearing.

"Have you any idea what you've done?" she whispered.

"I do now. But at the time, I was crazy. She really wanted to see my eye color. And I really wanted to look at her—without the goggles..."

"What was it like?" she whispered.

"I can't talk about it. Not here."

"You said she reacted badly."

"It was terrible."

"How was she when you saw her last?"

"When I dropped her off, she was fine. But I have to see her again. And you should see her, too. She told me something unbelievable. A rumor. One that involves you, and me, and anyone else who has to wear these goggles."

Slue said nothing. Her face remained blank, but a terrible fear seemed to radiate from every muscle in her face. Last time, it was she who brought the subject up. And he did not want to talk about it.

Ninety-four years ago there were camps on the far side of the Moon...

But that was not what Hieronymus was about to tell her. His concern was over certain hidden current events—which were, naturally, intertwined with certain hidden historical events.

"There is a rumor going round on Earth. The Earth girl I had this misadventure with—"

"Wait," interrupted Slue. "She was from Earth?"

"Yes. Listen. She told me this rumor that she claims to have substantiated."

Hieronymus told Slue what he had heard about the Mega Cruisers. He stopped speaking as Slue's face switched from fear to panic. Out of sight of the screen, she appeared to have grabbed something, and furiously wrote the following sentence on her tablet with her stylo-point and held it up to the screen for Hieronymus to see:

STOP TALKING ABOUT THIS NOW.

I DON'T KNOW IF THIS LINE IS SAFE.

WE'LL SPEAK ABOUT IT IN SCHOOL.

CHANGE THE SUBJECT.

Hieronymus paused. *Where were we? Oh, yes. Tonight. The Ferris wheel. The girl from Earth. The Ginger Kang Kangs playing at the Dog Shelter. Bruegel. I have to convince Slue to come along. She won't want to. But she must. She has to…*

"So. Slue. Like I said, I met this really cool girl from Earth, and I'm supposed to meet her tonight at eight. You would like her. And how often do you get a chance to hang with a girl from Earth? It would be so excellent! After we pick her up, the four of us can head over to the Dog Shelter and check out the Ginger Kang Kangs. It will be so much fun. Please come. Bruegel won't drive me unless you come with us."

"Wait. Who is this Bruegel guy?"

"You must have seen him. He's big. He has a really loud voice. He's not ugly."

"He's not ugly. That's good to know. Almost as good as knowing that he's a Loopie. And he won't drive you unless I come along, which is a little creepy. Anyway, I have other plans tonight, so I can't go."

"Really? What can possibly be more important than this?"

"More important than traveling two hundred kilometers in a car with you and your Loopie friend to see an obscure band play at the Dog Shelter? I can think of a lot of things."

"Well, what are you doing tonight?"

Slue sighed, as she always did whenever she was slightly embarrassed.

"I'm going out with Pete tonight. You remember Pete from the rotunda? I told him that I'd go see *Trapezoids Crunchdown* with him."

"I don't think Pete will be seeing you tonight."

"What makes you say that?"

"Believe me, Slue, my very accurate sources that tell me Pete will be doing something else entirely different tonight."

"Hieronymus, what are you talking about? You don't even know Pete! You just met him once, and you almost got into a fight with him."

"On the contrary, Pete and I hung out on the transporter yesterday morning on the way to LEM Zone One. I misjudged him entirely. He is a truly excellent fellow. He and I are great pals now. In fact, if he was not committed to do this *thing* tonight, I would invite him along with us. But you'll see. He has other plans, probably in the vicinity of Telstar Towers, and he will cancel on you."

"Telstar Towers? Are you kidding me? No way would Pete even dream of going over there. You are not talking about the same Pete I am, Hieronymus."

"I'll make you a deal. If Pete cancels, as I predict he will, you will come out with me and Bruegel tonight on a double date. You and Bruegel. Me and the Earth girl."

For a split second, Slue's face curled up in total disgust.

"Double date? Are you out of your mind? What are in Jesus Pixie are you talking about?"

"I am talking about trying to get myself back to LEM Zone One so I can meet this girl. I can't take the subway because it's totally messed up—I got in last night at five in the morning because of that. The only one I know who has a car is Bruegel. He will drive me out there on one condition—that I set us all up on a double date. Him and you, me and the girl I met last night."

"This is so nauseating, Hieronymus."

"Why do you care? You just told me that you are supposed to meet Pete, right?"

"I am meeting Peter tonight. Yes. This is true."

"But I know for a fact that he will cancel."

"He will not cancel. Peter is a very upstanding young man, unlike all of your Loopie friends. He does not cancel dates."

"So you admit that you are going out on a date with him?"

"Stop it, Hieronymus. Yes. I have a date with Pete."

"You are dating him?"

"I hate that word dating. It is so embarrassing, I get chills of nausea."

"Answer the question."

"Okay. Yes, Hieronymus, I am dating Pete. Happy? Satisfied?"

"Almost. Now answer this next question. Is he your boyfriend?"

"I don't know. What does that mean, anyway? Boyfriend, girlfriend, it's so stupid."

"So you would not get upset if Pete called you up and canceled because he said that he was sick or something like that, then you found out that he was actually having a wild sexy love affair with an unbelievably hot girl who just so happens to be in the Loopie class?"

"You are...insane. I'm not even going to answer that."

"So I can safely assume that you are not willing to bet that Pete might cancel his date with you?"

"Okay, I'll bet. If it shuts you up, I'll bet."

"Excellent. So, if Pete does not cancel his date, I am wrong. I will be humiliated and I will tell everyone in class what an insane kazzer-bat I really am. And that I take classes with the Loopies. Because I'm stupid. But, if Pete does indeed cancel, like I know he will, then you will have to come out on a harmless double date with me and Bruegel and the girl I met last night. We will pick her up from the Ferris wheel at LEM Zone One, and then we will all go to the Dog Shelter to see the Ginger Kang Kangs, which Bruegel informs me is a really happening band."

Slue sighed. "Okay, Hieronymus. Whatever you say."

"It's a deal?"

"Sure."

"We'll be by to pick you up in about two hours."

"It will never happen."

"Five thirty. Be ready."

"Wait. Five thirty? That's a bit early, isn't it?"

"It's a long drive. But don't worry, you get to sit up front with the driver—your date, that is."

"It's all set, big guy," Hieronymus smiled as he approached his friend and slapped him on the shoulder.

"What's all set?" Bruegel asked with a glassy-eyed stare of profound momentary confusion. He shifted his mind from the cookies' ingredients list to whatever Hieronymus must have been talking about.

"Tonight. It's all set. Slue is coming with us."

"Slue?"

"Yes. Slue. The girl with the blue hair."

Bruegel stared up from his comfortable place on the linoleum floor among the piles of cookie boxes all around him. "Slue…" he said, repeating the word silently several times before making an obvious mental connection, and his eye shifted out of whatever trance he had happened to find himself in. "Slue, yes, of course. Oh, that's wonderful! Wonderful! I knew you'd do it! That foxentrotter with the blue hair! You are a true friend, Hieronymus, a true friend! Wow! I have a date tonight with the girl with the blue hair whom every guy in school thinks is really hot! Let's see, what jacket should I wear… maybe my purple suede tuxedo? Hieronymus, do you think I should wear my spats on my shoes? Girls dig those. Also, I was wondering, I have this wonderful top hat, a real stovetop that my mother's last boyfriend left behind before he split on us. It's really cool. Should I wear that? It's made of alligator skin—very rare, from Earth! What do you think?"

Hieronymus did not think anything at all. He just started picking up the boxes of cookies that his friend had been studying and proceeded to put them back in their proper places on the shelves.

They purchased a case of Peterray's Extra Special Beer for Bruegel's mother. They split the cost and handed the wrinkled cash to Mr. O'Looney. An elderly homeless couple lay sleeping and snoring on a large ripped antique sofa that was propped up against the Plexiglas window. Even as they slept, this man and woman had odd expressions on their faces, as if their dreams returned them to their youth, but a youth of such apprehension and uncertainty, and one that would lead them to the unpleasant reality they found themselves in.

The two boys left through the front door of O'Looney's, the neon streets before them glowing in the constant twilight, the flocks of large white hummingbirds forming clouds and ascending to the tops of the highest towers that surrounded them.

Hieronymus was back in his room. He sneaked in through the living room hoping to avoid his father, who was still furious at him for coming in at five in the morning. He did not have a Hell of a lot of time, so he sorted through the piles of clothes he had never bothered to put away. Everything was a mess. *Why am I always leaving my crap all over the floor?* he wondered. *I always tell myself that I'm going to hang things up, and yet, here I am, rummaging through all my shirts and my trousers, my socks, ugh. What's wrong with me? I was going to wear that shirt tonight, but I left those socks on it and now it smells like someone's feet...* He was in a bit of a quandary—everything was either wrinkled, or was filthy, or stank because he didn't bother to put it into the laundry hamper. And it was always the same cycle. The only time he ever gave a damn about tidiness were those moments he suffered from his lack of it.

Suddenly, he realized there was a figure at the doorway, observing him. His father.

Ringo was not in a good mood. He had huge bags under his dark brown eyes. He had been under a lot of pressure at his job the whole week, and last night's disaster was an over-the-top episode of extreme stress. Pacing all night. Sometimes, the worry got to him so much he had to curl up in a fetal position on the couch and scream into a pillow to deal with the anxiety of *where the Hell is my Pixiedamned son, it's three thirty in the Pixiedamned morning* but that didn't improve matters—not one bit.

When Hieronymus finally got in, Ringo was too exhausted to press him for details. It was difficult for Hieronymus to lie to him because he never had anything to hide, except for the fact that he hung out a lot at O'Looney's, and that was not exactly something worth lying about, it just never came up. So any lie told to his father, even the smallest one, took on an extreme weight for him. He felt sorry for his father, but he was not sure exactly why. The man was not that old—but the lines of disappointment he carried on his forehead betrayed a life where something, somewhere long ago passed him by. It was hard to be dishonest to a guy like that. Especially when he's your own father.

"So where in Hades were you last night."

"I told you, Da. I was at LEM Zone One on a class field trip. I wandered off with a couple of friends, which I know I shouldn't have done. I got lost, and I missed the transporter ride back. The subway took forever. You know that. Look it up, they always list the previous night's subway problems on the transport channel. I can even show you the tickets of the rides I went on at the amusement park there."

"Amusement park?"

"Yes, Da, there's an amusement park at LEM Zone One."

"So you wandered off to go on some childish rides and that caused you to miss your transport ride back? What's wrong with you? Have you any idea how far away LEM Zone One is?"

"I do now."

"Don't be a wise guy."

"I'm not. Sorry. I just agree with you that now, after this experience, I understand how far away that place is."

"That's not really the point, Hieronymus. What I'm angry about is the fact that you put yourself at risk over something so utterly stupid. The subway at three in the morning, getting in at five—"

"I got on at about midnight. Normally, it should have taken only an hour and a half, tops. It's not my fault the train broke down, or whatever it did."

Ringo's voice grew slightly louder.

"No. It is completely your fault. What kind of a jackass waits till midnight to take a train that has to cross the *entire* Sea of Tranquility? You've got to be kidding me! That train is a notorious, undependable wreck! You wait till midnight? You don't even call me and let me know where you are?"

"Sorry…"

"Have you any idea how dangerous the train is? You know about what happened two nights ago? That couple that was murdered? The man was killed because he was a One Hundred Percent…"

"Yes, I know, Da."

"You want to know what else, Hieronymus? The school did not even have you listed as being on that field trip. I called them at six."

"You called the school at six?"

"Yes. Remember? Your uncle Reno was coming over. We were going to have dinner with him. You never showed up. So I called the school, and they said that your class canceled out on the field trip. There is no trace of you being anywhere."

"I'm sorry, Da. I don't know why they listed my class as being canceled. Most of the kids cut, so I guess that's why the teacher—actually, we had a sub again—listed the class as being cancelled from the trip because everyone just cut. But I was there. I was with Bruegel and Clellen. They didn't cut."

"Clellen. Doesn't that girl live over in Telstar?"

"Yeah."

Ringo seemed to drift for a fleeting moment as soon as Clellen's name came up. He thought she was one of the wackiest, most eccentric human beings he had ever met. And, of course, so badly beautiful, so blindingly gorgeous, he felt like a horrible old lecher just thinking of her. He dutifully pushed her image from his mind. He was both appalled and delighted his son associated with her...

The bubblephone rang. Ringo went into the living room to answer it. Hieronymus followed at a distance, wary of who might call. And the fact that his class was canceled turned out to be a stroke of luck for Hieronymus, as the caller himself turned out to be none other than Lieutenant Dogumanhed Schmet, Detective, Sea of Tranquility Police Department.

His screen image, that inhuman, waxen face, sent horrible shivers up the spines of both father and son. Hieronymus remembered him.

"Hello? Hello," he said. "Excuse me, I am looking for a Mr. Ringo Rexaphin. Is that you, sir?"

"Yes," replied Ringo with as neutral voice as he could muster. "Can I help you?"

"Good afternoon, sir. I am Lieutenant Dogumanhed Schmet of the STPD. We're just making a routine check of all LOS-bearing males between the ages of fifteen and twenty. This is just a routine check, but we have to ask you a couple of questions, if that's all right with you."

"Of course," replied Ringo. "I have nothing to hide."

"Thank you, sir. Your cooperation in this matter is much appreciated. Now, before we go any further, I would like to ask you, as a parent of a child who bears lunarcroptic ocular symbolanosis, you are familiar with Quarantine Directive Number Sixty-Seven, are you not?

"Yes, I am."

"Good. Now, sir, I should just point out, that this is a very serious regulation regarding the rights and protections of all Lunar citizens, and as law enforcement officials, it is our duty to uphold this regulation to the utmost level as the law applies. You have the right to be informed that this law pertains not only to those who directly bear lunarcroptic ocular symbolanosis, but to those who may try to protect those who bear this affliction. Do you understand what it is that I am telling you, sir?"

"Officer, as I mentioned earlier, I have nothing to hide."

"Thank you, Mr. Rexaphin. As I stated earlier, your cooperation with the STPD is most valued and is indeed an example of good citizenship..."

Ringo was annoyed with this man daring to lecture him on citizenship, and he was also annoyed with the droning quality of his voice. As if he was reading it all from a card. Which, in fact, he was. Starting early that morning, Detective Schmet called up all the families of male children who fit the vague description of a One Hundred Percent Lunar Boy who was in the amusement park. He was keeping the Earth girl in custody, but after that ride into the atmosphere and back, he could not ask her any more questions. He chose not to. Her look of disappointment had been so immense. She got to him. He would not press her, but as a result he had no more leads, so he was looking for suspects the hard way.

"A couple of questions, Mr. Rexaphin, then I'll be on my merry way. You have a son who goes by the name Hieronymus Rexaphin, yes?"

"That is true."

"Funny—you may not know this, but I met your son two years ago."

"Yes. I remember."

"That boy, what was his name? Lester? Am I correct?"

"I do not recall the name of the boy who died of a drug overdose."

"Yes. Drug overdose. Well, that is what they said, didn't they?"

"Is this the reason you are calling us? To ask me about a case that I thought was closed two years ago?"

"Certainly not. No, sir. That case is shut and closed and as dead as that dead boy's shocked rigor mortis face. Yes, that case was shelved a long time ago, of course he died of an overdose and your son showing him the mind-boggling sight of his ferocious eye color, which does not legally exist, certainly had nothing to do with his actual death."

Ringo did not respond to Detective Schmet's insinuations. He just hoped he would ask what he had to ask, then be on his way. However, the fact that Hieronymus came in so late, and now, a call from the police, was suddenly very worrying. He kept his face stone still.

"Anyway, Mr. Rexaphin, I'll get to the point. Just a routine check. Can you please tell me where your son was between the hours of eight PM and midnight last night?"

"He was here," Ringo lied without hesitation. "With me. And his mother."

"Really? Because I just called his school. It appears, according their records, that there was a field trip yesterday to LEM Zone One. Did your son travel out to LEM Zone One with his class by any chance?"

"Absolutely not. Indeed, his class was originally supposed to go on that trip. That is true. But because so many of my son's classmates had cut school that morning, as punishment, his section was not allowed to go—for them, the trip was canceled. A few rotten eggs spoiled it for the entire bunch. Well, I should add that that particular class has a lot of rotten eggs…"

"Yes," said Detective Schmet. "I remember."

"You can call back the school and double check with them yourself. Just ask them if the Loopie class was canceled from the field trip."

"The Loopie class? Is that their official name?"

"No. But it's what everyone calls them."

"Ah, yes, of course. The Loopies. And they *are* Loopies. Every last one of them. You know, I don't think it will be necessary for me to call back the school if you can vouch for him. I'm just going through a list of names and I have a Hell of a lot more people to call. I'm just trying to track down some kid with LOS who broke Quarantine Directive Number Sixty-Seven—he showed his illegal eye color to some tourist girl from Earth, it nearly killed her. What can I say. If your son is around, you might want to ask him about it. He might have a friend of a friend who knows someone who was there, it's a small world and the Moon is even smaller, as they say. If you hear anything, even the smallest bit of information, just call me back on this number, if you please. Thank you very much for your cooperation, Mr. Rexaphin."

Hieronymus was very fast. He ran to his closet and grabbed the only clothes left that were not in a heap on the floor. His dark blue velvet suit. A pink shirt he never wore. He grabbed one black sock and one white sock. He had to act and think quickly because the detective was wrapping things up and his father was doing a great job at pretending to be surprised for the officer—but if he was not out the door and halfway down the elevator shaft before that phone conversation was over, he was going to get grounded on the spot and that would mean missing his chance to see Windows Falling On Sparrows. He had to see her again, and no call from the police was going to stop that. He refused to consider the real significance of it all—that Lieutenant Schmet himself had called less than twenty-four hours after showing his eyes to the girl from Earth. That it was already too late. That they were on to him. He didn't want to think of that. He wanted to be just another normal boy afraid of getting grounded instead of an abnormal boy afraid of getting tossed into a secret prison. He ran. He scooped up his shoes with one hand and sprinted out the door. The elevator down the hall was a large, gaping welcome box into which he dashed, the doors closing just as he heard his father ferociously shouting his name with all the anger and pain that a father could yell upon learning his son was in serious, serious trouble.

The elevator went directly down. He sat on the carpeted floor and slipped both of his shoes on in a frenzy.

He sprinted through the lobby. One of the old men whom Bruegel had earlier tossed into the street was walking, his face a swollen mass of bloated bumps. He spat a tooth out of his mouth. He instantly recognized Hieronymus. "Your friend is a dead man!" the old gentleman croaked. "You tell him that! He is dead!" Hieronymus had no time for that and left the ancient gangster behind him. He made a sharp left turn, zoomed right past O'Looney's, and hopped over several concrete benches and the large dirt-filled pots meant to hold trees but only held emptiness. Tower Ayler was behind him. Tower Zhoug was in front of him.

He ran faster. He knew his father would not come chasing after him. Later, he would tell Ringo everything, after he saw the Earth girl again. He had to see her. He had to return to the scene of the crime. He had to meet her, and by meeting her, it would be proof that his ability to see the fourth primary color was not such a big damn deal. That he could not predict the future action of movement. That he was practically normal.

He ran. The concrete plazas and rundown streets were nearly empty. The sky above was red. The Earth looked down upon him. In the distance, the buildings sizzled in their worn-out neon. Straight ahead, at the foot of Tower Zhoug, stood Bruegel right next to his mother's car, wearing a ridiculous top hat made from alligator skin. A hummingbird hovered close to it, as if the cyndrical shape of it were a gigantic flower. The big Loopie smiled at the running boy in the goggles, who wore a blue velvet suit but whose socks did not match.

chapter ten

Hieronymus was immediately alarmed that Bruegel's car was a Pacer.

"A Pacer?" he exclaimed, slightly out of breath.

"Yeah. What's wrong with Pacers?"

"You are going to drive us two hundred kilometers out to LEM Zone One in a Pacer? An old Pacer?"

"Yes, Hieronymus. I fail to see the problem."

Pacers were famous for their undependability. They always broke down. Bruegel's Pacer was an old car, with the standard shape—a gyroscopically balanced sphere hanging within a five-meter-high rubber wheel. This Pacer had a lot of window space and its body was a dark maroon with the paint chipping off—a quality it shared with the Ferris wheel from the previous night. It sat four people, two in the front and two in the back. Hieronymus stared warily at it. It was old, clunky, and ridiculous looking. It was also covered in a layer of sticky dust. He ran one of his hands across the window. The grime pile on his fingertips was dark gray and gooey.

"When was the last time you took this *thing* to the car wash?"

"What?" Bruegel replied.

"This car is the filthiest looking piece of skuk I've ever seen."

Bruegel acted like he did not hear and instead pointed out the incredibly ridiculous-looking tie he was wearing. It was a printed reproduction of a famous painting of nude figures on an Earth beach playing volleyball.

"Do you think Slue will like my tie?"

"I think that tie is the least of your worries. More pressing is the condition of your car. Do you really think we will make it to LEM Zone One?"

"I got this tie on the Waxboy Exchange."

Realizing he was not going to get a sensible answer, Hieronymus changed the subject.

"I thought your mother's car was a Windbird, or at least a Lancer…"

"Why are you complaining, man?" Bruegel sighed as they climbed inside, where an even worse mess greeted them.

The first thing Hieronymus' feet touched as he got into the passenger seat were empty beer bottles. In the back were numerous collections of crinkled plastic bags, each one with a junk food label of some sort. The car upholstery was ripped in several embarrassing places. There was an odor wafting in the stale air of the car's interior.

Bruegel started up the car engine, which whirred incoherently, coughing as if it were diseased. They lurched forward, and Hieronymus felt the car wobble. The drive to Tower Pelikanhopper, where Slue lived, was not a long one—just on the other side of the Sun King Tower housing projects—but Hieronymus quickly realized that this idea of asking Bruegel to drive him out to LEM Zone One was not only foolish, but clearly self-destructive. He figured Slue would last about ten minutes in this jalopy, providing they did not die in a car crash resulting from severe mechanical failure.

"Listen, I really have to tell you something, Bruegel…"

"Yes, Hieronymus?" replied the driver, who concentrated on the street in front of him with the nervousness of someone who had just gotten his license.

"This car really looks like skuk, you know that?"

"You think so? In what way?"

"In what way? Well, just forgetting the filthy exterior for a moment, which has probably stained my hand for life, you have beer bottles and candy wrappers and junk food bags all over the place."

"So?"

"Do you think girls like Slue don't notice things like that? It's embarrassing, this mess! What on Earth 'n Moon were you thinking?"

Bruegel did not respond. Hieronymus noticed a few beads of sweat forming on his brow, as if he were suddenly nervous.

"Did you hear what I just said?"

"What?"

"I just told you that your car looks like a hellhole and for the most part, girls don't like cars filled with beer bottles and junk. We should at least stop and dump half the skuk out of here."

"What are you talking about? This car's a classic. My mother's exboyfriend told me that. He said the Pacer is an underrated classic."

"I'm not talking about whether this car is a classic or not. All I'm saying is that it is a disgusting disaster. It smells and it looks like your mother and her boyfriend had several parties in here without ever cleaning up."

"It's all right. Slue seems pretty cool. I don't think she'll mind."

"You don't even know her. I know her. She'll mind."

"You think so?"

"I know so."

"Well, it's too late."

They turned a corner and began the drive up to Pelikanhopper, which was the nicest of all the residential buildings in Sun King Towers.

"You should think about this," Hieronymus warned as they pulled into a parking space not too far from the entrance. "Slue has been going out with Pete."

"Yeah, so?"

"Pete has a Prokong-90."

"Really?"

"That's right. He told us about it yesterday. Don't you remember? He said it's only three years old, but he keeps it in great shape. He talked about how Slue loves his car—that they go for long rides under the Earthlight in it."

"Wow. A Prokong-90…"

"Yeah. And you're about to take her out in a dodgy Pacer that looks, feels, and smells like the toilet at O'Looney's."

—

Slue's mother answered the door with an incredibly worried expression. It was rare to see her like this, as she was generally so cheerful. She had an incredibly strong resemblance to her daughter, but, of course, without the goggles and the blue hair. Behind her, from somewhere in the apartment, Hieronymus heard the exasperated voice of Slue's father, pleading with someone on the phone. This too was unusual. Slue's mother was caught between letting them in where they might hear what was going on, or being rude and asking them to wait, which was difficult as she had known Hieronymus for many years.

"Don't be stupid, Raskar! I don't care what you found out, stay out of it! You or those radical friends of yours cannot change a thing! Are you crazy? Do you know what you are up against? Have you any idea what they will do if they find out what you have been up to? You want to throw your life away? All those years in law school, Raskar? Your whole life is in front of you! If you get caught, you will go to jail, or much worse, and you will not be helpful to your sister or anyone of her kind!"

Distracted by the family drama, nearly shaking, Slue's mother let them in. The conversation inside the apartment immediately stopped, and the older woman presented a falsely cheerful demeanor for Hieronymus. It shifted somewhat when she met Bruegel, who lumbered into the family's apartment, awkwardly trying to remain low-key and failing.

"My name is Dertorphi. I'm Slue's mother." She held out her hand, but Bruegel did not shake it. He was so nervous. He only grinned, and when he spoke, she could barely hear the insanely quiet words, *Hi, I'm Bruegel.*

"Is everything all right, Mrs. Memling?" Hieronymus asked.

"Oh, everything is splendid, Hieronymus. You remember Slue's brother Raskar, of course. He's just giving your father and me a bit of grief. Now that he is a lawyer, the first thing he wants to do is make up for lost time with all the teenage rebellion he suppressed and missed out on as a youngster."

Hieronymus nodded. He assumed it was much more complicated. Especially the part about being helpful to Slue, or others like her. That, of course, meant only one thing.

Their living room was large, with a wonderful view of the Sea of

Tranquility spread out before them in all its neon-lit urban luster under the perpetual twilight. Far away, clouds of hummingbirds traversed the endless panorama. Dertorphi quickly changed the subject and told Hieronymus that she had heard about his wonderful presentation of *The Random Treewolf*. Bruegel walked over to the sofa and rudely plopped himself down while taking the liberty of grabbing a colossal fistful of potato chips and shoving them into his mouth. Slue's mother looked on disapprovingly.

Slue's father, Geoffken, entered, along with her younger brother Ned. Geoffken looked exasperated, but also appeared to welcome the distraction of visitors. They said hello to Hieronymus, then looked over at Bruegel, who, within seconds, had managed to wolf down half the bowl of chips. Geoffken frowned at the large apparition sitting in his living room—the strange teenage boy who did not even have the simple manners to acknowledge them in their own home. Bruegel reached forward to help himself to more, and Hieronymus watched as he stuffed them into his mouth. *So embarrassing.* He studied his friend with a tiny bit of resentment. He knew he was thinking Slue was already his girlfriend, he just knew it, just by the way the big boy chewed those chips with his mouth open and his slight cockiness toward everyone there.

Slue entered. She saw Bruegel and immediately turned around and left the room.

"Hey!" said Ned. "I know you! I've seen you around the school."

Bruegel looked up at Slue's younger brother. He stared at him, chewing with his mouth open.

"Yeah, you hang out with all those hoods by the Woolburth wall just next to the school."

Bruegel only stared and chewed and swallowed. He looked over at Dertorphi. "Can I have some more chips? These are really good."

Then he belched.

Within moments, Bruegel was alone in the living room. The family had moved to the kitchen to find Slue and discreetly ask Hieronymus who exactly the stranger was in their living room.

"Who is that boy, Hieronymus?" asked Dertorphi. "He is very rude! He did not even take his hat off—if you can even call that thing a hat."

"He's a Loopie." Ned laughed. "He's in that insane class with all the retards."

"Really?" asked Dertorphi. "Hieronymus, you are not associating with Loopies, are you?"

Before he could come up with an explanation, Slue finally spoke.

"That boy out there is Hieronymus' friend, and they are friends because Hieronymus is in the remedial math and science classes."

The silence that followed only served to amplify the chewing sounds of Bruegel and his loud chip-eating in the living room.

Dertorphi's face twisted in absolute shock. For the first time, a tiny measure of contempt crept into her voice as she looked at Hieronymus.

"No. I don't believe you. Hieronymus, certainly Slue is joking..."

Hieronymus looked at her, his face completely neutral. "You didn't know that? Slue never told you that I spend half my day in the Loopie class?"

Ned burst out laughing. "Loopies! Slue is hanging out with Loopies!"

"Ned, leave the kitchen!" Dertorphi demanded.

"Hieronymus," Geoffken interjected. "You never told us this before. This is a very serious matter. Why have you kept this a secret from us?"

Hieronymus was annoyed with Slue's parents, whom he had known for years, as they suddenly began to look at him like some kind of a stranger.

"Well, Geoffken," he said. "I don't see what the problem is. I'm terrible in math and I'm terrible in science. I do very well in the remedial classes, but in any other class, in those subjects, I would fail, and I would still be two years behind. And the problem is not really the remedial classes—the problem is our society itself, where a large number of kids from underprivileged families or families with social problems always end up in the..."

"But they are criminals!" Dertorphi interrupted. "Those kids are rotten hoodlums! Everyone knows that! How can you stand to be around them? Aren't you afraid of them?"

"Actually," Hieronymous began in an icy neutral voice, "they are more afraid of me than I am of them..."

"It's an outrage!" Geoffken bellowed. "A boy like you, a star, the number one student of the Advanced Honors section in history, philosophy, and literature, should be thrown in with that human detritus! Your father allows this?"

"My father has no control over this."

"What about your mother? Your parents are divorced, right? Can't you go live with your mother—maybe she lives in a school district where they can bend the rules a little…"

"Actually, sir, my mother lives at home with me and my da."

Behind her goggles, Slue rolled her eyeballs at her father's lack of tact.

"Your mother lives with you? I've never seen her. At school, it's always just you and your da. A lot of people think your parents are separated. We used to think that your mother was dead, but I remember Ringo mentioning her, so I assumed that they had divorced."

"No. She lives at home. But my mother is not well."

"What's wrong with her?"

Before Hieronymus could answer, Slue interrupted, glaring at her father.

"Enough, Da! This is none of your business!"

Ned returned to the kitchen, laughing.

"You're not going to believe this, but that Loopie out there not only finished the second bowl of chips, but he got up and went to the bathroom to grab a big wad of toilet paper to wipe his hands with!"

"Ugh!" Dertorphi sighed. "Slue, kindly ask your friends to leave."

"Yeah, Ma, they just came by to pick me up, so we're leaving…"

Both of Slue's parents stared at her in shock.

"You are not planning to go out with these thugs, are you?" her father yelled.

"Da! I have known Hieronymus since the third grade! I have been friends with him since the third grade! You have known him this entire time! He has been here a countless number of times and you have always liked him! He is one of my best friends! How can you suddenly call him a thug!? How dare you? You know him so well, Da!"

"In fact, Slue," her father yelled back. "It appears that I don't know him at all! He takes half his classes with Loopies? How could we not know that? He brings big, strange, psychotic-looking men, like that guy in the living room, into our home?"

Ned remained at the kitchen door, laughing. "Hey, Slue," he taunted his older sister. "So is that your date tonight? You going out with the giant screwball who just finished all the chips—and uses toilet paper like it's a napkin?"

Dertorphi was quick to remedy the entire situation.

"Slue, shouldn't you be getting ready for your date with Pete tonight?"

Hieronymus could not help but grin from ear to ear, and the humiliated look of complete and utter resignation over Slue's face was a priceless moment that more than made up for the embarrassing exchange with her parents.

"No, Ma. I'm not going out with Pete tonight. He called about an hour ago. He canceled."

"Pete? Your new boyfriend? Weren't you two supposed to go to—"

"No, Ma. Pete had to cancel. He said there was an emergency."

Hieronymus continued smiling.

"That Pete is a fine boy," Dertorphi continued. "I hope it's nothing serious."

Hieronymus tried desperately not to laugh. "Yes, Slue. I'm sure whatever Pete is doing can't be very serious. I mean, it *could* be serious."

"Hieronymus! Don't even start."

From the doorway, a new voice entered the conversation. "Are you talking about Pete?" Bruegel asked, his voice a little less shy than before, but not yet at its characteristic loud volume. Then he continued, a huge smile on his face, oblivious to the awkwardness his total honesty was about to conjure.

"I know where Pete is tonight! He's with Clellen."

"Clellen?" asked Ned, his face lighting up. "Is that that really hot-looking babe who dresses really weird and is in the Loop—I mean—in the same class as you?"

"Yeah." Bruegel smiled. "She's taking him over to Telstar so they can check into her favorite motel. They are definitely going to be swimming in each others sweat all night long, that lucky stinker in a bell pot. Pete, man, she has him tongue-tied around love's icicle with a hot-jamming tug on the plexinister go-round jelly-bed."

Nobody really understood the last part of Bruegel's report on Pete and Clellen, but it was clear that Pete had dumped Slue for the notorious

Clellen, and any contempt her parents may have had for the two boys somehow shifted toward the absent Pete instead. When the evening's plans were explained—that they were driving out to see the Ginger Kang Kangs—Slue's father was moderately impressed, as he had heard they really were an excellent band. It did not really matter what they told Geoffken and Dertorphi—the two elders were completely distraught that their daughter's proper and athletic and handsome and gentlemanly boyfriend, whom she had been dating for the past few weeks, was in fact as fiendish as they had imagined. *Clellen!* thought her mother. *That infamous little slattern! A Loopie slut! He discards our lovely daughter so he can have a cheap rendezvous with that queen of cheapness and strange clothes and bizarre hairstyles?!*

The thought of Pete's surprise transgression distracted them so much, they hardly noticed their daughter leaving with the big Loopie and the half-Loopie, not saying goodbye, not even closing the door behind them, the clanking sound of the elevator up the hall echoing and entering their living room.

Ned, deep in thought as he sat on the sofa, wished that he himself could once, just once, be as lucky as Pete in getting a girl like Clellen to go with him to a sleazy motel in Telstar. *Some guys got all the luck,* he thought, staring out at the red sky filled with Mega Cruisers landing and floating and going away.

On the slow-moving elevator down, Hieronymus finally introduced his two friends to each other. It was an embarrassing non-event. Bruegel was sweating like a pig on a frying pan, and Slue could not have been more uninterested in meeting him.

"Slue, this is Bruegel," he said, very formally. "Bruegel, this is Slue."

They shook hands. Slue appeared to be a million craters away as she said, "Nice to meet you."

Bruegel simply grunted in reply.

Hieronymus thought to himself, *This is swell. The evening is starting off as a smashing success…*

Bruegel remained frighteningly quiet as the elevator continued downward.

Slue stood, completely dressed in black velvet for the evening, except for her stockings, which were the exact same blue as her hair. She wore black suede boots. She wore a large black velvet poncho over everything. Both of the boys in the elevator with her thought she was, as usual, supremely excellent-looking in every way.

Hieronymus grinned. "This elevator is always so slow!" he said to Slue, but she didn't even look at him. He then glanced over at Bruegel, who stood as still as a statue, his eyes darting from Slue, to Hieronymus, back to Slue, to Hieronymus, as if watching a tennis match.

Then Bruegel attempted to break the ice. "So, uh, Slue. Do you like Pacers?"

"What?" she asked in a completely neutral, almost rude voice.

"Pacers. You know."

"No, Bruegel. I don't know what you're talking about."

"Oh," he said, his voice trailing off with renewed cowardice.

A few seconds of total embarrassing silence passed by until Hieronymus added his own thoughts on the evening's transportation.

"Don't worry, Slue—Bruegel always gets nervous on long elevator rides. He'll be a regular bag of laughs later on when we're driving in his Pacer on the way to see the Ginger Kang Kangs—"

"Yes," Bruegel then added in a halting, dry voice. "The Pacer. It's a good car. You'll see."

Slue said nothing and stared at Hieronymus for a good three or four seconds with a look of extreme annoyance on her face.

"What time do we have to meet your friend?" she asked. "The girl from Earth."

"Eight. Eight o'clock. At the Ferris wheel in the amusement park at LEM Zone One."

Slue looked at her own watch on her wrist and sighed out loud.

"We don't have much time," she uttered. Then she turned to Bruegel. "You—how fast is your car?"

"M-m-m-my Pacer?" he asked in a frightened little-boy voice.

"Yes. Your Pacer."

"It's…it's a good car…"

"I didn't ask if your Pacer was a good car—I asked if it was fast."

"Fast? Yes, the Pacer can go very fast."

"Can you take it off road?"

"Uh, I don't know. I think so."

The elevator finally reached the bottom of Tower Pelikanhopper, and the three of them walked through the lobby.

As they left the building, Bruegel interjected once more with something completely unrelated.

"Uh, Slue, uh, do you like the Ginger Kang Kangs?"

She ignored him and kept her gaze at Hieronymus as she continued.

"We'll have to take a shortcut I know—it cuts through a deserted part of the Sea of Tranquility—if we want to get there on time."

"You think we'll be late?"

"It's Saturday night. Have you any idea of how packed that highway is going to be?"

"You know a shortcut?"

"Yeah. If the highway is too crowded, it will definitely get us there on time, but it does go through the middle of nowhere, so I hope your friend's car is in good shape…"

But Slue nearly bit her own tongue as the three of them came upon the vehicle in question.

The Pacer.

"Jesus Pixie," she said.

Late or not, Slue refused to get into the vehicle unless the boys got rid of at least half the crap and junk, mostly bottles and cans and old bags of food. Luckily, there were a couple of empty large plastic bags in the glove compartment to expedite this task. Still, Slue was completely disgusted. Bruegel's Pacer was an old car. It was a standard gyroscopically balanced sphere hanging within a five-meter-high rubber wheel, and even Pete's Prokong-90, the last car she had ridden in, looked like this. But Pete kept his car clean and sharp and inviting for passengers, unlike this piece of klud she was about to enter. What a disaster! To imagine, at this moment, Pete was with Clellen! That clown! Clellen! Not that she was so taken with Pete—she would smack him if he even suggested going to one of those motels in Telstar—but what a thought! Indeed, the idea of sitting through *Trapezoids Crunchdown* was not truly appealing, but still, to be passed over, lied to, to have your date broken so he could go out with *her,* that…lunatic Loopie! And now here she was, with two losers, one of whom she'd known since third grade, whom she had always secretly liked, and this weird guy from the Loopie class. A weird guy with a crummy car full of junk. A weird guy who somehow had it in his weird mind that this was some kind of date!

Several hairline cracks in the vehicle's large vulgar windows. Maroon paint flaking off. Dents. One of the headlights slightly dimmer than the other. Spots of rust. The exhaust pipe hanging at an awkward angle. On the back of the spherical body sphere, several utterly embarrassing bumper stickers that referred to bars or tourist attractions. The large single tire itself, almost bald. She could not believe that she was about to take a journey in such an outlandish pile of junk.

Hieronymus and Bruegel filled the two plastic bags with as many beer cans and bottles and as they could gather and tossed them out the door where the trash landed with a glass-breaking thud upon the concrete sidewalk next to the run-down vehicle.

"Come on, Slue!" Hieronymus shouted from the Pacer. "We're late!"

Slue was seated on the edge of the curb.

"Yeah…Slue," echoed Bruegel with a forced tone of familiarity. "We have to go."

"I can't believe you boys have just dumped all that skuk on the sidewalk like that without putting it into a garbage can."

Bruegel turned the key and the mediocre engine began its infected coughing, almost drowning out Hieronymus as he called to her again.

"Come on, Slue. I don't want the Earth girl to think we're not coming."

She stood up, went over to the two garbage bags, picked them up, and with one in each hand, began walking with long determined steps up the avenue toward a large trash receptacle. The Pacer slowly followed and waited as she shoved both bags into the already crowded bin that in of itself was big enough to hold fifty such bags. Three or four filth-covered hummingbirds flew up in a panic from the pile of trash, then hovered, waiting for the girl to leave. Bottles fell, and one of them shattered. The smell of old beer wafted up. She was beyond disgust, but back to the Pacer she went, climbing aboard to sit next to Bruegel in the passenger's seat while Hieronymus stayed in the back.

—

Bruegel's driving was as careful as his personality was random—he drove with an attentiveness that was borderline annoying as the Pacer swerved through the streets and then into tubes and tunnels that led away from the enormous housing complex of Sun King Towers. His eyes were constantly on the lookout for something.

"Hey, Bruegel!" Hieronymus called from the back seat, where he had stretched himself out now that the junk had been removed. "You *do* have your driver's license, right?"

Bruegel, lost in his own careful driving, did not acknowledged his friend's question.

"Uh, let's see…" he mumbled. "Three traffic lights, make a left, Boulevard Queen Maria direction north three kilometers to exit 43, then onto Highway 16-61, straight on through to LEM Zone One…"

Slue glared over at Bruegel.

"Hey," she could not bear to even mention his name at this point. "Hey—didn't you hear Hieronymus? He asked you if you really have a driver's license. Do you?"

Bruegel stared straight ahead, both of his sweaty hands on the large, skinny steering wheel.

"Yeah. Don't worry. I got my license. I just don't want to get stopped by cops."

Slue stared at him with utter disbelief.

"If your license is okay, why are you so afraid of the cops? Are they looking for you?"

"No. If the cops were looking for me, all they'd have to do is pick me up at school."

"Then what's the problem? Why are you driving like such an old lady?"

"I'm driving like an old lady?"

Hieronymus was getting very bored by this exchange between Bruegel and Slue—the big fellow's driving was bad enough, but every time she distracted him, he only slowed down to about half the speed he was already moving at. The night was young, and they were having a miserable time already.

Plodding along the Boulevard Queen Maria, the traffic clustered up around them. They hit every single red light. Saturday night and all the cities in the Sea of Tranquility were abuzz, a massive party on the near side of the Moon—horns honking, neon flashing, crowds gathering along the sidewalks.

"What the Hell is going on!" Hieronymus gasped. "I've never seen the Queen Maria this crowded before! Is there a holiday or something I'm unaware of?"

Slue turned around from the front seat to face him. She had that annoyed expression. She was so lovely. The purple tint of her lenses. Her blue hair. Her cheekbones. Her poncho. *I love you,* he said to her in his mind. *I love you, and yet here we are, on our way trying to meet up with another girl. I love her also, at least I think I do, but I don't even believe that she is really going to be there, but I desperately want her to be there, despite what I saw with my uncovered eyes. If she is there, then it is proof that our eyes cannot read into the projections of the future. You and I will have proof that we are more normal than we realize. But if she is gone, then it is true—and I am doomed, as you are, Slue, we are doomed. Sooner or later, they will snatch us away and force us to pilot ships from one end of the solar system to the next, we will be separated by the vastness, imprisoned by what we can see, we will spend our lives as lost specks in the endless vacuum, our fates are the same, we will be caught, separated, exiled, and still, I am incapable of telling you the simple truth of how much you are to me, how you are the only reason I can continue living in this nightmarish world of neon and goggles and Loopies and Toppers and loser fathers and crying mothers and crowded places full of artificial people breathing the artificial air while the forbidden Earth above laughs down upon us with all its radiated, smoke-filled mess and mud and madness...*

Slue continued to look at him from the front seat. Outside, the crowds of people lining Boulevard Queen Maria gathered in massive groups as the traffic ground to a depressing halt. Someone was blowing a tin horn just outside, and the thousands of conversations created a low timbered hum in the twilight that nearly drowned out the sound of the car engine.

Why is she looking at me?

"So," began Slue, deliberately. "This girl from Earth."

"I told you what happened."

"Over the phone."

"And..."

"We can't speak safely over the phone. But here, in this hunk of trash that your friend thinks is a car, you can tell me exactly what happened. No one can hear us. Not even my date right here—he's too nervous trying to drive, he won't understand anything."

This was true. And so, as the car inched forward, and with Slue's face in the exact same position, looking back into the rear seat where Hieronymus sat, he told her the entire sordid, wonderful story. Including the part when they kissed.

Do you like her?

What do you mean, do I like her?

What I really mean is, do you love her?

I don't know.

You must know. You showed her your eyes. You did it because she asked you.

She had the ability to keep herself as still as a stone. Hieronymus wondered, is this what women do when they are sad? She did not move the entire time they were stuck in traffic on the Boulevard Queen Maria. She sat in the front next to Bruegel, but she remained in that three-quarter-turn position, and she could have been a still photograph for all he knew. Why was she asking him these questions? Two pairs of goggles separated their eyes. She wanted to know if he loved the Earth girl. That seemed to be the whole point of this, even more so than the extraordinary crime he had committed the night before. It was more important that she knew. Did you love her? Do you love her?

In fact, what Hieronymus really wanted to do was jump up, take Slue by the hand, run with her, run with her, run with her, together, run through the crowds on the boulevard that surrounded them, away from Bruegel and his trashy car, away from the neon, from the towers and the roads, run deep into a field where the only light by which to see came from the muddy planet above, run to where there was no one, and at last do what had been on both their minds since the moment they met so many years ago—that is, to take the goggles off and look at each other.

"The Earth girl?"

"Who else, Hieronymus?"

"Yes. I love her."

Slue looked at him for another two or three seconds, then she slowly turned away. A minute went by. Hieronymus could hardly breathe. Why did he tell her that? Why did he do that? *I don't know what I am talking about,* he thought to himself.

Suddenly, the Pacer lurched forward at a green light, then made a left turn onto a ramp that led onto Highway 16-61. Leaving the traffic behind them, it appeared for a while that it would be a smooth and uninterrupted ride to LEM Zone One.

Slue opened her window. Hieronymus watched her blue hair as the wind from the outside swept into the car, the strands silhouetting against the headlights of the incoming traffic. They sped along the highway, the lunar landscape on both sides of the elevated concrete route glistening with bright, sizzling neon. It all became a blur. The traffic was fairly heavy—in front of them was a crowded mosaic of thousands of other cars all going in the same direction. Towers on both sides of the expressway went off into the horizon. Above them, hundreds of Mega Cruisers traversed the red-colored heavens. Hieronymus looked at the back of Slue's head, and all he could feel was heartbreak.

I'm sorry.

They passed under several huge highway signs, all of them green with bright white lettering. LEM Zone One—200 km. Then, all of a sudden, the traffic began to slow down again, like an accordion collapsing into its final low note, then stopping completely.

The three of them sat there. For three long, agonizing minutes. Then the traffic began to inch along.

"Okay," Slue said to Bruegel in a very neutral, business-like voice. "We can't stay on this highway if we're gonna be on time to meet Hieronymus' Earth girl."

"I know," replied Bruegel. "You said something about a shortcut?"

"Yeah. Get off at Exit 94. It's up there, just beyond those three station wagons. That will take us to a small road called Sheng Avenue. We stay on Sheng till we pass a water crater that's actually a seaweed farm, then we make a right turn into the countryside, we head due north into the middle of nowhere. We travel through the countryside for about an hour till we get to a whole bunch of lakes—this is the back way into LEM Zone One—then we're there. Hieronymus gets to pick up his girlfriend, and then we go see the Ginger Kang Kangs at the Dog Shelter."

Bruegel just nodded.

"How do you know this shortcut, Slue?" Hieronymus asked from the back seat.

Slue kept her face pointed ahead, and Hieronymus had to struggle to hear her as she made no effort to raise her voice for him.

"Pete showed me this shortcut. We went to LEM Zone One about ten days ago to go see one of his favorite tellball teams. We were late, the traffic was bad, so we took his Prokong-90 through the same shortcut."

As the Pacer inched forward, an opening appeared between cars and Bruegel steered them all directly onto the ramp at Exit 94. They turned onto Sheng Avenue, which was completely empty.

"I'm not sure this jalopy will be as fast as Pete's Prokong-90," Hieronymus muttered.

"Don't worry," replied Slue with a weary sigh, completely uninterested in the upcoming activities of the evening.

Sheng Avenue led through a dark and deserted industrial wasteland. Closed-down factories. Gray, low buildings with smokestacks. One old brick structure in the distance attracted a massive swarm of hummingbirds—thousands and thousands of them all flew in through a single window, then out through an abandoned doorway as if forming a single fuzzy dragon—colorless, white-gray in the distance, smoke-like, directionless. They passed a fence with incomprehensible graffiti sprayed on it. A bizarre odor permeated the air. Between two wrecked cars, a man appeared to be cooking something in a barrel. Flames lapped up, casting an orange glow in the dilapidated buildings that surrounded him. A white-furred moose drank from a filthy puddle. It looked up as the Pacer sped by. The beast had a bell around its neck, and a low-toned clang was heard as the teenagers left it behind. They passed a car stripped of its many body parts—a shell of a vehicle, a Saturn-shaped machine no longer up on the edge of its wheel, but on its side, resembling a rusted version of the ringed planet that was more familiar—sitting among tall weeds, two or three filthy plastic bags fluttering in the wind, caught on the destroyed frame.

They continued along this route for several minutes. They passed the seaweed farm and made a right turn into the open countryside.

Five minutes later there was no more neon, no roads, no sign of buildings, and certainly no other cars. Humanity was nowhere in sight, and all they could hear was the crunching of the dirt under the revolving rubber wheel of the Pacer.

Bruegel stepped on the pedal, and soon they were speeding. They were alone, and far up ahead loomed the silhouettes of distant mountains.

chapter eleven

Hieronymus held his head between his hands, so angry about the way things had turned out, so hopelessly frustrated and furious at his friends. He felt like screaming. Of course, it was his own fault. He had to involve them. He could not go by himself—he had to ask for a dumb favor from his dumb friend who would ask for an even dumber favor in return, and this meant getting Slue, of all people, in on this ridiculous project of trying to get back to LEM Zone One by eight o'clock. So stupid. A circle of stupidity.

He punched the upholstery of the car's back seat. He grabbed his own gut and gritted his teeth, but this was a waste of time. There was nothing, nothing, not a damn thing he could do about the simple harsh fact that they were late, and they were lost.

Of course, he knew that Windows Falling On Sparrows had left the Moon. He should have accepted it, but the uncertainty had driven him completely mad. He did not want to believe that the fourth primary color allowed him to see past the constraints of time. He did not want to believe in what he was capable of seeing. He wanted to be moderately normal. Just a little normal.

He sat in the Pacer, fuming at his bad and stupid luck, unaware that

he was only half right. The ship that carried Windows Falling On Sparrows really did ascend into the Lunar sky, exactly where he saw it would.
It did point toward the Earth. What he failed to understand was that
everything pointed toward Earth. She went up. She circled the Moon.
She returned, and he had no way of knowing.

"I know which eye of yours is real, and which one is false," Windows
Falling On Sparrows said to the doll-like man who sat next to her.

"How can you tell?" he asked very quietly.

"There are tears in the real one."

"Indeed."

"We are not going back to Earth, are we?"

"We are not. We are going to Aldrin City. I lied. It was a ploy. It was
a trick so you would admit that you did meet a One Hundred Percent
Lunar Boy. We are going to hold you there, at our station, and keep you
here on the Moon until we catch him. The sooner you tell us, I don't
know, his name for example, the sooner we will reunite you with your
mother and father, who are being kept under house arrest at their hotel.
You might even make that flight out to your vacation resort after all."

"My mother hates that hotel."

"Indeed she does. Most unfortunate."

"And the prospect of leaving the Moon for Chez Cracken San, I
must be honest, is not too appealing."

"It sounds like a dreadful place."

"So why would I be in any hurry to help you locate the boy I met
last night?"

"Beats me."

"You don't care if I tell you his name."

"I don't care. I'll find him."

"You're a little like that cat tattoo on your hand."

Lieutenant Schmet said nothing. Belwin announced something
about landing. Windows Falling On Sparrows looked out the window
by her seat. She thought of Hieronymus as the neon Lunar world grew,
its bright colors and spiderwebbed highways looming below. *I will see
you again.* She smiled.

———

Everyone at the station was very kind. Schmet did not even put her handcuffs back on, and as she was processed, Belwin talked to her about such subjects as consciousness and inanimate material and Lunar cinema. Lieutenant Schmet took great pains to make sure that her detention cell was very comfortable, and he paid for the delivery of dinner from one of Aldrin City's finest restaurants. He forbid all personnel and all officers from the Ocular Investigative Division to interrogate her. She was not to mix with any other prisoners. No one was to know she was there, including her parents, and certainly not the Earth embassy. He knew that if he put his nastiest instincts forward and began a serious interrogation, he would have the name of the creature that looked at her without the goggles, but something prevented him. She was already so dear to him he couldn't stand the thought of making her sad in the slightest. She apologized to him. That made her a golden fortress he refused to breach.

Schmet went home. He climbed into bed after taking the usual medications. He had the usual terrifying nightmares. He got up early the next morning and went to his office and spent the entire day calling scores of families with One Hundred Percent Lunar Boys who lived within a reasonable distance of where the incident occurred. Eventually, he came upon a name he recognized. From two years ago. The fish that got away.

*   *   *

Hieronymus opened his window, stuck his head out, and looked over at the Earth, which was no longer high in the sky but extremely close to the horizon. The distant silhouette of a cloud of hummingbirds drifted in front of it.

The unforeseen problem of driving in the open countryside of the Moon is that any vehicle can easily start driving in circles. Or end up driving in the opposite direction from which it intended to go. Especially if one is driving a car with a faulty navigation system, as was the case with Bruegel's Pacer.

—

Bruegel and Slue were arguing.

"You stupid doofus!" Slue yelled at her date. "You mean to tell me that your car does not have a navigation system?"

"I do have one. But it's broken. Anyway, I never needed one before."

"Have you ever driven before?"

"Yes, I told you already that I have my license—"

"I don't believe you!"

"Fine, don't believe me. I don't care what you think. Especially now that your directions have turned out to be such utter klud—"

"My directions are fine. I took this route a week and a half ago in Pete's Prokong-90, and we got there in under an hour! But with you and this pile of skuk you call a car—do you realize that we have been driving for two and a half hours?"

Bruegel was silent for a few moments, then he retorted with what he thought to be a killer line, one that would put this fresh little fox right back in her fresh little cage.

"Yeah, well, don't you go bragging about Pete right now. Pete is at this very moment in a motel with Clellen and you can be sure that they are fixing the steampipe to go bursting in a pigbarn with yo-yos going up and down, up and down…"

"What are you, completely retarded? What kind of a sentence is that?"

"Your friend Pete and his Prokong-90, he…he's…doing the icebox firehouse maranga-style with that bag o' box Clellen!"

"What kind of language is that? What are you, sick? Insane?"

"You think Pete is so hot, how come you're not in a motel with him in Telstar like Clellen? You're just a fake fox, you're just a rusty nail, princess! Pete's with Clellen because she gives out the showstopper, unlike you, you moldy old pig!"

"I should smack you! How dare you! You sick boy! I don't give a damn what Pete and your weird friend Clellen are doing!"

Hieronymus brought his head back into the car.

"Let's go home," he said with extreme resignation in his voice. His eyes were still wide open and scanning the horizon for a glimpse of neon.

"Go home?" Slue declared as she glared back at Hieronymus. "Your genius navigator here has no idea where we are. How are we going to go home?"

"I say we skip LEM Zone One and head directly over to the Dog Shelter," Bruegel announced, as if there was absolutely nothing wrong with the fact that he had no idea where he was driving. "One of you can call the Earth girl and tell her to meet us there."

A lull in the heated conversation quickly followed. Slue was aware that Hieronymus had a deep hatred of any kind of mobile communication device. One look at Bruegel, and she knew he probably didn't bother with such things as well. As for herself, she simply left her mobile-screen and her watch phone on the kitchen counter by accident.

"Does this car have a phone?" she asked the driver.

He glanced over at her as if she had asked the most absurd thing imaginable. "Phone? Absolutely not. That's dangerous. You can't talk on the phone while driving. People think they can do that, but they can't…"

Slue cut him off.

"Great! No way to call anyone!"

"That's not our fault, Slue." Hieronymus sighed. "You always carry around phones and screens and communication watches. If you forgot to bring it, well, don't blame us…"

"I don't blame you and I don't blame your moronic friend either, Hieronymus. I blame myself for even agreeing to go on this utterly stupid trip in the first place!"

"You should blame Pete," Bruegel added in all honesty. "If Pete did not cancel on you so he can go…well, you know, with Clellen…then you'd be having a blast at *Trapezoids Crunchdown* instead of hanging out with us in my mother's Pacer…"

"Just get me to any train station. First sign of civilization, just stop there and drop me off. I can walk from there."

"Maybe you can walk from here?"

"Maybe you can shut your mouth and drive."

"I am driving—unfortunately, I followed your directions."

"My directions are sound—it is your bad driving and your car's lack of proper navigation equipment that have gotten us lost."

"Sorry, *Sluuuue*," Bruegel retorted, dragging out her name, trying to make a mockery of it, but only sounding like a seven year old. "Sorry I don't drive a *Proooookong Ninetyyyyyy…*"

"Hieronymus," Slue said as she ignored the latest infantile burst from Bruegel and turned to face the dejected fellow in the back. "Where are we. Where are we?"

"Well, Slue, it appears that we're just jackassing around the countryside in a crummy Pacer like three losers with nowhere to go."

"Jackassing?"

"Yeah. Jackassing all the way out there, just to turn around and jackass all the way back."

Their conversation on jackassing was about to go into greater depths of detail until they all heard it—a clanky metallic pop. It came from the engine, directly below the passenger compartment.

"Oh!" shouted Bruegel. "What in the name of the holy toilet was that?"

Slue covered her face in her hands as the car slowed down and then came to a complete dead and lifeless stop in the horrifying middle of absolute nowhere.

The silence was overpowering. The red sky appeared a little darker than normal. They were on a flat and endless plain. Mountains in the distance, on all sides. The only movement came from the distant hummingbirds moving in their gigantic clouds so far away. The ground was just gray dirt. Clumps of grass periodically spotted the bleakness. Not a single Mega Cruiser could be spotted. The Earth hung closer to the horizon, almost touching the world's end. Slue knew what this meant, but she was too hesitant to point this dreadful conclusion out to the others. She stared straight ahead, and as her ears became accustomed to the quiet, she was certain she heard the fragile hiss of steam escaping from somewhere.

Bruegel opened his door and jumped out. The exterior of the vehicle was extremely hot. He crawled under the automobile's spherical body and opened the trunk. Slue left the car as well and began walking away. She stopped, staring at the Earth on the horizon.

Hieronymus remained in his seat, as still as a statue, full of anguish and regret.

He thought of his father.

He walked out on his father at the very moment his father was lying to the police about him. How could he have done such a thing? Ringo was probably calling everyone he knew, trying to figure out what the Hell had happened. And if by some chance the police figured out that it really was Hieronymus, then his da would be arrested, too.

The sounds of Bruegel working on the engine filled the passenger compartment. Restless with anger and despair, Hieronymus breathed as slowly as he could and tried to reason himself into a state of calm. His only recourse was to look at Slue, standing in her poncho, her back to him, a figure in the wasteland, looking at the far-away world of everyone's ancestor.

A long time passed. He opened one of the doors, climbed out, and almost fell on Bruegel, who was under the vehicle and still poking around the engine.

"How's it going?" Hieronymus asked him, noticing that his hands were covered in black greasy oil. There was also a streak across his face, as if he had scratched his cheek with one of his filthy fingers, leaving a long track of soot-colored goo.

"Not bad. Just a ruptured hose between the ganfoil and the friddercod. I think the best thing would be to shorten what's left of the hose and connect the ganfoil to the channer instead."

Bruegel held up a mechanical device for Hieronymus to see.

"You're not worried about the friddercod?"

"No," he answered. "The friddercod can get enough acetone coolant if I tape this other tube here—from the blonzelarator. I mean, it's not perfect, but it should last for a few days till I get a new hose."

"How long do you think before we can get moving again?"

Bruegel sighed.

"Well, I have to be careful about cutting and refitting these hoses. If I screw it up, we'll be stuck out here—and Jesus Pixie only knows where 'here' actually is. I think I can get us going in about an hour."

Hieronymus nodded his head and slowly began walking toward Slue, who was still standing about fifty yards away. He heard Bruegel call his name.

"Hieronymus?"

He turned around.

"Yes, Bruegel?"

"I'm sorry. I'm really sorry, man. You know, getting us lost, then my car breaking down."

Hieronymus waved his arm in a *don't worry* kind of gesture.

Slue found a patch of grass and was sitting in it by the time Hieronymus had reached her. He found a grassy spot nearby and laid down. At first he rested his face in the dry green grass. Then he looked over at her. She looked at him, then she looked at the Earth.

"I'm really afraid of something," he said.

"What," she answered, barely audible.

"Well, a detective called my father. I overheard him asking my father where I was last night. My father lied and told him that I was at home."

"So," Slue replied, "that's good. You're lucky your father covered for you…"

"Yeah, well, it's not so simple. I know the detective. I remember him from two years ago. When that boy died after pulling off my goggles. I remembered his name. And I know he remembers me."

"And…"

"Well, me and that girl, we messed up in one serious way. I took her to her hotel, and in the lobby, the clerk and some other people, I think they were hookers, got a pretty good look at me when I brought her back. This one woman even made a nasty remark about it. The clerk offered to call an ambulance."

"So? What are you afraid of?"

"I'm thinking that maybe this detective will start to add things up. Maybe he could tell that my father was lying. Two years ago, he really wanted to nail me for killing that boy. The guy even mentioned it—he was baiting Da about it. He has a reputation for really hating people like you and me. I have this feeling that, as soon as he got off the phone, maybe he pondered to himself—remembering that *I'm the one who got away.* What's to prevent him from, you know, on a wild hunch, or even out of spite, getting a picture of me from the school, and then asking the clerk at the hotel if that was me who brought the girl home?"

"You're going to drive yourself nuts if you begin to worry about that."

He looked up. They could hear the sounds of clanking metal as Bruegel worked on the car, and in the dark red sky, a shooting star fell. Slue looked at it also.

"See that shooting star?" he asked her. "That's our fate. To be specks cast into the cosmos. To drive ships across the solar system till it burns us out. Sooner or later, they're going to get us. One by one. We're already in the net—it's just up to them to decide when to pull us out and stick us in the pilot seats. Of course it's true. Who else can drive those Mega Cruisers?"

Slue said nothing. Her silence confirmed that she thought the same thing...

"It has to be true. If we take our goggles off, we can see the direction of everything before it gets there. It's confusing here on the surface of the Moon, but of course, out there, going as fast as any of those ships can go, in the midst of those incredible distances, we know that in order to get from point A to point B, you have to visualize where point C will be as it crosses its own way between D and E as it intersects A and B. At those speeds and those distances, you need to see where time and space bend. No normal person can do that, and certainly no machine can as machines cannot see the fourth primary color."

Slue pulled some grass up with her hands.

"All of a sudden, you're good in math. Point A, point B..."

"No, I still suck at math. But no normal mathematician can do what we can do—see the fourth primary color, which exists everywhere."

"It is logical, but it's also frightening."

"You know I'm right. You know it's true. How many One Hundred Percenters do you know past the age of twenty-five? How long do they let us live among normal people before we're taken away for doing something as normal as looking at another human being?"

Slue looked at him for a long time. The wind blew her hair. The sound of the car repair continued like a clanky drum in a garbage yard.

"Slue, what was your father talking about on the phone"

"My father? What do you mean?"

"When Bruegel and I got to your apartment, your father was talking with your brother Raskar. He sounded really mad."

"Yes," she sighed. "I don't want to talk about that."

"Something about Raskar getting involved with something dangerous? With his 'radical friends' and things that they 'found out' about?" Hieronymus pushed.

"Raskar. You know he's a lawyer. He just started working at the Federal Courthouse down in the District of Copernicus. He thinks he may have uncovered evidence that…there are those in the government and in the corporate power structures who want to revive certain parts of the Regime of Blindness."

"What?"

"It's just a theory, but there are others who agree with him. Those are the 'radicals' my father referred to. One of them is a very powerful judge. He has also discovered that laws are being electronically altered. A little like *The Random Treewolf*. The crime of updating, but applied to the lawbooks. Laws that refer to LOS, specifically. And the high numbers of LOS people who disappear—maybe your friend from Earth is right about the Mega Cruiser pilots. He is not sure how to prove it, but he is very afraid, and he wants to do something drastic, but he doesn't know what."

"Your brother Raskar told you this?"

"Some of Raskar's friends are LOS people. I met them. They told me about the fourth primary color—there is more to our eye color than we can even imagine. You have no idea what I heard. And the lies we've been told…"

"Go on."

"Please," Slue said. "Not now. I don't want to think about this. It's too upsetting." Hieronymus wanted to insist, but she quickly changed the subject. "Have you noticed the position of the Earth?"

"Yes. We've gone a long way."

"Have you noticed something else?" she pressed.

"Something else?"

"Everything around here is a little darker."

"Are you serious?"

"Yeah. Look at Bruegel's pathetic jalopy. Doesn't it look darker than before? And the ground—much darker than when we got off the highway a few hours ago. Wouldn't you agree that the light out here is, well, different than when we started?"

Hieronymus looked around.

"We are a lot further out of our way than I imagined."

"So far out," Slue added, "that if we keep going in this direction, we'll be on the far side of the Moon, and then we'll really be lost."

As if by providence, as soon as the word "lost" came out of her mouth, they noticed something on the horizon that pulled them back from the abyss of helplessness. A flashing blue light in the extreme distance. Slue immediately took off her poncho and turned it inside out— its interior was bright red, and she began to wave it in the air with both hands, the wind fluttering it high above her head.

"What the Hell are you doing?" Hieronymus shouted.

"The police, you dummy!" she yelled back. "That's a police beacon!"

"Are you crazy?" Hieronymus exclaimed. "What if they start asking me about last night?"

"They won't. There are thousands of police officers, Hieronymus, and the vast majority of them are not out looking for One Hundred Percent Lunar Boys. Besides, you told me that your father covered for you."

Slue waved her inside-out poncho even higher.

Hieronymus instinctively walked backward, away from her.

"What's wrong with you? You're just like your idiot friend over there—he's afraid of the cops, too! Is that what you learn in the Loopie classes? Fear of the police?"

Hieronymus was at a loss for words. All he could think about was that detective with the wax-like face calling his father a few hours earlier.

In the distance, the flashing light appeared to change direction and grow slightly brighter.

"They saw us!" Slue shouted. She turned again to face Hieronymus, who continued to walk toward the car.

"Don't be stupid, Hieronymus! They're here to help us! We're lucky! Do you know what would have happened if we ended up on the far side? We'd get lost! We'd keep on driving and we'd run out of fuel then we'd have to walk, and then we'd starve to death! Don't you know what it is to be rescued? Don't you know?"

The distant vehicle began to take on a definitive shape as it got closer, and as expected, it really was a police car. It slowed down, coming in their direction like a Saturn on its side, riding on the rings. Slue continued to wave her poncho. Hieronymus turned and realized Bruegel was obviously perplexed by this latest development.

"Hey! What's going on? Who's coming—oh, damn! The police!"

The cop car came to a stop in front of Slue and Hieronymus. The first thing they noticed was its wheel—the rubber treads were about ten times thicker and deeper than the treads on the wheel of Bruegel's car. There was also a strange scoop thing attached to the front and a metal plate under the sphere. The engine turned off. Two police officers climbed out. They wore the characteristic stovetop hats and capes that cops everywhere wore.

They approached Hieronymus and Slue, their faces the very definition of neutrality.

"Good evening," one of them said politely. "What are you kids doing out here?"

"Our car broke down," Slue volunteered without hesitation.

"You took an old Pacer all the way out here?" the other one asked.

"Yes, we did, Officer. We thought we were taking a shortcut—but we got lost."

"How did you get lost?" the other officer asked. "Where were you going?"

"We were going to…" Slue was about to say LEM Zone One, till she realized how paranoid Hieronymus must have been feeling. "Well, we were looking for a club called the Dog Shelter. We wanted to see a band called the Ginger Kang Kangs…"

"What? The Dog Shelter? You think there's a club out here?"

"Well, Officer, unfortunately for us, the highway was jammed, so we decided to take some back roads."

"Miss, you are not even on a back road. This is open country."

"Yeah, we stupidly thought we would cross a field, but we couldn't find the road we were on, and I think the field just turned into this big expanse of wilderness."

"Where is this club you were heading to?"

Slue paused.

"Well, it's…"

Hieronymus decided to offer up the incriminating words himself.

"LEM Zone One, sir. The club is next to that place they call LEM Zone One, but because we've never been there before, we had no idea where we were going—well, we thought we knew how get there, but we messed up in following our directions."

The two officers looked at each other, and one of them sighed.

"If you kids were on your way to LEM Zone One, you are way, way off the mark."

"Really?" Slue asked.

"Yes, really. Is that your car over there?"

"It's our friend's car."

"Well, come on then," the officer said, indicating that he wanted Slue and Hieronymus to follow him to the Pacer. The second cop returned to the police car, began its engine, and slowly followed them, the beacon still spinning its raw blue light. They approached the stranded car, Bruegel standing next to the trunk, an incredibly guilty expression on his face.

"H-h-h-hello, Officer," he said.

"Is that your car?"

"It's my mother's car, sir."

"You were driving it?"

"Yes, sir."

"It's a Pacer. You were driving a Pacer in the open countryside?"

"I, uh, I'm sorry, sir, I don't understand."

"A Pacer is a class A road vehicle. Only class D vehicles are allowed out in open terrain like this."

Bruegel expressed total shock but Hieronymus knew he was faking it. He knew perfectly well his Pacer was not supposed to be out in the open country like this.

"I…I had no idea, sir…"

"Your license and registration, please."

Bruegel frowned as he reached into his pocket to get his wallet. The same cop then turned to Slue and Hieronymus.

"I'd like to see some ID please."

"I don't get this, Officer." Slue searched through her bag, looking for her Lunar identity card. "Have we done anything wrong?"

"This is a restricted area, young lady."

"Restricted? I didn't see any signs."

"It's quite possible you may not have seen any signs if you turned off the road back there in the Sea of Tranquility, but you are still breaking the law."

"Wait," Bruegel interrupted. "We're not in the Sea of Tranquility?"

"No," answered the cop. "You are nowhere near the S.O.T.—in fact, judging from the tracks you were making, it seems you were heading directly toward the Far Side, which begins only a couple of kilometers from here."

Bruegel's jaw dropped. Slue and Hieronymus had already figured that out by the position of the Earth, but Bruegel was truly perplexed.

They handed their ID cards over to the officer. Bruegel reluctantly gave him his driver's license, which the policeman studied with great interest. Then the cop looked up with an almost accusatory expression in his eyes.

"Your name is Houseman Reckfannible?"

"Yes."

"And…let me see what it says here…you are a graduate student at Gagarin University, doing research on…what does this say, Economic Theories of Roubustion Defaltiker? I don't even know what that means."

Bruegel forced himself to smile, hoping he would not be asked to explain.

"You are twenty-seven years old?"

"Yes." Bruegel gulped.

"Really?"

"I look…much younger than I am."

"Is that so?" said the officer, who then started scratching the surface of the card Bruegel gave him with his fingernail.

"What have we got?" the other officer asked.

"Oh, the usual." The first officer cracked a slight smile, nodding his head as he managed to peel Bruegel's photo off the card to reveal the image of the actual owner of the driver's license he held in his hand.

"Bruegel!" Slue was boiling mad.

Hieronymus, had he not been through his own law-breaking adventure the previous night, would have been laughing at the clumsy predicament his friend had suddenly put them in. Instead, his dread drove him into even deeper pits of insane worry.

But the officer was oddly sympathetic.

"Look, kid. I know where you're coming from. Let me guess. You normally use this fake ID to go to bars and buy alcohol from places that don't look too carefully at ID. Tonight, I don't doubt what your friend here says. There's a band that you all wanted to see, but the only way to get there was to borrow—I hope this is your mother or your father's car—someone's car. But because you don't really know how to drive, you got lost. Right?"

Bruegel nodded. Then he spoke in a really quiet voice.

"I know how to drive, sir. I took driver's ed last year."

"There is a difference between knowing how to drive and *knowing how to drive*. Do you at least have a learner's permit?"

"It…it…expired a few months ago, sir…"

"What is your name, kid?"

"Bruegel. Bruegel Westminster."

"Okay, Bruegel. This is what we are going to do. We are all going to be as honest as we can to try and get you and your friends back home safe. Where you are right now is a very dangerous place. I am assuming that the navigation system in your car is broken, yes?"

"Yes, sir. How did you know?"

"Because only a broken system would let your car wander this far. If your car had a normal navigation setup, you would have been warned that you were entering the wilderness, and even worse, heading for the far side of the Moon."

Bruegel shrugged and nodded his head.

"Okay. The three of you look like nice kids. You don't look like you are dressed up to go exploring the far side of the Moon. Or to go looking for trouble in restricted areas. You look like you are all going to a club. I take your word for that."

The officer went over to the Pacer.

"Tell me the truth. Whose car is this?"

"My mother's."

"So if I were to punch in the number on the license plate on our computer over there in our police cruiser, whose name would appear?"

"Elizabeth Westminster. My mother."

"Your mother would be surprised if I told her that you were driving with a fake license?"

"Yes. She thinks I have a real license."

"You realize that we cannot allow you to drive this car home? We will have to call a tow truck to come get it. It's going to be very expensive. Your mother will have to pay for it."

"Please, sir," said Bruegel, his voice wavering, almost crying. "My mother has no money. She's unemployed."

Hieronymus had never seen his usually confident friend behave in such a pathetic manner before.

Bruegel's face crunched up, and he began to sob. "Please, sir. Please, Officer. Don't call my mother. We have no money. We can barely pay for anything. My mother, she's in a lot of trouble as it is. Please, Officer…"

"What about your father. Can your father deal with this?"

"I…I don't even know who my father is. I don't even know if he lives on the Moon…"

The two police officers looked at each other. The one who asked all the questions shrugged his shoulders. The second one nodded his head, then he went forward to speak to Bruegel.

"Listen, kid. The fact is that you broke the law. You were driving without a license. And this is a restricted area. But in many ways, you're lucky we caught you out here in the middle of nowhere. In fact, we didn't even catch you driving, technically. You are lucky your car broke down. What if you were driving around in a crowded urban area? What if you were in an accident? What if you and your friends had a couple of drinks, and then you accidentally hit someone? Then you would go to jail. But you have not done anything to put you in jail."

"Really?" Bruegel's eyes filled with tears. "You're not arresting me?"

"No. But you *are* in trouble. We're going to give you a ticket for presenting a fake ID to a police officer. And a ticket for—" the officer paused, then looked over at his colleague.

"Technically, we cannot actually give this boy a ticket for driving without a license. He is just out here working on a car. We know he drove it here, but we can't give him a ticket, because the car is parked. We did not catch him physically driving. But because it's his mother's car, she's the one who is ultimately responsible."

Both police officers were suddenly unsure how to proceed. It was obvious to the three teenagers that they were trying to find a fair solution because it was clear they should not have been out there in the middle of nowhere like that. Another team of officers could have really busted their chops, but luckily, this was not the case. And both Hieronymus and Slue were aware that these officers made no mention of their goggles, or their being One Hundred Percent Lunar kids—they did not even appear to notice it.

The officers walked over to their vehicle. Slue glared at Bruegel. She was temped to unleash her fury on him—after all, he had lied to her about having a driver's license.

But he just sat on the ground, covering his face with his hands...crying.

One of the officers came back. He spoke to Bruegel.

"What's wrong with your mother's car?"

"Ruptured ganfoil hose, Officer."

The cop scratched his chin.

"Were you able to fix it?"

"Yeah. I finished with it just before you got here."

"That's good, because I think this is what we're going to do. You and your friends are going to ride with me in the cruiser, and Officer Duebelex over there is going to drive your mother's Pacer. About twenty kilometers from here is a station. We'll drop the Pacer off there, and then you three can take the bus or the train back home. You will have to tell your mother the truth about what you did, and your mother will have to pay a fine if she wants to get her car back. That's the law. You will also have to appear in court to deal with the fake ID, and that's going to be another fine. Still, it's the only thing we can do. If I have to call a towing truck out here to get your mother's Pacer, the charge is going to be astronomical."

Of course the kids understood these two were bending over backward to help them out of a difficult situation. But then Hieronymus froze. While this officer was explaining to them the most reasonable way to deal with the situation, the other officer, the one he referred to as Duebelex, was sitting inside the police cruiser looking at something on the vehicle's computer. He had his ID card. He must have been scanning it.

Hieronymus knew that his life was over.

Finished.

Duebelex stared at something on his vehicle's dashboard. He spoke into a radio. He looked directly at Hieronymus. He shook his head in disbelief. He double-checked something on his screen. He looked at Hieronymus, then he made an expression that seemed to say something to the effect of *I can't believe this. I just can't believe this…*

He exited the police cruiser.

Walking quickly in Hieronymus' direction, he drew a pistol.

"Hieronymus Rexaphin," he announced in a loud voice. "Please put your hands up."

Hieronymus complied. Slue's jaw fell open with shock. The first officer who had been dealing with Bruegel appeared just as surprised.

"Duebelex," he said to his comrade. "What's going on?"

"I was checking their cards. This young man is in heaps of trouble. He's a One Hundred Percent Lunar Boy, and he showed his eyes to a girl from Earth last night. There's a bulletin out for his arrest."

"Okay, let's take him in," said the first policeman as he walked away from Bruegel.

Hieronymus said nothing. He stood with his hands in the air.

"Your name is Hieronymus Rexaphin, is it not?"

"Yes, sir. It is."

"You are to keep your hands in the air. You are to face the ground. Do not speak to your friends. If you'd be so kind as to kneel until we get proper handcuffs."

"Certainly," replied Hieronymus as he got down on his knees, only looking at the dirt and sparse tufts of grass below him.

Slue was pleading with the officers, but Hieronymus was so nervous he could not understand what she was saying. He turned slightly, and he thought he saw Bruegel sitting in the dirt next to the Pacer, absolutely flabbergasted over how the focus of law enforcement could shift so suddenly. There was an odd buzz of panic in the air. He couldn't comprehend words, only the sound of voices—and Slue was clearly distraught, and the police were calmly explaining something to her.

"Slue," he called. "Don't be upset."

But one of the officers spoke before she could answer.

"Hieronymus, please do not speak to your friend."

"Officer? Where will you take me?"

"Normally, we would take you to the station, of course. But your arrest warrant has special instructions. We are to drive you all the way to Aldrin City, to the Ocular Investigative Division."

"And what about my friends?"

"They will be fine. We will make sure they get home safe."

"Officer, I need to call my father."

"I'm sorry, young man, but according to our instructions, you are not allowed to call anyone. We are to treat you as a very dangerous criminal and we are to deliver you personally to a certain Lieutenant Schmeet."

"Schmet," Hieronymus corrected him.

"Schmet?"

"Yes. His name is Lieutenant Schmet, not Schmeet."

"So you've been in trouble with this type of thing before?"

"No, sir. I'm just the fish that got away."

Still staring at the ground, Hieronymus focused on a pebble as he felt the officers gently move his arms around his back and lock his wrists with plastic cuffs.

The police spoke to each other in hushed tones.

"Something has just occurred to me. Maybe these kids are not lost at all. Maybe they knew exactly what they're doing out here. Maybe they were helping this guy Hieronymus escape to the far side of the Moon."

"Excuse me, Officers?" Slue interrupted.

Then there was silence, followed by incoherent mumbling, panic-like praying and frightened crying, and when he finally turned around and looked up, Hieronymus saw the two police officers crawling on their knees in states of absolute confusion and Slue just standing there before them, her goggles up on her forehead, her wonderful, beautiful eyes so vivid in their fourth primary color. She smiled at Hieronymus as the two symbols of authority were reduced to groveling at her feet, as if she were an avenging goddess.

chapter twelve

Hieronymus ran over to Bruegel, who still sat in the dirt by his mother's Pacer. The large fellow was in a state of complete bewilderment. He was about to get arrested. Then the cops were going to do him an enormous favor. Then the cops suddenly arrest Hieronymus. Then Slue just looks at them and they collapse.

"Bruegel. Whatever you do—don't look at Slue in the eyes."

"What's going on?"

"It's very hard to explain. Listen. We have to get out of here right now. Do you have a knife or something sharp?"

"In the toolbox."

"Good. Get a blade and cut these handcuffs off."

One of the police officers had curled himself up into a fetal position. The other was slowly attempting to crawl away. The first thing Slue did was take their pistols away from them and toss them into the distance as far as she could. Then she went back to the officer who was on his hands and knees, and with her goggles still up on her forehead, knelt before him, blocking his way. He stopped, unable to resist glancing again at the forbidden, illogical eye color again. His face went blank, and his mouth hung wide open. She knelt forward, and cupped his cheeks in the palm of her hands. "Don't be afraid," she said to him.

You will have no memory of this. This incident with the three teenagers and the Pacer in the middle of the wilderness never happened. Look me in the eyes. It never happened. You never met us. The name Hieronymus Rexaphin means nothing to you. You will go back to the car, and you will completely erase all data that you may have downloaded on the car's computer during the past half hour. You and your partner will completely forget this incident. You will drive back to the exact spot where you only thought you saw a girl waving a cloth. You will be convinced that it was an optical illusion. If you have had any communication with any authorities regarding three teenagers in a Pacer, you will tell them that it was a mistake. You do not have your pistols because you both misplaced them somewhere at the station. If you feel disoriented, it is because you were overcome with car exhaust, and you both had to stop and rest. This conversation we are having now will be completely forgotten. If at any time you should see our faces again, you will not recognize us. You have never seen me. You have never seen my eyes. As far as you are concerned, the fourth primary color does not exist. You know nothing of the case of Hieronymus Rexaphin...

By the time Bruegel finished cutting through the plastic handcuffs to release Hieronymus, Slue had repeated the same thing to the other disoriented officer, who remained shivering in a fetal position. She then went over to the cruiser and retrieved their ID cards. She also took a handheld device.

Her goggles were back in place over her eyes when she approached the two boys.

"You are out of your mind." Hieronymus said to her matter-of-factly.

"You should be thanking me."

"Technically, you have just willingly assaulted two police officers. You are now in much worse trouble than I am."

"Bruegel," she said, ignoring Hieronymus. "Is it true what you told the policeman? That you fixed the Pacer?"

"Yes."

"Then let's go."

"We are not going anywhere!" Hieronymus looked over at the disoriented cops crawling on the barren surface of the Moon. "We can't leave them like that! We have to take them to the hospital!"

"They tried to arrest you!"

"What am I, a criminal? If they're told to arrest me, then they have to arrest me. I am not going to go around hurting anyone trying to escape the fact that I broke the law last night! I did something last night that is extremely illegal! I should not have looked at that girl! But I'm stupid and I'm weak and I did it and now I have dragged you and Bruegel into it! I'm going over to that police cruiser, I'm turning on their radio, I'm calling an ambulance, and I'm going to wait right here and I'm going to turn myself in! I'll tell them that I was the one who looked at them. I'm taking full responsibility!"

But Slue would have none of that.

"That's just a load of skuk, Hieronymus! You're a coward! You're passive, as usual! It won't help you to do that, anyway."

"Slue, there is nothing in the world that will make me leave this spot!"

"Really?" she asked him.

"Really! Nothing!"

Slue walked up to him and kissed him on the mouth.

Within minutes, they were in the Pacer. Bruegel was driving, and they were heading in the direction of the far side of the Moon.

Clearly, Slue was now in charge of the expedition. She told Bruegel to drive directly toward a pair of high, craggy mountains on the horizon. Bruegel was beside himself with embarrassment over the discovery that he did not really have a driver's license, and so his usual cocky and anarchistic exterior was replaced by this new and rarely seen side—that of a boy so shy he could hardly speak, and yet, for the first time in his life, emboldened with a newfound sense of focus.

Hieronymus kept wondering to himself, *how long did we kiss? She kissed me…and she did it…as if it were the most logical thing to do…*

Those police officers could be dying.

Don't worry, they're not.

How do you know? Not only did you look at them, you took their faces in your hands and you forced them to look at you again! What did you say to them?

I told them what I knew they were about to do.

What are you talking about?

You know full well, Hieronymus. As soon as I looked at those two officers, I knew, judging by their trail of projected color, that they would lay on the ground for a while, then they would get up, they would walk to their vehicle, they would sit and wait till they felt normal again, they would forget all about meeting us here, then they would drive back to where they came from.

Why are you telling Bruegel to drive to the far side of the Moon?

Because when I looked at the Pacer, I saw and thus I knew that the three of us would climb back inside. I saw the direction the Pacer would go. Its color projection traveled exactly to where those two mountains are.

You knew that we were going to go there?

Yes.

Did you know that you were going to kiss me?

Yes. But…

But what?

I don't think I needed to take my goggles off to know that.

Bruegel was driving incredibly fast, but the mountains ahead of them appeared only slightly bigger. Slue took out the handheld object she had taken from the police car.

"What are you holding?" Hieronymus asked her.

"It's a Police Omni-Tracker."

"What the Pixie is that?"

"It's a portable navigation device—but a very special one. Only the police are allowed to use these. In theory, it is supposed to keep track of every person on the surface of the Moon."

Slue pressed a button, and a flat translucent projected map-like image bounced into the air in front of her. A flashing red dot appeared upon what could only have been a representation of the countryside. The dot moved swiftly. Slue pointed to it.

"This is us," she said. "This red dot indicates the position of the Omni-Tracker."

"At least we know where we are," said Hieronymus. "So not only have you showed your eyes to a pair of police officers, which is the same as assault, in case you forgot—but you have also stolen state property."

"The police won't notice right away that this is missing, but when they do, they will think they left it along with their guns at the station."

"How are you so certain of this?"

The mountains loomed larger in the distance. The Pacer was moving with a greater fluidity than ever before. What Bruegel was unaware of was that in making his repairs, he unintentionally flushed away a blockage in the fuel-feeder that had been hampering the vehicle's performance for years.

Slue looked at Hieronymus.

"I am certain because…there is another reason the authorities are so fearful of the fourth primary color. It is not just that a person becomes disoriented. The mind becomes so unhinged while viewing this color that memories can be taken away and false memories can be inserted…"

"You mean, as in hypnotized?"

"No," Slue replied, a sad expression on her face. "Much deeper than that. When a normal person sees the fourth primary color, as you know, their mind becomes deeply confused. It has to reboot itself. A human being becomes like putty during those moments. They can be told anything, and for them, it becomes the truth. By now, those police officers are emerging from their confused state. And they will both be convinced of the exact same thing. That the exhaust of their cruiser made them pass out. That I was an optical illusion when I waved my poncho at them. That they never met us. And all this because I told them so."

"How did you know this, Slue?"

She looked at him, and with the hills to the side of her passing, the light outside fading, her blue hair becoming a neutral mass of waving strands in the wind that passed through her partially opened window, she smiled at him.

"How do you know this, Slue?"

———

The Pacer passed between the two mountains and continued directly into the abyss. Hieronymus and Slue both knew they were on the far side of the Moon, as the Earth was nowhere in sight. The sky above was no longer red, but a dull, dark purple. The light was dim. The terraformation of the far side was very different from the near side. There were sections where the grass grew taller, wavier, and covered the hilly countryside in ominous patches.

A hummingbird the size of a dog flew directly in front of them, almost colliding with the Pacer. Bruegel was shocked. "Did you see that bird!" he shouted.

Slue returned her attention to the projected image from the Omni-Tracker. Then she began typing on the small device.

"What are you doing?" Hieronymus asked.

"Preparing your defense."

"Defense? I have no defense," Hieronymous slumped back into his seat with a sigh of inevitability. "No matter what we do, they will find me. They will put me away. And then—"

"—they will force you to pilot Mega Cruisers till your eyes pop out. Yes, well, we are going to see to it that you don't."

"How is that?"

The engine beneath them purred as the wheel that encircled their vehicle ran over the bumpy terrain.

"By challenging the way the law is applied. By exposing the government's methods of abusing Quarantine Directive Number Sixty-Seven. By exposing the fact that the laws that govern us have been edited without the public's knowledge. Because of 'updating'. It is the printed word of law that controls everything, but you know, my brother Raskar, is right. Those printed words have been changed and not to our benefit. Do you know that there has never been a trial for any One Hundred Percenter accused of looking at anyone without their goggles?"

"What?"

"Indeed. Your goggles fall off. You look at someone. That person is momentarily incapacitated. You are arrested. And you disappear. No trial. Nothing. Nobody questions anything because most people are terrified of us. And we are all terrified of one another. But it is unconstitutional, it is illegal, and I am sure, now that I think about it, considering what the girl from Earth told you, that there are secret deals between the Lunar Government and the corporations that run the Mega Cruiser lines, if not all the high-speed traffic throughout the solar system. They break the law, they use us, they make money."

Slue pressed another button, and a map of a familiar lunar city appeared in front of her. Aldrin City, which was not too far from Sun King Towers. A flashing blue dot appeared in the middle of what appeared to be an elaborate compound of roads and tall concrete buildings.

"Okay," Slue continued, pointing to the blue dot. "That's your father. That's the Aldrin City Prison. No surprise. Your father is in jail."

Hieronymus only gritted his teeth. He felt sick at this realization, and he felt horribly guilty.

"Are you sure he is in jail?" he asked, hoping that maybe his father was just there for questioning.

"Oh, he's incarcerated for sure. Look at this." Slue pressed another button on the handheld machine, and additional text appeared. She read it out loud.

"Ringo Rexaphin. Charged and held without bail for aiding an Ocular Fugitive. Charged with the crime of lying to a detective of the Ocular Investigative Division. Charged with breaking Quarantine Directive Number Sixty-Seven. Charged with terrorism. Awaiting trial."

"Terrorism?" Hieronymus gasped. "All he did was cover for me."

"There is nothing we can do for him right now," said Slue, looking back into the rear seat. "But I have a question. Your uncle. The one who got you that ancient copy of *The Random Treewolf* that you showed me in the rotunda at school."

"My uncle Reno."

"Right. You told me that he comes to the Moon to do research at that giant library, right?"

"Yes."

"That incredible library that's on the far side of the Moon?"

Hieronymus stared at her. They passed a tall white tree without leaves. It had been painted white. Then someone had spraypainted graffiti on its trunk.

"Do you think your uncle might be there *right now?*"

"I don't think my uncle Reno can be of any help."

"Your uncle Reno is about to be incredibly helpful. By allowing us into the library. By showing me the Lunar Law section, where I will find every civil code, in printed paper form, that relates to Quarantine Directive Number Sixty-Seven. And I am certain that there is no code at all that spells out the exact circumstances that lead to the unjustified punishment we are all sooner or later subjected to. Not in the original, not in the paper form that has obviously been updated for decades. If I can get there and scan the original, and then get it to my brother…"

They passed another tree that had been painted white.

"Why are the trees painted white?" Bruegel asked.

Slue ignored him as she turned to Hieronymus again.

"The Earth girl…"

Hieronymus stared at Slue. "Yes. The Earth girl."

"Did you really expect to see her tonight?"

"I was hoping to see her."

"That is not what I asked. I want to know if you were *really expecting* to see her."

Hieronymus looked away.

Slue continued. "You did not really believe that she would be there tonight, did you?"

"I don't know what to believe."

"This whole trip was an experiment for you, wasn't it? To prove that what you saw with your goggles off was not the absolute truth. Am I right?"

Hieronymus nodded.

"But when you saw her without your goggles on, you were certain that you would never see her again?"

"Slue…" was all he could manage as she spelled out what he knew to be true.

"But isn't it odd, Hieronymus, that if you really, really wanted to be certain, you would have found a much more dependable method of returning to LEM Zone One? Instead, you decided to rely on your friend Bruegel here, and look where that has led you. Yet you must have known that. You *chose* to depend on Bruegel because he is undependable, and you knew that he would complicate things by proposing to bring me along. Is this not true?"

They passed several white moon moose in the distance. Two of them were nose to nose, fighting over something they both had in their mouths at the same time. It was another of the dog-sized humming-birds, a dead one.

"She…" Hieronymus began, "is not even on the Moon. Last night, I saw her projected color…turn upward into the sky, and return to Earth…I am certain that the authorities figured out what happened, and she refused to cooperate, and they sent her back."

"You did not want to believe it," Slue whispered.

"No. But we had this deal. To meet at the Ferris wheel. To see if it was true. I knew it was a ridiculous thing. I was as certain of her departure as you are certain that those police officers will go back to their station, oblivious as to what happened."

"But if you really wanted to test this out, you would have just paid a few extra bucks to take the express transport or the TGV back to LEM Zone One."

"Yes. I must have subconsciously wanted to fail. If I failed to return to LEM Zone One, then the possibility would remain that she was still there. That my failure to get to the Ferris wheel was nothing more than a self-fulfilling prophecy, with nothing to do with being a One Hundred Percent Lunar Boy."

"Like a normal person."

"Like a normal person who screws things up because he plans things badly."

"But we are not normal people," said Slue, a hint of finality in her voice.

Because of the Omni-Tracker, the three students from Lunar Public 777 at least knew the direction they were going in. However, Slue was worried that sooner or later, someone in some police station would notice the unusual path that one of their Omni-Trackers was taking, and she knew that it would not be long before they had to ditch the machine somewhere.

But first, she had to make a couple of phone calls.

On the device's keyboard, she typed in the name Reno Rexaphin. On the translucent screen in front of her, the map landscape changed, and a small green dot flashed inside of what appeared to be a vast subterranean structure within a mountain. She checked the coordinates. It was about three hundred kilometers from their present position.

The giant library. Filled with books made of paper.

"Bruegel," she asked the big fellow sitting next to her in the driver's seat. "Bruegel?"

"Ugh, hi, Slue. Are you having a good time?"

"Yeah, listen, Bruegel, how much fuel do we have left?"

The big fellow squinted forward to look at the instrument panel. From what he could gather, the news was not encouraging.

"We should have enough to get us to the Dog Shelter," he replied optimistically.

"Bruegel," continued Slue. "We are nowhere near the Dog Shelter."

She referred once again to the positioning of the Omni-Tracker. There was only one single highway that snaked through the entire far side of the Moon, and throughout this entire time, she had been directing Bruegel to drive in its direction. When she looked at the fuel level that remained in the vehicle, she was able to conclude (as she was quite good in mathematical reasoning, unlike her two companions) that they might reach the highway, but they most certainly would not reach a fuel station. However, almost hidden on the map that floated in front of her, just half a kilometer off the highway, was an indicator for an abandoned town. Or mining camp. Or something from long ago no longer in use. It was simply called JOYTOWN 8 (ABANDONED). It was the "abandoned" part of the name in parenthesis that got her attention. She realized there was only one available option. She checked the coordinates and told Bruegel to head there, which was not too difficult—they were heading in that direction anyway.

She turned to Hieronymus.

"Your uncle Reno. He lives at the library?"

"Yeah," replied the exhausted Hieronymus. "Because it is so out of the way, all the researchers usually stay there."

"Is he the kind of guy who stays up late? You know, past midnight?"

Hieronymus shrugged. "I don't know. Give me the Omni-Tracker —I'll try to call him."

Slue already knew that it was possible to use the Omni-Tracker as a telephone, but she adamantly refused to allow Hieronymus to call his uncle. She didn't even want to use it to call her own family, whom she figured were probably getting worried, as it was already quite late.

"We should be really careful about who we call with this machine," the One Hundred Percent Lunar Girl told him. "Any calls to anyone in our families would send up red flags with the police—we know that they are looking for you right now. A call to your uncle Reno would probably catch the attention of the authorities, as you are missing, you are wanted, and your uncle is your only known relative on the Moon. Anyway, there is only one person on this entire round rock who is going to help us right now, and he is the only one I am going to call."

"Who is that?" asked Hieronymus.

Slue smiled at him as she punched in the number in the Omni-Tracker.

Pete was extremely surprised to get a late-night call from Slue. And highly embarrassed. There was no way she could not hear the sounds of the Ginger Kang Kangs in the background as he and Clellen were having a totally excellent time at the Dog Shelter. The only thing he was thankful for was the fact that she did not call a few hours earlier while he and Clellen were checked into that sleazy motel over by Telstar.

"Pete! Hi, it's Slue!"

"Oh…hi, Slue. Uh…how's it going?"

"Great, Pete! Wow, I can hardly hear you! Are you at a club? What band is that? I know that song!"

"Oh. Yeah. That's the…ah…Ginger Kang Kangs."

"Wow! That's so funny, Pete! You must be at the Dog Shelter!"

"Yeah, I'm at the Dog Shelter…"

"Guess what, Pete? I'm with Hieronymus and Bruegel and we were supposed to go the Dog Shelter tonight too! We were going to see the Ginger Kang Kangs also!"

"Really?" Pete was beyond embarrassed.

"Yes, Pete. I had nothing to do tonight after you canceled our date. Remember, you canceled on me tonight because you said you had an emergency? I hope it turned out all right—this emergency of yours. I was very worried. Whenever someone says that they have an emergency, you know, it can be worrisome for others. So Hieronymus and Bruegel offered to take me to the Dog Shelter to see the Ginger Kang Kangs because your emergency was stressing me out. But we never made it! We had an emergency of our own!"

"Really?" Pete asked, completely perplexed over what Slue was telling him.

"Yes. A real emergency. Now, Pete, can I please speak to Clellen?"

"Clellen? You want to speak to Clellen? Uh, Clellen who?"

"Now, now, Pete. Don't be coy. I know she's there. I need to speak to Clellen."

"Really?"

"Pete. Just pass your phone to her."

There was a moment where all Slue could hear was noise, shuffling sounds, people's voices, and the loud sound of the band. Then Clellen's unmistakable voice.

"Hello?"

"Hi, is this Clellen?"

"Yes, this is Clellen. Whom do I have the pleasure of *conversating* with?"

"Slue! Remember me?"

"Slue?" The noise in the background appeared to diminish as Clellen obviously took the phone with her to a less noisy part of the club. It was clear she did not remember the name Slue. "Are you from school? Do I know you?"

"Of course you do! I'm the girl with the goggles and the blue hair…"

"Oh! Of course! We met in the rotunda! You're one of the Toppers! You're the friend of Mus!"

"Yes. I'm the friend of Mus…"

"You are so cute and so gorgeous! You know, I almost dyed my hair blue after I saw how hot it looked on you, but then I didn't want anyone to think I was copying you."

"No one would think that, Clellen. You can dye your hair whatever color you want—who cares what anyone thinks. Besides, you already have beautiful hair."

"You think so? I'm always doing things with it, like jelling it up or putting rollers in it."

"It always looks good."

"Thank you so much, Slue! You're so sweet! We should hang out soon!"

"Let's hang out tonight."

"Tonight?"

"Yeah. You're with Pete, right? He has his incredible car, that Pro-kong-90, right?"

"I think that's what his car is. It's really fast. We were in a motel earlier this evening so we could be alone and have some luv-fun and after a few hours of wrapping the rainbow we then remembered that the Ginger Kang Kangs were playing tonight and I looooove the Ginger Kang Kangs but we thought we would be late because the Dog Shelter is pretty far from Telstar, but his car is so fast that we got here in forty minutes!"

"That's amazing."

"Yeah, and Pete is so nice, he's such a honey…"

"I'm sure he is, Clellen."

"You really want to meet up tonight? All of us?"

"Why not? That's why I called you and Pete. I heard about a really cool party tonight out here where we are."

"Where are you?"

"We're on the far side of the Moon."

"Really?"

"Yeah, and there is this place called Joytown 8—it's an abandoned outpost. Some kids from Gagarin University are organizing an all-night dance party there. It's going to be so much fun! You and Pete have to come!"

"Oh, Slue! That is so nice of you to invite us! And Mus is there?"

"Mus is here."

"So it will be like a double date! Me and Pete, you and Mus!"

"Well, I guess so. Except Bruegel is here, too."

"Oh, that Bruegel," Clellen said with an affectionately dismissive tone in her voice. "He's always the odd man out, I suppose."

Hieronymus was amazed at how well Slue arranged it all, but he was reluctant to get any more of his friends involved with his snowballing troubles. He knew full well there was no all night party at the abandoned Joytown 8. None of them were sure anything even remained of what-ever this Joytown 8 may have been. All through Lunar history, hundreds of towns and outposts were created on the far side of the Moon, and the vast majority of them failed. Sometimes they were completely disassembled, but sometimes they remained as empty ruins. Slue was hoping that at least some buildings were left standing. Her plan was to park and hide Bruegel's Pacer, which was quickly running out of fuel, and then, with Pete's Prokong-90, head out deeper into the far side of the Moon till they got to the gigantic library. Once they were there, they would somehow sneak in. Slue would find the law library and get all the proof she needed that prosecutions against One Hundred Percent Lunar people were in fact illegal, that what had happened between Hieronymus and the Earth girl could not be proven, and that she herself deserved to live a life unencumbered by the whims of a paranoid partnership between the government and powerful transportation corporations that snatched people like her away to be cast into the deepest corners of the solar system simply because her eyes are able to see where time bends space and space bends time.

Slue needed the Omni-Tracker to guide them directly into Joytown 8. It was not really a town. The first indications of anything man made were the tall decrepit poles that sprung up across the horizon, as if long ago, over a hundred years ago, a wall of some sort had existed there. The Pacer slowed down. The sky was an even darker purple than before. The visibility was dimmer. It was not nighttime. On the Moon, daytime and nighttime did not really exist. But the further they drove into the far side, the less clear and the more shadowy and ominous the world became. The grass was longer, but in many places flat and matted. The color of the grass was lighter, almost gray. The hills were more extreme. The Earth was nowhere to be seen. Above them, past the clumsy thick artificial atmosphere, was infinity.

"Stop." Hieronymus said it softly, but another strange quality to the far side of the Moon was the amplification of sound. Even whispers seemed incredibly loud.

The Pacer paused at what appeared to be an entrance. A gate. Beyond it, the remains of a paved road overrun with dead weeds. The frame of the gate remained in its foreboding stature, a terrible structure, and its hinges on the ground, covered with a strange ochre-colored silt just like the hundreds of poles that went off in two directions on either side of it.

"What is that?" Hieronymus asked, pointing out a large white spherical object at the foot of the gate. Bruegel drove the Pacer closer, and what it appeared to be was an old plastic ball, about a meter in diameter. It had holes in it, and its interior was a hollow metal wire mesh. From the faded paint of its exterior, it was clear this had been a large eyeball, and many of the wires draped down from the top of the gate, as if this giant eyeball had at one time served as an ornament suspended above the entrance.

"How odd," Slue said. "This must have been a strange town if they had that big floating eyeball hovering over the front gate like that."

"I'm not sure if this was an actual town," Hieronymus said grimly.

Bruegel drove the Pacer farther in the direction of a few abandoned concrete buildings that appeared once they drove past the main gate. These first few buildings were all very uniform—all were constructed on a grid, and they all had the same rectangular shapes, all made from cinderblocks, none had a second floor, and from what the teenagers could see, all the roofs appeared to have been blown off long ago. Every window in every building had been shattered. Thousands of bright white hummingbirds flew in and out of the ruins or crawled on walls or descended into holes on the ground. They populated the ghost town with darting movements and eerie buzzing silence.

"Could this have been an old military base?" Slue whispered, slightly frightened.

"I don't know. There has never been a Lunar military as far as I know. And it does not look old enough to be an ancient Earth base. Perhaps it was a training center for the police? Housing for construction workers when they made the highway?"

"We're almost out of gas..." Bruegel said.

They scanned the surroundings for a structure they could hide the Pacer in. Directly ahead were a number of taller buildings—one of them had been partially caved in, leaving just enough room to put the car away for a few days.

"I'm not too keen on leaving my mother's car here," Bruegel grumbled as they drove toward the ruin.

"We have to," Hieronymus replied. "We won't make it to a gas station, and then you'll really be in trouble. You'll be stuck on the highway. The cops will find it, then find you, and we'll have a repeat of that sweet little scene of a couple of hours ago. We'll find someone who will drive us back with some extra fuel. Do you think your mother will be too upset if she sees you returning without her car?"

Bruegel shrugged his shoulders as he turned the steering wheel.

"She has no idea I even took her car out tonight. She was already passed out when I took the keys from the kitchen cabinet. She never uses it."

They found an old plastic sheet covered in silt and dust and they tossed it over Bruegel's car, which had been safely hidden inside the collapsed building.

The ground crunched below their feet as they walked between the abandoned cinder block buildings. A hundred years of long-ago broken glass. Pebbles everywhere. The sky was a dull purple. Large hummingbirds darted past them, or hovered from safe distances. They were all that same brutal, blank white. Lunar white. The absence of color in their feathers and on their long beaks. Thick and thin cables covered the ground and draped many of the buildings. In one spot, at the corner of a tall building with an enormous antenna, they came upon a sad sight. Tangled among a large cluster of cables lay the mummified corpse of a moon moose, its normally white fur now gray and yellow with lifeless age, its face a strange flattened pulp. It must have wandered into the abandoned town decades ago, got tangled and trapped in the pile of cables, and starved to death.

"This is a dreadful place," Slue said.

But as they walked away from the corpse of the animal, they came upon something even stranger. Parked in front of the large shell of a circular building with a cracked dome for a roof were seven or eight vehicles. Two of them looked like they had been there as long as the moose, for they were covered in silt and dust. The rest sat in their spots as still as stones, but one of them must have just parked there. Its red tail lights were still on.

Strange mumblings sounded from inside the circular building. Human voices, suffering.

chapter thirteen

The first thing that came to their minds was *run*.

But to Slue and Hieronymus, there was a terrible familiarity to the voices they heard moaning.

It was unmistakable.

There must have been another One Hundred Percent Lunar Person inside that building, and whoever it was, they had just shown their eyes to someone.

Then another voice joined in. The usual mumbling, prayer-like chanting, Jesus and Pixie, obscure references to confused childhood imagery, sadness, confusion…

Slue took the Omni-Tracker from her bag and handed it to Bruegel.

"Take this, and run down about three blocks. Hide in that building on the corner, the one with the crack on its side. Keep this machine on because Pete and Clellen are going to be here really soon, and this Omni-Tracker is sending out a signal for them to find us."

"Pete and Clellen?" Bruegel asked with an utterly clueless expression on his face.

"Yes. You don't remember our plan? Pete and Clellen are coming here to pick us up. We thought that there was going to be a party here tonight, but now we have to tell them that it's been moved."

"What are you doing? Where are you and Hieronymus going?"

"We are going to find out what is going on in that building over there. You can't come."

"Why not?"

"Because we think that something is going on in that building that might be dangerous for people with normal eyes. Hieronymus and I don't have normal eyes. That's why we have to wear these goggles. There could be others like us in that building who aren't wearing goggles, and if they look at you in the eye, you can get hurt."

"I thought you were supposed to be *my* date tonight?"

"I *am* your date tonight."

"But you kissed Hieronymus."

"Sometimes that sort of thing happens."

She pressed the Omni-Tracker into Bruegel's hand. Then she kissed him on the cheek. "Run! Run like the wind and wait for us! Wait till Pete and Clellen arrive. We'll be back in a few minutes, but if you see someone other than ourselves leave that building, keep the Omni-Tracker on and meet Pete and Clellen at the highway, go back to Sun King Towers, and never tell anyone what happened tonight!"

Still hiding, they watched the shadowy form of Bruegel as he ran, hopping over cables and crumbling cinder blocks, still wearing his purple suede tuxedo and alligator skin stovetop hat.

They had no idea what to expect. They ran between some parked cars in the lot just before the domed building where the voices were coming from. Judging by the amount of dust on each car, it was easy to see that they had all arrived at different periods of time. *Who would leave their cars here?* Hieronymus wondered. *Here, of all places…*

They approached the front wall of the structure. The door had long ago fallen off, and it lay before the entrance like a cracked plastic doormat. There were no lights inside, but the interior of the building appeared to have enough light from the large dome of its roof, which, on closer observation, was another white translucent plastic formation, not unlike the big, strange eyeball they encountered on the way in.

Inside, they found themselves in a lobby full of shredded couches.

On one wall was a full-sized oil painting of a man in an odd uniform, the sort of which neither Slue nor Hieronymus had ever seen before. It was crooked and dusty. Next to the portrait, embossed into the wall, was an odd sentence: Obscura Camera Projection Techbolsinator.

None of this made any sense to the boy and the girl except that the moaning of the human voices became slightly louder from the building's interior. To Hieronymus, he figured that there must have been at least six or seven people chanting and crying at once.

Then they saw him. A man. Exceptionally skinny. Sitting on the floor right in front of them just under the mysterious words. He looked half-dead, sleep deprived, and drunk. He had a shaggy blond beard and long, filthy hair. He did not look as if he had washed himself in weeks. He wore a light green wool sweater, and his corduroy slacks had holes at the knees. His eyes were so bloodshot that the whites were bright red, and his pupils were extremely dilated. He looked up and smiled when he saw Hieronymus and Slue. Then he began to chant…

Jesus and Pixie, how your hour is bright.
Oh Pixie, Fairy of the Lord, I tunnel in my tracks
through fire, and flood and smashed automobile
He sees the colors of salt and blood
through his eyes, the demon portholes
witness him and his eyes that slay the normal light…

Hieronymus knelt beside him.

"Who are you? What the Hell is this place?"

The bearded man tried to utter a few words, but nothing came out.

"Those voices!" Slue said, also kneeling down close to him. "Are there One Hundred Percent Lunar People here? Has anyone shown you their eyes without their goggles on?"

The strange fellow looked at her for a long time, then laughed while exhaling. He then very slowly brought himself up. He was utterly filthy.

"Follow me," he grinned. "I'm ready for more anyway…"

Slue and Hieronymus cautiously followed him into a dark corridor that curved around the back of the circular building's interior. Then the teenagers gasped as their weary host stepped over three mummified skeletons sprawled out on the floor.

"Don't worry about them…" He grinned as they continued to follow him. "They've been dead for a long time. They were dead when I got here. Sometimes, it is very hard to leave. I'm not even sure I could leave, I love it here so much…"

"You look like you're starving!" Slue declared. "When was the last time you had anything to eat?"

The skinny guy turned and grinned at her.

"Nobody eats here." He smiled.

He pushed open the door to a large circular room where Hieronymus and Slue were confronted with the most unexpected sight they could possibly imagine.

The entire wall of the circular room was covered in the fourth primary color.

On the floor, sitting or lying on thin mattresses, were dozens of people, staring at the forbidden color, their faces in a trance. They were moaning, they were on their knees, some were sleeping, and more than a few were obviously dead.

The odor was beyond repugnant. Rot. Sweat. Decomposition. Feces. Urine. Some of these people were as emaciated as the bearded one, and others appeared to have just arrived.

The sound was deafening and horrifying. They mumbled incoherently, and they were all staring at the walls surrounding them, all looking into the incomprehensible pigment that their minds refused to accept.

Where did they get this color? wondered Hieronymus. *Did someone manage to find it in pigment form? Perhaps on another planet?*

He walked up to investigate and discovered the true horror of it all. And then he understood what Joytown 8 must have been. And its secret, awful place in history. And why some people flock to it…

He grabbed Slue by the hand.

"We have to go," he shouted. "NOW!" Slue, stunned by the scene around them herself, broke free from his hand and went to look at the wall up close, and once she realized what the entire wall was made from, that it was not paint, but a gruesome mosaic, preserved under a clear protective varnish, she covered her face in her hands and screamed, her voice just another of the hysterical human chorus that ebbed and flowed from that awful, awful place.

Hieronymus fell into a pile of glass that must have shattered over a century ago. Luckily, he did not cut himself as the cracked edges of the broken shards had been dulled by time and the elements. Slue grabbed him by the elbow and pulled him up, and within seconds they were blindly running from building to building in Joytown 8. Hummingbirds flew next to them and crisscrossed just before them like strange, silent phantoms. The complicated dead cityscape unfolded before their terrified eyes. It was an endless jungle of concrete and wires and broken and bashed electrical parts. And junk—machinery that made no sense to them. Rubber objects tossed about. The farther they ran, the more they felt trapped and suffocated. They were trying to find Bruegel, but they were not sure which direction they had charged into as they left the horrible domed building.

They passed through one caved-in structure. They guessed it must have been a guardhouse of some sort, because there appeared to be old and crude weapons on the concrete floor, along with a strange metal bowl that Hieronymus deducted must have been an ancient helmet. They were not anxious to stay and examine anything. The entire complex was unbearably sinister. There was nothing written. No letters, no typography. If there had at one time been words printed in ink on the walls, they had long since vanished. If the people from those days used paper to write information on, that was gone as well. The only thing remaining was that circular wall of fourth primary color—preserved, and now an illegal and forgotten attraction for a very special group of thrillseekers—or addicts.

"Bruegel!" Hieronymus shouted, suddenly panicking. "Bruegel! Where are you?"

All he heard was the echo of his own voice.

He shouted his friend's name again, and from another concrete ruin of a building a line of gigantic hummingbirds swarmed from one of the collapsed windows. They avoided the strange swarm of fluttering creatures, and ducked into an alley where they viewed, on an avenue, a herd of white-furred moose all heading in the same direction on the boulevard. The beasts were moving below a gigantic radar dish that hung suspended between two brick towers—long ago it must have fallen into this position when its own structure began to crumble.

In the alley, they found an open doorway and ducked inside. The herd of moose continued to pass on the outside avenue, all of them making strange, deep bellows with their open mouths. Exhausted and frightened, Slue and Hieronymus sat on the concrete floor against a metallic wall. In the center of the floor was a drain. There were endless lines of old pipe running across and hanging from the ceiling, all of it covered in a strange copper-and-tan crystallized silt. Some formations were so old stalactites formed out of it and hung down among the ancient plumbing.

They were cold, and Slue began to shiver under her velvet poncho. Hieronymus put his arm around her. He was cold as well.

"This place…" she said, staring at the drain. "You know what this place is…"

He nodded.

He had an idea when they first passed that dilapidated gate with the ancient eyeball. This was never a town. This was, at one time, a true horror.

How long could humanity live on the Moon and remain human? There was no percentage below One Hundred. Either you were human or you were something else entirely. The Moon was a stone in space. The air they breathed was artificial. The water they drank came from melted comets.

She dyed her hair blue.

The endless clacking of a thousand moose hooves continued just outside. Then two or three of the gigantic animals sauntered into the alleyway from where they entered, one poking his head into the room where the two teenagers sat huddled on the floor. It casually walked inside, wandered over to the drain in the middle of the floor, bent down, and with an incredibly long snakelike tongue, began to lick the interior of the drain.

"What the Hell is it doing?" Hieronymus asked in an urgent half-whisper.

"Shut up!" hissed Slue.

The beast looked up and stared at the two directly in the eye. Its eyes were a bland pink. Its teeth were crooked, and its lips were coated in a strange green material. A large black beetle crawled on its side, disappearing into its fur, reappearing, disappearing again.

The staring contest did not last very long—after a few seconds, the creature went back to licking whatever moist horrors it could find in the drain. Its tongue was wet. Awful. Its hooves were huge, caked with unknown matter accumulated from a lifetime of wandering around the far side of the Moon.

The teenagers held each other tight, and somewhere under the poncho, one of his hands met one of her hands and their fingers intertwined in a way that only frightened lovers' could.

The moose looked up again as seven or eight huge hummingbirds entered the chamber, flying in circles. The white-furred beast let out a strange howl, jumped up on its hind legs, and tried to bite the fast birds. They flew through the doorway and the mammal followed in confused, shadowy pursuit, barking and howling.

Their hands stayed together.

There was a loud and hollow echo of metal on metal that rang throughout the avenue. Outside, the fallen radar dish must have shifted.

More hummingbirds entered, and some perched up on the pipes that ran across the ceiling, while others just hovered, staring at the lost teenagers. Three or four landed on the floor, then disappeared down the same drain where the moose had just stuck his long tongue.

Do you remember the last time we worked together in school?
The rotunda? We were working on The Random Treewolf.
You started to tell me something.
What did I tell you?
About something that happened on the Moon ninety-four years ago.
I wanted to speak about the Regime of Blindness. But you didn't want to listen...
Do you think that this is one of those camps?
Yes.

I thought so, too. The remains of the gate. The big eyeball…

Anyone like us, they would round up. They would do unspeakable things to us. That wall…you know what that wall was made of…

That time, you began to tell me something else.

What else did I begin to tell you?

The reason I am called a One Hundred Percent Lunar Boy. The reason why you are called a One Hundred Percent Lunar Girl.

It's an old expression from former times. Back then, a person was labeled as being either One Hundred Percent Lunar, or One Hundred Percent Human. There was no in-between.

A strange silence had descended. The moose had all left the area, but the hummingbirds remained. Only the sounds of the creaking ancient antennas and broken radar dishes in the wind could be heard over the refined buzzing of the floating birds' swifting wings.

They were alone on the far side of the Moon. They were alone. Alone. Far away from everyone. Not a trace of neon light. No authorities. Just them, hiding in shadows.

"We won't die," she said to him, both of their hearts beating so uncontrollably.

"And even if we do…" He smiled.

With only inches separating their faces, they took off their goggles and looked at each other.

An outstanding thing happened. The hummingbirds all launched into the air with an excited vigor and suddenly, as if by clarion call, hundreds more swarmed into the room with an inexplicable urgency, empowered. They came in through the open windows where the glass had long vanished. They crawled out of the drain on the floor. They emerged from pipes. They squeezed in through cracks on the walls, filling the room with the fluttering of thousands of feathers, no longer white, as these birds were suddenly triumphant in their natural lunar color, the fourth primary color. They swarmed around the boy and the girl, astonished, on the concrete floor, eyes to eyes, a cloud of hummingbirds, a cloud of hummingbirds enveloping them. Filling the void, these hovering beasts matched their eye color, birds of the fourth primary color electrically shifting the cavernous room from empty ruin to palace of bright splendid forbidden hue. They transformed and they arrived by the thousands, all at once, from all corners, to create a sphere around the two, a moving sphere of fast moving birds glowing and pulsating as the fourth primary color. Huge birds, pointed beaks, hovering, forming an orb that breaks free of the obscure, the resplendent glowing announcement to all eyes that this fourth primary color cannot be hidden nor diluted nor outlawed, that it exists loudly as the Moon's color of all things lunar. Where blank white once lay as a non-pigment, it arises on the wings of magnificent hummingbirds answering the call of the lovers' long suppressed eyes.

Surrounded by thousands of swarming birds, bathed in their nameless color, everything felt truly normal for the boy and the girl. For the first time in their lives, they were each able to look at another person, directly, no goggles, no consequence, no drama. It was normal. *Your eyes are beautiful* he told her, and she laughed, the blue-haired girl. *You know what?* she replied *your eyes are beautiful too* and she reached forward and touched the side of his face, and he did the same, his fingertips tracing the surface of her cheek. *I have never looked another person in the eyes like this before.* It was true. It was remarkable. They could have looked away, they could have seen the future and past projections of their own selves, objects, the bending of time with space, they could have looked up into the wondrous void of the infinity, but they wanted only to look at each other. The normal wonderfulness of a young man and a young woman looking at each other. The light of the purple sky, the cold murky concrete floor, the dark sinister walls, all comprised of blue, yellow, red, all obscured now by the true lunar color, vivid in the feathers of a thousand hummingbirds and their own eyes before them, meshed together to make their world normal. Normal. *You look so different,* he said, smiling at her. *You look like a girl from the countryside. I don't even notice that you have blue hair.* She laughed. *You look different too, for the first time, you don't look uptight. I can't believe how not-uptight you are!*

They continued with these revelations until they had nothing left to say. Then at last they kissed, and that too was a completely normal and wonderful thing to do.

chapter fourteen

They heard the sound of a car. The hummingbirds around them pointed their beaks in the direction of the mechanical hum. Then they dispersed as quickly as they came. They returned to their blank-white, colorless selves as soon as the teenagers stopped looking at each other. The birds all fled, like bats from a cave. And they feared the reverberation of the human industrial machine. It got louder. A deep, purring engine, humming along with the crackle of glass and pebbles getting crushed under a large tire.

Hieronymus and Slue got up from the concrete floor and ran over to the square hole in the wall that at one time had held a window.

Pete's Prokong-90 was cautiously moving up the boulevard.

They saw Pete in the driver's seat, Clellen right next to him, and Bruegel in the back. And as they did not wear their goggles, they also saw the projection of the car continuing farther, themselves entering the car, then the vehicle driving in a straight line under the collapsed radar and out of sight.

"It appears that it is our fate that we should run out and meet them…" Hieronymus said, putting his goggles back on.

"Wait," Slue said, a genuine sadness in her voice. "Let me look at you one last time before you do that."

—

Pete and Clellen could not figure out just what kind of a place they had driven into, and to them, Bruegel's explanation made no sense at all. When they finally discovered Slue and Hieronymus running out from the building they were hiding in, they were, of course, relieved, and for a few moments, Pete was utterly embarrassed, till he saw that they were holding hands. Clellen was overjoyed to see her friend Hieronymus, and she giggled and turned to Pete, exclaiming, "See! I told you! They *are* together!"

Pete was a little confused about all of this. For weeks he was dating Slue. Then he met Clellen and decided to cheat on Slue for some action with this…more adventurous…young lady. He did not exactly intend for Clellen to automatically become his girlfriend, but, in the space of a few hours, he managed to get light-years with her as opposed to the admittedly boring time he spent with Slue. Clellen was up for going to a motel *right away!* With Slue, such a fun subject like that never even came up. Slue was, despite being really good looking, a snob. She was not a good kisser either, and the goggles thing got tiresome after a while. Clellen, on the other hand—hot, good looking, hilariously funny, liked sports (or at least she claimed she did), and best of all, *she did it*—well, he had never known anyone who *did it* like her before.

Bruegel remained quiet as he sat in the back. He too saw Hieronymus and Slue approach the car holding hands. All he could do was quietly sulk. He liked Clellen, but she chose Pete. He liked Slue, but alas, she chose Hieronymus. He knew for a fact that Clellen had made out with Hieronymus, and that Pete had dated, and thus probably kissed, Slue. Another night where the other guys get all the girls. *The girls I like don't like me.* He pondered at the injustice of it all. *And the girls I don't like, they like me.*

Hieronymus opened the door and slid into the back seat of the vehicle next to Bruegel. Slue followed, sat next to Hieronymus, and closed the door after herself.

"Well." The One Hundred Percent Lunar Boy grinned. "Here we all are…"

"So, Mus…" Clellen smiled as she turned from her position in the front passenger seat, her winning smile hiding the utter madness that navigated every moment of her life. "What about this party! Slue-Blue told me about this amazing party, but Bruegel has just informed us that the party was moved?"

Slue was about to answer when, at that moment, the Prokong-90 turned a corner, and they suddenly found themselves on an avenue they had been on before. Straight up ahead was the terrible domed building. The number of cars parked outside caught Pete's attention.

"Hey! That must be the party you guys were talking about!"

"NO!" Slue shouted. "Pete! Turn around! Don't go there! Don't go there!"

But Pete just glanced at Slue for a quick, grinning second. "I don't know," he declared, heading directly for the building with the wall inside. "If Slue thinks we should stay away, that can only mean that it must be FUN!"

Hieronymus leaned forward to Pete.

"Listen, man, you don't even want to go *near* that place. It's not a party."

As they drove closer, Hieronymus and Slue realized yet another car had arrived a short time earlier and parked very close to the entrance. There were three men in their early twenties who were busy with a rope—one fellow had tied it around his waist and the other end of the line was attached to the car. He was walking toward the entrance and his comrades were uncoiling the rope.

Pete drove right up to them.

"Hey!" he called out from his window. "What's up? What are you guys doing?"

They looked up at him with worried expressions.

"Are you a cop?" one of them called.

"Do I look like a cop?"

They exchanged glances, their eyes wide with nervousness. Then Pete continued before they could answer.

"Look, I'm not a cop, okay? I'm still in high school for crying out loud. What's going on—is there a party in there?"

"Pete!" insisted Hieronymus. "I told you, it's not a party!"

"What's with the rope?" Pete then added.

"We need it. We can only go in one at a time. After twenty minutes, we pull the other out, and then another one of us gets to go in."

Pete laughed. "What's going on in there? You need a rope to pull each other out? Don't tell me—it's an orgy!"

"No, no, nothing like that!" one of the fellows insisted.

Slue leaned forward. "Pete! We have to get out of here!"

Then Clellen leaned forward.

"Did you just say there was an orgy in there?" she asked with an odd sort of spark.

Before Pete could answer, he sniffed the air.

"Ugh! What is that rank odor?"

The stumbling figure of a nineteen-year-old girl emerged. Like the bearded fellow they had encountered earlier, she looked and smelled like she had not bathed in weeks. She wore a disheveled paisley dress. Her dark hair was hopelessly matted into large filthy clumps. One of her stockings was ripped all the way down to her ankle. She wandered right up to Pete as he poked his head from the car window, her eyes extraordinarily bloodshot. For the first time, the athletic teenager heard the moaning and bizarre chanting from the domed building. The filthy girl pressed herself against his car.

"Hey!" the healthy tellball player exclaimed as he rolled up his window. "Don't touch my car!"

"Obscura Camera Projection Techbolsinator!" the girl exclaimed with a parched voice.

Pete stepped on the gas pedal and the vehicle began to go forward, but Slue reached forward and touched his shoulder.

"Wait. Don't go yet."

"That weird girl outside touched my car!" complained Pete, who stopped the vehicle nevertheless. The mysterious girl with the bloodshot eyes caught up to them and pressed her face to the glass. Clellen laughed, then said mockingly to her fellow Loopie, "Bruegel! Your girlfriend is here!"

"Shut that rat cage you call a mouth, Clellen!"

Hieronymus reached forward and faced Clellen just inches from her nose, mouthing the words *Don't don't don't…let it ride, don't answer.* And while Clellen fumed, Slue leaned over to speak to Bruegel, who was quietly brooding.

"Bruegel, do you have the Omni-Tracker I gave you earlier?"

He nodded, reaching into his pocket and handed her the instrument.

Without explaining anything to anyone, Slue quickly exclaimed, "I'll be right back!" and opened the door and jumped out.

"Slue!" Hieronymus shouted as he watched her jump over discarded cables and piles of junk, carrying the Omni-Tracker, running past the boys with the rope, running right back into the entrance of the domed building.

"Would someone please explain to me," Pete, who was utterly confused, shouted, "just what the Pixie Hades is going on!?"

Hieronymus didn't answer, all he said was "Wait!" as he too jumped out and ran directly toward the terrible domed building.

One of the young men who was preparing the rope so his friend could go inside without getting trapped, realized Hieronymus was wearing goggles.

"Hey! Look! It's a One Hundred Percenter!" one of them shouted. They automatically blocked his way.

"Show us your eyes!" they immediately demanded.

"There's plenty of this eye color where you're going," he answered.

They paused, and then just nodded to each other. "True," one of them simply remarked. Then the fellow who had the rope attached to him came up with a bold proposal.

"How would you like to make some money?"

"Guys, in case you haven't noticed, I'm not here to hang out. I know what's in there, and the only reason I'm even standing here talking to you is because you are in my way, and I have to get my friend, who just disappeared into that hellhole you three seem so eager to visit."

"Yeah, but you have LOS—that color in there won't have any effect on you. You can be our guide. You bring us in, make sure we have a nice place to sit, then bring us out so we don't get all caught up in it all and starve to death. We'll pay you."

"There are dead people in there!" Hieronymus shouted. "The place smells! And that color! You shouldn't even be looking at it! Don't you know what it does to your head?"

One of them smiled.

"Oh, we know. We've been here before."

"You're crazy! You spend enough time in there and you will destroy yourselves!"

"That's why we have this rope, man."

"You are a complete fool! You're willing to mess up your head just so you can have a cheap thrill like this?"

"Dude, you are so wrong," the fellow who stood in the middle of the three added.

"Wrong?" exclaimed Hieronymus.

"Wrong. We are not here for any kind of cheap thrill. We are here to experience truth. Just because we cannot comprehend the fourth primary color does not mean it can't exist."

"You're right about that. It exists. But you shouldn't mess with it, either."

"We are not messing with anything. That color exists in nature—your eyes prove that. We have the right to experience it just as much as it is your right to live your life without having your eyes covered by goggles!"

"Fellas, I would love to get into a discussion with you on this matter, but you don't understand—"

"You are the one who does not understand. Your eyes and your mind accept this color, so you miss out on the incomparable experience that we have when we see it."

"I have to go. I don't know what happened to my friend. My other friends are waiting back there in the car."

But the three young men continued to block his path. Hieronymus noticed that one of them wore a sweatshirt that had Sea of Nectar State University spelled out in big letters.

"Suppose I were to tell you that if you were to go into that room, you would experience something incomprehensible, something like death, for example," the man said.

"Death?"

"Death."

"There are dead people in there already. Why don't you ask them?"

"What if, in that room, the incomprehensible spectre of death could be experienced for a temporary moment. Would you not be curious?"

"That's a false and morbid and stupid comparison. Now get out of my way."

"I only say death because it's impossible to imagine. It's the opposite of consciousness. The fourth primary color exists because you say it does, and the government says it does not. When we look at it, we see it for a brief and strange moment, but then our minds push it away, like a forgotten dream. That's why there are all those silly stories about Jesus and Pixie and how it is the Devil's color, but in reality, our mind is simply comprehending the abyss of truth, and in that moment, the truth of physical reality far surpasses our own means to comprehend it."

Hieronymus looked at the young man's sweatshirt. Of course it made sense. These fellows were all students at the Moon's most notorious party school.

"Is that what you study at Sea of Nectar State University?"

"Not officially. The three of us are philosophy students."

"Oh. And is this your homework assignment?"

"No, but our professor told us about this place."

"Yeah, well he sounds like an irresponsible kazzer-bat. There are dead people in there."

"Don't knock SONSU. Gordon Chazkoffer, one of greatest philosophers ever, wrote *The Perceptive Analysis of Social Mercantile Transgression* when he was a graduate student there."

"Right. A hundred years ago. When it was a good place. Now it's nothing more than a beer distributor's wet dream. Look at you guys. You're just a bunch of stoners."

"Do you know that we have an original edition of *The Perceptive Analysis* in the philosophy department?"

"Sweet. Ask me if I care. I read it last year. It's a wonderful book, but there is nothing in it that says you should tie a rope around yourself and go into a room full of half-dead people so you can blow your mind on a color you should not even look at."

"The original edition has three missing chapters—all of which go into great detail on the fourth primary color."

Their conversation was suddenly interrupted by the loud honking of the Prokong-90's horn. Pete was getting impatient. Slue was taking forever, and the three students just told Hieronymus something unbelievable.

He looked at the boys with the rope.

"What did you say?"

"We have an original edition of *The Perceptive Analysis of Social Mercantile Transgression*. It has the three missing chapters that put Gordon Chazkoffer in jail. It's the only published analysis on the fourth primary color. Of course, it was banned."

This was new. Hieronymus paused.

These college stoners. Losers. Could they be serious?

"What does he write about?"

"He talks about what happens to a human being who sees the fourth primary color in a controlled way—how exposure to it in short intervals, over a long period of time, can lead to the most profound intellectual enlightenment."

"Intellectual enlightenment? By looking at a color?"

"You see? Already you don't understand. But it's real. The mind shuts down. It reboots. And you come out different. You are better. You are sharper. The greatest philosopher of the last century did it. Short intervals over a long period of time. It changes you."

Hieronymus did not know what to make of these guys. They looked like enlightened barrelheads. Or barrelheads who just got too lazy to play tellball. But philosophy students? They stood there outside the most horrific place on the Moon, trying to figure out a way to go inside as if they were mountain climbers preparing to descend into a live volcano. Three guys with a rope long enough to hang themselves if they decided to travel to the very bowels of Hell itself.

*   *   *

Seconds later, Slue emerged from the building, running. She brushed past the rope holders, took Hieronymus' hand, and led him back to Pete's Prokong-90, whose engine was still idling in that perfect humming kind of way.

The girl with the matted hair sat on a bundle of cables, saying that strange word again over and over, *techbolsinator, techbolsinator, techbolsinator…*

They climbed back inside, and the Prokong-90 began to move.

"Drug addicts," Pete sighed. "Disgusting!"

"That must be a real Buzz parlor," Clellen commented in a strangely neutral voice, as if she could not decide whether it was a good thing or not. "That girl looked like she was flying on a refrigerated popsicle of three-tone S-Jam, or maybe she just looped her veins in a knot of Kip-Kap. Sledgehammer chozen-burr, those boys with the ropes were prepping on a disskener cycle kan from the seven ache. What do you think, Bruegel?"

Bruegel appeared to be so depressed that he only looked up and shrugged while Pete gave Clellen a slightly wary glance. He was a little uncomfortable with Clellen's sudden knowledge of drug terms that were so alien to him.

But only the One Hundred Percent Lunar kids in the car knew that all that activity at the domed building had nothing to do with drugs.

"What did you do?" Hieronymus quietly asked Slue as the vehicle sped up an abandoned avenue, away from the horrible domed building.

"I took the Omni-Tracker in there, pressed the special alert button for the police, and I left it in the center of that room."

"Why did you do that?"

"Why? Are you as insane as those guys with the rope? That place has to be destroyed. All those people walk in there and half of them starve to death because they can't figure how to walk out. I think this is a matter for the police…"

But Hieronymus did not pay much attention. He was thinking about what those fellows had told him. The desire they, and many others, had to see the incomprehensible. Then it occurred to him: Of course that was why, from time to time, a One Hundred Percenter was murdered and their eyes stolen. The need to experience that color was so enormous that some people resort to murder to see it. Or, like the fellows with the rope, they're willing to put their own lives at risk. Three missing chapters from one of the greatest philosophical texts—that explained what happened if a normal person saw that color in a *controlled* way. Such mad curiosity, he thought he could not imagine—but in fact, when he considered his own indulgence with the Earth girl, and the highly illegal thing he just did with Slue, it became clear that these same curiosities were what the authorities wanted suppressed at all costs…

—

They sped past the decrepit poles that had, at one time, formed a pe-
rimeter around Joytown 8, and after a bumpy ride over a grassy plain,
the lone highway on the far side of the Moon appeared—Highway Zero.
Within moments, they were on it, a dark, winding four-lane pavement
with only periodic lamps upon tall metal towers every half kilometer.
There was no speed limit on the far side of the Moon. Pete stepped
on the gas pedal. The strange countryside passed them by, and directly
above, Hieronymus noticed there was a comet, a bright fat slash in the
evening sky, hanging just under the dark purple abyss.

Slue continued to tell half-truths to Pete and Clellen.

"How did you three get all the way out here?" Pete asked, keeping
his eyes on the road ahead of him.

"Bruegel drove us in his mom's Pacer," Slue answered.

Clellen laughed out loud.

"Bruegel, you don't even have a license! And that Pacer! I can't
imagine that thing even rolling up the street!"

"It's actually a wonderful car!" Slue lied. "And Bruegel is an excellent driver. Unfortunately, the fuel station we had planned to go to was
closed, so we had to park it in Joytown 8. We'll come back during the
week with some fuel and pick it up."

Completely uninterested in Bruegel's plight, Clellen changed the
subject to something she was far more curious about.

"So," she grinned, "You and Mus? Are you and Mus…?"

"Mus and I," Slue began, a thin smile spreading across her face,
"have invited you, and Pete, to *another* incredible party tonight!"

Pete glanced back for a quick second.

"I hope this next party is better than that smelly drug thing we almost went to just now," he said with some dismay. "We missed the last
two songs of the Ginger Kang Kangs for that!"

"That was not the actual party, *Peter*," Slue continued, purposefully
calling him Peter because she knew he hated it. "The real party was
moved to a huge underground library that's farther up the highway.
It was supposed to be in that strange domed building, but my friends
from Gagarin University who are holding the party had to move it at
the last minute because all of those drug addicts got to the site first

and decided to have a drug party there. That's why I ran back into the building, to get directions from one of the druggies."

"Where is this library?" Pete asked.

"Exit 399. Go on to West Gong Road off Highway Zero. It's just farther up, and at this speed, we'll get there in an hour."

"A library is a weird place for a party, Slue," Pete added.

"Not this library. The books there are made of paper."

"What? Paper? You've got to be kidding!"

"Yeah. Billions of them. But the party itself will be held in a special reception area, and I think the Rapoozles are playing."

"Who are the Rapoozles?" Clellen asked.

"A really great band from Saint Exupéry," she lied, making the whole thing up as she went along. Hieronymus looked at her. *Are you completely insane? There is no party. There is no band called the Rapoozles. They are going to be so pissed off at us once we get there and they see there is no party and we forced them to drive hundreds of kilometers for nothing.*

But Slue was not the least bit worried. She had yet another plan on top of this one, and an even further plan beneath that one. She was prepared to lie and cheat her way into that library if necessary, right to the law section, right to that one page in the code book of Lunar law that would nullify all these illegal proceedings currently chasing Hieronymus Rexaphin to the far side of the Moon, and filling her own future with a terrible expectation of dread, and even worse, defeat.

Hieronymus fell asleep, his head resting against Slue. The purring of the Prokong-90's engine had a very soothing effect on him...

People are not supposed to live here!

Like the Angel of Death who does not understand what death is.

You don't even know what that color is. But you see it. And yet, you don't understand it.

You belong here, on the Moon. A false world. An artificial blight.

If you ask the Angel of Death what death is, he won't be able to answer you.

So I ask you, what is the color you see? You don't know.

It has no name. But it is yours. It is yours.

You know it because you dream in this color.

You are dreaming of it now. Do you have a name, your own name for this color? A secret name?

Whisper it. Whisper it as would an angel who understands the secret of mortality, but cannot explain it to mortals for fear of having his wings torn from his back and placed in an oven…

Hieronymus awoke, snuggled together with Slue, who was also asleep. Bruegel slept against the car door, and Clellen, up front. He stuck his fingers under his goggle lenses to rub his eyes. It was a dream he was familiar with. The same questions, over and over, asked by a voice he had never met. He leaned forward.

"Hi, Pete."

"How's it going, Hieronymus?"

"Good. I fell asleep."

"I know. Everyone fell asleep."

"How long have I been out?"

"Maybe an hour."

"You don't mind driving this far out?"

"Not at all. I've taken this route before. A couple of years ago, my da and I drove from one end of the far side to the other. I like it out here. It's very quiet."

The landscape had changed, and there was less grass and more rocky soil, and the sky was even darker—not as dark as the nighttime on Earth, but almost. The hills on all sides of them were pointy and in some cases even twisted. The comet above had moved to a different place in the sky.

"Oh my…" Pete said, slowing down slightly. "Look at that."

Off to the left, and standing about a hundred meters from the highway, was the distinct figure of a lunar gorilla. It stood erect, just like a man, its long arms hanging down its side. It watched the approaching car with great curiosity.

"Have you ever seen one of those before?" Pete asked Hieronymus.

"Once. When I was a boy. A gorilla was lost and wandered into town. It was very strange, because a lot of people thought it was a man in a gorilla costume. He just walked up the street, looking around. He didn't bother anyone, and nobody bothered him. I was in a park with some friends, we were playing soccer, and the gorilla walked through the middle of the field, and we stopped the game, and one kid insulted him because we also thought that it was a guy in a costume, and the kid was pissed off because the walking gorilla prevented him from scoring. Later, I told my father that there was a man in a gorilla suit who walked through our game, but he told me that in fact that was no man, that was a genuine gorilla who walked all the way from the far side of the Moon and was lost."

As the car passed the mysterious figure, Hieronymus could not help but think that the creature was looking at him, directly in the eye, as if the gorilla knew all about his plight and how much trouble he was in and how much he was endangering all those around him.

"Listen, Pete, I think you should know something. I'm in a lot of trouble. I'm wanted by the police."

Pete glanced over at Hieronymus for a quick second.

"I didn't hear that last part about you being wanted by the police."

"But you heard the part about me being in trouble."

"Yeah, I figured that."

"You should just drop me off here. Take everyone else home."

"We're in the middle of nowhere."

"That's not your problem. But if you keep hanging around with me, I know it, I'm going to drag you down and you're going to end up going to jail."

Pete just laughed.

"I'm not going to jail. That's such a silly thing to think, going to jail. I haven't done anything wrong, and neither have you."

"Oh, I did something wrong. Last night..."

"Let me guess. You showed your eyes to someone."

"How did you know?"

"I didn't know, but what else can a One Hundred Percent Lunar Boy do that would get him in trouble with the police?"

"You're right. Anyway, you should know that we're not really going to a party tonight."

"I figured that."

"You knew?"

"Yeah, Slue is a terrible liar. Clellen believed her, though, which is funny in and of itself. I figured that it must be something really important for her to go to such lengths to get someone to drive her so far into the other side of the Moon. I also feel pretty bad about punking out on her tonight—you know, hooking up with Clellen behind her back and all—but it seems to be okay. I think she likes you a lot more than me, and it's fine, nothing was really happening between me and her anyway. Whenever we'd go out, she would talk about you *a lot*. So it's cool, and besides, what Clellen and I did earlier, at this motel in Telstar, oh man, she is one wild girl…"

"Well, I've known Clellen for a long time," added Hieronymus. "A lot of people misunderstand her. I'm really glad you met her because you and her…sort of compliment each other, in a weird but good kind of way."

"You think so?"

"Yeah. You're like one of the big athletes in school, and she's really one of the most eccentric kids in my class, and, I don't know, it's the kind of thing we always like to imagine…"

"Listen, I'm just curious about something, and you don't have to answer if you don't want to. When we were driving through that ghost town back there, and you and Slue came out of that abandoned building and you were holding hands. And with me it's cool, I think its good and I'm glad. Really glad. But I was wondering, was she seeing the both of us at the same time?"

The highway ahead was empty. The white line was never ending in its faded journey before them. The lights along the side, atop their lonely poles, passed like the solitary stranded sentinels they were.

"No. I kissed her for the first time tonight. And this was after she found out about you and Clellen. We were never both going out with her at the same time."

Then Hieronymus did something that surprised himself. He leaned forward so he was certain that only Pete could hear, despite the fact that the others were sleeping, and in a barely audible whisper said, "I've been in love with Slue since I first met her in the third grade."

Eventually, the others woke up. Bruegel rubbed his eyes, wishing he had brought some beer or vodmoonka or something like that, and then asked out loud, *Where are we going, really? It is so incredibly late. Where are we? What the Hell kind of place is this?* Clellen was adamant that the party they were going to was going to more than make up for the journey out here—it was going to be at a library where they had books made of paper, and Clellen herself was not entirely sure what that meant, but it sounded *way awesome,* and besides, if it got too late, they would just find some place to sleep, maybe a motel. It would be a nice excuse to go to a motel again, and she was sure that out there in the middle of nowhere, a motel would have a lot of rooms, one for her and Pete, one for Slue and Hieronymus, and one for Bruegel, where he could just go off by his mopey self.

Slue did not listen to any of this. She kept quiet and wondered, *Yes, when we get there, how are we going to get in, how are we going to get in, how are we going to get in?*

chapter fifteen

It was a ghastly scene. The first police officers to arrive did not even know Joytown 8 actually existed. When they were told to trace the distress signal on the Omni-Tracker Slue had activated, and when they first came upon the domed building, they could not believe the sight and, most of all, the terrible odor. Like Pete, they too simply thought it was some kind of drug party or bizarre cult event filled to the gills with lunatics. They drew their guns and went inside, walked past the bearded fellow, past the broken rope, past the long-dead mummified corpses, and, following the Omni-Tracker's signal and the inexplicable human sounds, entered the circular room.

Three separate squads were dispatched to the location of the Omni-Tracker. All three disappeared.

Naturally, this chain of events sent alerts up and down the communication structure of the police that something very bizarre had happened in some long forgotten corner over on the far side.

Lieutenant Dogumanhed Schmet had gone to bed. He was immensely pleased with himself. There was something so deeply satisfying about a hunch that reveals itself as truth. That is why he was an excellent detective. A small tickle in the back of the brain. A microscopic idea floats up. It is normal for a father to tell a lie to protect his son. If he had had a son of his own, he would tell a million lies a day to protect him, too, if he had to. But as it turned out, he did not have a son, nor a wife, nor a family—he only had his work as a detective, and part of that lonely existence was to find out who broke the law and who didn't. That man, Ringo Rexaphin, broke the law. You cannot lie to the police. It is a severe crime to do so. His son, Hieronymus Rexaphin, had been identified as the ocular assailant, to use the technical term. And, of course, it was a hunch of his very own that led him to single out this One Hundred Percent Lunar Boy amongst so many others. It started with the way the father had lied. All lies are apparent to anyone who knows what a lie really is, and Lieutenant Schmet could feel them. Like a feather tickling the top of his spinal chord, just under the skull. A guilty fabrication. That boy was the one who had gotten away two years ago. If they had locked him up then, he would not be out in the streets, showing those dangerous eyes of his to innocent people. Clearly, the young man was a genuine menace, and now he was on the run.

Where is your son?

I don't know.

Where is your son?

I told you, I have no idea.

Give me the names of all your son's friends.

I don't know who his friends are.

Some father you are.

Are you here to insult me?

I am here to find out where your son is.

Well, I don't know where he is. He left a few hours ago.

He was seen at LEM Zone One, in a hotel lobby, accompanying a girl from Earth who had obviously been negatively affected by exposure to the fourth primary color.

I thought the fourth primary color didn't exist?

You should stop covering for your son. There are two witnesses.

I told you. My son was at home. He was tired. He went to sleep early.

How do you explain my witnesses?

I don't. They are confusing my son with someone else. Or they are lying. Those goggles can make a lot of sixteen-year-old boys look alike.

Where is he now?

I don't know.

Well, I guess you will have to stay here until you decide to cooperate.

I am cooperating. Now let me go home. My wife is a very sick woman. She is unable to take care of herself.

I'm sure she'll be fine. She's an adult. Anyway, we'll let you go as soon as you confess that you have lied to us, and that your son was out all night.

I need to call someone who can go over to our apartment. My wife needs someone to take care of her.

No.

I have the right to call a lawyer.

No, you don't.

Excuse me?

Just kidding. Of course you have that right. We all do. But you need my permission to call a lawyer. As it turns out, I have a lot of administrative work to do right now, so I don't have the time to speak to you any longer. The very second you sign a confession, my administrative duties shall cease, and then I can hear your request regarding phone calls to wives and friends and lawyers.

You are a complete bastard. I will get you into a lot of trouble for this.

You will do nothing of the sort. You will wait. You will worry about your wife. Eventually, you will resent your son for putting you into this predicament. Then you will sign the confession that I have drafted for you. In this confession, you will state that you knew full well that your son, Hieronymus Rexaphin, was at LEM Zone One during the evening I have specified and that you have lied to authorities to cover up for your son's illegal activities. This confession will also make it clear that you or your family were under no threats from me and that you signed it under your own free will.

Lieutenant, you are a very strange-looking man. Has anyone ever told you that your face looks like it's made out of waxy plastic? It's as if you were just a doll, a badly manufactured doll. Just looking at you, I can't help but wonder—if someone were to slice your head in half, would it be a solid mass of the same strange material that all those beads of sweat run across?

—

That night, Lieutenant Schmet was certain Hieronymus Rexaphin would turn up somewhere. Probably by morning, the boy would be spotted sneaking out of a friend's house, or would get stuck anywhere he needed to show his identification, or he would be found sleeping in a car. The girl from Earth was still in her cell, and she told him nothing because he asked her nothing. She knew the boy's name, but he refused to ask her. She only mentioned the Ferris wheel as their rendezvous point by accident, and that was before she realized the boy was still a fugitive. The lieutenant decided to post extra agents in the amusement park at LEM Zone One just in case the kid decided to return to the scene of the crime, which they often did, for inexplicable reasons. Of course, the biggest expectation was for Hieronymus to go home and see to his crazy mother, especially once he got wind of the fact that his father was gone. Schmet figured that the One Hundred Percent Lunar Boy would last about five minutes at home before twenty squads showed up to arrest him. And that would be that.

He left instructions with several police department jurisdictions to alert him if anything unusual were to happen during the night that might have to do with lunarcroptic ocular symbolanosis. He slept well, but he had the usual horrible dream about an unfortunate event that happened to him as a boy. He woke up in a furious sweat, and then he calmed down. He sat up. He looked for his medication. He closed his eye. The image of her slapping on the glass, trying to get away from the fire, and he shook his head as if sad thoughts could be cast away from his mind like sand from a shovel. Mathematically, it was impossible to make sense of it, but at least once an hour for his entire life he would ponder why they were there at that particular time. *If only we had left five minutes later…*

He bowed his head. He had a strange, inexplicable desire in his fervent post-nightmare state to rush to the door of her cell and make sure she was all right and curl up on the floor just outside her room, like a sleeping guard dog, protecting her from the unpredictability of the horrible accidents conjured in his mind. But as his senses returned, he realized, alas, she was not Selene.

In the small table next to his bed, he had a small square box. About two inches square, it was made of brushed aluminum. Sometimes he secretly carried it with him. He never dared show it to anyone, and it had been a terribly long time since he opened it himself. But he kept it as a reminder—all tragedies could be avoided. All fires need not ignite. All routes have their detours. And memories are tattoos that haunt the unfortunate with images of what could have been.

And then they called. It was not about the boy, Hieronymus Rexaphin.

When he arrived in Joytown 8, he found the abandoned buildings swarming with an army of police, all of them keeping a distance from the domed building, which they had surrounded. He shook his head at their clumsiness. Accompanying him was the slim and completely silver figure of a rescue robot—Belwin, on permanent loan from his friend in the Lunar Fire Command. The robot, despite the fact that it had no face at all, spoke in a very elegant manner and walked as gracefully as a deer in a field.

"So, Belwin," Detective Schmet said. "Once more, this is not a normal fire rescue mission."

"I understand that, Lieutenant."

"You are familiar with the phenomena of lunarcroptic ocular symbol-anosis?"

"I am, now that I have uploaded the files you have sent me."

"You understand, of course, that this fourth primary eye color will have no effect on you?"

"How could it? I am not a living thing. I don't even have eyes, and even if I did, what good are eyes to a robot if there is no consciousness to perceive meaning out of a visual field?"

"True, Belwin. Very true. Indeed, I borrowed you tonight because I have a feeling this event has a lot to do with the fourth primary color."

"I am at your service, Lieutenant Schmet."

They arrived at a makeshift command barricade in an old run-down garage directly opposite the domed building and its parking lot of forgotten cars. There were police officers everywhere, but none could be seen out in the open. Captain Wiis Begflendopple was organizing squads of riot police with helmets and shields and rifles poking in every direction. He was a stout man with a long and large red handlebar moustache. He was dressed in a thick padded police SWAT uniform. As soon as he saw Lieutenant Schmet, his eyes lit up.

"Ah! Dogumanhed! I am so happy you have come! And just in time. We are getting ready to storm that building over there."

"Which one?"

The captain pointed with his gloved hand

"The big one with the dome. That is where they are hiding."

"Who?"

"Renegade drug dealing goggle-freaks, that's who!"

"You think there is a group of people with lunarcroptic ocular sym-bolanosis in there? You are certain of this?"

"Am I certain? Listen to this…"

The captain picked up a small silver object—a police radio—and increased the volume. It was the unmistakable sound of people lost in the trance of exposure to the fourth primary eye color. Lieutenant Schmet had never heard so many voices making that particular type of moan all at the same time.

"We lost another two-man squad just under an hour ago. That makes eight. Eight police officers assaulted by those lunatics with their insane eye color!"

"Explain to me what happened," Schmet said to the nervous captain.

"Well, as you know, we received a report that a missing Omni-Tracker was giving out a distress signal. We sent out a normal squad of two officers to investigate. They came to the scene, they reported that there was an abandoned 'town,' or former base of some kind—"

"It was an Ocular Internment Camp," Schmet, who was well aware of this place's history, interrupted.

"Whatever," Captain Begflendopple continued. "As the officers ar-rived, they noticed several people milling about the outside. College students, drifters, drug addicts, homeless, the usual riffraff that decide to form squat parties. The officers were surprised that anyone would travel this far over to the far side of the Moon when there were already enough abandoned buildings in our urban areas. As they entered the building, they reported seeing corpses. Then a few moments later, nothing. Just the sounds of what you hear on their radio."

Detective Schmet watched more of the clumsily dressed police

officers arrive and take positions in the concrete shells of all the dilapidated buildings in the area. These guys were amateurs. They couldn't
give a damn—they'd rather be off doing traffic duty somewhere or sitting in a cozy office down in Glennville. To them, this was a sort of
game, and they had no idea, *no idea*, what they had just stumbled upon!

What a big mess, and in more ways than one. All these camps were
supposed to have been completely razed to the ground—how could
this one have survived? Did some bureaucrat eighty-five years ago just
forget to cover up his tracks? Perhaps they thought no one would be
able to figure out what Joytown 8 was. This police captain here certainly did not, nor did the officers who went into what was most certainly a genuine Obscura Camera Projection Techbolsinator. Their idea
that there were One Hundred Percent Lunar People hiding out in that
building was absurd—anyone with the fourth primary color in their
eyes would have fled long ago. Only a real Techbolsinator, left over from
the Regime of Courage, could affect so many people like that. If only
he could pry off a piece of it—or even better, take possession of that
whole building. But how could he? Even he would be susceptible to the
color of its wall inside. Still, there had to be a way.

The captain continued, but Lieutenant Schmet was only half listening, the sweat rolling down his face as he contemplated the enormous power that sat in the building across the parking lot.

"Naturally, whenever a squad disappears like that, another is automatically assigned to follow up. In this case, two more pairs of officers
were swallowed up by whatever is going on in that building. So, more
of us came in and surrounded the place. Once it was clear that a large
police presence was in the area, all the riffraff that were milling about
went inside. We sent in two more officers to negotiate with the terrorists, but they too disappeared."

"There are no terrorists inside there," commented Schmet with a
certitude the captain found a little off-putting.

"No? Well then what do you suppose had happened to my men?"

"They are fine for now. Most likely, they are having a reaction to the
fourth primary color."

"I think they are hostages who need to be rescued."

"No one is being held hostage."

"Really? Well, in about ten minutes, we are going to storm that building. There are already dead people in there, and the smell—did you get a whiff of it?"

Dogumanhed Schmet did not answer, as he had lost his own sense of smell many years ago.

"Captain, if you go in there with your guns blazing, you will only accomplish two things. You will accidentally kill innocent people. And the officers that you send in there will all succumb to whatever is paralyzing the other officers. You will be in the exact same predicament you find yourself in right now, only worse."

It did not take very much for Detective Schmet to convince the captain and the other police brass around him to try his own plan, which was incredibly simple. Let Belwin the robot go in there first and report back. As no one, even the SWAT team, nor the fifty or so other police officers who had been dragged from their comfortable beds to provide back up in this perplexing situation were in any way enthusiastic about storming the old domed building, it appeared to be a logical solution. Everyone just wanted to go home. And to go back to bed.

The detective and the robot walked across the parking lot, past the cars that had been parked there for months, and others more recently left. One car had a rope tied to it leading directly into the building. They climbed up the three or four steps, then entered into the disheveled lobby with the shredded furniture. Dogumanhed Schmet stopped before the old deteriorating painting.

"Wilson MacToolie," he uttered, recognizing the portrait.

"Sir?" Belwin asked.

"Oh, nothing. That's a portrait of a wonderful man. His name was Wilson MacToolie. He was a political leader who was in charge of a movement known as the Regime of Courage. It happened about ninety years ago. Some misguided people today would call it the Regime of Blindness, but they are wrong. It was a courageous thing to do, to build these places, these camps. You see, Belwin, human beings don't naturally belong on the Moon, but we've forced ourselves to come here, and we forced the Moon to change to accommodate us. As a result, nature itself stepped in and decided to try and change us. This change is manifested in lunarcroptic ocular symbolanosis, but the ones who are born with this condition are completely incompatible with the rest of humanity. They should live separately, and Wilson MacToolie tried to do just that. Either remove their eyesight, or banish them. If someone with LOS has their eyes removed, then they can live with the rest of humanity. If not, then they should be banished, one way or another…"

Belwin studied the unusual face of the lieutenant. Even a machine could tell there was something cruel and inhuman about this man. He turned and walked into the curving hallway. Schmet stayed behind, naturally, and shifted his gaze to the official words carved in the wall.

"Obscura Camera Projection Techbolsinator," he quietly said to himself. "What an extraordinary discovery to find this here!"

In his pocket, his fingers touched the small aluminum box he decided to carry after all. He began to calculate. *Do I tell them about this? Or do I freelance with this? What a dilemma! They would bestow me with such honor if I presented them this discovery! Or, I could use it myself. If the MacToolie Group knew I was keeping this from them, they would throw me out, maybe even kill me. How could I hide it from them, those shadowy bastards, controlling everything behind the scenes. No. I must tell them, but under my conditions…*

He was thrilled—so thrilled that he almost brought the little box out and opened it.

Belwin did what he was manufactured to do. Rescue people. He entered the circular room. What he found were dozens of people on mattresses and on the floor in strange states of euphoric agitation. Some were unconscious, and some were dead. He immediately scanned the DNA, respiratory, circulation, and nervous systems of every person and determined within seconds who needed immediate medical care. He sent a message back to the assembled police officers that several ambulances had to be brought forward to the entrance of the building right away. He also scanned the circular wall surrounding him. The extreme presence of the fourth primary color would make it virtually impossible for any normal human being to enter this chamber, so he requested the assistance of several rescue robots to assist him in safely removing the incapacitated, as well as the deceased, from this den of horror.

The kind robot went to a young woman who lay emaciated on the floor. He sensed she was about to die, so he chose her first, and with the agility of a ballet dancer, he gently picked her up and carried her outside, where a waiting ambulance sat with its lanterns spinning, its medics waiting, its oxygen tanks full, its IV solutions ready, and its antibiotics prepared in clean little packages designed to save as many lives as possible.

While Belwin set about his task, Schmet wandered back to his friend, Captain Wiis Begflendopple, who was happily ordering his officers to return home. Crisis solved—send for more rescue robots, ambulances, coffee, and snacks. The captain went up to the lieutenant and good naturedly slapped him on the back.

"Well done, Dogumanhed! Well done! You were right! You were right to send in that rescue robot! No terrorists, no crazed drug addicts, no hostage situation. Just a goddamned wall with that goddamned color! What a story! I just hope no one has any more of that paint!"

"Paint, Captain?"

"Yes, Dogumanhed, paint!" Begflendopple laughed while twirling the pointy tip of his moustache with his thick fingers. "Imagine if punks like these find more of that paint to start coating more walls in other squats like this one!"

"That wasn't paint, Wiis," Schmet whispered. "Listen, I suggest you keep this as quiet as possible. That room is a relic from a past era. This ghost town? Someone should reconstruct the wall that used to surround it, and nobody—NOBODY should talk about what happened today."

Before the captain could answer the detective's curious position on the sensational event that had just occurred, another police officer arrived with two young men in handcuffs. They each had the glazed eyes which Lieutenant Schmet immediately recognized. The arresting officer brought them to the captain.

"We found these two hiding in a shed just up the street."

"Really?" The jovial Begflendopple laughed some more, still twirling his moustache.

But Dogumanhed Schmet found nothing humorous about the

situation and immediately began interrogating the prisoners, both of whom were not entirely at their sharpest.

"What are you doing here?" the lieutenant asked sharply.

The two young men were instantly terrified by the waxen visage of this frightening investigator—his bright yellow hair, one blue eye and one brown eye, the same turquoise suit of plush velvet. One of them glanced at Schmet's hand, the one with the cat's screeching face.

"Dude, that is one awesome tattoo…"

"I have the power to put you both into a tiny holding cell, squeezed in together with a few unpleasant thugs who might want to rough you up while the guard takes a long coffee break. Would you like that? I doubt it, so kindly leave the 'dude' crap outside for now. Sit down, and if you answer my questions without a hassle, I'll let you get the Hell out of here so you can go home to your spoiled middle-class lives."

A guard brought over a pair of folding chairs, and the two terrified fellows sat.

"What are you doing here in Joytown 8?"

The taller of the two answered. "We came because there is a wall inside that building…"

"Yes," Schmet interrupted. "I figured that. How did you find out about this building with the wall?"

"I don't know. Everybody."

"Everybody? Who's everybody?"

"Everybody at school."

"Where do you go to school?"

"Sea of Nectar State University."

"Everybody at Sea of Nectar State University knows about the building with the wall?"

"A few kids."

"Can you give me the names of some of these 'few kids' who know about this place?"

"Most of them are here tonight."

"Any of them dead?"

"I don't know."

"The only good thing about tonight's charming discovery is that a few missing persons cases will be solved as soon as we identify the corpses."

"Oh."

"Yes. Oh. And while we are on the subject, can you fellows explain to me why you are out here and not stuck inside with the others?"

"Oh. Well, we had a plan."

"A plan?"

"Yes. A plan. Because any time we have been here before, we always got stuck inside—"

"You have been here before?"

"Yes, Officer. A bunch of times. Anyway, it is very hard to leave because of the color. It shuts down your brain. And if you look at the color while your brain is shut down, it keeps it turned off, and everything becomes unbelievable. The bad thing is that you forget to leave, and you forget where you are. So we figured out a system—we brought along a rope and we each took turns going in there. After twenty minutes, the other two would pull out whoever was in there. Then we'd trade places so everyone would get a turn—"

"I noticed that there was a rope. But there are only two of you. Where is the third?"

"He's still inside the building. As soon as we saw the cops, we tried to pull him out, but the rope broke. We just hung around because we didn't want to leave him."

"How noble of you. So the both of you can say with complete clarity that you were inside that building, purposefully exposing your minds to the fourth primary color."

"Yes. We each must have gone in twice."

"Here is the question of the day. The only reason we are sitting here in this dump and having this pleasant conversation instead of you two pulling each other by ropes so you can go into that Hellish room and freak yourselves out, the only reason why we are all here, is this…"

Lieutenant Schmet pulled out the Omni-Tracker Belwin had carefully retrieved after rescuing several of the more serious starvation cases. The device that Slue decided to leave behind. The device she stole from the police car.

Both boys looked at it, and one scratched his head. Schmet continued to speak, and the beads of sweat that ran down his face were truly offensive to look at.

"I'm a bit lost as to how this got there. A police Omni-Tracker. It was inside that room, smack in the middle of the mess, on the floor between a couple of mattresses, and most intriguing of all, its distress signal was turned on. Somebody placed it there. Somebody wanted the police to come here. I can't understand why. If you can help me figure out who left this here, then you two can leave."

"It's a tough one, Officer. No offense, but among ourselves and all our friends, the last thing we wanted tonight was for the police to show up."

"No offense taken. But, certainly, not everyone tonight was from your school."

"True, there were loads of people we didn't know."

"Anything strange about anyone tonight? Anything out of the ordinary? Was there anyone who might not have approved of this scene?"

Suddenly, the taller of the two perked up, as if he had just remembered something.

"Wait! There was somebody!" He turned to his friend. "Remember that kid with the goggles?"

"What?" Detective Schmet interjected. "Did you just say goggles?"

"Yeah. There was a One Hundred Percent Lunar Boy. He was with a group of friends. He was arguing with me about the room with the wall."

"If I were to show you a picture, do you think you could identify him?"

"Sure."

With his inhuman face barely expressing the slightest bit of the excitement he felt inside, Lieutenant Schmet lifted his arm and pressed a pair of small buttons on his wristband device. A two-dimensional, slightly translucent image of Hieronymus Rexaphin's high school yearbook portrait flashed into the air and hovered just in front of the two college students.

"Yeah, that's him!" they both said at the same time.

Schmet could hardly contain his pleasure. He knew, he could feel with that same feather that had tickled his spine, there had been a connection somewhere.

"Wonderful, fellas. Now, this boy with the goggles, think carefully.

Was he the one who carried the police Omni-Tracker?"

"Now that I think about it…" the other boy replied, his eyes half closed, wracking his brains to remember, "it was a girl. Yeah, a girl. Actually, she also wore goggles, but more stylish than his. He was with a One Hundred Percent Lunar Girl. And she had blue hair…"

"Really?" the detective exclaimed. "My gosh…" He pressed a few buttons on his wristband, searching for a menu that might be useful. "One Hundred Percent Lunar Girls with blue hair—now how unusual can that be?"

An image of Slue appeared in the air, replacing the one of Hieronymus, also taken from the Lunar Public 777 High School yearbook.

"Could it be her?"

"Definitely," one of them replied.

Schmet could not believe the gold mine of witness evidence he was uncovering with these two boneheads. Stoners. Absolute kazzer-bats. He hated them, but what they just told him confirmed his belief that sooner or later the lunarcroptic ocular symbolanosis vermin would start working together. First in teams of two or more. Then there would be armies of them. It was only a matter of time.

"Describe to me exactly what happened."

"Well, you see, the three of us arrive at the domed building over there, and we get out our rope and we tie one end to our car and just as we are ready to start taking turns going in, this really awesome-looking vehicle pulls up, I think it was a Prokong-90…"

"A Prokong-90?"

"Yes, now that I think about it, Officer, it was definitely a Prokong-90."

"Prokong-90…" Lieutenant Schmet said softly, no longer paying attention to the college student who proceeded to give detailed descriptions of the vehicle and the driver and especially the eccentric-looking girl in the front passenger seat. The students' words faded. He realized that he had heard everything he needed to hear from them.

"Captain Begflendopple," the man with the waxen, doll-like face said as he turned to his friend and commanding officer. "Captain Begflendopple, I request an all-points bulletin for any Prokong-90 traveling on this side of the Moon."

"Can we go, Officer?" one of the Sea of Nectar students asked.

"Yes—wait, no, not yet." Something came to the lieutenant's attention. His two eyes—one artificial, one real—stared intensely at them.

"You. And you. You said Sea of Nectar State University?"

They glanced at one another with expressions of terrible dread.

Schmet looked deeply into their bloodshot eyes with extreme contempt, then he stood up and ran to the door. Outside, rescue robots were piling the half-dead in front of ambulances, and the dead in front of morgue trucks.

"Belwin!" he shouted to the silver figures. "Belwin! Come here!"

The mirror-shiny mechanical man reported to the waxen detective. They returned to the frightened students.

"Belwin, won't you kindly scan these two gentlemen? Is it true that they are students at Sea of Nectar State University?"

"Yes, Lieutenant. They are enrolled as philosophy majors at SONSU."

"Have you scanned the people you have rescued from that lovely circular room where these fine young men before us were so intent numbing their brains?"

"I have indeed, Lieutenant."

"Have you scanned the corpses?"

"Of course. Identifying the deceased is a very important part of my—"

"Belwin, please do some math for me. Quickly. Tell me the percentage of people, both living and dead, whom you have removed from the Techbolsinator, that are associated with Sea of Nectar State University."

"Certainly—that would be sixty-six percent."

"Wonderful. Now, of that sixty-six percent, how many are philosophy majors?"

The robot had the answer before Lieutenant Schmet had even finished his question.

"My records indicate that one hundred percent of the SONSU students here tonight are philosophy majors."

This bit of curious information sent Schmet into a raging fit. Belwin was a little surprised, as it seemed so irrelevant.

"So! Boys! It appears that we are not here just for the thrill of it all!

How can it be that there are so many philosophy students from Sea of Nectar here?"

"Sir?"

"There is a rumor going around. It's an old rumor. A rumor about a book. With three missing chapters. I myself read them a long time ago, but I destroyed my copy because I know how dangerous these ideas are. How quaint it must be that a copy somehow turns up at Gordon Chazkoffer's wonderful little alma mater! Don't pretend you don't know what I am talking about!"

"Sir?" mumbled one of them, petrified.

"Nothing I hate more than a goddamned BARRELHEAD who thinks he is a philosopher because he looks at that goddamned color and thinks it makes him smarter! Real philosophers enlighten themselves with hard work! Years and years of intellectual dirt under the fingernails! Forgoing stupid parties because you have to finish reading Hegel and Decartes and Plato! You spoiled little bastards—bad enough you look at that damn color for kicks—but to be pretentious enough to think it can enlighten you!"

He turned to Captain Begflendopple, who had not the faintest idea what Schmet was upset about.

"Send these two and anyone they associate with to the compound at Aldrin City! Order an immediate police raid on the philosophy department at Sea of Nectar State University! All reading material, especially any older versions of any works by Gordon Chazkoffer, is to be impounded! Bring in all professors from that filthy department for questioning!"

Wiis Begflendopple stared at his old friend with the sweaty waxen face. Never in his life had he ever heard of such a preposterous request. And from *that* school?

Schmet didn't wait for objections.

"Belwin!" he yelled as he charged toward his own car. "Belwin! Come with me. The night is far from over!"

Next stop—traffic control. It should not be too difficult to track down the activities of a Pixiedamned Prokong-90 on this side of the round rock, especially if those kids decided to take Highway Zero. Where else could they go? He looked down at the cat tattoo on his hand.

If you quietly wait by the hole in the wall, sooner or later the mouse will forget you're there…

chapter sixteen

The library was indeed hidden away. It took them so long to find it, even Clellen, who had been the longest in held-out expectations for dancing and rockin' all night, was exhausted and bored and no longer cared about anything at all. Hieronymus had been wondering if he should try and call his uncle directly on one of Pete's communication devices when Slue announced, "There it is. Up ahead, Pete. Don't you see it?"

They had left Highway Zero at exit 399 and were riding along West Gong Road, which was little more than a dirt path through a series of small jagged mountains. Here, there was almost no plant life. It was a desert. The sky was darker, and Hieronymus thought to himself that this was probably what the entire Moon looked like before it was terra-formed, back in the days when the Moon was just a moon...

And their destination turned out to be a little anti-climactic. Here, the road came to an abrupt end. The entrance to the library was a simple door on the flat side of a concrete cylinder that led into the co-lossal mountain. The only indication this was a place for books was the neon tube sign just above the door—blue neon letters that flashed on and off every few seconds with one word: LIBRARY.

"Library?" Pete asked.

"Yeah," Slue replied. "We did tell you that we were on our way to a library."

"Right, but doesn't this library have a name? There is nothing for hundreds of kilometers in every direction and suddenly, we see this word, written in flashing neon, and it's like they couldn't decide to at least name it the something-something memorial library, or the Great Far Side of the Moon Library?" Pete put on the emergency brake and turned the engine off. There was nothing that signified any parking spaces, so he just decided to leave the vehicle exactly where they stopped.

As all five of them left the Prokong-90, Clellen decided to weigh in on the flashing sign.

"I don't know, Pete. I like it just the way it is. It's funny. It's also sexy. It looks like a forbidden club where only swingers go."

"I agree with Clellen." Slue was wondering how she was going to drop the pretense they were going to a happening party instead of an utterly boring excursion into the world of paper books deep in the bowels of an endless library where there was nothing to do but research authors and subjects, each long dead...

Pebbles crunched beneath their feet. They arrived at the door and when Hieronymus tried to pull it open, he discovered that the entrance was locked.

"Oh!" he exclaimed. "What the Hell is this? It's locked!"

"It *is* something like three-thirty in the morning," Pete said.

He banged on the door, but it had no effect. It must have been made of a very thick alloy.

"This must be a Hell of a party," Clellen remarked. "They keep the light flashing, but they don't let anyone in."

"There's no door buzzer?" asked Slue, a hint of desperation in her voice.

"Nothing." Hieronymus noticed a raised square plate off to the side. In the middle of the plate was a slot. "Wait, what's this for?"

Pete squinted as he bent over to take a closer look.

"Oh," he replied with a resigned disappointment in his face. "It's an old-fashioned card reader. My father used to have one at his old job. You need a special card, probably one that is associated with the library, to get in."

A collective sense of defeat overcame the five of them. Pete because he really wanted to come through for Slue after the clumsy and insensitive way he had dumped her. Clellen because that flashing neon light had re-ignited in her the hope they were going to get to a super-cool late night party after all. Bruegel because he was hoping to find a bar and maybe a number of less uptight college girls he could meet and stop being the stupid loser odd-man-out that he had spent the entire evening being. Slue because she knew, she knew, she knew that inside this mountain, in the law section, was all the proof she needed to keep Hieronymus out of prison. Hieronymus because that locked door represented the end. He would get caught. His life was over. Damn his life. Damn it all…

They stood staring at the door. All five of them. They could all hear the wind whistling through the nearby mountains and hills. The comet remained in the same position above their heads. Bright and illustrious, but only temporary.

Then Bruegel reached into his pocket, pulled out his fake ID, looked at it for a quick second, reached forward, and inserted it into the slot. Like magic, the forbidden door opened, and a mechanical voice rang out, "Welcome back to the Library, Houseman Reckfannible! We hope you have a pleasant research session!"

Slue hugged Bruegel and gave him another huge kiss on the cheek, and this time he smiled. "At least *my* date knows how to say *Open Sesame!*" she exclaimed.

They all laughed. Then the five friends entered the library entrance, shocked by what they had encountered.

Somewhere up ahead, deep inside the complex, was loud thumping music.

Hieronymus and Slue exchanged incredulous expressions.

Could it be? they both thought at the same time, *that there really is a party here?*

They walked through the cylindrical corridor. With its black painted walls, it already looked like a club. Clellen was walking right next to Pete, and she was just in front of Hieronymus as they traveled through the long tunnel. As the music got louder, she turned around and stuck her tongue out, then mouthed the letters P-A-R-T-Y with her wonderfully shaped lips, and Slue began to laugh. Bruegel began to boast in his old manner, and Hieronymus was relieved his old friend was returning to his old self…

"Clellen, my darling furtonibuster of Klaxon," he bellowed as loud as he usually did in class, making up words as he went along, "you can tongue-spell the words 'party' all you want, as soon as you show up, the festivities shall come to a follimigoshiner end as they will think, '*Alas, the queen of bad dancing has arrived! End the party now!*'"

Clellen turned around again to glance at Bruegel, and with her hand firmly in Pete's hand, she stuck her tongue out again, and this time retorted with a typical Clellen answer, and yet, with a different edge, words that would normally be considered a put down, and indeed, may have been meant as a put down, were spoken with only one real emotion: love.

"Bruegel, you don't know a kennel-kat five load about dancing—if you go out on the dance floor, your smell alone will drive the ladies into a volcanic rift-tango! You'll be alone again, dancing with the invisible girl of your invisible dreams, boy-o!"

"Oh, Clellen. Assembled ladies, of which I see only two, well, maybe one, as I'm not sure that I can really call Clellen a lady—but, out of respect for Pete, for the moment, let's suppose she is indeed a lady, you have both had your last chances to dance with genuine Lunar Royalty, as the Westminster clan are known throughout the solar system for our prowess on the disco-dance floor…"

But Slue interrupted him—she was walking with Hieronymus and she was holding his hand, but she turned to Bruegel with a look of cheerful admiration.

"Well, Bruegel, I guess I'll have to dance with you just to see how good you are!"

"Yeah, Bruegel," Clellen added. "I'll dance with you too. But you're not as good as me."

Bruegel, pleased with the attention, continued, "Ladies, I'm afraid that as you are women who are already accompanied by gentlemen I like and admire, so I shall have to place you both down the list below the older and more experienced women who are destined to not just make repertoire with me on the dance floor, but, shall take me away into the deep wondrous realms of adult love-communion in palaces, in mansions, in fortresses of pleasure…"

Clellen laughed. "I see someone is planning his gigolo agenda for the evening."

They reached the end of the tunnel, which brought them to a pair of double doors. Pete opened them, and they all walked through into a large, high-ceilinged reception area with aluminum walls. There was a desk to the left. No one sat at it, but a big piece of cardboard was propped up on it with the word PARTY, followed by an arrow pointing to a door at the rear.

The reception room was as nondescript as possible, and the music was getting louder. The teenagers had no other recourse but to cross the reception room and head farther into the mysterious maze. The door they headed to had a sign over it: CONFERENCE ROOM 5. They entered, and despite the music they had heard since entering the library, they were still surprised at the level of outlandish behavior being exhibited by the fifty or so full-grown adults, all dancing and drinking under the flashing lights of the large conference room. The tables and chairs lay piled up against one of the walls to make room for the bar, the sound system, the DJ, and the extraordinary crowd of mostly drunken people who appeared to have already danced half the night away and were obviously enthused about continuing into the wee hours of the morning.

No one noticed the party crashers. Clellen, not wanting to waste a single second, dragged Pete with her into the abyss of music and dancing, where she threw out every outlandish move possible. Pete, although an unimaginative dancer himself, laughed uproariously at Clellen's antics. Hieronymus remained on the side and scanned the room for the one familiar face who might be able to help him, and certainly enough, there he was.

Uncle Reno.

Slue, still holding his hand, whispered in his ear, "Hieronymus, that man dancing with those two women—isn't that your father?"

"No," he answered. "That's my uncle Reno."

"He looks exactly like your father."

"He does. Except he's younger."

The man was surrounded by partiers, and they watched him hop up
and down, happily engage in all sorts of conversation, and laugh non-
stop among the loud music and general aura of cheerful debauchery.
He has no idea his brother—my father—is in jail! Hieronymus thought
to himself. *Which means the police don't really know of his connection
to this whole miserable ordeal. Which means this library might be a safe
place for a while.*

Bruegel had already found a place at the bar and was making the
bartender laugh about something while the man poured what must
have been two large glasses full of vodmoonka.

All along the walls were large, comfortable chairs, most of which
were filled by revelers of all sorts and ages. It was difficult to understand
the purpose of this party, or who these people were, except it was unde-
niably a stroke of luck it was happening at that moment, for now they
did not have to seek out his uncle or wake him up.

Hieronymus and Slue began to walk directly to him, and just as they
were about to start pressing themselves through the mass of dancers,
Reno Rexaphin turned his face in their direction and suddenly realized
who had just come to the party.

"Oh my God!" he shouted. "It's Hieronymus!" He touched the
elbow of a woman who was dancing next to him. "Look who's here! It's
my nephew!"

Reno barged through the crowd and ran to Hieronymus and
gave him a huge and unbalanced hug that almost brought them both
crashing to the floor. He had the unmistakable smell of liquor on his
breath. The man was drunk.

"I don't believe this!" he shouted. "What a wonderful surprise! How
did you find out about my party? Did your father tell you? Is he here?
Where is Ringo? Ringo, you old bastard!" he began to shout good naturedly, fully expecting Hieronymus' father to be there. Then his eyes
shifted to Slue.

"Oh my!" He grinned at Hieronymus for a second, then shifted his
clownish grin back to the One Hundred Percent Lunar Girl.

"Hello, dear lady." He took her hand and kissed it. Then he bowed.
"Reno Rexaphin, at your service." Unfortunately, he bowed down too far
and fell to the floor. The woman he was with, wearing a gold-sequined

dress, quickly knelt to help him up.

Hieronymus glanced over at Bruegel and watched him down two glasses of vodmoonka in the same number of seconds. Clellen and Pete were doing something called the bird-dance, which was currently a popular number where everyone circles each other with their arms waving about like crazed hummingbirds…

Reno jumped in front of Hieronymus and placed his hands upon this nephew's shoulders.

"I'm sorry, Hieronymus. I'm a little drunk."

"That's okay, Uncle Reno."

"Is your father here?"

"No."

"How did you get all the way out here?"

"It's a long story."

"Does your father know you're here?"

"No."

He nodded toward Slue. Then he half-whispered a question in Hieronymus' ear.

"Is…is…is that your…is that your girlfriend?"

Hieronymus hesitated as he looked over at Slue, who was talking to the woman in the gold-sequined dress.

He smiled at his uncle.

"She's your girlfriend, isn't she?" asked Reno. "Well done, nephew! Well done!"

Slue came over with the woman in the gold-sequined dress.

"Hieronymus!" she beamed. "We're in luck! This is Matilda—she's going to let me into the law library!"

"Law library?" laughed Reno as he looked at Slue. "You've come all this way, you have the good timing to show up while we are having this excellent party, and the first thing you want to do is go to the law library?"

Slue disappeared with the woman named Matilda, who, as it turned out, was a staff librarian at the gigantic complex. She was sober. Uncle Reno was trashed. The occasion for the party was non-existent—every couple of weeks, one of the staff members would decide to throw a party for whatever excuse. The real reason was they were bored because this library was so far away from everything else on the Moon, and the workload was intense—not only was it a library in the storage sense of the word, it was the last refuge for paper books in the entire solar system. It was also a massive archiving operation. Thousands of books a day had to be scanned—the old-fashioned way—page by page, and because of the fragility of the books themselves, the only way they could be handled was by human hands. Needless to say, this was an ongoing project that would probably, by all estimates, continue for the next three hundred years, at least. The library was also understaffed. Reno loved going there for two reasons: As a professor of ancient literature he had access to the most extraordinary sources—the paper editions themselves. The research he accomplished there was unparalleled, and he loved working with the librarians and archivists in his never-ending quest to solve the puzzles of ancient literature.

The other reason was no less important but much less public. Reno led a double life. Unbeknown to his wife on Earth, Reno had a girlfriend at the library. She was a librarian. They had been lovers for years. Her name was Matilda. Hieronymus had no idea of this when she took Slue down to the law library.

Hieronymus was exhausted. He went over to one of the many couches shoved back against the wall, and he sat. The dance crowd became a little thinner, and he noticed Clellen doing another completely original take on one of the current pop dance hits of the day. Naturally, some people thought she was a complete eccentric, but most of the crowd thought she brought an extraordinary enthusiasm. In the middle of it, she turned to Hieronymus. She caught his eye and gestured for him to come over, *Come on, Mus!* she must have yelled, although he couldn't hear her. *Come on, Mus! Join the party!* And just to her side, there was Pete, also shouting, *Come on, man! Get out here!* Even Bruegel was on another part of the dance floor, ripping it up with a group of drunken women who must have been in their thirties. They appeared to find him highly amusing. Hieronymous hesitated before jumping into the melee, after all, what fun was it to start dancing without Slue—on the other hand, he felt overwhelmed by an incredible melancholy. Soon, the police would catch up with him. Soon, he would never see his friends ever again. The feeling of certain doom, that time was running out, that this, the fun of being with friends from both the Loopie class and the Topper class, as well as the class in the middle as represented by Pete, was slipping away. They were coming to get him. It was time to dance. With Clellen, and with Slue as soon as she got back. With all the people there. To hop up and down, to wave his arms around, to be human, to have fun.

It was about to end, it was about to end…

He got up from the couch and jumped into the crowd, Clellen shrieking with delight, Pete bellowing out with laughter. Hieronymus let himself go, dancing his enormous troubles away on the far side of the Moon, deep within a cavernous vault, among thousands and millions and billions of books made of paper that had not been read for centuries and would most certainly never be read again.

You have never spoken to your mother?

Uncle Reno, you are drunk.

I knew your mother many years ago.

I figured that.

Not a word?

You know what she's like. All she does is cry.

I think my brother is an ass.

Please, Uncle, don't go there.

No, I'm serious. I love him. He's my older brother. But what an idiot. Such a loser.

I wish you'd stop. It's not easy to hear my uncle call my father those things.

Do you know why your mother cries all the time?

I don't know. Because she's stuck on the Moon? Stuck because of me?

No. That is not why she cries all the time.

Well, I guess it is very deep then. Very pathological.

Your father is the one who named you Hieronymus, right?

I guess so. I don't really know. Probably. What does that have to do with anything?

You know something, your mother was a wonderful writer. Did you know that?

I knew that she once wrote a book.

She did not write a book—she wrote a novel. A wonderful novel.

Okay. So she wrote a novel. Great.

You've never read it?

Da told me that it was out of print. Out of circulation. Impossible to find.

Haven't you ever been curious about your mother's novel?

Reno, the woman sits in bed in a plastic raincoat crying all day.

She was not always like that.

And you were not always a drunk.

I am not "a drunk." I AM drunk, right now. But I'll be sober tomorrow. I don't drink very often. Today is a special occasion.

What might that occasion be, Uncle Reno?

I forgot. I'll have to ask Matilda when she comes back with your amazing little blue-haired friend. What is her name?

Slue.

A lovely name. Tell me, what do you think of Matilda?

I didn't really get a good look at her.

Do you think she's nice looking?

Sure.

You know, don't tell your father, but me and her, we're, ugh, she and I, we...

Please, I don't want to hear this. You didn't tell me this, okay?

She is...she makes me very happy...she is so...

You want some coffee, Reno?

Your mother, she told me something once...

I think I'm going to go back and dance a little more with my friends.

When your mother was young...

Oh, I almost forgot. Uncle Reno, can me and my friends all crash here tonight?

Uhhh, sure, Hieronymus. When Matilda gets back, she'll set you all up in our dormitories. But before you crash, or before I pass out, there is something I have to give you. I discovered it last week, quite by accident. It's a present. I was going to give it to you yesterday, but you were gone, and I

had to get back here because we were having this wonderful party tonight.
Don't move from that couch. I'll be right back. I'll be…right…back…

Hieronymus sat for a while, so exhausted he could not get up. The music slowed down, and only a few couples were still out there, slow dancing. Among them were Pete and Clellen. During the entire time they were there, not once did they leave the dance floor. It must have been at least two hours. Hieronymus looked at his watch. It was about five thirty in the morning. Nobody appeared to be leaving, or even preparing to leave. The bartender was still pouring drinks. Bruegel was on a couch between two women, and they were all laughing and clinking glasses and laughing some more. One of them had taken his top hat from him and was wearing it. Through the entrance, another team of caterers arrived. They pushed a fancy-looking table on wheels into the noisy room. It had a wide selection of barbecued meat piled onto big oval plates. *What kind of a party is this?* Hieronymus wondered. *Everyone here seems determined to keep on partying…*

Then Reno returned and sat down next to him. In one hand was a plastic cup filled with ice cubes and amber-colored whiskey. In his other hand was a blue velvet pouch with an object inside. He handed it to Hieronymus. He took a long drink, the ice cubes making a crackly racket.

"Thank you, Uncle Reno," he said hesitantly, but his uncle stared ahead and only half smiled in a very sad sort of way.

Hieronymus reached into the bag and took it out. It was a book. A real book. Made from paper. It had a cover made of leather. He flipped through it without reading. Real ink on real pages. The feel of it was exquisite.

"This is a real book!"

"Well, we *are* in a place where we are surrounded by real books…"

"Did you steal it? Is this legal?"

"Totally legal. If we discover that there is more than three of the same edition, if it has no historical value, we're supposed to throw them out. Or we can keep them. I took this one because I think you should have it."

"It must be hundreds of years old." Hieronymus remarked. "But it looks new…"

Then he opened it up, expecting to see an ancient language. But on the first page he understood every word. It was the title. And the author.

THE FLOOD COUNTRY
BY BARBIE O'FALLIHORN

Hieronymus looked at his uncle.

"This is my mother's book. Where did you get this?"

"I told you. I found it. Completely by accident. I was looking for something else entirely. I came upon a container with four of them."

"I thought her book was completely lost. I also thought that nobody published paper books anymore."

"Indeed, we all thought that. But a while back, on Earth, a few publishers tried to make books the old-fashioned way again. We have so few things we can grasp in our hands these days. Everything floats and then is gone. Your mother's novel was chosen by a publisher of paper books. But she's a little stubborn, your mother—she refused any other format except paper once it was made. Anyway, it flopped commercially. But critically, it received enough notice that with a bit of effort, she could have carried on. But she started to slip into the woman she is today. She didn't want to even look at her books, and she destroyed all the copies she had."

"Take this back. I don't want it."

"Oh, you want it, One Hundred Percent Lunar Boy! You know exactly why you want to read it, too. Open it. She wrote it years before you were born. There she is. Barbie O'Fallihorn, and she…is going to… speak…to you now."

"I don't have to take this from you, Reno. You are as boring as my father."

"It must have been a terrible thing to grow up with your mother right there in the apartment, lying in bed in a plastic raincoat, crying, sleeping, crying, never even speaking to you, and your father pretending that she was completely normal."

"Yeah, well, what's it to you?"

"Oh, it's everything to me. How is this for irony? I miss your mother more than you do. I used to know her. She was like an older sister to me.

I miss her because I know some things about her life that your father has never told you. For example, have you ever wondered why she wears a raincoat to bed? A raincoat? It never rains on the Moon."

"I am going to leave."

"You are not going anywhere. Your blue-haired girlfriend has not returned from the law library yet. You have no choice but to listen to your uncle."

"You're drunk."

"Do you know what country on Earth your mother is from?"

"No."

"How can you not know something like that? Your mother is from a country that does not exist any more. It was a country where all it did was rain. Everyone wore raincoats. But, one day, it literally did not stop raining. Puddles turned into lakes, and creeks turned into rivers and the water got higher, and soon the ocean joined in and suddenly there was nowhere to go but to a watery grave. Out of a huge family of seven brothers, only your mother escaped—with her grandmother."

"Stop. Please don't continue…"

"You knew this already, Hieronymus. You knew that there was a tragedy to your mother that was deeper than your own dark shadow, and it follows you everywhere. It has literally cut you in half. One part of you is a conformist just like your father, and the other part of you is still in exile, just like your mother. Oh, you might have this whole business with the lunarcroptic ocular whatever-the-hell-they-call-it, but that is not really your problem. Your biggest problem is you have never spoken a single word to your mother, and you know that there is nothing you want more."

"I think you've said enough for tonight, Reno."

"You think so?"

"Yes. You've spoken much too much tonight…"

"How sad that you can say that to your uncle, but not to your own mother…"

"My mother is mad. Let's just leave it at that."

"A pity your father never took care of her, then."

"Maybe there was nothing he could have done about it."

"Ah, the passive approach. You look so much like your da when you speak like that. Whatever happens, happens. Going with the flow. Poor Barbie. I always thought she was way too good for my idiotic, passive brother. Loser brother. And you know he's a loser. You know it."

"Yeah, well, my loser father is in jail right now. He was covering for me."

"Is that so?"

"You're not fazed in any way that your brother is in jail at this moment?"

"No more than you, boy-o. You hate his guts more than I do. If you were concerned about your da, you would have told me a long time ago. Instead, you went dancing with that wacky girl over there."

Reno pointed out Clellen.

"She really is something, that one. I'll bet she has her own out-standing tragedies. Just like that guy she's dancing with, but he doesn't know it yet. Or your other friend over there who looks like he's going to have to decide which one of those women he's going to end up with to-night. He has tragedy written all over him. I have my own tragedy which is a mother lode all by itself. So does your father. My friend Matilda. Everyone in this room. This whole round rock is a tragic place. But you. You've got the Magic Mountain of tragedy and you have to figure out what the Hell you're going to do about it before it turns into a volcano and takes your head right off."

Hieronymus walked away from his uncle. He navigated through the couples on the dance floor. He walked right past Clellen and Pete. Clellen's eyes followed him, as did Pete's chin. They watched the solitary, shadow-like boy.

He found another couch. He sat down on it.

He opened up his mother's novel. He read the first two pages. Then he closed it and stuffed it into his jacket pocket.

He leaned forward. He buried his face in his hands.

His slid his fingers under the goggles to rub his sad, watery eyes.

chapter seventeen

Then it happened very quickly. Slue finally returned, followed by Matilda, who went to the couch where the nearly passed-out Uncle Reno lay sprawled, his eyes half closed. Slue went right up to Hieronymus, and she was smiling.

She sat right next to him and she kissed him on the mouth.

At that moment, the lights went on. Extremely bright lights.

Their lips parted, and entering the room, much to the chagrin of every person there, was Lieutenant Dogumanhed Schmet. Hieronymus immediately recognized him from the incident in the classroom two years earlier. *Oh, man, not this guy again. What happened, did someone complain about the noise?* Then he realized that this was the same officer who called his father, a real LOS-hater and certainly not the kind of police officer who simply went around breaking up parties.

He had ten other officers with him, maybe more, and they circled the crowd on the dance floor. The policemen all wore the characteristic top hats and capes, and they did not appear to carry any weapons. They all appeared to be a bit bored and tired, unlike Lieutenant Schmet, whose waxen, sweaty face was ecstatic.

"Ladies and gentlemen, please do not be alarmed. My name is

Lieutenant Dogumanhed Schmet of the Sea of Tranquility Police Department, Ocular Investigative Division. We do not mean to interrupt your wonderful party—you can return to your utterly wasteful distractions and pathetic little debaucheries as soon as I have apprehended the highly dangerous fugitive who is in your midst, hiding out among you now."

Slue got up and walked directly to Clellen. She put her arm around her and whispered very intently. Clellen returned a rather confused and frightened expression. Slue took a tiny object out of her pocket—a gray, finger-sized rectangular thing with a flashing red light on it—and passed it to the perplexed girl, who nodded with a sincerity seen only on young children who have been given an important assignment they must not fail.

"…the fugitive I am seeking," the detective continued, "wears those goggles that are common to a certain group of incompatible lunar citizens. This one has with him several accomplices, one of whom is a female goggle-wearer with blue hair, and a boy who drives a Prokong-90."

Listen, Clellen, I have something that I have to give to you right now. These men are here to arrest Hieronymus, and I am pretty sure they are going to arrest me, too. If that happens, you have to take this media transference chip directly to the Lunar Federal Court in the District of Copernicus. It's really important. It is the big white building that is shaped like a snail's shell. You know it? Its one of the most famous buildings on the Moon. You have to find someone there named Raskar Memling. He's my older brother. He works there, and you have to find him and give this to him. It has to be done in person. When I disappear, everyone will be worried about what happened. You must tell my brother everything. He has a friend who is a constitutional judge. This data cube I am giving you has all the proof we need that people like me and Hieronymous are being tossed into jail without trial, and it's being done illegally. There is a secret illegal arrangement between some people in the government and transportation corporations. I can't go into it right now, but when it breaks, it's going to be huge. Just take this, and give it to my brother. It's up to you, Clellen. They're going to arrest me, and probably question anyone I spoke to. But they won't take you. All you did was dance. And because of that, you're safe. You get the last word. Just remember what I told you. My brother. Tell him everything.

Concentrate. This might be the most important thing you ever do, Clellen.
I don't know if I'll ever see you again, but it has been wonderful to have
you as a friend. And I know that I can depend on you.

Lieutenant Schmet continued with the unpleasant address to the crowd.

"So as soon as we have the following in custody, the rest of you can continue with your foolish party. When I call your name, please step forward. Hieronymus Rexaphin. Slue Memling. Peter Cranach. Reno Rexaphin. Matilda Weyden…"

Hieronymus and Slue walked up to Detective Schmet.

Hieronymus spoke directly to the officer. "Look. You got me. Here I am. Just take me. Why are you arresting the others?"

But instead of answering, he just bellowed out the charges as if they were in a courtroom and he was already the judge, jury, and executioner.

"Hieronymus Rexaphin, you are being arrested and charged with the crime of Ocular Assault, by showing your uncovered eyes to an unsuspecting tourist from Earth. Slue Memling, you are being arrested and charged with possession of a stolen police Omni-Tracker and then subsequently and maliciously placing said Omni-Tracker into a highly dangerous environment, where no less than eight officers were severely injured while trying to retrieve it. Peter Cranach, you are being arrested and charged with the crime of transporting known criminals into forbidden areas of the Lunar Far Side, in particular, Joytown 8, a known magnet for gangs and drug smuggling operations."

Pete was beside himself with disbelief. He shouted at the lieutenant.

"What are you, crazy? We've done nothing wrong!!"

"Insulting a police officer can be interpreted as assault, depending on the discretion of the officer. You have just insulted me. You have hurt my feelings. I charge you with assault, young man."

Pete rushed at him in a tantrum of fury, but Schmet was fast, and with a tiny flick of his own wrist, the big tellball player was on the floor, writhing in agony with a broken arm. "Your loyalty to your friends is admirable, but your stupidity is not," the detective said before continuing on with his announcement.

"Reno Rexaphin, you are being arrested and charged with the crime of aiding and abetting these known criminals. Matilda Weyden, while you are not technically under arrest, you are hereby required to come with us for questioning."

Then the detective began pointing out several random people in the crowd.

"You. You. And you. We are taking you in for questioning. Anyone who by any chance allowed these terrorists to have access to this library's research terminals must come with us."

There was a great murmur in the crowd, as most of the people thought the demands of this lieutenant were a bit outlandish. Then one officer brought forward Clellen and Bruegel.

"Lieutenant," he said. "What about these two? They're teenagers—they must be friends of the accused."

Schmet looked at them and laughed—he recognized Clellen and Bruegel from that day he was called to that miserable school where Hieronymus killed that boy with his eyesight. Total lowlifes. Losers. Failures.

"No, let them go. They're too dumb to know anything. They're just a couple of stupid Loopies. That's what they call them at their school. Loopies. Everyone calls them Loopies. That girl is an insane filthy slut and that boy is just mental."

Normally, Clellen would have shouted a wall of insults at the detective, but she just stood there staring at his strange, doll-like face. She felt completely different from that moment on, as if the old Clellen had been left behind somewhere. In one second, she was transformed. She listened to his every word, her eyes on his. She clutched the data cube in her hand with a steely determination to quietly stare him down. Indeed, she knew she *would* have the last word.

Bruegel, on the contrary, could not resist. The entire time the detective was speaking, the big fellow just looked at him with an amused expression, his head slightly cocked to one side, his open mouth chewing potato chips from an open bag he held in one of his hands. "Excuse me, Detective, but I was wondering about something. You have the most bizarre complexion on your face—you look like a plastic action figure that was coated in wax! If someone were to slice your entire head in half with a machete, I am sure that it would be the same unpleasant material all the way through—"

"On second thought," Schmet interrupted, "take the big oafish one in for questioning as well."

And then he turned to Clellen one more time.

"Looks like you're all alone now. All your friends are arrested. Now just how do you intend to get back to the other side of the Moon? Maybe you'll just *slut* your way back?"

A couple of the other officers laughed at his crude remark, but Clellen only stared straight ahead.

Hieronymus and Slue were handcuffed and placed into the back of the same vehicle as Lieutenant Schmet and Belwin, the rescue robot, who was instructed to drive. The others were transported in separate police cruisers, and Pete was taken away to a prison hospital because of his broken arm.

Most of the journey back to the near side of the Moon was uneventful. All Hieronymus could do was watch the landscape change as they returned to the more familiar sights of remote cities covered in neon lights, crowded highways, and a sky perpetually red.

Clouds of hummingbirds flew in the distance. Some flew parallel with them. Others, farther away, snaked among distant skyscrapers. Their destinations random. Clouds shaped as far-away, colorless dragons, reigning over the lunar sky.

Today is the first day of my exile, Hieronymus thought.

He looked at Slue, and they smiled at each other. Soon, the police would separate them. They would be sent to different prisons. They would be trained as pilots. Then they would be cast off into the far and sad cosmos. Then they would live short and uneventful lives in the deepest loneliness possible.

"Lieutenant?" Slue asked. "Will we see you at our trial?"

"Trial?" the waxen-faced man replied with a laugh. "What makes you think you are getting a trial?"

"It's the law. We have the right to a fair trial."

"You have the right to keep your mouth shut, miss."

"If I robbed a bank, would I get a trail?"

"You? No."

"If I was a random guy on the street who did not have lunarcroptic ocular symbolanosis and I robbed a bank, would I then get a trial?"

"Indeed, you would."

"I see. So it is because I can see the fourth primary color that my rights are somehow altered."

"Your rights are not altered. You have no rights to begin with. If you can see the fourth primary color, you are no longer classified as a human being, and thus, you have no recourse to use the civil mechanisms of our state."

"And where in our civil code is this spelled out?"

"It is not. Because you are not a human being, in your case, it is irrelevant what the law says."

"So it is a question of the state not recognizing us as human beings."

"It is clear, in fact, that you and your boyfriend here are not human beings."

"If we are such non-citizens then, what gives you the right to arrest us?"

"I arrest you as I would arrest any public menace. For example, if a diseased dog were running around biting people and spreading rabies, I would have to capture it. Of course, I would not be having the pleasant conversation that we are currently having with such a beast, but still, I think you get the idea."

"So what happens next?"

"Well, I take you back to the station in Aldrin City, I register you, and then you will be transported to a holding chamber where you will await assignment to internment with a private detention facility."

"Private? We are not even kept in a state prison?"

"Oh, no. As you are not a human being, you are turned over to one of several corporations that handle creatures such as yourself."

"Show me the part of the law where this is encoded as something legal."

"Show me the part of the law where you are encoded as a human being."

"It is an outrage the way you speak to us."

"Miss Memling, how did you get a police Omni-Tracker?"

"How did you ever get to become a police officer? You are so clearly unqualified."

"Well, I must be good at it. After all, I tracked you two down."

"That didn't take much," Hieronymus interjected. "We're just a couple of kids, but you make us out to be dangerous outlaws, which we are not."

"In fact, you were an outlaw the moment you were born."

"Really? You know, one would think you would have better things to do with your time. The crime rate on the Moon is pretty high these days, but here you are wasting your time with us."

"I'm not wasting my time. Because of you, I've discovered the existence of a genuine Obscura Camera Projection Techbolsinator."

"That thing should be destroyed!" Slue declared.

"That thing is going to be incredibly useful."

"It is a horror! It's a morbid, morbid horror! How could someone even construct such a thing!" she continued, completely outraged.

"At one time, there were several of them. They were made during the Regime of Courage. Oops. I'm sorry. So politically incorrect of me. I forgot. You creatures like to call it the Regime of Blindness. Anyway, where was I? Oh, yes. You see, everyone is so fascinated by the fourth primary color, but nobody knows how to control it. As you may well know, a normal person who sees this color, once they are under the shock of it, and before they can fully recover, become highly susceptible to memory manipulation. That is the real reason people like you are such a menace. And that is why that circular room with its wall made up of thousands of real One Hundred Percent Lunar irises can be such a powerful tool. Anyone who goes in there forgets completely who he is. Before he can recover, you tell him whatever you want, and your suggestion becomes his memory. You can put twenty of the Moon's greatest scientists in there, and while they are under the shock of that color, you can tell them something as silly as the flat Earth revolves around the Moon, which is made of cheese, and they will come out convinced that this is a solid, indisputable fact."

"That is barbaric—"

"My darling blue-haired girl, it is an unstoppable fact. Why do you think One Hundred Percent Lunar People are sometimes randomly attacked and their eyes stolen? Sometimes there are those who *need to see* that color, and they will even resort to murder to obtain it. And sometimes, there are those who need to *use* that eye color on someone else. Just think of the countless possibilities—the ability to tell another person what their own memories are. Why should this fabulous power only be in the hands of the creatures who are born with it? The Regime of Courage set out to make proper use of this phenomenon—by keeping all of you away from the rest of humanity, then taking your eyes away from yourselves to build several rooms exactly like the one you saw in Joytown 8. These rooms were put to excellent use as far as manipulating the memory of politicians, judges, intellectuals, enemies of the state, whomever they felt needed a bit of reprogramming. I have already arranged for that room to be put under strict lock-up under the Ocular Investigative Division. And whoever owns the key to that place has a lot of power. Oh, did I mention that I'm the one with the key?"

"Something must really be driving you nuts," Hieronymus told the detective. "Something terrible happened to you. It's obvious. Look at your face. Your skin. You are the strangest-looking man I have ever seen. What was it? An accident? You were not born like that, so something awful happened to you and you are carrying this around with you…"

"I think you've said enough, young man."

"I think I touched a nerve."

Suddenly, a voice broke in that had been unheard of during the entire car ride. It was Belwin.

"Actually, Lieutenant Schmet, I was there."

"What? You? Mechanical man? What are you talking about?"

"I was there. I'm the one who pulled you out of the fire so many years ago. You must have been about twelve years old. It was that awful accident when the Mega Cruiser crashed on the highway just outside of Tycho. Hundreds of people died. I was brought to the scene, but it was too late to save most of the people on the bus you were traveling with. I was very sorry not to have been able to save the other members of your family. It was beyond tragic. Your mother. Your father. You had seven sisters, all killed in that fire. Happily, you survived, even though you were burned almost beyond recognition, but I can see that the plastic skin they have since coated you in appears to have taken to your body quite well."

Rescue robots are not known for their tact. Their talents lie in their abilities to walk into fire, discover people, and then rescue them. As polite a conversationalist as he always was, Belwin had no idea what he was saying was, indeed, very upsetting to Lieutenant Schmet.

"If you had a mouth, I would instruct you to shut it. Instead, I am ordering you to cease all comments and drive. As a matter of fact, stop this car."

The robot did as he was told. He stopped speaking and the vehicle was brought to an abrupt halt on the side of the highway.

"Just in case you two creatures are wondering, we did not stop because Belwin's big mouth caused me any amount of grief. That is none of your concern. We stopped because I have a bit of business to take care of. Now if you will just kindly remain in your seats, I will be right back."

Schmet opened the door and left the vehicle, his strange blond hair blown up and ruffled by the whizzing traffic. Parked just ahead of them was another police cruiser, its blue lanterns silently flashing. He ran ahead of them and stopped at it, engaging in a conversation with someone within.

Slue stared ahead, and her mouth opened, slowly. Her face conveyed nothing but shock.

"Schmet," she said, sleepily. "His name is Schmet, isn't it?"

Hieronymus looked at her.

"Yes. That is his name."

"He has one brown eye and one blue eye, doesn't he?"

"He does. But in case you have not noticed, only one of those eyes is real."

Slue addressed the robot in the front seat.

"Belwin, did you say that Schmet burned himself in that gigantic Mega Cruiser crash outside Tycho? It was many years ago, wasn't it?"

"Yes."

"And that Schmet lost seven sisters? In the ensuing fire?"

"That is correct."

"Hieronymus!" Slue gasped, turning to the boy next to her. "That is a famous fire! And not just because it was a catastrophic accident. In that fire, there was a boy. A boy with seven sisters. A twelve-year-old boy. With a name like Schmet. He was incredibly rare. This boy, he was reported killed—and you are not going to believe this—was one of the very, very few Fifty Percent Lunar Boys! He had one normal eye, and one eye that was colored with the fourth primary color!"

"Indeed," Belwin cut in. "He lost his LOS eye in the fire."

This was an outlandish revelation for Hieronymus.

"A Fifty Percent Lunar Boy! I didn't even know that was possible!"

"It is. Historically, there have only been a dozen. But doesn't it make sense? He knows everything we do before we do it."

"No wonder he hates all One Hundred Percenters. His family was killed by a Mega Cruiser. Guess who pilots Mega Cruisers…"

"Look at him," Slue said. "He's one of us."

As they watched the man with the false skin and the false eye, they saw he was talking to someone inside the police car parked in front of them. Then he opened the vehicle's side door, and the person he was conversing with climbed out and accompanied him as he strolled back to the car of Hieronymus and Slue.

It was a girl.

Hieronymus could not believe who it was.

The door swung open. Schmet poked his head into the back compartment where Hieronymus and Slue sat side by side. He had a huge smile on his artificial face. He looked directly at Hieronymus.

"Surprise!" he blurted out. Then he invited the girl outside to ride with them. She entered the interior and her face drew up in considerable surprise once she realized it was Hieronymus in the car. She gasped. Schmet sat down next to her, directly opposite his two LOS prisoners, and closed the door after himself. Belwin immediately started the vehicle, and they continued on their way among the fast-moving traffic.

"Hello, Windows Falling On Sparrows," Hieronymus said with total remorse in his voice.

Her shocked expression melted into complete sadness.

"I didn't betray you!"

"I know you didn't."

"He took me in a ship directly into the atmosphere. He lied and he told me we were going to Earth. What you saw, my forward projection of color, was not my leaving the Moon. He took me to Aldrin City. He figured all this out on his own. I did not betray you…"

"Indeed, she did not betray you, Mr. Rexaphin." Lieutenant Schmet laughed. "It was the clerk at the hotel who identified you. And, if I may say so, my considerable talent. In any event, you betrayed yourself. You all do that, you know. Eventually, all of you One Hundred Percenters betray yourselves."

"What about you Fifty Percenters?"

"What was that, Miss Memling?"

"You heard me. It must be rough—dedicating your life to rounding up those who are…let's say, complete, as opposed to the pathetic and confused half that you are."

"Keep digging your hole, blue-haired girl."

"Lieutenant Schmet, if I were to take my goggles off, I would see what the traffic ahead of us would be like. With my LOS vision, I could tell if I'm about to get into an accident, or I could see an accident about to happen, and I could avoid it. It must rip you up. If you were free to openly look at the world with your eye of the fourth primary color, you would have seen that Mega Cruiser fall out of the sky before it happened when you were twelve…"

If Windows Falling On Sparrows were not in the car, Schmet would have smacked Slue in the face for daring to say such a thing, which was, of course, completely true. Instead, he turned to the Earth girl, calling her by his adopted name for her.

"Selene, may I introduce to you, the lovely Slue Memling. She is Hieronymus Rexaphin's girlfriend."

Windows Falling On Sparrows looked at Slue, her expression completely neutral above the pang of sadness that sentence gave her.

"I'm not his girlfriend."

Schment looked at Hieronymus. "If only every man could have your problems! Look what we have here! My gosh! What do we do? These two girls! How can you not love the both of them? You lucky guy! How do we find ourselves in a police car with these two beauties? One from Earth! One from the Moon! And we are all in trouble! If you confess your love transgressions to either one of these young ladies, you are also confessing your criminal transgressions to me! What a fix we are in! Unless we all come clean right now. About everything. Love and crime! Right now! It has to come from you and you alone! The Earth girl won't betray you, your father won't betray you, it's up to you. Hieronymus Rexaphin, did you or did you not show your uncovered eyes to this girl, Windows Falling On Sparrows?"

Hieronymus looked at Windows Falling On Sparrows. Then he turned his head to the side and looked at Slue. His eyes stayed on her for a long time. Then he turned his goggled stare to Lieutenant Schmet.

"I confess to three things. I confess that I have always loved Slue Memling, from the moment I met her in the third grade, even though I also feel as if I have met her for the first time earlier this evening. I confess that I love Windows Falling On Sparrows, and despite having only met her two evenings ago, I feel as if I have known her all my life. And, Lieutenant, I confess to the crime of Ocular Assault."

"Charming," said Schmet with a smile.

"You can't put him in jail," Windows Falling On Sparrows protested. "I'm not pressing charges!"

"It is not a question of you pressing charges. Romeo has broken the law. And it's a serious one."

"Then you should arrest me, too. I'm the one who took his goggles off! I begged him to do it! I wanted to see that color with my own eyes! I'm just as guilty as he!"

"I am certainly not going to arrest you, Selene. We have no use for you."

"No use for me? Why, because I am not a One Hundred Percent Lunar Girl?"

Schmet smiled.

"It is true, then. They will be sent to camps on the far side of the Moon and then they will be forced to pilot Mega Cruisers till they die. If my eyes were of the fourth primary color, you'd arrest me, too!"

"Who do you work for?" Slue interjected. "The police, or one of those private detention facilities you mentioned?"

The plastic face remained still, locked in its false smile.

"Belwin!" Slue shouted. "Who is going to take custody of us?"

The rescue robot, who had been quiet because of Schmet's orders, was obliged to answer a direct question. It was part of his programming in the business of saving lives. To be as honest as possible.

"All processed LOS citizens who have been caught breaking Quarantine Directive Number Sixty-Seven are usually handed over to the MacToolie Group."

Slue and Hieronymus look at each other. That name. MacToolie.

"Wilson MacToolie," Slue whispered. "Of course. The painting of the uniformed man in the lobby of the Techbolsinator. Now I remember. Wilson MacToolie. He was the architect of the Regime of Blindness. The MacToolie Group. They must be his descendents—"

"Okay, enough of your conspiratorial blabbering, young lady." Schmet turned to Windows Falling On Sparrows. He was determined to keep the conversation off politics, and focused on the sentimental.

"And *that* is who Hieronymus has left you for. An unpleasant, paranoid girl like *that*. Blue hair—ugh. I told you already that these Lunar Boys with the goggles are all alike—they take advantage of girls from Earth. They seduce you with promises of incomprehensible colors, and they have fun with you for a while. But they always return to their own kind…"

"And what kind do you return to, sir?" Hieronymus asked, looking directly at Schmet. "Trying so damn hard to prove you are human. Of course, you are one of us. That is why you are so good at catching us. A part of you understands us completely. And always one step ahead. What normal person would think of flying her up into orbit like that? You understand the fourth primary color. You created the event of her leaving because you sensed that she saw it. No normal person would even think of such a thing, except for someone like you—a Fifty Percenter, one leg in the normal world, one leg in the LOS world. Of course, you no longer have your eye, so it's even worse. You spend your life chasing your other half. And you can't even see that color anymore, and that makes you crazier than anything else. You miss it, don't you?"

Schmet had no answer, and in that half second of silence, Hieronymus saw an opportunity. Windows Falling On Sparrows was not wearing handcuffs. Her hands, the same hands that had removed his goggles just two nights earlier, were free. He looked at her, and he spoke.

"They are arresting me because I looked at you. That's all I did. I only looked at you. You looked at me. And it's against the law. But you know what really frightens them? What really has the government terrified? They don't want people like Slue and I to look at each other. With our goggles off. That's their nightmare. That we will all find out the incredible, unbelievable thing that occurs when two of us look at each other. Slue and I discovered this for ourselves last night. We did not die, but the world around us became…spectacular."

He spoke the next sentence slowly and intently. In the background, the noise of the speeding traffic they were among intensified. Belwin was changing lanes.

"How nice of Lieutenant Schmet not to handcuff you."

Windows Falling On Sparrows understood immediately. It took only half a second. She reached forward with both her hands, grabbed the two pairs of goggles in front of her, and pulled them off.

Hieronymus and Slue looked at each other.

The windshield shattered into flying broken glass as a gigantic hummingbird smashed itself through and invaded the vehicle, followed by a dozen more. The car swerved, and there was another glass explosion as a side window vanished into screeching shards and hummingbirds charged into the vehicle. From all directions, the birds in the sky suddenly knew where to go—they flew down to their target, clouds of them changing direction and swarming down upon the fast-moving police cruiser. Hummingbirds from the tops of nearby houses instinctively knew where to find the two young people who had looked at each other's eyes of the fourth primary color, and even the hidden birds who tunneled under the ground to lay their eggs burst from the soil, as the silent clarion call to converge could not be broken. The spark to give them their righteous color, their lunar hue, their denied fourth primary plumage surpassed all other hummingbird activities, and they swarmed the car by mad instinct, and the closer they got to the people who looked at each other, the closer they felt the newly created circuit, the new inexplicable energy, and the brighter and more resplendent they became as lunar hummingbirds of the fourth primary color.

Within a fluttering few seconds, thousands of the hummingbirds converged on the vehicle, filled the interior and obscured the exterior in a circular pulsating cloud of the forbidden color. They dented the panels of the car, trying to get in, and they touched the occupants once they entered. The inside cabin was full of hummingbirds, all hovering and swarming and awash in the special chaos only wild birds could bring. The color, the fourth primary color was everywhere, and this time, Windows Falling On Sparrows was ready for it and she reveled in its finality and its complete shutting down of her mind.

This time, she smiled.

Schmet was too late. He tried to cover his good eye, but he too was engulfed within the endless swarming birds. He fell under the shock of the color and his mind shut down to its primordial state. He curled up into a fetal position halfway on the floor, crying out the names of his seven deceased sisters—including his favorite, the one named Selene.

Belwin was unaffected by the color. But he was extremely confused by the arrival of thousands of hummingbirds smashing the windshield and swarming the vehicle. None of it made any sense. He had no eyes, but his sensors were confounded by the mad flock nevertheless, and the police cruiser began to swerve uncontrollably.

Every car in the immediate vicinity saw the cloud of hummingbirds and their explosion of inexplicable color that enveloped the police car just in their area. Dozens of cars were suddenly driven by incapacitated drivers, and Hieronymus and Slue kept looking at each other as the explosions and cacophony of the highway crashes all around them filled their world.

They kissed, and then they felt themselves spinning, then upside down, the flying shards of glass on all sides, the horns, the screams of the colossal pileup unable to interrupt the meeting of their lips.

The vehicle smashed into the road divider, flipped over again, was hit by several other cars, and then tumbled off the highway, where it smashed through the side of a restaurant.

* * *

Hieronymus woke up laid out on a stretcher. There were dozens of people all around him, and off to the side, he saw an ambulance. There were also several other police cars, and he turned his head and saw the smashed-up vehicle they had been riding in now completely bent out of shape and jutting out of the wall of the restaurant. There were fires on the highway, and long pillars of thick black smoke reaching up into the red sky. Other people were on stretchers, but he didn't recognize any of them. Perhaps they were from some of the other cars, or maybe they were from the restaurant itself. He sat up. Where was Slue? Where was Windows Falling On Sparrows?

For a few seconds, he saw them both. Windows Falling On Sparrows was unconscious and on a stretcher. As none of the medics were fussing over her, she did not appear to be hurt. Only sleeping, or recovering from the fourth primary color. Slue stood over her, looking down at the Earth girl. She seemed completely unaffected by the accident, except for a scratch across her face and her blue hair in a tangle. She was still in handcuffs. A police officer came to her side and started to escort her to another police cruiser. Hieronymus watched as she was escorted to the door, then he watched as she climbed inside, still wearing her velvet poncho. She turned to him, and then she smiled, a look of genuine relief on her face the moment she realized he too was not injured. She ducked into the car and Hieronymus thought, *On what world will I see you again…*

Not too far away, and arguing with a pair of traffic officers, was Dogumanhed Schmet. The detective was covering his eye, but he appeared to be guided along by Belwin. He had his back to Hieronymus. He was completely disoriented, and certainly in trouble as he was responsible for his prisoners, and thus the accident was completely his fault. As he argued and pleaded, Hieronymus noticed the small aluminum box he gripped in his hand. He held it tight over his heart, as if he wanted to protect it with his own body from the chaos of such an accident-filled world.

Then Hieronymus noticed something too good to be true. His handcuffs had been removed. Of course! As soon as the ambulance arrived, the medics would have taken the cuffs off.

He looked around. He was surrounded, but nobody was paying much attention to him. Feeling a little wobbly, he stood up. He knew that there was one thing he had to do. One last thing he had to take care of before they got him for good. He walked toward a police car that sat unoccupied. In theory, he knew he could drive it. He did not have a license, but he had taken driver's ed. He was going to steal it. He was going to steal the police car.

"Hey! You!" a voice shouted from behind him. "Where do you think you're going?"

Hieronymus, halfway in the driver's seat, the door still open, turned around as five or six police officers began moving quickly toward him.

"Get back here!"

But before they could take another step, Hieronymus lifted his goggles up over his eyes and the cops fell to the pavement.

"Watch out!" cried a terrified voice. "The goggle-freak has taken his goggles off!" Everyone in the immediate area suddenly took cover behind cars and other objects, afraid to look into the direction of the boy whose eyes contained the color of the damned.

He started the car, and was surprised at how well he was able to drive. There was now only one place to go.

One place to go.

When he arrived home, he discovered the apartment was a complete mess. It must have happened when they had come to arrest his father. They must have turned the place upside down looking for him. Or could it have been his mother? It was only yesterday his da had been taken away—did she even know? Would she tear the house apart like that looking for something to eat? He walked into the hall, and as he got closer to her room, he could hear her sobbing. The same sound he had known all his life.

And then, he heard something else. Police sirens. They knew exactly where he was. They wanted to trap him—and that was fine, because he was home now, and what he had to do would not take long.

"Ma," he said as he entered the room. As expected, the bedroom was a catastrophe. A shelf on the wall had been completely overturned. A closet emptied and clothes tossed on the floor. A bottle of water lay on the floor in its own puddle. A vase cracked.

Barbie lay in the bed, wearing her plastic raincoat and crying, her bright red hair a tangled, tragic mess. She looked up at him, and she continued to cry.

The sounds of police sirens came up from the outside world.

"Ma. It's me! Your son. Hieronymus. I've come home. I've returned."

The mad woman buried her face in the pillow, still sobbing. Hieronymus knelt on the floor next to her bed so he could be closer to her.

"Listen, Ma. I'm not sure you can hear me. I'm not sure that you can. I've spent my whole life with a mother I could never speak to. It's not your fault, and it's not my fault, it is just the way it is. But I'm your son and all mothers and sons have to speak to each other, otherwise we all become nothing but orphans, and I'm tired of feeling like an orphan."

There was a crash from outside the bedroom. The first group of policemen must have smashed down the front door of the apartment. The unmistakable sound of rushing boots echoed through. The police sirens grew louder in the distance.

Hieronymus took his goggles off and he tossed them across the room. He knew exactly what was about to happen.

"Look at me, Ma," he said, with both desperation and confidence. "Please look at me. I don't have much time. I know for a fact that they are going to come in here and drag me away. Please look at me before they do that."

Barbie Rexaphin looked up at Hieronymus. Her reaction was different from all the others. Perhaps because she was already pretty much out of her mind, she looked at him, into his eyes of the fourth primary color, with more of an expression of curiosity than anything else.

There was another crash from the outside. Voices were commanding each other to do this, or do that. Three men rushed into Barbie's bedroom, but they all collapsed to a pile on the floor in a second as soon as Hieronymus looked up at them. "We found him!" someone shouted. "He's hiding in there—in the bedroom!"

Hieronymus turned back to his mother, who appeared to be really looking at him for the first time in his life.

"I know you can't speak to me. And that's fine. You see, Ma, I think I finally found a way for us…"

With that, he took out the copy of his mother's long lost novel, *The Flood Country.*

"This is your book, Mother. This is yours. You wrote this. And you know what I'd like to do? I'd like to read it to you right now. I'm going to read as much of this as I can before they take me away. We may never see each other ever again, Mother, but this is something they will never be able to take away from us."

With that, something that was almost a smile came to the red-haired woman's face. Hieronymus opened the book and began to read his mother's own words back to her.

> When I was a young girl, back home in the country I am ex-iled from, and will forever be exiled from, as this land no longer exists, I had a friend whom I am not entirely sure was real. My parents claimed that he was an imaginary friend. His name was Hieronymus, and he was a boy. You see, I, at one time, had seven brothers, but they were much older. Hieronymus was younger and whenever he emerged from the shadows around me, I was so pleased to be the older one, the older sister for a change. When I fell asleep, he would walk with me into my dreams. When I awoke he would stay with me during the day. He was my secret, and if anyone came into my room, Hieronymus would fade away, back into the shadows. That is why I kept my room dark, with the win-dows covered, so Hieronymus would be comfortable in his hiding place. Then each time he came to exist, my world would be full of light and I would no longer be lonely.
>
> He was a very smart boy and he was quite funny. If I was teased or made fun of, Hieronymus, riding within my ear, whis-pered the perfect response that would devastate any bully. He was my ally. He was always on my side. He knew me better than myself.
>
> And he rescued me. I had been struggling within a dark pit of mysterious melancholy. It paralyzed everything, and I only felt normal when in the presence of this dream-like boy. He listened to me. We would have tremendous amounts of fun. When I finally told my parents about him, they became very upset. They did not understand, but there was nothing they could do. He was my in-vention, and he was very real to me.
>
> What was remarkable about my darling Hieronymus were his luminous eyes. He could see in the dark, and he could see through walls, too. He could see through people, and he often knew what

you were going to do before you were going to do it. Once I got lost in a forest, and I had no light and I was so desperately afraid until Hieronymus emerged from the shadows of my tears, and led the way home as if his eyes were a pair of lanterns.

Of course, I am alive today because of my imaginary friend. During the horrific rains that within a week completely flooded and destroyed my entire country, I was with my family and we were climbing into a boat that came to the rooftop of our house as the water was rising so fast. The wind knocked me into the rushing current, and to the horror of my parents, I was pulled away from everyone else. Luckily, I found a large floating table and I climbed onto it, but I was so worried about my parents and my brothers that I started to cry. All I had was my raincoat. Suddenly I realized that Hieronymus was with me, and he told me not to worry. It got dark, but with his luminous eyes he was able to see where the higher land was, and that's where we went. As the rain was still falling and the water was still rising, Hieronymus took me to all the places where the water was not collecting, and he told me that he was able to see where the water was going to go before it got there, and that was because he had luminous eyes.

I was the only one in my immediate family who was rescued. It was the most terrible, loneliest time for me. My grandmother also survived, and as refugees, we went into exile.

After the flood, Hieronymus disappeared. What a loss. All family and friends, real and imagined, gone. It was difficult to adjust and I became angry at him for abandoning me. I just stayed in bed all day. I found a raincoat and I wore it when I slept, as my dreams took me back to the scene of the deluge. I wanted to rescue my family, and I wanted Hieronymus to rescue me. But all I did was cry. Nearly all of the time.

I got so depressed that I ended up in the hospital.

And it was there, one night, that my Hieronymus finally returned. He came to me out of the shadows, as my room in the hospital was so ominous and full of them. By that time, I was a young woman. My imaginary friend came to visit as a young man. I've come back, Barbie, he said to me, but you are no longer the same, and so I can't stay for too long. I was so happy to see him, and I asked him, Dear Hieronymus, with your luminous eyes, you see how dark my heart has become. Can't you guide me out of these halls of madness as you guided me out of the flood country? Can't you guide me from this exile of sadness, this far side of the heart where shadows are long and the night does not end?

But Hieronymus only smiled. The next time we meet, he told me, I will be a real person and I won't fade away into the shadows anymore. And you won't need anyone's luminous eyes, for only your own words will turn your exile into your home, your own words will turn your night to day, and your own words will guide you out of the flood that has made your world so wet with grief that the tears you cry are never ending. I will return and I will listen to all the words I've waited to hear from you all my life.

Someday, you will only wear your raincoat when it rains.

epilogue

I always pick up hitchhikers. The far side of the Moon really is the end of everything and I don't think I can just pass anyone who's stuck out there on Highway Zero. Well, you would not believe who I picked up last week. A really, really weird girl. A total foxentrotter, by the way. I thought she was on drugs when I first saw her, but no, she was straight-edge. I was out there in my mega rig doing my usual haul between the mines and Collinsberg when I spotted her, just standing off to the side of the highway. She didn't even have her thumb out. I told you, she was unbelievable looking! Hot. With a body that…well, you know what I mean. Of course I stop, and I say, "Hey, iceboxmelter! You wanna ride?" and she gives me this look and she says, "No, I'm fine walking," and so I ask her, "Where you going?" and this time she answers a little more squarely, and she says, "District of Copernicus."

I tell you, nobody out there ever turns down a ride. Her hair was really weird, like it had been gelled up but the gel got mixed up with dirt and dust and it was stuck in all these different directions. She looked like she was dressed for nightclubbing, but she was covered in filth. I asked her what she was doing out there, and she told me she was at a party and that her date got arrested. She said that now she was on a special mission to get to the Lunar Federal Court in District of Copernicus and was perfectly happy to walk. A nut. But I couldn't just leave her out there.

I finally convinced her to take a ride with me. As it turns out, she had been walking for three days already. Sleeping on the side of the road. She must have been starving. When I offered her some dried moose jerky, she refused. She said "not till I do what I have to do in the District of Copernicus." Here we were, in the middle of nowhere, and this girl, this *foxentrotter*, just kept staring ahead, just kept staring ahead, utterly in another world and completely determined to get to that big snail-shaped building in D.C. Well, I felt sorry for her. As it turns out, I always pass D.C. on the way to Collinsberg anyway, so what the Hell. I agreed to take her there. All the way there.

And that was that. I was completely exhausted. I tried to get her to come with me to a motel room, but she gave me this weird look and said, "I don't do that kind of thing anymore." I pulled over at the next rest stop which had a Lunemotel and I told her if she didn't want to come with me she could sleep in the rig. I went to bed by myself and got about seven hours of Z-time. I then went back to the truck and she was still there, sitting in the same place, waiting for me to take her to D.C.

I don't even know what her name was. She wouldn't tell me. I don't think I have ever seen anyone more focused or determined before this one. After another whole day of driving, we finally make it to the District of Copernicus. As you might know, the first thing you see is that gigantic building that is shaped like a snail's shell. She points it out to me. "There, take me there," she says about twenty times. Then she takes out this gray, finger-sized rectangular object with a flashing red light. She holds it in both hands. By that point, I was really glad to get rid of her.

I brought her right up to the front of the building. She said thanks and she got out. What a sight was she, walking up those huge steps, behaving like she had the weight of the Moon on her shoulders.